LINDA
HOWARD
DEBBIE
MACOMBER
LINDA
TURNER

CHRISTMAS KISSES

Silhouette Books

Published by Silhouette Books

America's Publisher of Contemporary Romance

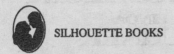

SILHOUETTE BOOKS

CHRISTMAS KISSES

Copyright © 1996 by Harlequin Books S.A.

ISBN 0-373-48328-7

The publisher acknowledges the copyright holders
of the individual works as follows:

MACKENZIE'S MAGIC
Copyright © 1996 by Linda Howington

SILVER BELLS
Copyright © 1996 by Debbie Macomber

A WILD WEST CHRISTMAS
Copyright © 1996 by Linda Turner

This edition published by arrangement with Harlequin Books S.A

® and TM are trademarks of Harlequin Books S.A, used under license.
Trademarks indicated with ® are registered in the United States Patent
and Trademark Office, the Canadian Trade Marks Office and in
other countries.

Printed in U.S.A.

CONTENTS

MACKENZIE'S MAGIC
Linda Howard

Dear Reader,

Not all that long ago, the world was a much slower place. Generations of a family would be born, grow up, marry, set up their own homes, and all stay within the same neighborhood. It wasn't unusual for a house to be home to three generations at the same time. Babies were born in the same house where grandparents died, and there was a wonderful sense of continuity, of roots, that has gone by the wayside now as families scatter to the four corners of the earth.

But we still have that yearning for the safe place of our hearts, the center of the family, and Christmas is the perfect expression of that. "Are you going home for Christmas?" is a phrase spoken thousands—millions—of times as the holiday nears. People seldom live in the same house their entire lives now, but the house isn't the home; the family is. The family is the sanctuary, and people travel untold miles to reach it every year at that special time, the time of Christmas.

I hope you reach your sanctuary, and I hope you have a wonderful Christmas.

Linda Howard

Chapter One

*H*er head hurt.

The pain thudded against the inside of her skull, pounded on her eyeballs. Her stomach stirred uneasily, as if awakened by all the commotion.

"My head hurts." Maris Mackenzie voiced the complaint in a low, vaguely puzzled tone. She never had headaches; despite her delicate appearance, she possessed in full the Mackenzie iron constitution. The oddity of her condition was what had startled her into speaking aloud.

She didn't open her eyes, didn't bother to look at the clock. The alarm hadn't gone off, so it wasn't time to get up. Perhaps if she went back to sleep the headache would go away.

"I'll get you some aspirin."

Maris's eyes snapped open, and the movement made her head give a sickening throb.

The voice was male, but even more startling, it had been right beside her; so close, in fact, that the man had only murmured the words and still his warm breath had stirred against her ear. The bed shifted as he sat up.

There was a soft click as he turned on the bedside lamp, and the light exploded in her head. Quickly she squeezed her eyes shut again, but not before she saw a man's broad, strongly muscled, naked back, and a well-shaped head covered with short, thick dark hair.

Confused panic seized her. Where *was* she? Even more important, who was *he?* She wasn't in her bedroom; one glance had told her that. The bed beneath her was firm, comfortable, but not hers.

An exhaust fan whirred to life when he turned on the bathroom light. She didn't risk opening her eyes again, but instead relied on her other senses to orient herself. A motel, then. That was it. And the strange whumping sound she had only now heard was the blower of the room's climate-control unit.

She had slept in plenty of motels, but never before with a man. Why was she in a motel, anyway, instead of her own comfortable little house close by the stables? The only time she stayed in motels was when she was traveling to or from a job, and since she had settled in Kentucky a couple of years ago the only traveling she'd done had been when she went home to visit the family.

It was an effort to think. She couldn't come up with any reason at all why she was in a motel with a strange man.

Sharp disappointment filled her, temporarily piercing the fogginess in her brain. She had never slept around before, and she was disgusted with herself for having done so now, an episode she didn't remember with a man she didn't know.

She knew she should leave, but she couldn't seem to muster the energy it would take to jump out of bed and escape. Escape? She wondered fuzzily at the strange choice of word. She was free to leave any time she wanted...if she could only manage to move. Her body felt heavily relaxed, content to do nothing more than lie there. She needed to do something, she was certain, but she couldn't quite grasp what that something was. Even aside from the pain in her head, her mind felt fuzzy, and her thoughts were vague and drifting.

The mattress shifted again as he sat down beside her, this time on the side of the bed closest to the wall, away from the hurtful light. Carefully Maris risked opening her eyes just a little; perhaps it was because she was prepared for the pain, but the resultant throb seemed to have lessened. She squinted up at the big man, who sat so close to her that his body heat penetrated the sheet that covered her.

He was facing her now; she could see more of him than just his back. Her eyes widened.

It was *him*.

"Here you go," he said, handing the aspirin to her. His voice was a smooth, quiet baritone, and though she didn't think she'd ever spoken to him before, something about that voice was strangely familiar.

She fumbled the aspirin from his hand and popped them into her mouth, making a face at both the bitter taste of the pills and her own idiocy. Of course his voice was familiar! After all, she'd been in bed with him, so she supposed she had talked to him beforehand, even if she couldn't remember meeting him, or how she'd gotten here.

He held out a glass of water. Maris tried to prop herself up on her elbow to take it, but her head throbbed so violently that she sank back against the pillow, wincing with pain as she put her hand to her forehead. What was wrong with her? She was never sick, never clumsy. This sudden uncooperativeness of her own body was alarming.

"Let me do it." He slipped his arm under her shoulders and effortlessly raised her to a sitting position, bracing her head in the curve of his arm and shoulder. He was warm and strong, his scent musky, and she wanted to press herself closer. The need surprised her, because she'd never before felt that way about a man. He held the glass to her lips, and she gulped thirstily, washing down the pills. When she was finished, he eased her down and removed his arm. She felt a pang of regret at the loss of his touch, astonishing herself.

Fuzzily she watched him walk around the bed. He was tall, muscular, his body showing the strength of a man who did physical work instead of sitting in an office all day. To her mingled relief and disappointment, he wasn't completely naked; he wore a pair of dark gray knit boxers, the fabric clinging snugly to his muscled butt and thighs. Dark hair covered his broad chest, and beard stubble darkened his jaw. He wasn't handsome, but he had a physical presence that drew the eye. It had drawn hers, anyway, since she'd first seen him two weeks ago, forking down hay in the barn.

Her reaction then had been so out of character that she had pushed it out of her mind and ignored it, or at least she had tried. She had deliberately not spoken to him whenever their paths crossed, she who had always taken pains to know everyone who worked with her horses. He threatened her, somehow, on some basic level that brought all her inner defenses screaming to alert. This man was dangerous.

He had watched her, too. She'd turned around occasionally and found his gaze on her, his expression guarded, but still, she'd felt the male heat of his attention. He was just temporary help, a drifter who needed a couple of weeks' pay in his pocket before he drifted away again, while she was the trainer at Solomon Green Horse Farms. It was a prestigious position for anyone, but for a woman to hold the job was a first. Her reputation in the horse world had made her a sort of celebrity, something she didn't particularly enjoy; she would rather be with the horses than putting on an expensive dress and adorning a party, but the Stonichers, who owned Solomon Green, often requested her presence. Maris wasn't a snob, but her position on the farm was worlds apart from that of a drifter hired to muck out the stables.

He knew his way around horses, though; she'd noticed that about him. He was comfortable with the big animals, and they liked him, which had drawn her helpless attention even more. She hadn't wanted to pay attention to the way his jeans stretched across his butt when he bent or squatted, something that he seemed to do a thousand times a day as he worked. She didn't want to notice the muscles that strained the shoulder seams of his shirts as he hefted loaded shovels or pitchforks. He had good hands, strong and lean; she hadn't wanted to notice them, either, or the intelligence in his blue eyes. He might be a drifter, but he drifted for his own reasons, not because he wasn't capable of making a more stable life for himself.

She'd never had time for a man in her life, hadn't particularly been interested. All her attention had been focused on horses, and building her career. In the privacy of her bed at night, when she wasn't able to sleep and her restless body felt too hot for comfort, she had admitted to herself the irony of her hormones finally being kicked into full gallop by a man who would likely be gone in a matter of weeks, if not days. The best thing to do, she'd decided, would be to continue ignoring him and the uncomfortable yearnings that made her want to be close to him.

Evidently she hadn't succeeded.

She lifted her hand to shield her eyes from the light as she watched him return the water glass to the bathroom, and only then did she notice what she herself was wearing. She wasn't naked; she was wearing her panties, and a big T-shirt that drooped off her shoulders. *His* T-shirt, specifically.

Had *he* undressed her, or had she done it herself? If she looked around, would she find their clothes haphazardly tossed together? The thought of him undressing her interfered with her lung function, constricting her chest and stifling her oxygen flow. She wanted to remember—she *needed* to remember—but the night was a blank. She should get up and put on her own clothes, she thought. She should, but she couldn't. All she could do was lie there and cope with the pain in her head while she tried to make sense of senseless things.

He was watching her as he came back to bed, his blue eyes narrowed, the color of his irises vivid even in the dim light. "Are you all right?"

She swallowed. "Yes." It was a lie, but for some reason she didn't want him to know she was as incapacitated as she really was. Her gaze drifted over his hairy chest and flat belly, down to the masculine bulge beneath those tight boxers. Had they really...? For what other reason would they be in a motel bed together? But if they had, why were they both wearing underwear?

Something about those sophisticated boxer shorts seemed a little out of place on a guy who did grunt work on a horse farm. She would have expected plain white briefs.

He turned off the lamp and stretched out beside her, the warmth of his body wrapping around her as he settled the sheet over them. He lay on his side, facing her, one arm curled under his pillow and the other resting across her belly, holding her close without actually wrapping her in his embrace. It struck her as a carefully measured position, close without being intimate.

She tried to remember his name, and couldn't.

She cleared her throat. She couldn't imagine what he would think of her, but she couldn't bear this fogginess in her mind any longer. She had to bring order to this confusion, and the best way to do that was to start with the basics. "I'm sorry," she said softly, almost whispering. "But I don't remember your name, or—or how we got here."

He went rigid, his arm tightening across her belly. For a long moment he didn't move. Then, with a muffled curse, he sat bolt upright, the action jarring her head and making her moan. He snapped on the bedside lamp again, and she closed her eyes against the stabbing light.

"Damn it," he muttered, bending over her. He sank his long fingers into her hair, sifting through the tousled silk as he stroked his fingertips over her skull. "Why didn't you tell me you were hurt?"

"I didn't know I was." It was the truth. What did he mean, hurt?

"I should have guessed." His voice was grim, his mouth set in a thin line. "I knew you were pale, and you didn't eat much, but I thought it was just stress." He continued probing, and his fingers brushed a place on the side of her head that made her suck in her breath as a sickening throb of pain sliced through her temples.

"Ah." Gently he turned her in to him, cradling her against his shoulder while he examined the injury. His fingers barely touched her scalp. "You have a nice goose egg here."

"Good," she mumbled. "I'd hate for it to be a bad goose egg."

He gave her another narrow-eyed look, something he had down to an art. "You have a concussion, damn it. Are you nauseated? How's your vision?"

"The light hurts," she admitted. "But my vision isn't blurred."

"What about nausea?"

"A little."

"And I've been letting you sleep," he growled to himself, half under his breath. "You need to be in a hospital."

"No," she said immediately, alarm jangling through her. The last thing she wanted was to go to a hospital. She didn't know why, but some instinct told her to stay away from public places. "It's safer here."

In a very controlled tone he said, "I can handle the safety. You need to see a doctor."

Again there was that nagging sense of familiarity, but she couldn't quite grasp what it was. There were other, more serious, things to worry about, however, so she let it go. She took stock of her physical condition, because a concussion could be serious, and she might indeed need to be in a hospital. There was the headache, the nausea... What else? Vision good, speech not slurred. Memory? Rapidly she ran through her family, remembering names and birthdays, thinking of her favorite horses through the years. Her memory was intact, except for... She tried to pinpoint her last memory. The last thing she could remember was eating lunch and walking down to the stables, but when had that been?

"I think I'm going to be okay," she said absently. "If you don't mind, answer a couple of questions for me. First, what's your name, and second, how did we wind up in bed together?"

"My name's MacNeil," he said, watching her closely.

MacNeil. MacNeil. Memory rushed back, bringing with it his first name, too. "I remember," she breathed. "Alex MacNeil." His name had struck her when she'd first heard it, because it was so similar to the name of one of her nephews, Alex Mackenzie, her brother Joe's second-oldest son. Not only were their first names the same, but their last names both indicated the same heritage.

"Right. As for your second question, I think what you're really asking is if we had sex. The answer is no."

She sighed with relief, then frowned a little. "Then why are we here?" she asked in bewilderment.

He shrugged. "We seem to have stolen a horse," he said.

Chapter Two

*S*tolen a horse? Maris blinked at him in total bewilderment, as if he'd said something in a foreign language. She'd asked him why they were in bed together, and he'd said they had stolen a horse. Not only was it ridiculous that she would steal a horse, but she couldn't see any connection at all between horse thievery and sleeping with Alex MacNeil.

Then a memory twinged in her aching head, and she went still as she tried to solidify the confused picture. She remembered moving rapidly, driven by an almost blinding sense of urgency, down the wide center aisle of the barn, toward the roomy, luxurious stall in the middle of the row. Sole Pleasure was a gregarious horse; he loved company, and that was why his stall was in the middle, so he would have companionship on both sides. She also remembered the fury that had gripped her; she'd never been so angry before in her life.

"What is it?" he asked, still watching her so intently that she imagined he knew every line of her face.

"The horse we 'seem' to have stolen—is it Sole Pleasure?"

"The one and only. If every cop in the country isn't already after us, they will be in a matter of hours." He paused. "What were you planning on doing with him?"

It was a good question. Sole Pleasure was the most famous horse in America right now, and very recognizable, with his sleek black coat, white star, and white stocking on the right foreleg. He'd been on the cover of *Sports Illustrated,* had been named their Athlete of the Year. He'd won over two million dollars in his short career and been retired at the grand old age of four to be syndicated at stud. The Stonichers were still weighing the offers, determined to make the best deal. The horse was black gold prancing around on four powerful, lightning-fast legs.

What *had* she been going to do with him? She stared at the ceiling, trying to bring the hours missing from her memory back to the surface of consciousness. Why would she steal Sole Pleasure? She wouldn't have sold him, or raced him—in disguise, of course—on her own. She rejected those possibilities out of hand. Stealing a horse was so foreign to her nature that she was at a loss to explain having apparently done exactly that. The only reason she could even imagine having for taking a horse would be the animal was in danger. She could see herself doing that, though she was more likely to take a whip to anyone mistreating one of her babies, or any horse at all, for that matter. She couldn't bear seeing them hurt.

Or *killed.*

The thought knifed through her, and suddenly she knew. Oh, God, she knew.

She jerked upright in bed. Instantly pain mushroomed inside her skull, the pressure almost blinding her for a second. She gave a gasping, almost soundless cry; a hard arm shot upward and closed around her, preventing her getting up, but it didn't matter anyway. She felt her muscles going slack, unable to support her, and she slumped over on him. The pain quickly subsided to a far more manageable level, but the moment of agony left her weak and shaking, collapsed on his chest, in his arms, her eyes closed as she tried to recover from the shock.

MacNeil gently turned so that she was flat on her back and he was half over her, one heavy, hairy, muscled leg thrown across her much slimmer ones, his arm under her neck, his broad shoulders blocking the light from her closed eyelids. One big hand covered her left breast, the contact brief and warm and electrifying, then moved up to her throat. She felt his fingers pressing against the artery there, then a soft sigh eased from him, and he briefly leaned down to press his forehead against hers, very gently, as if he were afraid the touch might hurt her. She swallowed, trying to control her breathing. That was the limit of her control, though, because there was nothing she could do about the speed at which her blood was thundering through her veins.

Only the thought of Sole Pleasure kept her focused. Maris gulped, opening her eyes and staring up at him. "They were going to *kill* him," she said in a stifled tone. "I remember. They were going to *kill* him!" Renewed rage bubbled in her bloodstream, giving force to the last sentence.

"So you stole him to save his life."

He said it much more as a statement than as a question, but Maris nodded anyway, remembering at the last second to limit herself to only a tiny movement of her head. The calmness of his voice again piqued her interest with its familiarity. Why wasn't he alarmed, indignant, or any number of other responses that could reasonably be expected? Maybe he'd already guessed, and she had only confirmed his suspicion.

He was a drifter, a man who routinely walked away from responsibility, but even though he'd guessed what she was doing, he had involved himself anyway. Their situation was highly precarious, because unless she could prove the charge she'd made, they would be arrested for stealing Sole Pleasure, the most valuable horse in the country. All she remembered now was the danger to the stallion, not who was behind it, so proving it could be a bit chancy.

Chancy... *Chance.* Chance and Zane. The thought of her brothers was like sunrise, bringing light to the darkness in her mind. No matter what was going on or who was behind it, all she had to do was call Zane, and he would get to the bottom of it. Maybe that had been her original plan, lost in the fog that obscured the past twelve hours. Get Sole Pleasure out of harm's way, contact Zane, and lay low until the danger was over.

She stared at the ceiling, trying to remember any other detail that would help clear up the situation.

Nothing. "Did I call anyone last night?" she asked. "Did I say anything about calling one of my brothers?"

"No. There was no time or opportunity to call anyone until we got here, and you were out like a light as soon as you hit the bed."

That information didn't clear up the question of whether she had undressed herself or he had done it. She scowled a little, annoyed at how the physical intimacy of the situation kept distracting her from the business at hand.

He was still watching her closely; she felt as if his attention hadn't wavered from her for so much as a split second. She could sense him analyzing every nuance of her expressions, and the knowledge was unsettling. She was accustomed to people paying attention to her; she was, after all, the boss. But this was different, on an entirely different level, as if he missed nothing going on around him.

"Were you going to call your family for help?" he asked when she didn't say anything else.

She pursed her lips. "That would have been the most logical thing to do. I should probably call them now." Since Zane had left the SEALs, he was much easier to contact; Barrie and the kids kept him closer to home. And he would know how to get in touch with Chance, though the odds of Chance even being in the country weren't good. It didn't matter; if she needed them, if she made the call, she knew her entire family would descend on Kentucky like the Vikings swooping down on a medieval coastal village—and heaven help those who were behind all this.

Maris tried to ease herself away from him so that she could sit up and reach the phone. To her amazement, he tightened his grip, holding her in place.

"I'm okay," she said in reassurance. "As long as I remember to move slowly and not jar my head, I can manage. I need to call my brother as soon as possible, so he can—"

"I can't let you do that," he said calmly.

She blinked, her dark eyes growing cool. "I beg your pardon?" Her tone was polite, but she let him hear the steel underlying it.

His lips twitched, and a ruefully amused look entered his eyes. "I said I can't let you do that." The amusement spread to his mouth, turning the twitch into a smile. "What are you going to do, fire me?"

Maris ignored the taunt, because if she couldn't prove Sole Pleasure was in danger, neither of them would have to worry about a job for some time. She lay still, considering this sudden change in the situation, possibilities running through her mind. He was too damn sure of himself, and she wondered why. He didn't want her to call for help. The only reason she could come up with was that he must be involved, somehow, in the plot to kill Sole Pleasure. Maybe he was the one who'd been hired to do it. Suddenly, looking up into those blue eyes, Maris felt the danger in him again. It wasn't just a sensual danger, but the inherent danger of a man who had known violence. Yes, this man could kill.

Sole Pleasure might already be dead. She thought of that big, sleek, powerful body lying stiff, never to move again, and a nearly crippling grief brought the sheen of tears to her eyes. She couldn't control that response, but she allowed herself no other. Maybe she was wrong about MacNeil, but for Sole Pleasure's sake, she couldn't take the chance.

"Don't cry," he murmured, his voice dropping into a lower note. He lifted his hand to gently stroke her hair away from her temple. "I'll take care of things."

This was going to hurt. Maris knew it, and accepted the pain. Her father had taught her to go into a fight *expecting* to get hurt; people who didn't expect the pain were stunned by it, incapacitated and, ultimately, defeated. Wolf Mackenzie had taught his children to win fights.

MacNeil was too close; she was also lying flat on her back, which took away a lot of her leverage. She had to do it anyway. The first blow had to count.

She snapped her left arm up at him, striking for his nose with the heel of her palm.

He moved like lightning, his right forearm coming up to block the blow. Her palm slammed into his arm with enough force to jar her to the teeth. Instantly she recoiled and struck again, this time aiming lower, for his solar plexus. Again that muscular forearm blocked her way, and this time he twisted, catching both of her arms and pinning them to the pillow on each side of her head. With another smooth motion he levered himself atop her, his full weight crushing her into the bed.

The entire thing took three seconds, maybe less. There had been no explosion of movement; anyone watching might not even have realized a brief battle had taken place, so tight had been the movements of attack and response, then counterattack. Her head hadn't even been unduly jarred. But Maris knew. Not only had she been trained by her father, she had also watched Zane and Chance spar too often to have any doubts. She had just gone up against a highly trained professional—and lost.

His blue eyes were flinty, his expression cold and remote. His grip on her wrists didn't hurt, but when she tried to move her arms, she found that she couldn't.

"Now, what in hell was that about?" His voice was still calm, but edged with an icy sharpness.

Then it all fell together. His control, his utter self-confidence, the calmness that seemed so familiar. Of course it was familiar—she saw it constantly, in her brothers. Zane had just that way of speaking, as if he could handle anything that might happen. MacNeil hadn't hurt her, even when she had definitely tried to hurt *him*. She couldn't have expected such concern from a thug hired to kill a horse. The clues were there, even those sexy gray boxers. This was no drifter.

"My God," she blurted. "You're a cop."

Chapter Three

"**I**s that why you attacked?" If anything, those blue eyes were even colder.

"No," she said absently, staring up at his face as if she'd never seen a man before. She felt stunned, as if she really hadn't. Something had just happened, but she wasn't sure what. It was like the way she'd felt when she first saw him, only more intense, primally exciting. She frowned a little as she tried to pin down the exact thought, or sensation, or whatever it was. His hands tightened on her wrists, drawing her back to the question he'd asked and the answer he wanted, and reluctantly she gathered her thoughts. "I just now realized that you're a cop. The reason I tried to hit you was because you wouldn't let me call my family, and I was afraid you might be one of the bad guys."

"So you were going to try to take me out?" He looked furious at the idea. "You have a concussion. How in hell did you expect to fight me? And who taught you those moves, anyway?"

"My father. He taught all of us how to fight. And I could have won, against most men," she said simply. "But you—I know professional training when I see it."

"So the fact that I know how to fight makes you think I'm a cop?"

She could have told him about Zane and Chance, who, even though they weren't cops, had many of the same characteristics she'd noticed in him. She didn't, though, because she wasn't one hundred percent certain their organization or agency or whatever it was was exactly squared away with either the State or Justice Department. Instead, she gave MacNeil a secret little smile. "Actually, it was your shorts."

He was startled out of his control, his blue eyes widening. "My *shorts?*"

"They aren't briefs. They're not white. They're too sexy."

"And that's a dead giveaway for being a cop?" he asked incredulously, color staining his cheekbones.

"Drifters don't wear sexy gray boxers," she pointed out. She didn't mention the interest she could feel stirring in those sexy gray boxers. Perhaps, under the circumstances, she shouldn't have mentioned his underwear. Not that his reaction was unexpected, she thought. She was barely clothed, and he wore even less. She could feel the hard, hairy bareness of his legs against hers, the pressure of his hips. Just minutes before, she had thought his touch carefully controlled, so that there was no intimacy, despite his closeness. She didn't feel that way now. It wasn't just his arousal; there was something *very* intimate in the way he held her beneath him, as if their brief battle had startled him out of his careful control and provoked him into a heated, purely male response. She took a deep breath as an unfamiliar excitement made her heart beat faster, made every cell in her body tingle with life. The secret part of her, the wildness that she had always known was there but which no man had ever before managed to touch, shivered in fierce satisfaction at the way he held her.

"Cops don't necessarily wear them, either."

Her comment about his shorts had definitely disturbed him. She smiled again, her dark eyes half closing in sensual delight as she absorbed the novel sensation of having a hard male body on top of her—an extremely *aroused* male body. "If you say so. I've never seen one undressed before. What kind of cop are you, specifically?"

He was silent for a moment, studying her face. She didn't know what he saw there, but the set of his mouth eased, and if anything, he settled even more heavily against her. "Specifically, FBI. Special agent."

A *federal* agent? Startled out of her sensual preoccupation, she gave him a puzzled look. "I didn't think stealing a horse was a federal crime."

He almost smiled. "It isn't. Look, if I let go of your hands, are you going to try to kill me again?"

"No. I promise," she said. "Besides, I wasn't trying to kill you, and even if I had been, I'm not as good as you are, so you don't have to worry."

"I can't tell you how reassuring that is," he said dryly, but he released her hands and shifted his position a little, propping himself over her on his forearms. The change forced his hips more firmly against hers, forced her thighs slightly apart to accommodate the pressure. She caught her breath. His interest had grown, to the point that there was no politely ignoring it. But he *was* ignoring it, not in the least embarrassed by his body's response to her.

Maris took another deep breath, delighting in the way the simple action rubbed her breasts against the hard, muscled planes of his chest, making her nipples tingle. Oh, God, that felt so good. She would gladly lie in his arms and do nothing more than *breathe,* if they didn't have a stolen champion horse stashed somewhere and someone presumably on their trail, trying to kill both them and the stallion.

But they did have a stolen horse hidden away, and a big problem on their hands. She focused her thoughts, and despite the fact that she was lying helplessly pinned beneath him, she fixed him with a dark, penetrating gaze. "So why was a federal special agent mucking out my stables?"

"Trying to find out who's been killing horses and collecting the insurance money on them—boss." He added the last word in a dry tone, responding to her arrogant claiming of the Solomon Green stables as her own.

She ignored the not-so-subtle teasing, because she'd heard it so often from her family. What she loved, she claimed; it was as simple as that. She drew her head back deeper into the pillow and gave him a frankly skeptical look. "Insurance fraud rates a special agent?"

"It does when it involves kidnapping, crossing state lines and murder."

Murder. So she'd been right: Someone *was* trying to kill them. Had this someone hit her on the head, or had she gained the goose egg by a more mundane method, such as falling?

"What brought you to Solomon Green?"

"A tip." One corner of his mouth curved slightly. His face was so close to hers that she could see the tiny lines created by the movement, as if he smiled easily. "Law enforcement agencies couldn't operate without snitches."

"So you knew Sole Pleasure was in danger?" She didn't like that. Anger began to smolder in her dark eyes. "Why didn't you tell me? I could have been on guard without causing any suspicion. You didn't have a right to gamble with his life."

"All of the horses are insured. Any of them could have been targeted. Sole Pleasure should have been their least likely target, because he's so well-known. His death would raise a lot of questions, attract a lot of attention." He paused, watching her carefully. "And, until last night, you were on my list of suspects."

She absorbed that, her only reaction a slight tightening of her mouth. "How did last night change your mind? What happened?" It was both frustrating and frightening, not being able to remember.

"You came to me for help. You were so angry you could barely speak, and you were scared. You said we had to get Sole Pleasure out of there, and if I didn't want to help, you'd manage on your own.''

"Did I say who was after him?''

He gave a slight shake of his head. ''No. Like I said, you were barely speaking. You wouldn't answer any questions. I thought at the time you were too scared, and once we had the horse safe, I was going to give you a little time to settle down before I started questioning you. Then I noticed how pale and shaky you were, maybe a little shocky from the adrenaline crash. You wanted to go on, but I made you stop here. You conked out as soon as we got in the room.''

That reminded her again of both the interesting question of whether she had undressed herself or he had done it for her and his rather irritating assumption that he could *make* her do anything. She frowned when she realized that he could back up that assumption with action; her current position proved it. He hadn't hurt her, but physically she was still very much under his control.

Her frown deepened as she grew more annoyed with herself than before. She was doing it again, letting her attention drift. She could keep letting herself get sidetracked by her undeniable attraction to him, or she could keep her mind on the problem at hand. Sole Pleasure's life, and perhaps her own, depended on doing whatever she could to help this man.

There was no question which was most important.

"The Stonichers,'' she said slowly. ''They're the only ones who would benefit financially from Sole Pleasure's death, but they'd make more by syndicating him for stud, so killing him doesn't make sense.''

''That's another reason I didn't think he was in danger. I was watching all the other horses. The insurance on them wouldn't be as much, but neither would their deaths cause much of a stir.''

''How did I find you?'' she asked. ''Did I come to your room? Call you? Did anyone see us, or did you see anyone?'' His room was one of ten, tiny but private, in a long, narrow block building the Stonichers had built specifically to house the employees who were transient and had no other quarters, as well as those who needed to be on-site. As the trainer, Maris was important enough to have her own small three-room cottage on the premises. The foaling man, Mr. Wyse, also had his own quarters, an upstairs apartment in the foaling barn, where he watched the mothers-to-be on video monitors. There were always people around; someone had to have seen them.

''I wasn't in my room. I'd been in the number two barn, checking around, and had just gone out the back door when you rode by on Sole Pleasure. It was dark, so I didn't think you'd seen me, but you stopped and told me I had to help you. The truck and trailer that brought in that little sorrel mare this afternoon were still sitting there, hooked up, so we loaded Sole Pleasure in and took off. If anyone saw us, I doubt they could even have seen there was a horse in the trailer, much less recognized it as Sole Pleasure.''

It was possible, she thought. The number two barn was where the mares who had been sent to the farm for breeding were stabled. Night came early in December, and the horses were already settled down, the workers relaxing or at supper. The truck and trailer didn't belong to Solomon Green, and everyone knew they had brought in a mare that afternoon, so no one would think anything of the rig leaving, except the driver, who had decided to spend the night and start back at dawn the next day. And Sole Pleasure was exceptionally easy to load; he never made a fuss and, in fact, seemed to enjoy traveling. Loading him wouldn't have taken more than a minute, and then they would have been on their way.

"I didn't have a chance to call my family," she said, "but did you call anyone while I was asleep?"

"I went out to a pay phone and let my office know what was going on. They'll try to run interference for us, but they can't be too obvious without blowing the operation. We still don't know who's involved in the ring—unless you've remembered something else in the past few minutes?"

"No," she said regretfully. "My last clear memory is of walking down to the stables yesterday afternoon. I know it was after lunch, but I don't know the exact time. What little else I remember is just flashes of being angry, and scared, and running to Pleasure's stall."

"If you remember anything else, even the smallest detail, tell me immediately. By taking the horse, we've given them the perfect opportunity to kill him and blame it on us, or at least they'll see it that way, since they don't know I'm FBI. They'll be after us hot and heavy, and I need to know who to expect.''

''Where's Pleasure now?'' she asked in alarm, putting her hands on his shoulders and pushing. She squirmed under him, trying to slip free of his weight so that she could get up, get dressed and get to the horse. It wasn't like her to be so lax about a horse's comfort and security, and though she had watched MacNeil enough to know that he was conscientious with the animals, the final responsibility was hers.

''Calm down. He's all right.'' MacNeil caught her hands, once more holding them down on the pillow. ''I've got him stashed in the woods. No one's going to find him. I couldn't make it easy for them. Leaving him in the parking lot, where anyone could get at him, would have made even a fool suspicious. They're going to have to come to us in order to find him.''

She relaxed against the pillows, reassured about Pleasure's safety. ''All right. What are we going to do now?''

He hesitated. ''My original plan was to find out what you knew, then put you somewhere safe until we had everything settled.''

''Where were you going to put me, in the trailer with Pleasure?'' she asked, a slight caustic edge to her voice. ''Well, too bad. I can't tell you what I know, and you need to keep me handy in case I do remember something. You're stuck with me, MacNeil, and you aren't putting me anywhere.''

"There's only one place I'd like to put you," he said slowly. "And I already have you there.''

Chapter Four

It wasn't a surprise, given all the evidence at hand.

Pure male possessiveness was in Alex MacNeil's attitude, in every line of his body, staring plainly down at her from those sharp blue eyes.

Maris knew she wasn't mistaken about that look. She had grown up seeing it in her father's eyes every time he looked at her mother, seen the way he stood so close to her, touched her, a subtle alertness in every muscle of his body. She had also seen it innumerable times in her five brothers, first with their girlfriends and later, for four of them, with their wives. It was a look of desire, heated and potent.

It was both scary and exhilarating, startling her, and yet at the same time it was as if she had known, from the moment she first saw him, that there was something between them and eventually she would have to deal with it.

That was why she'd been at such pains to avoid him, not wanting the complication of an involvement with him, or having to endure the resultant gossip among the other employees. She had dated, some, but she had instinctively shied away whenever a boy or man showed signs of becoming too involved, possessive. She'd never had much time or patience for anything that interfered with her concentration on her horses and her career, nor had she ever wanted to let anyone that close to her.

She had a strong private core that she'd never let anyone touch, except for her family. It seemed to be a Mackenzie trait, the ability to be alone and be perfectly content, and even though all her brothers except Chance had eventually married and were frighteningly in love with their wives, they had married *because* they were in love. Maris had always been content to wait until that once-in-a-lifetime love happened to her, too, rather than waste time by flinging herself without thought into a brief affair with any man who just happened to have the right physical chemistry with her.

The chemistry was there with MacNeil, all right. The proof of it, on his part, was pressing urgently against the soft notch of her legs, tempting her to open her thighs wider and allow herself to feel that rigid length full against her loins. The fact that she wanted to do so was proof of the right chemistry on her part. She should move away, she knew she should, but she didn't. There wasn't a cell in her body that wanted to move, unless it was closer into his embrace.

She stared up into his beard-stubbled face, into blue eyes that were hard and darkened by sharp desire, a desire he was ruthlessly containing. Her own eyes were dark, bottomless pools as she met that sharp gaze. "The question is," she said slowly, "what are you going to do about it?"

"Not very damn much," he muttered, shifting rest-lessly against her. His jaw tightened at the sensations resulting from that movement, and his breath sighed out between his teeth. "You have a concussion. You have a killer headache. We have an unknown number of unknown people looking for us, so I have to keep my mind on the situation, instead of thinking about getting into your little panties. And even if you said yes, damn it, I'd have to say no, because the concus-sion could be causing mental impairment!" The last sentence was raw with frustration, ground out as if every word hurt him.

She lay very still beneath him, though her instinct was to part her thighs and cradle him against her, pull-ing him into her soft heat. Her eyes went as dark as night, softening, something mysterious and eternal moving there. "My headache is better." Her voice was low, her gaze drawing him in. "And I'm not mentally impaired."

"Oh, God," he groaned, resting his forehead against hers and closing his eyes. "Two out of four."

Maris moved her hands, and he immediately freed them. She laid her palms against his shoulders, and he tensed, waiting for her to push him away, knowing it was for the best but dreading the loss of contact. She didn't push. Instead, she curved her hands over the powerful muscles that cushioned the balls of his shoulder joints, trailed her fingers over the curve of his collarbone and finally flattened her hands against the hard planes of his chest. His crisp black chest hair tickled her palms. His tiny flat nipples hardened to pinpoints, intriguing her. His heartbeat was hard and strong, throbbing beneath her touch.

She was amazed, a little taken aback, by the intensity of the desire that shook her. No, not just desire—*need*. Need, hot and strong. She had seen sexual attraction all her life, at the most basic level in her horses and the other animals on the ranch, and in her own family as something powerful and tender and somehow both straightforward and complicated at the same time. She didn't underestimate the compelling power of sex. She had seen it, but she'd never before *felt* it, not this heat and ache, this emptiness that could be filled only by him, this melting sensation deep inside. She had always thought that if she ever felt this way it would be associated with love, and love was impossible here, because she didn't know him, not really. She knew his name and his occupation, but nothing about the type of person he was, and it was impossible to love a stranger. Be attracted, yes, but not love.

But her sister-in-law Barrie had once said that within five minutes of meeting Zane she had known the kind of person he was, and loved him. They had been strangers, but extraordinary circumstances had forced them into an intimate situation and shown them facets of each other's characters that otherwise would have taken months for them to discover.

Maris considered her own situation and the stranger who was so intimately sharing it with her. What had she learned about him since awakening—or regaining consciousness—in his arms?

He wasn't pushing her. He wanted her, but he wasn't pushing. The circumstances weren't right, so he was waiting. He was a patient man, or at least a man who knew how to be patient when he had to be, something that was entirely different. He was intelligent; she would have seen that days—weeks—ago, if she had let herself study him. She wasn't certain, but she thought that an FBI special agent had to have a law degree. He had some working medical knowledge, at least about concussions. He was evidently strong-willed enough to have gotten her to do something she didn't want to do, though, of course, with a concussion she wouldn't have been at her best. He had taken care of her. And most of all, despite the fact that she had slept almost naked in his arms, he hadn't taken sexual advantage of her.

That was quite a list. He was patient, intelligent, educated, strong-willed, caring and honorable. And there was something else, the subtle quality of danger and controlled power. She remembered the quiet, authoritative tone of his voice, the utter confidence that he could take care of any problem that might arise. In that he was like her brothers, particularly Zane and Chance, and they were two of the most dangerous men she could imagine.

She had always known that one of the reasons she'd never fallen in love was that so few men could compare favorably with the men in her family. She had been content to dedicate herself to her career, unwilling to settle for less than what she knew a man could be. But Alex MacNeil was of that stamp, and her heart lurched. Suddenly, for the first time in her life, she was in danger of falling in love.

And then, looking into those eyes so blue it was like drowning in the ocean, she knew. She remembered the change inside herself, the quiet recognition of her mate.

"Oh, dear," she said softly. "I have a very important question to ask you."

"Shoot," he said, then gave a wry shrug of apology at his word choice.

"Are you married, or otherwise involved with anyone?"

He knew why she was asking the question. He would have had to be dead not to feel the electricity between them, and his state of arousal proved that he was far from it. "No. No involvements, period." He didn't ask the same question of her; the background check he'd run on all the employees at Solomon Green had given him the basic information that she was single and had no record of prior arrests. In the time he'd worked at the farm, from the questions he'd asked, he had also found out that she didn't date any one man on a steady basis. The other guys had kidded him about having the hots for the boss, and he'd gone along with the idea. Hell, it was true, so why not use it as part of his cover?

Maris took a deep breath. This was it, then. With the directness with which she faced life, and the fey quality with which she saw things so clearly, she gave him a tiny smile. "If you aren't already thinking of marrying me," she said, "you'd better get used to the idea."

Mac kept his expression still, not allowing it to betray the shock that was reverberating through him. *Marriage?* He hadn't even kissed her yet, and she was talking marriage!

A sane man would get up and get his mind back on the business at hand, which included keeping them alive through the next few hours. A sane man wouldn't continue to lie here with this woman in his arms, not if he wanted to preserve his enjoyable single state.

He wanted her, no doubt about that. He was familiar with desire, having indulged that particular urge since the age of fourteen, and knew how to ignore it when indulgence would interfere with work. The work was absorbing, and he'd thrown himself into it with the cool, incisive intelligence that he also used to govern his personal life. He'd always been the one in control in his relationships, the one who called an end to things whenever he thought a woman was beginning to cling, to expect more from him than he was willing to give. It wasn't fair to string a woman along and let her hope when there was no hope, so he always simply ended the affair before it got to the tears-and-recriminations stage.

But then, he'd never met Maris Mackenzie before.

He didn't get up. More disturbing, he didn't laugh and say the concussion must have impaired her mentally after all. She was small, delicately built, even fragile, so it was ridiculous for him to dread making her angry or, even worse, hurting her feelings. He wanted to continue holding her, wanted to cradle her close to him and protectively cover her, keep her safe from the danger that would erupt around them within the next couple of hours, shield her from everything—except himself. He wanted her open to him, vulnerable, naked, completely at his disposal. He wanted to sink into those beguiling, mysterious black eyes and forget everything but the feverish delight of thrusting into her.

The sharp turn of events had thrown him off balance, that was all. Until last night, she and everyone else at Solomon Green had been on his list of possible suspects, and he had refused to let himself dwell on the heat that ran through him every time her slight, disconcertingly female body came within sight. Hell, she hadn't even had to be in sight; the thought of her had slipped into his consciousness at odd times during the day and disturbed his sleep at night.

He had resented his inability to ignore her as easily as she ignored him. She had a very still, intense quality about her, a focus that bespoke a will of iron. She was as absorbed in her job as he was in his, to the point that he'd thought she didn't even know he existed as a person, much less as a man. The idea had been strangely disturbing. He'd needed to blend in, but instead he'd found himself wanting to stand out, so that she would look at him with recognition in her eyes instead of a blank stare. Night after night he'd lain alone and thought about her, resenting both the fact that he couldn't seem to stop and the fact that she was oblivious to him. He wanted her to be as aware of him as he was of her, wanted to know that she, too, twisted on lonely sheets and thought of him in bed with her.

He wanted her with an intensity that infuriated him. Everything about her appealed to him, and that was surprising in itself, because there was nothing overtly sexual about her manner. She was pure business; she never flirted, never played favorites with the men under her authority, never made a suggestive remark, didn't go out of her way to make herself more attractive. Not that she had to; he couldn't have been more aware of her than if she made a practice of parading naked in front of him.

He knew exactly how her jeans clung to her curvy little ass, had imagined more than once gripping those round cheeks in his hands and lifting her into his thrust. He'd studied the shape of her high, round breasts underneath the flannel shirts she wore and, considering the slightness of her build, driven himself crazy thinking about how tight she would be when he slid into her. He'd had all the normal, heated sexual thoughts. But he'd also found himself absorbed in the satiny texture of her skin, as flawless as if she didn't spend countless hours outdoors. No woman should have skin like that, as pure as a child's, and so translucent he could see the fragile blue veins in her temples. He would look at her pale brown hair, bleached by the sun into streaks of ashy blond, and think of how it would trail across his arm like a fall of silk. Her eyes were as black as night, fey and unfathomable, tempting a man to try to plumb those mysterious depths.

Desire, like heat, was measured in degrees, and ran the gamut from lukewarm to vaporization. She had long since turned him to steam, he thought; it was nothing short of a miracle that he'd held her in his arms all night and done nothing more than that, even though all she was wearing was a pair of skimpy, blood-pressure-raising panties and his own T-shirt, which was so large on her that it kept slipping down to reveal one silky shoulder.

This was desire, all right—and more. It was want carried to a higher degree than he'd ever before experienced, a fever that refused to cool, a need he hadn't let himself satisfy. Until last night, he hadn't even let himself talk to her, even though he'd known he should, to see what, if anything, he could find out from her. Oddly enough, she had seemed to avoid him, too, though he'd noticed immediately that Ms. Mackenzie was a hands-on trainer who knew everyone working under her and was on easy terms with them. She was pure magic with the horses and a tyrant when it came to their care, but a benevolent tyrant, and everyone from the stable hands to the riders seemed to treat her with varying degrees of respect and adoration. It was out of character for her to avoid him, but that was exactly what she'd done.

It had made him suspicious. It was his job to be suspicious, to notice anything out of the ordinary, and her behavior toward him had made him wonder if something about him had made *her* suspicious, put her on guard. With his background, he was familiar with horses, which had made him the logical choice for the job, and he'd tried to blend in. Still, he was always aware that his training had permanently changed him, and a sharp eye might be able to spot the little things that forever set him apart from others: the extraordinary alertness, so that he was aware of every little detail of the activity going on around him; his sharp, fast reflexes; his unconscious habit of placing himself in positions that could be defended.

And she had spotted those details, known what they meant. He didn't at all like the swiftness with which she had sized him up and said, "You're a cop," even if her actions of the night before had already convinced him that she wasn't involved in the ring that killed race-horses and collected the insurance money. She saw too much, with those black eyes of hers, and now she was looking at him as if she could see into his soul.

Honesty prodded at him. Even though every hormone in his body was roaring at him not to do anything to jeopardize his current position, to stay right where he was, on top of her and all but between her legs, he ground his teeth and said what he knew he had to say.

"Marriage? You must be hurt worse than I thought, since you're delirious."

She didn't take offense. Instead, she curled her arms around his neck and gave him that small, inscrutable, damnably *female* smile again. "I understand," she said gently. "You need time to get used to the idea, and you have a job to do. This can wait. Right now, you have to catch some damn horse killers."

Chapter Five

She needed to clear her head, needed some time away from him so that her nerves would settle down. Maris pushed lightly against his shoulders; he hesitated, but then rolled to the side, freeing her from his weight. The loss of that heavy pressure, the vital heat, was so unexpectedly painful that she almost reached out to pull him over her again. One glance at the straining fabric of his shorts told her that he might not be able to withstand any more temptation, and while her entire body yearned for him, she wanted to be able to fully enjoy their first time together. She had a concussion, and there were an unknown number of people after them who would likely try to kill them, as well as Sole Pleasure—powerful distractions, indeed.

Gingerly she sat up on the side of the bed, being very careful to hold her head as still as possible. The aspirin had helped; the pain was still there, but it didn't throb as sickeningly as it had before. She eased into a standing position and was relieved when the room remained stable.

Instantly he was on his feet beside her, his hand on her arm. "What are you doing? You need to rest as much as possible."

"I'm going to take a shower and get dressed. If I'm going to be shot at, I want to be on my feet and wearing clothes when it happens." God, he was big, and there was all that naked flesh right in front of her. She took a deep breath, fighting the urge to press herself against him, to find out exactly where her head would fit against his shoulder now that they were standing up. His body was so beautiful, his shoulders wide and powerful, his arms and legs thick with muscle. How silly she'd been to avoid him all these weeks, when she could have been getting to know him! Silently she mourned those wasted days. She should have realized sooner why her reaction to him had been so sharp, why she'd felt that odd sense of fright.

This was the man with whom she would spend the rest of her life. No matter where her career had taken her, home had always been a mountain in Wyoming, and Alex MacNeil was going to change that. Her home would be with him, wherever he was, and an FBI special agent could be assigned anywhere. Though her life would never be completely without horses, he might be assigned to a city, where she wouldn't be able to find a job as trainer. She had never before met a man whom she would even consider putting ahead of her horses— but she looked at him and instinctively thought, *No contest*.

He was hers. She was his. She recognized it at every level of her being, as if she were vibrating to a resonance that only he produced.

But danger surrounded them, and she had to be prepared.

He had been watching her face with that narrow-eyed, intensely focused way of his. He didn't release her, but drew her closer, his arm circling her narrow waist. "Forget whatever you're thinking. You don't have to do anything but stay out of the way."

His nearness was too tempting. Maris leaned her head on his chest, rubbing her cheek against the hairy roughness as an almost painful tenderness filled her. "I won't let you do this alone." His nipple was right there, only a few inches from her mouth, and as irresistible as catnip to a kitten. She moved those few inches, and her tongue darted out, delicately licking the flat brown circle.

He shuddered, his arm tightening convulsively around her. But his gaze was grim and determined as he cupped her chin with his other hand and gently lifted her face. "It's my job," he said in the even, quietly implacable tone she had heard before. "You're a civilian, and you're hurt. The best way you can help me is by staying out of the way."

She smiled in wry amusement. "If you knew me better, you wouldn't say that." She was fiercely, instinctively, protective of those she loved, and the thought of letting him face danger alone made her blood freeze in horror. Unfortunately, fate had decreed that she love a man whose profession was putting himself between the lawless elements in society and those he had sworn to protect. She couldn't demand that he quit his job any more than her family had demanded that she quit the dangerous work of gentling unbroken horses. He was what he was, and loving him meant not trying to change him.

She straightened away from him. "I'm still going to shower and dress. I still don't want to face anyone in just my panties and a T-shirt...." She paused. "Except you."

He inhaled sharply, his nostrils flaring, and she saw his hand flex as if he wanted to reach for her again. Because time had to be growing short, she stepped away from him, away from temptation, and gathered up her clothes. Just as she reached the bathroom door a thought occurred to her, and she stopped, looking back at him. *Was* he alone? Though Zane and Chance never talked about their assignments, they had sometimes discussed techniques, back in their training days, and she had absorbed a lot. It would be very unusual for an FBI agent to be working without backup.

"Your partner should be close by," she said. "Am I right?"

His eyebrows lifted in faint surprise; then he smiled. "In the parking lot. He got into position an hour or so after we got here. No one's going to take us by surprise."

If his partner hadn't been on watch, Maris realized, MacNeil never would have relaxed his guard enough to be in bed with her or let himself be distracted by the sexual attraction between them. Still, she was certain he hadn't slept but had remained awake in case his partner signaled him.

"What's his name? What does he look like? I need to be able to tell the good guys from the bad."

"Dean Pearsall. He's five-eleven, skinny, dark hair and eyes, receding hairline. He's from Maine. You can't miss the accent."

"It's cold out there," she said. "He must be frozen."

"Like I said, he's from Maine. This is nothing new to him. He has a thermos of coffee, and he lets the car run enough to keep the frost off the windshield, so he can see."

"Won't that be a dead giveaway, no frost on the car?"

"Only if someone knows how long the car has been there, and it isn't a detail most people notice." He picked up his jeans and stepped into them, never taking his eyes off her as he considered the somewhat startling workings of her nimble brain. "Why did *you* think of it?"

She gave him a sweet smile, her mother's smile. "You'll understand when you meet my family." Then she went into the bathroom and closed the door.

Her smile faded immediately once she was alone. Though she fully realized and accepted the wisdom of not interfering with a trained professional and his partner, she was also sharply aware that plans could go wrong and people could get hurt. It happened, no matter how good or careful someone was. Chance had been wounded several times; he always tried to keep it from their mother, but somehow Mary always sensed when he'd been hurt, and Maris did, too. She could feel it deep inside, in a secret place that only those she loved had managed to touch. She had been almost insane with fear that time when Zane was nearly killed rescuing Barrie from terrorists in Libya, until she saw him for herself and felt his steely life force undiminished.

It had happened to Zane, and he was the best planner in the business. In fact, expecting things to go wrong was one of the things that made Zane so good at what he did. There was always a wild card in the deck, he said, and she had to be prepared for it, no matter how it was played.

Her advantages were that she was trained in self-defense, was a very good shot, and knew more about battle tactics than anyone could expect. On the other hand, her pistol was in her cottage, so she was unarmed, unless she could talk MacNeil into giving her a weapon. Considering how implacable his expression had been, she didn't think she had much chance of that. She was also concussed, and though the headache had lessened and she was feeling better now, she wasn't certain how well she could function if the situation called for fast movement. The fact that her memory hadn't returned was worrisome; the injury could be more severe than she'd initally thought, even though her other symptoms had lessened.

Who had hit her? Why was someone trying to kill Sole Pleasure? Damn it, if only she could remember!

She wrapped a towel around her head to keep her hair dry and stood under a lukewarm spray of water, going over and over the parts she remembered, as if she could badger her bruised brain into giving up its secrets. Everything had been normal when she went back to the stables after lunch. It had been after dark, say around six or six-thirty, when she stumbled across MacNeil. Sometime during those five hours she had learned that Sole Pleasure was in danger and either surprised someone trying to kill him or confronted the person beforehand and earned herself a knock on the head.

It didn't make sense, but the Stonichers had to be behind the threat to their prize stallion, because they were the only ones who could benefit financially from his death. Since they would make much more by syndicating him for stud, the only way killing him made any sense at all was if he had some problem that would prevent them from syndicating him.

It wasn't a question of health; Maris had grown up around horses, loved them with a passion and devotion that had consumed her life, and she knew every detail of the well-being of her charges. Sole Pleasure was in perfect health, an unusually strong, fast horse who was full of energy and good spirits. He was a big, cheerful athlete who ran for the sheer love of running, sometimes mischievous but remarkably free of bad habits. She loved all her horses, but Pleasure was special to her. It was unthinkable that anyone would want to kill him, destroy forever that big, good-natured heart and matchless physical ability.

The only thing she could think of that would interfere with his syndication, the only possible reason anyone would grab for insurance money rather than hold out for the much larger fortune to be gained from syndicating him, was if the fertility tests had proved him sterile.

If that was the case, the Stonichers might as well geld him and race him as long as he was healthy. But injuries happened to even the hardiest animals, and a racing career could be ended in a heartbeat. The great filly Ruffian had been on the way to victory, well ahead of her male opponent in a special match race, when an awkward step shattered her leg and she had to be put down. Given the uncertainties of winning purses on the track and the given of insurance money, if Sole Pleasure was sterile, the Stonichers could conceivably be going for the sure thing and have hired someone to kill him.

She didn't want to think it of them. Joan and Ronald Stonicher had always seemed like decent people to her, though not the kind with whom she would ever be close friends. They were Kentucky blue bloods, born into the life, but Ronald particularly seemed to be involved in raising horses only *because* he'd inherited the farm. While Joan knew the horses better and was a better rider than her husband, she was a cool, emotionally detached woman who paid more attention to social functions than she did to the earthy functions in the stables. The question was, could they deliberately kill a champion Thoroughbred for the insurance money?

No one else was in a position to collect, so it had to be them.

They wouldn't do it themselves, however. Maris couldn't imagine either one of them actually doing the deed. They had hired someone to kill Pleasure, but who? It had to be someone she saw every day, someone whose presence near the horses wouldn't attract attention. It was likely one of the temporary hands, but she couldn't rule out a longtime employee; a couple hundred thousand would be terribly tempting to someone who didn't care how he earned it.

She turned off the shower and stepped out, turning the situation around and around in her head. By the time she was dressed, one thought was clear: MacNeil knew who the killer was.

She opened the door and stepped out, almost stumbling over him. He was propped against the countertop in the small dressing area, his arms crossed and his long legs stretched out, patiently waiting in case she became dizzy and needed him. He, too, had dressed, and though he looked mouth-wateringly tough and sexy in jeans, flannel shirt and boots, she regretted no longer being able to see him in nothing more than tight-fitting boxers.

Maris jabbed a slender finger at his chest. "You know who it is, don't you?"

He looked down at the small hand so imperiously poking him, and one dark brow lifted in bemusement. He probably wasn't accustomed to being called to account by someone he could have picked up with one hand. "Why do you think that?" he asked in a mild voice, but even so he stood so that he towered over her, silently reestablishing his dominance.

It might have worked if she hadn't grown up watching her petite mother rule over a household populated by brawny males. She was very much her mother's daughter; it never occurred to her to be intimidated. Instead she poked him harder.

"You said a tip led you to Solomon Green. Obviously the FBI has been working on this for a while, so just as obviously you have to have a list of suspects you're watching. One of those suspects is now working at Solomon Green, isn't he? That's what tipped you off." She scowled up at him. "Why did you say I was a suspect, when you know darn good and well—"

"Hold it." He held up a staying hand, interrupting her. "You *were* a suspect. Everyone was. I know who my main suspect is, but he isn't working alone. This ring has to have the collusion of a lot of people. The owners are the main ones to profit, but any of the employees could also be in on it."

She didn't like to think any of her people would be involved in murdering a horse for profit, but she had to admit it was possible. "So you followed him there and you've been watching him, trying to catch him in the act so you'll have proof against him." Her dark eyes caught fire. "Were you going to let him actually kill a horse, so there would be no doubt?"

"That isn't the outcome we'd like," he said carefully, watching her. "But we're aware that could be the scenario."

Her eyes narrowed. She wasn't fooled by his formal "official speak," used by both the military and law-enforcement organizations. Reading between the lines, she knew that while he might not like letting a horse be harmed, he'd been willing to let it happen if that was what it took.

She wasn't thinking of slugging him; she was angry, but not foolish. He's already proven he was more than a match for her. Still, the expression on her face must have made him think she was about to try again to take him down, because his hand came up in one of those lightning-fast movements and caught her wrist, holding it against his chest.

She drew herself up to her full five feet almost three inches and lifted her chin. "I refuse to sacrifice a horse. Any horse."

"That isn't what I want, either." He gently cupped her stubborn chin, his fingertips tracing over the satiny skin of her jaw. "But we can't make our move until they do something conclusive, something we can make stick in the courts. We have to tie everything together in a knot some slick lawyer can't undo, or a murderer is going to walk. This isn't just about horses and insurance fraud. A stable hand was killed, a kid just sixteen years old. He must have stumbled across something the way you did, but he wasn't as lucky. The next morning there was a dead horse in the stall and the kid was missing. That was in Connecticut. A week later his body was found in Pennsylvania.''

She stared at him, her dark eyes stark. The Stonichers might just be after the money, but they had aligned themselves with people who were truly evil. Any regret she might have felt for them vanished.

MacNeil's face was like stone. ''I won't move too soon and blow the investigation. No matter what, I'm going to nail these bastards. Do you understand?''

She did. Completely. That left only one thing to do. ''You refuse to compromise the case, and I won't let Pleasure be hurt. That means you'll have to use me as the bait.''

Chapter Six

"Absolutely not." The words were flat and implacable. "No way in hell."

"You have to."

He looked down at her with mingled exasperation and amusement. "Sweetheart, you've been the boss for so long that you've forgotten how to take orders. I'm running this show, not you, and you'll damn well do what I tell you to do, when I tell you to do it, or you're going to find yourself handcuffed and gagged and your sweet little ass stuffed in a closet until this is over."

Maris batted her long eyelashes at him. "So you think my ass is sweet, huh?"

"So sweet I'll probably be biting it before too much longer." The concept appealed to him; she could tell by the way his eyes darkened. She was rather taken by it, herself. Then he shrugged the moment away and grinned. "But no matter how good you taste or how fast you flutter those eyelashes, you aren't going to change my mind about this."

She crossed her arms and offered him an irrefutable fact. "You need me. I don't know what I saw or who hit me. It could have been one of the Stonichers, or it could have been whoever they hired. But they don't know that I can't remember, and they don't know about *you,* so they think I'm the biggest threat to them."

"That's exactly why you're staying out of sight. If it's one of the Stonichers holding the gun, I can't predict how he or she will act. Give me a professional killer any day, rather than an amateur, who's likely to panic and do something really stupid, like shooting you in front of a bunch of witnesses."

"God forbid you should have to deal with anyone who would get rattled by committing murder," she said, sweetly sarcastic, and he gave her another of those patented narrow looks of his. She continued with her argument. "They're probably surprised that I haven't already called the cops on them. By now they're figuring I was either hurt more than they'd thought at first and I'm lying unconscious somewhere, or that I've realized I have no proof to take to the cops, so I have no excuse for stealing a priceless horse. Either way, they want me. I'm the perfect patsy. They can kill Pleasure, make it look like I did it, and then kill me. Everything's tied up nice and clean, and who knows, the insurance policy may even pay double indemnity, which is more money in everyone's pocket. Nothing will make them commit faster than seeing me."

"Damn it, *no.*" He shook his head in exasperation. "I can't believe the way your mind works. You must read a lot of thrillers."

She glared at him, affronted. Her argument was perfectly logical, and he knew it. That didn't mean he liked it. It didn't even mean he would agree with it; she was fast learning that she could add *protective* to the list of his characteristics. And *stubborn*. God forbid she should forget stubborn.

"Sweetheart..." He smoothed his hands over her shoulders, an unfamiliar, tender ache in his chest as he felt the delicacy of her bones. He tried to think of the words that would convince her to leave this business to him and Dean. It was their job; they were trained for it. She would be in the way, and worrying about her would drive him crazy. God, she evidently thought she was seven feet tall and made of pig iron, but he could see how pale she was, how carefully she moved. She wasn't normally fragile, despite the slightness of her build; he'd seen her ride, effortlessly controlling stallions that most men would have trouble handling, so he knew she was strong. She was also alarmingly valiant, and he didn't know if his nerves could stand the stress.

"Look at it this way," she said. "As long as they don't know where Pleasure is, I'm safe. They need me to get to him."

He didn't argue, didn't try to convince her. He just shook his head and said, "No."

She gave his forehead an experimental rap with her knuckles, a puzzled look on her face.

He drew back a little, blinking in surprise. "What are you doing?"

"Seeing if your head's made out of wood," she retorted, her exasperation showing through. "You're letting your emotions interfere with your job. I'm your best bet—so use me!"

Mac stood motionless. He couldn't have been more stunned if this delicate fire-eater had suddenly lifted him over her head and tossed him through the window. *He* was letting his emotions interfere with the job? That was the last thing he'd ever imagined anyone would say to him. What made him so good at his job was his ability to divorce himself from the emotions that could hamper his actions. He'd always been the one who kept his head, who remained cool no matter how tense the situation. He might have some sleepless nights afterward, he might sweat bullets, but while the job was going down he was an iceman.

He couldn't be emotional about her; it wasn't logical. Okay, so he'd had the hots for her since he'd first seen her. Chemistry happened. With her, it had happened in a big way. And he liked her; he'd learned a lot about her since she had practically commandeered him the night before. She was quick-thinking, had a sense of humor, and was too damned gutsy for his peace of mind. She also responded to his slightest touch, her soft body melting against him, with a sheer delight that went to his head faster than a hit of whiskey.

He frowned. Only the fact that she was concussed had kept him from taking her, and even then, it had been a near thing. Never mind that they were waiting for a killer to come after them, that he had deliberately left a trail that was just difficult enough to keep from being obvious. He never should have undressed last night; he knew that. But the fact was, he had wanted to feel her against his skin, and so he'd taken off everything but his shorts and slipped into bed with her. Dean would beep him when anyone showed up; if Mac had timed it right, he figured it would take another hour at least before anything happened, but still he should have been dressed and ready in case something went wrong. Instead, he had been on top of her, between her legs, and thinking that only two thin layers of cotton were keeping him from her. It would have taken him maybe five seconds to get those two layers out of the way, and then he would have been inside her and to hell with anything else.

But none of that was emotion. That was liking, and a powerful lust. So she had this crazy idea, after spending only a few hours with him—and being asleep most of that time—that they were going to get married. Just because she felt that way didn't mean he did, and he sure as hell wasn't going to let himself be buffaloed into something like marriage, no matter how hard he got whenever she was anywhere around.

The thought of using her as bait almost made the top of his head come off, but that wasn't emotion, it was common sense.

"You're concussed," he finally said. "You're moving like a snail, and you don't need to be moving at all. You'd be more of a hindrance than a help, because I'd have to watch you, as well as myself."

"Then give me a weapon," she replied, her tone so unruffled that he wasn't sure he'd heard right.

"A weapon?" he echoed incredulously. "Good God, you think I'm going to arm a *civilian*?"

She straightened away from his grasp, and his palms ached from the loss of contact. All of a sudden her black eyes weren't bottomless at all, they were cool and flat, and the recognition of what he was seeing jolted him.

"I can handle a pistol as well as you, maybe better."

She wasn't exaggerating. He'd seen that look in the eyes of snipers, and in the eyes of some fellow agents who had been there, done that, and had the guts to do it again. He had seen it in his own eyes, and he'd understood when some women had shied away from him, frightened by the dangerous edge they sensed in him.

Maris wouldn't shy away. She looked delicate, but she was pure steel.

He could use her. The thought flashed into his brain, and he couldn't dismiss it. Policy said that no civilians should be involved if it could be avoided, but too many times it *couldn't* be avoided. She was right; she was his best bet, and he would be a fool if he compromised the investigation by not using her. It wrenched every instinct he had to do it, but he had to put his feelings aside and concentrate on the job.

Damn it, he thought in surprise, he *had* been letting his emotions cloud his thinking. That wasn't a good sign, and he had to put a stop to that kind of idiocy right now.

"All right," he said swiftly, wheeling around to get their jackets. He jerked his on and began stuffing Maris into hers. "Time's short, so we have to move fast. First we need to get the stallion out of the trailer and hidden somewhere else, then position the trailer so that whoever comes can't see that he isn't in it. Then we come back here. You drive the truck, I'll be hidden in the truck bed, under some blankets or something.'' He turned out the bathroom light and began ushering her toward the door. ''We'll post Dean down the road, where he can see them arrive. He'll leave then and get into position at the trailer. He'll give us warning. You leave by the back way just as they arrive, let them get a glimpse of the truck. They follow.''

They reached the door. MacNeil turned out the lights and took a small radio out of his pocket, keying it. ''Is everything clear?'' he asked. ''We're coming out.''

''What?'' His partner's voice was startled. ''Yeah, everything's clear. What's up?''

''Tell you in a minute.''

He slipped the radio back into his pocket and unchained the door. He paused then, looking down at her. ''Are you sure you can do this? If your head is hurting too much, let me know now, before it goes any further.''

''I can do it.'' Her voice was calm, matter-of-fact, and he gave a short nod.

''Okay, then.'' He opened the door, and cold air slapped her in the face. She shivered, even though she was wearing her thick down jacket. The weather bureau had been predicting the arrival of a cold front, she remembered. She had watched the noon news and weather yesterday; perhaps that was why she now had this thick jacket instead of the flannel-lined denim jacket she had been wearing yesterday morning. She was glad she had changed coats, because the temperature now had to be in the twenties.

She looked around as she left the cozy warmth of the motel room. The motel office and the highway were on her right. MacNeil took her arm and steered her to the left, circling her behind a late-model pickup truck that was covered over with frost. "Hold it a minute," he said, and left her hidden by the truck's bulk while he went around to the driver's side. He opened the door and leaned in. She caught the faint metallic jingle of keys; then the motor started and settled into a quiet idle. She noticed with approval that the interior light hadn't come on, which meant he had taken care of that little detail earlier.

Interior lights. As he closed the truck door with a barely audible click, the neon light from the motel sign slanted across his high cheekbones, and a door opened in her mind.

She remembered the way his face had looked last night as he drove, the grimness of his expression highlighted by the faint green glow from the dash.

She remembered the desperation with which she had hidden her condition from him. She had been afraid to let him know how weak she was, how terribly her head hurt, that she was vulnerable in any way. He hadn't said much, just driven in dark silence, but even through her pain she had felt the physical awareness running between them like a live electrical wire. If she showed any vulnerability, she'd thought, he would be on her.

That was why he'd come with her, not because he was concerned about Sole Pleasure.

Her thinking had been muddled by the knock she'd taken on the head. She had been terrified for Pleasure's safety, trying to think of the best way to protect him, and she hadn't been certain she could trust MacNeil. She had taken a big chance in asking for his help; he had given it without question, but afterward she'd been too unbalanced by the concussion and the strength and unfamiliarity of her own sensual awareness of him to think straight.

She had wound up exactly where she was afraid she would, under him in bed. And he hadn't done a darn thing, except make her fall in love with him.

"Come on," he said softly, not looking at her. In fact, he was looking at everything except her, his head swiveling, restless eyes noting every detail of their surroundings.

The early morning was dark and silent, so cold that their breath fogged into ice crystals. No stars winked overhead, and she knew why when a few white flakes began drifting soundlessly to the ground. A cold breeze sliced through her jeans, freezing her legs.

He led her across to a nondescript tan Oldsmobile that was backed into a parking slot between a scraggly bush, the motel's attempt at landscaping, and a Volvo station wagon. She walked carefully, and her headache obliged by remaining bearable.

He opened the rear door of the four-door car and put her inside, then he got into the front, beside his partner. Dean Pearsall was exactly as MacNeil had described him, thin and dark, as well as definitely puzzled. "What the hell's going on?"

Briefly MacNeil outlined the plan. Pearsall's head swiveled, and he looked over the seat at Maris, doubt plain in his expression.

"I can do it," she said, not giving him time to voice that doubt.

"We have to work fast," MacNeil said. "Can you get the video equipment set up?"

"Yeah," Pearsall replied. "Maybe. We're cutting it damn close, though."

"Then let's not waste any more time." MacNeil popped open the glove box and removed a holstered pistol. He took it out, checked it, then slid it back into the holster before handing it back to Maris. "It's a .38 revolver, five shots, and there's a round under the hammer."

She nodded and checked the weapon herself. A faint smile eased the grim line of his mouth as he watched her; he wouldn't have taken someone else's word on the state of a weapon's readiness, either.

"There's a Kevlar vest on the seat beside you. It'll be way too big for you, but put it on anyway," he instructed.

"That's your vest," Pearsall said.

"Yeah, but she's going to wear it."

Maris slipped the revolver into her coat pocket and grabbed the vest. "I'll put it on in the truck," she said as she opened the door and slid out. "We have to hurry."

The snowflakes were still drifting down, ghostly in the predawn quiet. Their footsteps crunched on the gravel as she and MacNeil crossed the parking lot to the truck. The defroster had cleared the bottom half of the windshield, and that was enough for him to drive.

He didn't turn on the headlights until they were on the highway and he could tell there was nothing in sight in either direction except for the tan Oldsmobile, which had pulled out behind them. Then he hit the switch, and the green dash lights illuminated his face just as they had earlier.

Maris shrugged out of her coat and into the Kevlar vest. It was heavy and far too big, so big it covered her hips, but she didn't waste her time arguing about wearing the cumbersome garment, because she knew MacNeil would never give in on this.

"I remember driving with you last night," she said.

He glanced at her. "Your memory's back?"

"Not all of it. I still don't remember who hit me on the head, or taking Pleasure. By the way, don't you think you should tell me?"

He grunted. "I don't know who hit you. There's a choice between at least three people, maybe more."

"Ronald and Joan are two. Who's the one you followed to Solomon Green?"

"The new vet. Randy Yu."

Maris was silent. That name surprised her; she would have thought of a lot of other people before she would have come up with the vet's name. She'd been impressed with his skill, and he'd never shown anything but the utmost care for his four-legged patients. He was a quarter Chinese, in his middle thirties, and with the strength a veterinarian needed. If he was the one she'd tangled with, she was surprised she'd managed to get away from him with no more than a bump on the head. Of course, whoever she'd fought with wouldn't have expected her to know how to fight, much less fight hard and dirty.

"It makes sense," she said, thinking about it. "A quick injection, Pleasure dies of cardiac arrest, and it looks like natural causes. Not nearly as messy as a bullet."

"But you ruined that plan for them," MacNeil said, harshness underlying the calm of his tone. "Now they'll be planning to use bullets—for both you *and* the horse."

Chapter Seven

Sole Pleasure wasn't happy. He didn't like being alone, he didn't like being cramped in a small trailer for so long, and he was both hungry and thirsty. MacNeil had backed the horse trailer deep into a section of woods, so deep she didn't know how he'd managed it, and Pleasure didn't like the unfamiliar surroundings, either. He was a horse accustomed to open pastures, roomy stalls, noise and people. As soon as they got out of the truck they heard his angry neighing and the thud of one of his rear hooves repeatedly kicking against the back of the trailer.

"He'll hurt himself!" Maris hurried to the trailer, moving faster than she should have for the sake of her head, but if Pleasure managed to break his leg, he would *have* to be put down. "Easy, baby, easy," she crooned as she unlatched the back gate, the special note she used for her horses entering her tone. The kicking stopped immediately, and she could almost see the alert black ears swiveling to catch her voice.

"Hold it." MacNeil's hand came down on top of hers as she started to open the gate. "I'll get him out. He's fractious, and I don't want him bumping you around. You stand over there and keep talking to him."

She gave him a considering look as she moved to the side. Really, the man was acting as if this were the first time she'd ever been hurt. Anyone who worked with horses could expect to be kicked, bitten, bruised and bucked off—though she hadn't been thrown since she'd been a kid. Still, she'd collected her share of injuries: Both arms had been broken, as well as her collarbone. She'd had a concussion before, too. What was the best way to handle an overprotective man, especially after you were married?

Exactly the way her mother handled her father, she thought, grinning. By standing her ground, talking rings around him, and distracting him with sex, and by choosing her battles and sometimes actually letting him have his way. This was one of the times to not kick up a fuss. She would ignore him later, when the stakes were greater.

MacNeil skillfully backed the big stallion out of the trailer; Pleasure came eagerly, happy to have company again, relieved to be unconfined. He showed his happiness by dancing around and playing, shoving MacNeil with his head and generally acting like any four-year-old. All things considered, Maris was just as happy not to be on the receiving end of those head butts, or to have to control all that power as he danced around. He would have been quieter for her—the horses found her especially soothing—but any jolt right now wasn't fun.

MacNeil led Pleasure away from the trailer, the stallion's hooves almost soundless on the thick pad of pine needles and decomposing leaves that carpeted the forest floor. He tied the reins to a sapling and patted the animal's glossy neck. "Okay, you can come over now," he called to Maris. "Keep him happy while I reposition the trailer."

She took control of the stallion, calming him with her voice and hands. He was still hungry and thirsty, but he was such a curious, gregarious horse that his interest in the proceedings kept him occupied. Dean Pearsall had stopped the Oldsmobile farther back, positioning the car so its headlights lit the area. MacNeil got in the truck and put it in reverse, leaning out the open door to check his position as he backed the truck up to the trailer. He was good at it; it took some people forever to get the trailer hitch in the right position, but MacNeil did it on the first try. Pretty good for an FBI agent, Maris thought. He was a fed now, but he'd obviously spent a lot of time around horses in the past.

It was snowing a little more heavily now, the headlight beams catching the drifting flakes as they sifted through the bare branches of the hardwoods. The pines were beginning to acquire a dusting of white. MacNeil maneuvered the trailer around, threading it through the trees, repositioning it so that it directly faced the narrow trail they'd made and anyone coming down it wouldn't be able to see that Pleasure wasn't inside. There were high, narrow side windows in the trailer, but none in front.

As soon as the trailer was in position and MacNeil had unhooked the truck and pulled away, Pearsall went to work, squirming underneath the trailer and setting up a video camera so that it couldn't easily be seen but would still have a good angle on anyone approaching the trailer.

MacNeil turned to Maris. "While Dean's working, let's get Pleasure tucked away back in the woods." He checked the luminous hands on his watch. "We need to be out of here in five minutes, ten tops."

The trailer contained blankets that had been used to cover the mare who had been brought to Solomon Green the day before. Maris got the darkest one and spread it across Pleasure's broad back. He liked that, swaying his muscular rump as if he were doing the hootchie-cootchie, and blowing in the particular way he did when he was pleased. She laughed, the sound quiet and loving, as she reached up to hug his big neck. He lipped her hair, but gently, as if he'd somehow realized by the way she moved that she wasn't quite up to speed.

"This way." MacNeil's voice held an odd note as he handed a flashlight to Maris, then untied the reins and began leading Pleasure deeper into the trees. He curved his other arm around Maris, holding her close to his side as they walked. Between the oversize Kevlar vest and her thick down jacket, he couldn't feel *her,* so he slipped his hand under the coat, under the vest, resting it on the swell of her hip. "How are you feeling?" he asked as they picked their way through the dark woods, stepping over fallen limbs and evading bushes that clutched at their clothes.

"Okay." She smiled up at him, letting herself lean closer into the heat and strength of his big body. "I've had a concussion before, and though this one isn't any fun, I don't think it's as bad as the first one. The pain is going away faster, so I don't understand why I can't remember what happened."

Her bewilderment was plain, and his fingers tightened on her hip. "A different part of your brain is affected, I guess. And parts of your memory are already coming back, so by tomorrow you'll probably remember everything."

She hoped so; these blank holes in her life were unsettling. It was just a matter of a few hours now, as she regained partial memory of things that had happened both before and after she was hit, but she didn't like not knowing everything that had happened. She remembered driving with MacNeil, but why couldn't she remember arriving at the motel?

Only one way to find out what she wanted to know. "Did I undress myself?"

Glancing up, she saw him smile at the abrupt change of subject. His voice deepened, evidence of the way the memory affected him. "It was a joint effort."

Maybe she would have been embarrassed an hour ago, but not now. Instead she felt a sort of aroused contentment fill her at the thought of him pulling off his T-shirt and putting it on her, the soft cotton still warm from his body.

"Did you touch me?" The whispered words were like heated honey, flowing over him, telling him how much she liked the idea.

"No, you were too out of it." But he'd wanted to, he thought. God, how he'd wanted to. He helped her over a fallen tree, supporting her so that she wouldn't stumble, but he was remembering how she'd looked sitting on the side of the bed, wearing nothing but her panties, her eyes closing, her pale hair floating around her delicate, satiny shoulders. Her breasts were high, firm, small but deliciously round, her nipples like dark pink little crowns. His right hand clenched on the reins; his palm was actually aching to touch her now, to fill his hand with that cool, richly resilient flesh and warm it with his loving.

"Well, darn," she said sedately, and in the glow of the flashlight he saw the welcome in her night-dark eyes.

He inhaled deeply, reaching for control. They had no time for any delay, much less one that would last an hour. An hour? He gave a mental snort. Who was he kidding? He was so worked up that five minutes was more like it, and that was only if his self-control turned out to be a lot stronger than it felt right now.

"Later," he promised, his voice a rough growl of need. Later, when this was settled and his job done. Later, when he could take the time with her that he wanted to take, behind a locked door and with the telephone off the hook. Later, when she felt better, damn it, and wasn't dealing with a concussion. He figured it would be two days, at least, before her head-ache was gone—two long, hellish days.

He stopped and looked back. They had gone far enough that he could no longer see the headlights through the trees. A small hollow dipped just ahead, and he led Sole Pleasure into it. The hollow blocked the wind, and tall trees leaning overhead protected him from the light snow. "You'll be okay here for a couple of hours," he told the horse as he tied the reins to a low, sturdy branch. Pleasure would be able to move around some, and if there were any edible leaves or stray blades of grass, he would be able to graze within a small area.

"Be good," Maris admonished the horse, stroking his forehead. "We won't be gone long. Then we'll take you back to your big, comfortable stall, and you can have your favorite feed, and an apple for dessert." He blew softly, then bobbed his head up and down in agreement. She didn't know how many actual words he understood, but he definitely understood the love in her voice, and he knew she was telling him good stuff.

MacNeil took the flashlight from her hand and set-tled his arm around her again as they walked back to the truck. Pleasure neighed his disapproval of being left alone, but soon the trees blotted out the sound and there was only the rustle of their feet in the leaves.

"You know what to do," he said. "They won't fol-low you too closely on the highway, because they won't want to make you suspicious. Let them see where you leave the road, but then drive as fast as you can, to give yourself as much time as possible. They'll be able to follow the tracks. Pull up to the trailer, get out of the truck and get into the trees. Don't waste time, don't look back to see what I'm doing. Get into a protected place and stay there until either Dean or I come for you. If anyone else shows up, use that pistol.''

''You need the vest more than I do.'' Worry gnawed at her. He was sending her out of harm's way, while he would be right in the middle of it, without protection.

''They might pull in before you're completely out of sight and get a shot off at you. The only way I'll let you do this is if you're wearing the vest.''

There that stubborn streak was again, she thought. Streak? Ha! He was permeated with it. She was beginning to think that if she scratched his skin, stubbornness would ooze out instead of blood. Living with him was going to be interesting; as he'd noted, she was used to being the boss, and so was he. She looked forward to the fights—and to the making up.

Pearsall was waiting for them when they got back. ''Everything's ready,'' he said. ''There's a six-hour tape in the camera, and the battery pack is fully charged. Now, if we can just get back into position before the bad guys show up, we're set.''

MacNeil nodded. ''You leave first. We'll let you get out of sight before we follow. Radio if you see anything suspicious.''

''Give me an extra minute so I can swing through the motel parking lot to make sure there aren't any new arrivals. Then I'll pull back and take up position.''

Pearsall got into the car and backed out, his head-lights bobbing through the trees.

Darkness settled around them as they listened to the sound of the car fading in the distance. MacNeil opened the passenger door of the truck and put his hands on Maris's waist, lifting her onto the seat. In the darkness, his face was only a pale blur. "Whatever happens, make sure you stay safe," he growled, and bent his head to her.

His lips were cold, and firm. Maris wound her arms around his neck and opened her mouth to him as he deepened the kiss, slanting his head for better contact. His tongue wasn't cold at all, but hot and strong, and her entire body tightened with excitement as she leaned closer to him. It wasn't enough; with the pleasure came frustration. She swiveled on the seat to face him, part-ing her legs so that he stood between them, pressed hard against her as the kiss changed yet again, into something fierce with need.

It was their first kiss, but there was no tentative-ness, no searching. They already knew each other, had already made the inner adjustment to the hot ache of physical desire, and accepted the hunger. They were already lovers, though their bodies hadn't yet been joined. The pact had been made. Invisible strands of attraction had been pulling them together from the first, and the web was almost complete.

He tore his mouth away from hers, breathing hard, his breath fogging in the cold air. "No more," he said, the words strained. "Not now. I'm as hard as a rock already, and if we—'' He broke off. ''We have to go. Now.''

''Have we given Dean enough time?''

''Hell, I don't know! All I know is that I'm about ten seconds away from pulling your jeans off, and if we don't go now, the whole plan is blown.''

She didn't want to let him go. Her arms didn't want to release their hold on him, her thighs didn't want to loosen from around his hips. But she did it, forced herself to open her embrace, because she could feel the truth pushing against her.

In silence he stepped back, and she turned in the seat so that she faced forward. He closed the door, then walked stiffly around the truck to climb in under the steering wheel, a look of acute discomfort on his face.

She wasn't good for his sanity, he thought as he started the truck and put it in gear. She made him forget about the job and think only about sex. Not sex in general, but sex in particular. Sex with her. Again and again, holding that slim body beneath him until he was satisfied.

He tried to imagine being sated with her, and he couldn't. Alarm tingled through him. He tried to think of some of the other women he'd slept with over the years, but their names wouldn't come to mind, their faces eluded him, and there was no concrete memory of how any of them had felt. There was only her mouth, her breasts, her legs. Her voice, her body in his arms, her hair spread across the pillow. He could imagine her in the shower with him, her face across the table from him every morning, her clothes hanging beside his in the closet.

The most frightening thing was that it was so damn easy to imagine it all. The only thing that frightened him more was the thought that it might not happen, that he was actually using her in a setup where she could be hurt, despite all the pains he was taking to keep her safe.

They left the cover of the woods, and he eased the truck across the rutted ditch and onto the highway. No headlights appeared in either direction. Fat snow-flakes swirled and danced in the beams of their own headlights, and the low clouds blocked any hint of the approaching dawn.

The radio remained silent, meaning Dean hadn't seen anything suspicious. After several minutes the lights of the motel sign came into view, and a few seconds after that they passed the Oldsmobile, pulled off on the side of the road and were facing back the way they'd come. It looked unoccupied, but Mac knew Dean was there, watching everything. No vehicle could approach the motel without being seen.

He pulled into the parking lot and backed into a slot, so that she could get out faster. He left the engine running, though he killed the lights. He turned to face her. "You know what to do. Do exactly that and nothing else. Understand?"

"Yes."

"All right. I'm going to get into the back of the truck now. If the fools start shooting early, hit the floorboards and stay there."

"Yes, sir," she said, this time with a hint of dryness.

He paused with his hand on the door handle. He looked at her and muttered something under his breath. Then she was in his arms again, and his mouth was hard, urgent, as he kissed her. He let her go as abruptly as he'd grabbed her, and got out of the truck. Without another word, he closed the door, then vaulted lightly into the truck bed, where he lay down out of sight and waited for a killer to appear.

Chapter Eight

The motel was located where a small side road entered the main highway. The highway ran in front of the motel, the secondary road along the right side. Dean had checked out the little road as soon as he arrived and found that it wandered aimlessly through the rural area. No one looking for them was likely to arrive by that route, because it went nowhere and took its time getting there. The Stonichers and/or their hired killer would be on the highway, checking motels, following the faint but deliberate trail Mac had left. The plan was for Maris to let their pursuers catch a glimpse of her as she drove around the back of the motel and onto the secondary road. She would turn left, then right, onto the highway. They would notice immediately that she wasn't pulling the horse trailer, so instead of trying to cut her off, they would hang back and follow her, expecting her to lead them to Sole Pleasure.

At least Mac hoped that was how it worked. If Yu was the only one following them, that was how it would go down. Yu was a professional; he would keep his head. If anyone else was with him, the unpredictability factor shot sky-high.

It was cold in the back of the truck. He had forgotten to get any blankets to cover himself, and the snow was still falling. Mac huddled deeper into his coat and tried to be thankful he was out of the wind. It wasn't working.

The minutes dragged by, drawn out agonizingly by his tension as he waited. Dawn finally began to penetrate the cloud cover, the darkness fading to a deep gray, though true daylight was at least an hour away. Traffic would begin picking up soon, making it difficult for Dean to spot their tail. People would begin leaving the motel, complicating the traffic pattern even more. And better light would make it more difficult for Maris to hide in the woods.

"Come on, come on," he muttered. Had he made the trail *too* difficult?

Right on cue, the radio clicked. Mac keyed it once in reply, then gave a single rap on the back of the cab to alert Maris, who had shifted into position behind the wheel.

The radio clicked again, twice this time. Quickly he rapped twice on the cab. Maris put the truck into gear and eased out of the parking slot. She was turning the corner behind the motel when headlights flashed across the cab as a vehicle pulled into the lot, and Mac knew the lure had been cast. In a few seconds they would know if the bait had been taken.

Maris kept the truck at an even pace. Her instinct was to hurry, but she didn't want whoever was following them to know they'd been spotted. The car hadn't turned the corner behind them by the time she pulled onto the secondary road, so if it *was* them, they were hanging back, not wanting her to spot them.

She stopped at the stop sign, then turned right onto the highway. Watching her rearview mirror as she turned, she saw the car easing out from behind the motel. Its lights were off now, and its gray color made it difficult to spot in the faint light; she wouldn't have noticed it at all if she hadn't been looking for it.

They were driving Ronald's gray Cadillac. Maris had only seen it once or twice, because she usually dealt with Joan, who drove a white BMW. The driveway wasn't visible from the stables, and she seldom paid attention to the comings and goings at the big house. All that interested her was at the stables.

Still, she wondered that they would drive one of their personal cars at all, until she realized that it didn't matter. Sole Pleasure was their horse, and no crime had been committed. If she had called the police, it would have been their word against hers that a crime had even been attempted, and no one in the world would believe the Stonichers were willing to kill a horse worth over twenty million dollars.

Dean's Oldsmobile was nowhere in sight. Maris hoped she was giving him the time he needed to drive the car deep enough into the woods that it couldn't be seen and to work his way into position on foot.

Watching the mirror, she saw the Cadillac turn onto the highway behind her. Without its headlights on, and with the swirling snow cutting visibility, she could barely make out the gray bulk. They would be able to see her much better than she could see them, though, because her lights were on; that was why they were hanging back so far, because they were unable to judge how visible they themselves were.

Their caution was working for her and against them. The distance would give her a few extra seconds to get out of the truck and hide, a few seconds longer for Dean to get set, a few seconds longer that Mac was safe. She tried not to think of him lying on the cold metal bed, unprotected from any stray bullets except by a thin sheet of metal that wouldn't even slow down a lead slug.

It was only a few miles to the place where she would leave the road and drive into the woods. A couple of times the snow became so heavy that she couldn't see the Cadillac behind her. The white flakes were beginning to dust the ground, but it was a dry, fluffy snow that swirled up with every breath of wind, and the passage of the truck blew it off the highway.

She maintained a steady speed, assuming they could see her, even though she couldn't see the Cadillac. She couldn't do anything that would make them suspicious. Finally she passed the mile marker that told her she was close, and she began braking, looking for the tire ruts where they'd driven before. *There*. She steered the truck off the highway, bouncing across the ditch faster than, for the sake of her head, she wanted to, but she didn't want to go any slower than she already was. Now that they had seen her leave the highway, she wanted to go as fast as she could, to gain a few more of those precious seconds.

Her headache, which had lessened but never disappeared, increased in severity with each bounce. She ignored it, gritting her teeth against the pain, concentrating on steering the truck on the narrow, winding path MacNeil had already blazed through the trees. She couldn't begin to imagine how difficult it must have been to do this with the trailer in tow, but it was a testament to both his stubbornness and skill that he had.

The Cadillac wouldn't be able to take the bumps and holes as fast as the truck did; it was too low to the ground. More seconds gained.

A bare limb scraped over the windshield, then her headlights caught the dark bulk of the trailer, almost concealed among the trees. Now. She parked the truck in the exact position MacNeil had decreed, killed the lights so the glare wouldn't blind the camera hidden under the trailer, then slipped out the door and walked swiftly to the trailer and then beyond it. She cut sharply to the left, stepping in places where the snow hadn't sifted down. She left no tracks as she removed herself from the scene so he could do his job without worrying about her.

She'd caught movement in her peripheral vision as she walked away, a big, dark shape silently rolling over the side of the truck bed to conceal himself behind one of the tires. At least he would have *some* protection, she thought, trying to console herself with that. His mind might be easier now, but hers certainly wasn't. He needed the vest she was wearing; she would never forgive herself if he was killed because she'd agreed to take his vest. It would have been better to remove herself entirely, even if it meant they wouldn't be able to get any solid evidence against the Stonichers. The FBI would get another crack at Randy Yu, but she would never find another MacNeil.

She'd gone far enough. She stopped, her back against a big oak. Snowflakes drifted silently down in the gray dawn, settling in a lacy cap on her unprotected head. She leaned her aching head against the tree and closed her eyes, listening, waiting, her breath almost halted, her heart barely beating, waiting.

Mac waited, his eyes never leaving the rutted trail. They might drive right up to the truck, but if Yu was in charge, they would probably get out of the car and come the rest of the way on foot. He and Dean were prepared for both circumstances. The underbrush was thick; if they tried to force their way through it, they would make a lot of noise. The best thing to do was to walk up the trail, staying close to the edges. Maris had parked the truck so that they could bypass it only on the driver's side; the tailgate on the passenger side was right up against the bushes. Anyone coming along that trail would be funneled into the camera's view and duly recorded on tape.

After what seemed an interminable length of time, he heard a twig snap. He didn't move. His position, crouched by the right front tire, was secure; he couldn't be seen until they walked in front of the truck, but by then they would have looked into the cab and seen it was empty, and wouldn't pay any more attention to the truck. They would be looking instead at the trailer, and at Maris's small footprints in the thin layer of snow, leading right up to it.

There were other sounds now, rustles from careless feet, more than one pair; the brushing sounds of clothing, the harshness of someone who was slightly winded trying to regulate their breathing. They were close, very close.

The footsteps stopped. "She isn't in the truck." The whisper was barely audible, sexless.

"Look! Her footprints go right up to the trailer." It was another whisper, excitement making it louder than the first.

"Shut . . . up." The two words were hissed between clenched teeth, as if they had already been said more than once.

"Don't tell me to shut up. We have her cornered. What are you waiting for?"

Though still whispering, the speaker's voice was so forceful that it was almost as audible as if he—or she—had spoken aloud. The mike might have caught it, Mac thought. With enhanced sound-extraction techniques, which the Bureau had, he was certain the words were now on tape. The only problem was, they hadn't exactly been damning.

"You hired me to do a job. Now stay out of my way and let me do it." There was fury evident now, in both words and tone.

"You're the one who bungled it the first time, so don't act as if you're Mr. Infallible. If you'd been half as smart as you seem to think you are, the horse would already be dead and Maris Mackenzie wouldn't suspect a thing. I didn't bargain on murder when I hired you."

That should do it, Mac thought with grim satisfaction. They had just talked themselves into a prison sentence.

He tightened the muscles in his legs, preparing to step out and identify himself, pistol trained and ready. A crashing, thudding noise behind him made him freeze in place. He looked over his shoulder and almost groaned aloud. A big, black, graceful horse was prancing through the trees toward them, proudly shaking his head as if wanting them to admire his cleverness in getting free.

"There he is! Shoot him!" It was a shout. Pleasure's unexpected appearance had started them out of caution. Almost instantaneously there was the sharp crack of a shot, and bark exploded from the tree just behind the horse.

Damn amateurs! He silently cursed. Pleasure was behind him; if he stood up now, he would be looking straight down the barrel, caught between the shooter and the target. He couldn't do anything but wait for the next shot to hit the beautiful, friendly stallion, who had evidently caught their scent and pulled free so he could join the party.

Dean realized Mac's predicament and stepped from concealment, pistol braced in both hands. "FBI! Drop your weapons on the ground—*now.*"

Mac surged upward, bracing his arms across the hood of the truck. He saw Randy Yu, his hands already reaching upward as his pistol thudded to the ground. You could always trust a professional to know how to do things. But Joan Stonicher was startled by Mac's sudden movement, and she wheeled toward him, her eyes wide with panic and rage. She froze, the pistol in her hand and her finger on the trigger.

"Ease off, lady," Mac said softly. "Don't do anything stupid. If I don't get you, my partner will. Just take your finger off the trigger and let the gun drop. That's all you have to do, and we'll all be okay."

She didn't move. From the excellent viewpoint he had, Mac could see her finger trembling.

"Do as he says," Randy Yu said wearily. The two agents had them caught in an excellent cross field. There was nothing they could do, and no sense in making things worse.

Pleasure had shied at the noise of the shot, neighing his alarm, but his life had been too secure for him to panic. He trotted closer, his scooped nostrils flaring as he examined their familiar scents, searching for the special one he could detect. He came straight for Mac.

Joan's eyes left Mac and fastened on the horse. He saw the exact instant when her control shattered, saw her pupils contract and her hand jerk.

A shrill whistle shattered the air a split second before the shot.

A lot of things happened simultaneously. Dean shouted. Randy Yu dropped to the ground, his hands covering his head. Pleasure screamed in pain, rearing. Joan's hand jerked again, back toward Mac.

And there was another whistle, this one earsplitting.

Maris stepped from behind a tree, her black eyes glittering with rage. The pistol was in her hand, trained on Joan. Joan wheeled back toward this new threat, and without hesitation Mac fired.

Chapter Nine

He was mad enough to murder her, Maris thought.

She was still so enraged herself that it didn't matter. Fury burned through her. It was all she could do to keep from dismantling Joan Stonicher on the spot, and only the knowledge that Pleasure needed her kept her even remotely under control.

The woods were swarming with people, with medics and deputies and highway patrol officers, with on-lookers, even some reporters already there. Pleasure was accustomed to crowds, but he'd never before been shot, and pain and shock were making him unruly. He'd wheeled at Maris's whistle, and his lightning reflexes had saved his life; Joan's bullet had gouged a deep furrow in his chest, tearing the muscle at an angle but not penetrating any internal organs. Now it took all of Maris's skill to keep him calm so she could stop the bleeding; he kept moving restlessly in circles, bumping her, trying to pay attention to her softly crooning voice but distracted by the pain.

Her head was throbbing, both from Pleasure's skittishness and from her own desperate run through the woods. She'd heard him moving through the trees, and in a flash she'd known exactly what had happened, what he would do. How he'd gotten free didn't matter; he had heard and smelled them, and pranced happily to greet them, sure of his welcome. She'd known he would catch her scent on MacNeil's clothes and go straight to him. It had been a toss-up which of them would be shot first, MacNeil or Pleasure. All she could do was try to get there in time to draw the horse's attention, as well as everyone else's.

For one awful, hellish moment, when Pleasure screamed and she saw Joan swing back toward MacNeil, she'd thought she'd lost everything. She had stepped out from the trees, moving in what felt like slow motion. She couldn't hear anything then, not even Pleasure; she hadn't been able to see anything except Joan, her vision narrowing to a tunnel with her target as the focus. She hadn't been aware of whistling again, or of taking the pistol from her pocket, but the weapon had been in her hand and her finger had been smoothly tightening on the trigger when Joan jerked yet again, panicked, this time aiming at Maris. That was when Mac had shot her. At such close range, just across the hood of the truck, his aim had been perfect. The bullet had shattered her upper arm.

Joan would probably never have use of that arm again, Maris thought dispassionately. She couldn't bring herself to care.

The entire scene had been recorded, complete with audio. The camera had playback capability and Dean had obliged the sheriff by playing the tape for him. Both Yu and Joan were nailed, and Yu, being the professional he was, was currently bargaining for all he was worth. He was willing to carry others down with him if it would lighten his sentence.

It had stopped snowing, though the day hadn't gotten any warmer. Her hands were icy, but she couldn't leave Pleasure to warm them. Blood glistened on his black chest and down his legs, staining his white stocking, splattering on the snow-frosted leaves and on Maris. She whispered to him, controlling him mostly with her voice, crooning reassurance and love to him while she held his bridle in one hand and with the other held some gauze the medics had given her to the wound on his chest. She had asked a deputy to contact a vet, but as yet no one had shown up.

Yu could have seen to the horse, but he hadn't offered, and Maris wouldn't have trusted him, anyway. It was he who had hit her on the head. As soon as she saw him again she had remembered that much, remembered his upraised arm, the cold, remorseless expression in his dark eyes. Other memories were still vague, and there were still blank spots, but they were gradually filling in.

She must have gone to the big house to see Joan about something. She didn't know why, but she remembered standing with her hand raised to knock, and freezing as Joan's voice filtered through the door.

"Randy's going to do it tonight. While everyone's eating will be a good time. I told him we couldn't wait any longer, the syndicates are pushing for a decision."

"Damn, I hate this," Ronald Stonicher had said. "Poor Pleasure's been a good horse. Are you certain the drug won't be detected?"

"Randy says it won't, and it's his can on the line," Joan had coolly replied.

Maris had backed away, so angry she could barely contain herself. Her first concern had been for Pleasure. It was the time when the stable hands would either be eating or have gone home for the night. She couldn't delay a moment.

Her next memory was of running down the aisle to his stall. She must have surprised Randy Yu there, though she didn't remember actually coming up on him. She remembered enough to testify, though, even if she never remembered anything else, and assuming her testimony was needed. The tape was solid evidence.

Another vehicle joined the tangle, and a roly-poly man in his late fifties, sporting a crew cut, got out of a battered pickup truck. He trudged wearily toward Maris, clutching a big black bag in his hand. Finally, the vet, she thought. Dark circles under his eyes told her that he'd probably been up late, possibly all night, with an ailing animal.

Tired or not, he knew horses. He stopped, taking in Pleasure's magnificent lines, the star on his forehead, the bloodstained white stocking. "That's Sole Pleasure," he said in astonishment.

"Yes, and he's been shot," Maris said tersely. Her head was throbbing; even her eyeballs ached. If Pleasure didn't settle down soon, her head would likely explode. "No internal organs affected, but some chest muscle torn. He won't settle down and let the bleeding stop."

"Let's take care of that problem, first off. I'm George Norton, the vet hereabouts." He was working as he spoke, setting down the bag and opening it. He prepared a hypodermic and stepped forward, smoothly injecting the sedative into one of the bulging veins in Pleasure's neck. The stallion danced nervously, his shoulder shoving her once again. She clenched her teeth, enduring.

"He'll quiet down in a minute." The vet gave her a sharp glance as he peeled away the blood-soaked gauze she'd been holding to the wound. "No offense, but even with the blood, the horse looks in better shape than you do. Are you all right?"

"Concussion."

"Then for God's sake stop letting him bump you around like that," he said sharply. "Sit down somewhere before you fall down."

Even in the midst of everything that was going on, as the medics readied Joan for transport, Mac somehow heard the vet. All of a sudden he was there, looming behind her, reaching over her shoulder for Pleasure's bridle. "I'll hold him." The words sounded as if he were spitting them out one at a time, like bullets. "Sit down."

"I—" She'd started to say "I think I will," but she didn't have a chance to finish the sentence.

He assumed she was about to mount an argument, and barked out one word. *"Sit!"*

"I wasn't going to argue," she snapped back. What did he think she was, a dog? Sit, indeed. She felt more like lying down.

She decided to do just that. Pleasure was going to be all right; as soon as he quieted and let the vet do his work, the bleeding would stop. The torn muscle would have to be stitched, antibiotics administered, a bandage secured, but the horse would heal. Even though the truck and trailer were stolen, under the circumstances she couldn't imagine that there would be any problem with using them to transport Pleasure back to Solomon Green. Until the vet was finished and Pleasure was loaded in the trailer, she intended to stretch out on the truck seat.

Wearily she climbed into the cab. The keys were still in the ignition, so she started the engine and turned on the heater. She took off her coat, removed the Kevlar vest and placed it in the floorboards, then lay down on the seat and pulled the coat over her.

She almost cried with relief as the pain immediately began easing now that she was still. She closed her eyes, letting the tension drain out of her, along with the terror and absolute rage. She might have killed Joan. If the woman had shot Mac, she would have done it. Enveloped in that strange vacuum of despair and rage, she had been going for a head shot. She hadn't even thought about Pleasure, not in that awful moment when Joan turned on Mac. She was glad she hadn't had to pull the trigger, but she knew she would have. Knowing her own fiercely protective nature was one thing, but this was the first time she had been faced with the true extent of it. The jolt of self-knowledge was searing.

Mac had already faced this; it was in his eyes. She had seen it in her father, in her brothers, the willingness to do what was necessary to protect those they loved and those who were weaker. It wasn't easy. It was gut-wrenching, and those who were willing to stand on the front lines paid for it in a thousand little ways she was only beginning to understand. She hadn't had to take that final, irrevocable step, but she knew how close it had been.

Her mother also had that willingness, and a couple of her sisters-in-law. Valiant Mary, intrepid Caroline, sweet Barrie. They had each, in different circumstances, faced death and seen the bottom line. They would understand the wrenching she felt. Well, maybe Caroline wouldn't. Caroline was so utterly straightforward, so focused, that Joe had once compared her to a guided missile.

The door by her head was wrenched open, and cold air poured in. "Maris! Wake up!" Mac barked, his voice right over her. His hand closed on her shoulder as if he intended to shake her.

"I am awake," she said, without opening her eyes. "The headache's better, now that I'm still. How much longer will it be before I can take Pleasure back?"

"*You* aren't taking him anywhere. You're going to a hospital to be checked out."

"We can't just leave him here."

"I've arranged for him to be driven back."

She could hear the effort he was making to be calm; it was evident in his careful tone.

"Are things about wrapped up here?"

"Close enough that I can leave it with Dean and take you to a hospital."

He wouldn't let it go until a doctor had told him she was all right, Maris realized, and with a sigh she opened her eyes and sat up. She understood. If their situations were reversed, she would be doing the same thing.

"All right," she said, slipping on her coat. She turned off the ignition and picked up the Kevlar vest. "I'm ready."

Her willingness scared him. She saw his eyes darken, saw his jaw clench. "I'll be okay," she said softly, touching his hand. "I'm going because I know you're worried, and I don't want you to be."

His expression changed, something achingly tender moving in his eyes. Gently he scooped her into his arms and lifted her from the truck.

Dean had brought the Oldsmobile out of its hiding place. Mac carried her to it and deposited her on the front seat as carefully as if she were made of the most fragile crystal. He got in on the driver's side and started the car; the milling crowd in front of them parted, allowing them through. She saw Pleasure, standing quietly now. The bandage was in place, and the wild look was gone from his eyes. He was watching the activity with his characteristic friendly curiosity.

As they drove by, Dean lifted his hand to wave. "What about Dean?" Maris asked.

"He'll get transport. It isn't a problem."

She paused. "What about you? When do you leave? Your job here is finished, isn't it?" She didn't intend to let him get away, but she wasn't sure exactly how much he understood of their situation.

"It's finished." The words were clipped. The look he gave her was one of restrained violence. "I'll have to do the paperwork, tie up some loose ends. I may have to leave tonight, tomorrow at the latest, but I'll be back, damn it!"

"You don't sound happy about it," she observed.

"Happy? You expect me to be *happy?*" His jaw clenched. "You didn't obey orders. You stepped right out into the open, instead of staying hidden the way you were supposed to. That idiot woman could have killed you!"

"I was wearing the vest." She pointed that out rather mildly, she thought.

"The damn vest only improves the odds, it isn't a guarantee! The issue here is that you didn't follow the plan. You risked your life for that damn horse! I didn't want him hurt, either, but—"

"It wasn't for Pleasure," she said, interrupting him. "It was for you." She looked out the window at the snow-dusted pastures they were passing.

It was quiet in the car for a moment.

"Me?" He was using that careful tone again.

"You. I knew he'd go straight to you, that he'd catch my scent on your clothes. At the very least he would distract you, bump you with his head. It was even possible he'd give away your position."

Mac was silent, absorbing the shock of the realization that she was willing to risk her own life to protect his. He did the same thing on a fairly regular basis, but it was his job to take risks and protect others. But he'd never before felt the terror he'd known when he saw Maris draw Joan's attention, and he hoped he never felt it again.

"I love you," she said quietly.

Damn. Sighing inwardly, Mac kissed his bachelorhood goodbye. Her courage stunned him, humbled him. No other woman he'd known would have put herself on the line the way Maris had done, both physically and emotionally. She didn't play games, didn't jockey for control. She simply knew, and accepted; he'd seen it in the soft depths of her black eyes, an instinctive inner knowledge that few people ever achieved. If he didn't snatch her up, it would be the biggest mistake of his life.

Mac didn't believe in making mistakes.

"How long does it take to get married in Kentucky?" he asked abruptly. "If we can't get it done tomorrow, we'll go to Las Vegas—assuming the doctor says you're all right."

He hadn't said he loved her, but she knew he did. She sat back, pleased with the situation. "I'm all right," she said, completely confident.

Chapter Ten

"Getting married in Las Vegas seems to be a tradition in my family," she mused the next day as her new husband ushered her into their suite. "Two of my brothers have done it."

"Two? How many brothers do you have?"

"Five. All of them older." She smiled sweetly at him over her shoulder as she walked to the window to look out at the blazing red sunset. It was odd how completely connected to him she felt, when they hadn't had time to talk much, to share the details of their lives. Events had swept them along like gulls before a hurricane.

The emergency room doctor had pronounced her concussion mild and told her to take it easy for a day or so. He had agreed with her that, if she had been going to lapse into a coma, she would already have done so. Over the course of the day her memory had completely returned, filling in the blank spots, so she knew she was okay.

Reassured, Mac had driven her back to Solomon Green and turned his attention to the job, ruthlessly clearing up details and paperwork so he could concentrate on the business of getting married. While she slept, he and Dean had worked. He had arranged for time off, checked into the details of marriage in Kentucky, decided it couldn't be done fast enough to suit him and booked them on a flight to Las Vegas.

Ronald Stonicher had been arrested for conspiracy to commit fraud; he'd had no idea his wife and Randy Yu planned to kill Maris, too, and was shattered by what had happened. Joan had undergone surgery on her arm, and according to the surgeon the nerve and tissue damage was extensive; he expected her to regain some use of the arm, but she would never again be able to write with her right hand, or eat, do or anything else requiring precise movements. Randy was spilling his guts to the feds, implicating a lot of people in the horse world in the scheme to kill off horses for the insurance money. He hadn't been charged with killing the sixteen-year-old boy. Evidently he had some information on it, though, and was holding that in reserve to bargain for an even bigger break on the charges.

Maris had called her mother, briefly filled her in on what had happened and told her she was getting married. "Have fun, baby," Mary had told her daughter. "You know your father will want to walk you down the aisle, so we'll plan another wedding for Christmas. That gives me three weeks. There shouldn't be any problem."

Most people would have screamed in panic at the thought of organizing a wedding in three weeks. Mary saw no problem, and from experience Maris knew that while other people might have problems accomplishing what her mother wanted, in the end she would have her way.

Mac had phoned his family, which consisted of his mother, stepfather and two half-sisters. They would be joining the Mackenzies in Wyoming for the wedding at Christmas.

During the ceremony an hour before, Maris had learned that her husband's full name was William Alexander MacNeil. "A few people call me Will," he told her afterward, when she mentioned how difficult it was for her to think of him as Alex. "Most people call me Mac." Since in her mind she had already begun shortening MacNeil to Mac, that suited her fine.

"*Five* older brothers?" Mac asked now, walking up behind her and slipping his arm around her waist. He bent his head to nuzzle her pale hair.

"Five. Plus twelve nephews and one niece."

He chuckled. "Holidays must be lively."

"*Riotous* would be a better word. Wait until you see."

He turned her in his arms. "What I can't wait to see is my wife, in bed with me."

She clung to his neck as he lifted her and carried her into the bedroom. His mouth closed on hers as he lowered her to the bed, and the aching passion that had subsided but never vanished surged back at full force. He crushed her into the mattress in his need, but at the same time he tried not to be rough as he eased her out of her clothes.

She squirmed against him, pulling at his clothes, the roughness of the fabric against her nakedness driving her crazy. Mac drew back, staring down at her delicate body with open hunger. He was breathing hard, obviously struggling for control, his eyes hard and glittering with lust. Gently he shaped her breasts with his hand, each in turn, rubbing his thumb over her nipples and bringing them to aching hardness.

"Hurry," she whispered, reaching for his belt.

He laughed a little, though there was no humor in the sound; instead, it was raw with need. He shed his clothes, kicking them away, and rolled on top of her. A groan of deep satisfaction tore from her throat as his heavy weight settled on her, and she opened her legs to cradle him close. She wanted him with a ferocity that would brook no delay, wanted him as she had never wanted or needed anything else in her life.

Mac positioned himself, then framed her face with his hands and kissed her as he slowly pushed into her body. Her flesh resisted, and she gasped, surprised by the painful difficulty. She had expected all her riding to have eased the way, but the lack of a barrier had in no way prepared her for his size.

He lifted his mouth, staring down at her as realization dawned. He didn't say anything, didn't ask any questions, but something hot and primitive flared deep in his gaze. As gently as possible, he completed his penetration, and when he was fully home inside her he waited, waited until the tension left her and her body softened beneath him, around him. Then he began moving, a slight rocking at first that did no more than nudge him back and forth, but enough to make her gasp again, this time with sensual urgency, and lift herself to him.

He took exquisite care with her, restraining the power of his thrusts, maintaining a slow, easy pace even when anticipation clawed at him, making him groan aloud with each movement. She clung to him, desperately searching for her own ease, trying to take him as deep inside her as possible, because instinct led her to that satisfaction. She cried out, overwhelmed by the sheer glory of this dance and struggle they shared, by the generosity of his loving.

She surged upward, unable to bear it a moment longer, and everything inside her shattered with a burst of pleasure so intense that she lost herself, sucked down in the whirlpool of sensation, a mindless creature knowing only the feel of his body, and hers. And she felt him join her, convulsing, thrusting, hotly emptying.

He cradled her afterward, stroking her with shaking hands as if to reassure himself she was real, that both of them were still whole.

"How did this happen?" he asked roughly. He tilted her chin so he could look into her face, and she saw that the glitter in his eyes was wetness now, not lust. "How could I love you so much, so fast? What kind of magic did you use?"

Tears burned her own eyes. "I just loved you," she said, the words simple. "That's all. I just loved you."

The mountain was wreathed with snow, and her heart lifted when she saw it. "There," she said, pointing. "That's Mackenzie's Mountain."

Mac stared with interest at the massive bulk. He'd never known anyone before who owned an entire mountain, and he wondered about the people, and the way of life, that had nurtured this magical creature beside him. In the two days they had been married, he had come to wonder how he'd ever existed without her. Loving her was like becoming whole, when he hadn't even known anything was missing. She was so delicate and fairylike, with her pale hair streaming over her shoulders and her great black eyes that held all the knowledge of centuries of women, but he'd learned that she was strong, and that the heart of a lion beat beneath her lovely breasts.

His *wife!* The unexpected marvelousness of it kept waking him in the middle of the night to look at her, to wonder at how fast it had happened. Only three days before, she had awakened in his arms and politely said, "I'm sorry, but I don't remember your name," and the realization that she'd been hurt had jarred him down to his toes. Only three days, and yet now he couldn't imagine sleeping without her, or waking without seeing her sleepy urchin's grin as she curled into his arms.

He had only five days off, so they had to make the best of it. Yesterday they had made a fast trip to San Antonio, where he had introduced her to his family. Both of his sisters had arrived with their broods of kids, three each, husbands in tow, but after the crowd

Maris was accustomed to, she hadn't turned a hair at any of it. His mother had been absolutely thrilled that he'd married at last, thrilled at the prospect of a Christmas wedding on top of a snow-covered mountain in Wyoming. Having gotten the telephone number from Maris, her mother had already called his mother, and they'd evidently become fast friends, judging from the number of times his mother referred to what Mary had said.

Today they were in Wyoming, and Mac wondered why he was getting a tight feeling in the pit of his stomach. "Tell me about your brothers," he murmured. "All five of them." He knew something about older brothers, being one himself.

She smiled, her eyes going soft. "Well, let's see. My oldest brother, Joe, is a general in the air force—on the Joint Chiefs of Staff, as a matter of fact. His wife, Caroline, has doctoral degrees in physics and computer science, and they have five sons.

"My next-oldest brother, Mike, owns one of the largest cattle ranches in the state. He and Shea have two sons.

"Next is Josh. He was a navy fighter pilot, aircraft carrier, until a crash stiffened his knee and the navy grounded him. Now he's a civilian test pilot. His wife, Loren, is an orthopedic surgeon. They have three sons."

"Do any of your brothers have anything but sons?" Mac asked, fascinated by the recital, and growing more worried by the minute. He tried to focus on the mundane. He thought he remembered Maris saying she had a niece, but perhaps he'd been mistaken.

"Zane has a daughter." There was a different note in Maris's voice and he raised his eyebrows in inquiry, but she ignored him. "He and Barrie also have twin sons, two months old. Zane was a Navy SEAL. Barrie's an ambassador's daughter."

A SEAL. He wondered how much worse this could get.

"Then there's Chance. He and Zane might as well be twins. They're the same age, and I think their brains are linked. Chance was in Naval Intelligence. He isn't married." She deliberately didn't mention what Zane and Chance did now, because it seemed safer not to.

"I wonder," Mac murmured to himself as he steered their rented four-wheel-drive up the mountain, "why I expected you to have a normal family."

She lifted delicate brows at him. "You're a special agent with the FBI," she pointed out. "There isn't one of those standing on every street corner, you know."

"Yeah, but my *family* is normal."

"Well, so is mine. We're just overachievers." Her smile turned into a grin, the urchin's grin that had laced itself around his heart and tightened the bonds every time he saw it. He stopped the Jeep in the middle of the road and reached for her. His kiss was hard, urgent with hunger. Her eyes were slumberous when he released her. "What was that for?" she murmured, her hand curling around his neck.

"Because I love you." He wanted to tell her one last time, in case he didn't survive the coming confrontation. She might think her family would welcome him with open arms, but he had a much better understanding of the male psyche and he knew better. He put the Jeep in gear again, and they resumed their drive up the snow-covered road.

When they topped the crest and saw the big ranch house sprawling in front of them, Maris said happily, "Oh, good, everyone's here," and Mac knew he was a dead man. Never mind that he'd married her before sleeping with her; he was an unknown quantity, and he was making love to their darling every night. She was the only daughter, the *baby,* for God's sake. He understood. If he lived, and he and Maris ever had a daughter, there was no way in hell he was going to let some horny teenage boy anywhere near his little girl.

He looked at the array of vehicles parked in front of the house, enough vehicles to form a good parade, and wondered if they would give chase if he turned around and headed back down the mountain.

Well, it had to be done. Resigned, he parked the Jeep and came around to open the door for Maris, clasping his hands around her narrow waist and lifting her to the ground. She took his hand and led him up the steps, all but running in her eagerness.

They stepped into warmth, into noise, into confusion. A very small person wearing red overalls suddenly exploded from the crowd, racing forward on chubby legs and shrieking, "Marwee, Marwee," at the top of her lungs. Maris laughed and dropped to her knees, holding out her arms in time to catch the tiny tornado as she launched herself forward. Mac looked down at the little girl, not much more than a baby, and fell in love. He lost his heart. It was that simple.

She was beautiful. She was perfect, from the silky black hair on her round little head to her crystal-blue eyes, dimpled cheeks, rosebud mouth and dainty, dimpled hands. She was so small she was like a doll, and his arms ached to hold her. Little kids and babies had never affected him like this before, and it shook him.

"This is Nick," Maris said, rising to her feet with her niece in her arms. "She's the one and only grand-daughter."

Nick reached out a tiny hand and poked him in the chest, in a movement so exactly like Maris's that Mac couldn't help grinning. "Who dat?" the little angel asked.

"This is Mac," Maris said, and kissed the soft, chubby cheek. Nick solemnly regarded him for a moment, then stretched out her arms in the manner of someone who is absolutely sure of their welcome. Automatically he reached out and took her, sighing with pleasure as the little body nestled against his chest.

Mac became aware of a spreading silence in the room, of what looked like an entire football team of big men getting to their feet, menace in every movement, in the hard faces turned toward him.

Maris looked at them, her face radiant, and he saw her eyes widen with surprise at their militant stances.

He eyed the competition. His father-in-law had iron gray hair and the black eyes Maris had inherited, and looked as if he ate nails for breakfast. His brothers-in-law looked just as lethal. Expertly Mac assessed each one, trying to pick out the most dangerous one. They all looked like bad asses. The one with the graying temples and the laser blue eyes, that would be the general, and damn if he didn't look as if he went into combat every day. *That* one would be the rancher, whipcord lean, iron hard, a man who faced down Mother Nature every day. The test pilot...let's see, that would be the one standing with his feet apart in the instinctive cocky stance of someone who cooly gambled with death and never blinked an eye.

Then Mac's gaze met a pair of deadly, icy eyes. *That one,* he thought. That was the most dangerous one, the one with the quiet face and eyes like blue-gray frost. That one. He would be the one in naval intelligence.

He was in big trouble. Instinctively he moved, depositing Nick in Maris's arms and stepping in front of them both, shielding them with his body.

Six pairs of fierce eyes noted the action.

Maris peeked around his shoulder, assessing the situation. *"Moth-er!"* she called urgently, stressing both syllables as she brought in reinforcements.

"Maris!" There was utter delight in the soft voice that came from what Mac assumed was the kitchen, the cry followed by light, fast footsteps. A small, delicate woman, no bigger than Maris and with the same exquisite, translucent skin, burst into the room. She was laughing as she grabbed her daughter, hugging her and doing the same to him, even though he stood rigidly, not daring to take his eyes off the threat looming in front of them like a wall.

"Mom," Maris said, directing her mother's attention across the room. "What's wrong with them?"

Mary took one look at her husband and sons and put her hands on her hips. "Stop that right now," she ordered. "I refuse to have this, do you hear?"

Her voice was sweetly Southern, as light as a breeze, but Wolf Mackenzie's black eyes flickered to her. "We just want to know a little about him," he said in a voice as deep and dark as thunder.

"Maris chose him," Mary replied firmly. "What else could you possibly need to know?"

"A lot," the one with the quiet, lethal eyes said. "This happened too fast."

"Zane Mackenzie!" a pretty redhead exclaimed, stepping out of the kitchen and eyeing him in amazement. "I can't believe you said that! We got married after knowing each other for *one day!*" She crossed the no-man's-land between the two battle lines, hugged Maris and turned to glare at her husband.

So he'd been right, Mac thought. That was the SEAL. It would look good on his tombstone: He Was Right.

"This is different," said the general, a perfect clone of Wolf Mackenzie except for his light blue eyes. He, too, looked as if nails were a regular part of his diet.

"Different, how?" asked a crisp voice, and a stylish blonde stepped out of the kitchen. She pinned a sharp green gaze on the six men. "You're all suffering from an overdose of testosterone. The main symptom is an inability to think." Marching forward, she aligned herself on Mac's other side. Something that was both heated and amused lit the general's eyes as he looked at his wife.

Another bruiser, the test pilot, said, "Maris is—"

"A grown woman," another feminine voice said, interrupting. A tall, curvy woman with chestnut hair and serene blue eyes took up a position beside the blonde. "Hi, I'm Loren," she said to Mac. "The one who just spoke is Josh, my husband, who usually exhibits better sense."

"And I'm Shea, Mike's wife." Another reinforcement arrived. She was dark haired, and sweetly shy. She stood beside Loren, crossed her arms over her chest and calmly looked across at her husband.

The two sides looked at each other, the men glaring at their turncoat wives, the women lined up protectively beside Mac. He was a little stunned to find himself surrounded by this perfumed wall of femininity.

Caroline gave her husband glare for glare. "Every one of us was welcomed with open arms when we married into this family, and I expect you to extend the same courtesy to Maris's husband—or else!"

Joe considered the challenge, his pale blue eyes glittering as he cocked his head. "Or else, what?" he asked, his deep voice silky and full of something that might have been anticipation.

Silence fell in the room, even the kids were quiet as they watched their parents. Mac looked at the six women ranged on either side of him, and his face softened into tender amusement. "It's okay," he said. "I understand."

"I'm glad you do, because I don't," Maris growled. "It's a—"

"Don't say it's a man thing," Mary warned, interrupting, and he bit back the words.

"No, ma'am," he said meekly.

Wolf's dark face lightened, and his lips twitched. Those two words were very familiar to him.

Nick squirmed to get down, and Maris leaned over to deposit her on her feet. The little girl patted Mac on the knee and said, "Mac," with great satisfaction in her tone. She trotted across to her father, holding up her arms to be picked up. Zane leaned down and lifted her, settling her on one brawny arm. "Dat's Mac," she said, pointing. "I wike him."

Suddenly that hard, deadly face softened into a smile, and a big hand smoothed a silky tendril of hair away from her face. "I noticed," he said dryly. "He took one look at you and turned into your slave, just like the rest of us. That's what you really like, isn't it?"

Her little head bobbed up and down, very definitely. Zane chuckled as he shot an amused glance across the room at her mother. "I thought you would."

From somewhere down the hall came a baby's wail. "Cam's awake," Barrie said, and immediately abandoned Mac to go to her baby.

"How does she *do* that?" Chance asked of the room in general. "They're only two months old. How do you tell twins apart by their cries?"

The females, Nick included, had won. The tension in the room dissipated, smiles breaking out as Chance followed his sister-in-law down the hall, intent on finding out if she'd been right. Before he walked out he winked at Mac, in a moment of male understanding. The crisis had come and gone, because when it came down to it, the Mackenzie men were unwilling to distress their women. The women had liked Mac on sight, and that was that.

Barrie was back in only a moment, a squirming bundle in her arms. Chance followed her, expertly holding another one. "She was right," he announced, shaking his head in bewilderment.

Mac looked at the two tiny faces, finding them as identical as if they were mirror images. It was impossible to tell them apart even by looking at them; how in hell did Chance know if she was right or not?

"Cameron," Barrie said, indicating her burden and smiling at his skeptical look. "Chance is holding Zack." She also carried two small, milk-filled bottles.

"How do you know?" He shook his head, still looking for any distinguishing difference in the babies.

"Cameron's the most impatient, but Zack is more determined."

"You can tell that in their *cries?*"

"Well, of course," she said, as if anyone should be able to do the same.

Nick was climbing up on her father's shoulder, gripping his hair for leverage. "Wook, Unca Dance," she exclaimed, standing upright and releasing her safety hold.

Zane reached up and snagged his daughter off his shoulder. "Here, swap with me," he said, and he and Chance exchanged kids. Zane settled the baby in the crook of his arm and took one of the bottles from Barrie, expertly slipping the nipple into the rapacious little mouth.

Chance balanced Nick on his hands, firmly holding her feet while she straightened and crowed with delight at her achievement. "Chance," he coaxed. "My name is Chance. *Chance.*"

Nick placed her little hands on each side of his face, leaning close to peer into his eyes and impress him with her seriousness. "No," she said with great finality. "*Dance.* Oo say it wong."

The room exploded with laughter at Chance's expression. He eyed the pint-size dictator in his hands, then shook his head and gave up. "Are you sure you want to marry into this family?'' He directed the question at Mac.

Mac looked at Maris and winked. "Yeah," he said.

Zane was watching him while the baby took the bottle, his calm eyes measuring. "Maris said you're an FBI special agent," he said, and something in his tone must have alerted Maris.

"No," she said firmly, pushing Mac toward the kitchen. "You can't have him. Being in the FBI is enough. You absolutely can't have him."

Mac found himself borne along on the tide of women, because they all wanted to discuss the wedding, but before he left the room he looked back. His gaze met Zane's . . . and Zane Mackenzie smiled.

"Welcome to the family," he said.

Epilogue

"You so *pwetty*," Nick sighed, her big blue eyes rapt as she propped her elbows on Maris's knee and stared at her aunt. The entire process of preparing for a wedding had fascinated the little girl. She had intently scrutinized everything as the women of the household had painstakingly made hundreds of tiny net bags, filled them with bird seed and tied them with ribbons. She had stood on her tiptoes, clinging to the table's edge, and watched as Shea, who made wonderful cakes, practiced making dozens of roses from icing before decorating Maris's wedding cake. Before long the practice roses had all borne evidence of a tiny, investigative finger. Once Nick had determined they were edible, they'd gradually disappeared, and her little face wore telltale smears.

Maris's gown held her absolutely enthralled. The long skirt, the lace, the veil, everything about it entranced her. When Maris had tried it on for the final fitting, Nick had clasped her hands under her chin and with shining eyes had said, "Oo a *pwincess!*"

"You're pretty, too, darling," Maris said. Nick was her flower girl. Zane had muttered about inviting disaster, and since Nick wasn't quite three years old, Maris was prepared for anything, including an outright re-

fusal to perform her role. At the rehearsal the night
before, however, Nick had strutted down the aisle with
her little basket of rose petals and proudly strewn them,
aware that every eye was on her. Whether she would do
so when watched by a huge crowd was another question, but she was undeniably adorable in her long,
blush pink dress, with ribbons and flowers in her silky
black hair.

"I know," Nick replied matter-of-factly, and left her
post at Maris's knee to return to the mirror to admire
herself. It was something she had done every five minutes since Barrie had dressed her.

Barrie and Caroline were the acknowledged fashion
mavens of the Mackenzie family, and they had taken
over the arrangement of Maris's hair and the applica-
tion of her makeup. They were astute enough to keep
things simple, rather than overwhelming Maris's dainty
face and frame with big hair and layers of makeup.
Barrie had finished her hair and retired to a rocking
chair to nurse the twins before the ceremony started.
She supplemented their feedings with a bottle, but
breast milk kept them contented longer, and she didn't
want to have to feed them again in the middle of the
reception.

Mary had quickly realized that the Mackenzie house,
as large as it was, simply couldn't hold the crowd that
was invited to the wedding. Because Christmas was on
a Wednesday, the church in Ruth had held its Christmas service on Sunday, freeing it for the ceremony. The
nine-foot-tall Christmas tree still stood in the corner,

its multitude of white lights twinkling. Holly and evergreen needles still decorated the windowsills, filling the church with a wonderful aroma. White lights outlined the arched doorway, the windows, the sanctuary and the steps leading up to it. Rows of white candles lent their mellow glow to the church. None of the overhead lights would be on, but the tree, the Christmas lights and the candles combined to give the setting a magical aura.

This was Christmas Eve, a time when most of the occupants of Ruth would normally have been at home either having their private celebrations or preparing for them the next day. This year they were attending a wedding. From the private room off the vestibule Maris could hear the swell of noise as more and more people arrived.

Mary stood quietly, a sheen of tears in her slate blue eyes as she watched her daughter prepare for her wedding. It didn't matter that Maris and Mac were already married; this was the wedding that counted. This was her beloved daughter who looked so delicate and beautiful in her silvery white gown, a color that turned Maris's pale, ash brown hair to a darker shade of silver. She remembered the first time she had seen her daughter, only seconds old, so tiny and lovely and already staring around with big, solemn black eyes, her father's eyes. She remembered the tears that had sheened Wolf's own black eyes as he'd taken Maris in his arms and hugged the little scrap to his chest as if she were the most precious thing he'd ever seen.

There were thousands of other memories. Her first tooth, her first step, her first word—predictably, "horsie." Maris sitting on a pony for the first time, her eyes huge with delight while Wolf kept a protective arm around her. Maris, a little shadow dogging her father's footsteps just as her older brothers had done. Maris in school, fiercely joining in any fight the boys had gotten into, her little fists flying as she rushed to their defense, utterly ignoring the fact that the boys were twice her size. Maris sobbing when her old pony had died, and her radiant joy when, the next Christmas, Wolf had given her her first "real" horse.

There had been Maris's first date, and Wolf's scowling, prowling nervousness until his baby was safely back under his roof. One of Mary's favorite memories was of Zane and Josh and Chance pacing along with their father; if Joe and Mike had been there, they would have been pacing, too. As it was, the poor boy who had been so brave as to take Maris out had been terrified when the four Mackenzie males met them on the front porch on their return and had never asked her out again. They had gotten better about it over the years, but Maris must have forgotten her first date or she wouldn't have been so surprised at their reaction to Mac when she'd brought him home. *Men.* Mary loved her men, but really, they could be so overbearing. Why, they *liked* Mac, once they'd gotten over their bristly protectiveness. If Maris didn't watch out, Zane would have Mac recruited into whatever it was he and Chance—

Zane. Mary stopped short in her thoughts, looking around the room. All three of his children were here, with Barrie. Usually he was tending to at least one of the babies, or riding herd on Nick. That meant Zane was free and unencumbered, and she was sure it wasn't by accident.

"Zane's free," she announced, because she thought Maris really ought to know.

Her daughter's head snapped up, and her lovely eyes caught fire. "I'll skin him alive," she said wrathfully. "I will *not* have Mac gone for months on end the way Chance is. I just got him, and I'm not letting him go."

Barrie looked startled; then she, too, realized the significance of having all three children with her. She shook her head in rueful acknowledgment of her husband's canniness. "It's too late to do anything about it now. He's had plenty of time to have a private talk with Mac, and you know Zane—he planned it perfectly."

Maris scowled, and Caroline drew back with the eye shadow brush in her hand. "I can't do this with your eyebrows all scrunched up," she admonished. Maris smoothed her expression, and Caroline went back to work. "I don't believe in letting hormone-driven men interfere in a woman's wedding. You can skin him alive tomorrow. Ambush him when he least expects it."

"Zane always expects everything," Barrie said, grinning. Then she looked at her daughter, who was twirling and dancing in front of the mirror, admiring herself. "Except Nick," she added. "He wasn't prepared for her."

"Was anyone?" Loren murmured, smiling fondly down at the little girl. Nick, hearing her name, stopped her pirouetting to favor them all with an angelic smile that didn't fool them for one second.

"Mac's besotted with her," Maris said. "He didn't turn a hair even when she polished his boots with the Magic Marker."

"An indication of true love if I've ever seen it," Caroline said dryly. She touched the mascara wand to Maris's already dark lashes, then stood back to admire her handiwork. "There! Mac would be crazy to leave you and go running around half-civilized countries where there's no sanitation and no shopping." Caroline's philosophy in life was to be comfortable, and she went to extraordinary lengths to accomplish it. She would gladly walk miles to find the perfect *comfortable* pair of shoes. It made perfect sense to her, since her work often required her to be on her feet for hours; how could she possibly concentrate if her toes were cramped?

"I don't think Mac would care about the shopping," Shea said. She picked Nick up and whirled around the room with the giggling little girl, humming a lively tune.

There was a knock on the door, and John poked his head inside. "It's time," he said. His pale blue gaze fell on Caroline. "Wow, Mom, you look great."

"Smart guy," she said approvingly. "I'll let you stay in my will."

He grinned and ducked out again. Maris stood, sucking in a deep breath. It was time. Never mind that they'd been married for three weeks already; this was a *production,* and practically the entire town was on hand to witness it.

Shea set Nick on her feet and got the basket of rose petals from the top of the closet, where they'd put it to keep Nick from scattering the flowers around the room. They'd already picked up the velvety petals once, and once was enough.

Barrie laid Zack beside Cameron. Both babies were sleeping peacefully, their little bellies full. Right on time, one of Shea's teenaged nieces arrived to watch them while Barrie attended the wedding.

The music began, their cue to begin entering the sanctuary.

One by one they began filing out, escorted by the Mackenzie men to their reserved seats. Zane's big form filled the doorway. Maris said, *"No,"* and he grinned as he held his hand out to Barrie.

"Just a minute." Barrie stooped in front of Nick, straightening the ribbons in her hair and at last placing the basket of flower petals in the eager, dimpled little hands. "Do the flowers just the way you did them last night, okay? Do you remember?"

Nick nodded. "I fwow dem aroun' on de fwoor."

"That's right, sweetheart." Having done all she could, Barrie stood and went to Zane, who slipped his arm around her waist and briefly hugged her close before they left to take their places.

Wolf came to the door, severely elegant in a black tuxedo. "It's time, honey," he said to Maris. His black eyes were tender as he wrapped his arms around her and rocked her back and forth, the way he had done all her life. Maris laid her head on her father's chest, almost overwhelmed by the sudden rush of love for him. She'd been so lucky in her parents!

"I was beginning to wonder if you'd ever forget about horses long enough to fall in love," he said, "but now that you have, I feel like we haven't had you long enough."

She chuckled against his chest. "That's exactly how I knew." She lifted her head, her eyes shining with both tears and laughter. "I kept forgetting about Sole Pleasure and thinking only about Mac. It had to be love."

He kissed her forehead. "In that case, I'll forgive him."

"Poppy!"

The imperious small voice came from the vicinity of his knee. They looked down. Nick was tugging on Wolf's pant leg. "We dotta *huwwy*. I dotta fwow fwowers."

As usual, her mangled English made him laugh. "All right, cupcake." He leaned down and took her free hand, to keep her from darting ahead of them and "fwowing fwowers" before they were ready.

He and Maris and Nick made their way into the vestibule, and Maris leaned down to kiss Nick's cheek. "Are you ready?" she asked.

Nick nodded, her slanted blue eyes wide and shining with excitement, and she clutched the flower basket with both hands.

"Here you go, then." Gently Maris urged Nick forward, into the center aisle. The church glowed with candlelight, and hundreds of smiling faces were turned toward them, it seemed.

Nick stepped out into the limelight like a Miss America taking her victory walk. She bestowed smiles to the left and the right, and she daintily reached into the basket for a rose petal. One. She held it out and let it drift downward. Then she reached for another. One by one she distributed the rose petals on the carpet with dainty precision, taking her time, even stooping once to adjust a petal that had fallen too close to another one.

"Oh, God." Beside her, Maris could feel Wolf shaking with laughter. "She's enjoying this too much. At this rate, you won't get to walk down the aisle until midnight."

People were turning and looking, and laughing at Nick's concentration on the task. Barrie buried her head in Zane's shoulder, lost in a helpless fit of giggling. Zane was grinning, and Chance was laughing out loud. Mac, standing at the altar, was beaming at the little imp who had so won his heart. The pianist, looking around, saw what was taking so long and gamely continued playing.

Tickled to be the center of attention, Nick began improvising. The next rose petal was tossed backward, over her shoulder. The minister choked, and his face turned red as he tried to hold back his guffaws.

She twirled on her tiptoes, flinging rose petals in a circle. Several flew out of the basket, and she frowned, stooping to pick them up and return them to the basket.

I can't laugh, Maris thought, feeling it bubbling inexorably upward. *If I laugh, I'll laugh until I cry, and it'll ruin my makeup.* She put her hand over her mouth to hold the mirth inside, but it didn't work. Her chest constricted, her throat worked and suddenly laughter burst joyously out of control.

Nick stopped and turned to look, beaming at them, waiting for them to tell her what a good job she was doing.

"*Fwow*—I mean, *throw* them," Maris managed to say between whoops.

The little head tilted to one side. "Wike dis?" she asked, taking a handful of petals from the basket and flinging them upward.

At least it was a handful, and not just one. "Like that," Maris said in approval, hoping it would speed the procedure.

It did. Another handful followed the first one, and Nick's progress down the aisle picked up speed. At last she reached the end, and bestowed an absolutely radiant smile on Mac. "I fwowed dem all," she told him.

"You did it just right," he said, barely able to speak for laughing. Her mission accomplished, she strutted to the pew where Zane and Barrie sat, and held up her arms to be lifted to the seat.

Relieved, the pianist launched into the familiar strains of "Here Comes the Bride," and at last Wolf and Maris began their stately walk down the aisle. Everyone rose to their feet and turned to watch, smiling.

Because time had been so short, there were no bridesmaids or groomsmen, no maid of honor or best man, so only Mac awaited Maris at the altar. He watched her approach, his hard face relaxed in a tender expression, his blue eyes still shining from his laughter. As soon as she stopped beside him, he gently took her hand in his, and behind them, they heard his mother give a teary, joyful little gasp.

Because Maris and Mac were already married, they had decided to skip the part about "who gives this woman." Wolf leaned down and kissed his daughter's cheek, hugged her tenderly, then shook hands with Mac and took a seat beside Mary.

"Dearly beloved," the minister began; then there was another gasp behind them. Recognizing Barrie's voice, Maris wasn't surprised when a little body slithered between her and Mac, taking a stance directly in front of them.

"I do it, too," Nick chirped, her little voice audible in every corner of the church.

Glancing over her shoulder, Maris saw Zane start to rise to retrieve his errant offspring. She shook her head, smiling. He winked and sank back into his seat.

So Nick stood pressed against their legs while the minister performed the service. They could feel her quivering with excitement, and Mac subtly gathered her closer to him so he would have a better chance of grabbing her if she started to do something startling, such as peek under the minister's cassock. She was already eyeing the garment with some curiosity. But she was content for the moment, completely taken with the ceremony, the candles, the twinkling Christmas tree, the beautiful clothes. When the minister said, "You may now kiss the bride," and Mac did so, Nick merely tilted her head back to watch.

"What's the best way to handle her when we leave?" Mac whispered against Maris's lips.

"Pick her up and hand her to Zane as we pass," she whispered back. "He'll be expecting it."

The pianist launched into the familiar stirring strains. Mac swooped Nick up with one arm, put the other around Maris, and they hurried up the aisle to the accompaniment of music, laughter, tears and a round of applause. As they passed the second pew, a tiny girl in a long dress was deftly passed from one pair of strong arms to another.

The reception was a long, glorious party. Maris danced endlessly with her husband, her father, all her brothers, several of her nephews, her brothers-in-law and an assortment of old friends. She danced with the sheriff, Clay Armstrong. She danced with Ambassador Lovejoy, Barrie's father. She danced with Shea's father and grandfather, with the ranchers and merchants and gas station attendants. Finally Mac claimed her again, holding her close and swaying to the music as he rested his cheek against hers.

"What did Zane say to you?" she demanded suddenly.

She felt him grin, though he didn't lift his head. "He said you'd know."

"Never mind that. What did he say?"

"You already know what he said."

"Then what did *you* say?"

"That I'm interested."

She growled. "I don't want you to spend months out of the country. I'm willing—barely—to let the FBI use you on investigations, but I don't like it. I want you with me every night, not thousands of miles away."

"That's exactly what I told Zane. Remember, I don't have to do what Chance does." He held her closer, dropping his voice to an intimate murmur. "Has your period started yet?"

"No." She was only two days late—but two days was two days, and she was normally very regular. It was possible her system had been disrupted by the concussion and the stress of everything that had happened, so she wasn't making any announcements yet. "Would you mind if I am pregnant so soon?"

"Mind?" He kissed her ear. "When we might get our own Nick?" His shoulders quivered under her embrace. "I didn't think she was *ever* going to get rid of those damn flower petals."

"She's one of a kind, I hope." But she leaned against him, feeling her breasts, her entire body, tighten with desire. If she wasn't already pregnant, she likely would be soon, given how often he made love to her.

They danced in silence for a moment, then Mac said, "Pleasure should have arrived by now."

She had to blink back tears, because Mac had given her the most wonderful gift for Christmas. With Sole Pleasure's worth hugely reduced now that the racing world had been rocked with news of his very low sperm count, the syndication offers had evaporated. It was *possible* Pleasure could sire a foal, but it was such a small possibility as to be negligible. He still had worth as a racehorse, and Ronald Stonicher might have gotten more for him than Mac had offered, but huge legal expenses had been staring him in the eye, and he'd jumped at the chance to sell the horse. Maris had worried so about Pleasure's future that Mac had made the offer for him without telling her, because he didn't want her to be disappointed in case the deal fell through.

"Dad can hardly wait to ride him," she said. "He's said several times that he envied me because I got to work with Pleasure."

They fell silent, simply enjoying the feel of being in each other's arms. Their wedding hadn't been a stately, solemn affair—Nick had seen to that—but it had been perfect. People had laughed and enjoyed themselves, and everyone for years would smile whenever they thought of Maris Mackenzie's wedding.

"It's time to throw the bouquet!"

The cry went up, and they swung around to see a crowd of giggling teenage girls gathering for the tradition, flipping back their hair, throwing sidelong glances at the older Mackenzie boys. There were more mature women there, too, giving Chance measuring looks.

"I thought you were supposed to throw it when we're ready to leave?" Mac said, amused.

"Evidently they can't wait."

She didn't mind hurrying things up a little; after that dance, she was ready to be alone with her husband.

Nick had been having the time of her short life, stuffing herself with cake and mints, and being whirled around the dance floor in the arms of her father, her grandfather and all her uncles and cousins. When she saw Maris get the bouquet that had so fascinated her earlier, with all the "pwetty" flowers and lace and ribbons, she squirmed away from Sam's grip on her hand and moved to where she had a better view of the situation, her little head cocked to the side as she intently watched.

Maris climbed on the dais, turned her back and threw the bouquet high over her shoulder. Cries of "Catch it! Catch it!" filled the reception hall.

Almost immediately there was a collective cry of alarm. Maris whirled. The crowd of girls and women was rushing forward, eyes lifted, intent on the bouquet sailing toward them. And directly in front of them, also concentrating on the bouquet as she darted forward, was a tiny figure in pale pink.

There was a surge of black-clad bodies moving forward as seventeen males, one MacNeil and sixteen Mackenzies, from six-year-old Benjy up to Wolf, all leapt for the little girl. Maris caught a glimpse of Zane's face, utterly white as he tried to reach his baby before she was trampled, and somehow she, too, was running, leaping from the dais, heedless of her dress.

Two crowds of people were moving toward each other at breakneck speed, with Nick caught in the middle. One of the teenage girls looked down, saw Nick and emitted a shrill scream of panic as she tried to stop, only to be shoved forward by the girl behind her.

Chance had been standing back, avoiding any contact with that wedding bouquet business, but as a result, his movements were less impeded. He reached Nick two steps ahead of Zane, scooping her up, enfolding her in his arms and rolling with her out of harm's way. Zane veered, putting himself between Chance and anyone who might stumble over him, and in another second there was practically a wall of boys and men protecting the two on the floor.

The bouquet hit Chance in the middle of the back.

Carefully he rolled over, and Nick's head popped out of the shield he'd made with his arms. "Wook!" she said, spying the bouquet. "Oo caught de fwowers, Unca Dance!"

Maris skidded to a stop beside them. Chance lay very still on the floor, with Nick on his chest. He glared up at Maris, his light, golden-hazel eyes narrow with suspicion. "You did that on purpose," he accused.

The MacNeils and the Mackenzies moved forward, smiles tugging at stern mouths. Maris crossed her arms. "There's no way I could have arranged this." She had to bite her lip to keep from laughing at his outraged expression.

"Hah. You've been doing spooky stuff all your life."

Nick leaned over and grasped one of the ribbons of the bouquet, pulling it toward her. Triumphantly she deposited it on Chance's chest. "Dere," she said with satisfaction, and patted it.

Zane rubbed the side of his nose, but he was less successful than Maris at hiding his grin. "You caught the bouquet," he said.

"I did not," Chance growled. "She hit me in the back with it!"

Mary walked up and stood beside Wolf, who automatically put his arm around her. Slowly a radiant smile spread across her face. "Why, Chance!" she exclaimed. "This means you're next."

"I—am—not—next." He ground the words out, sitting up with Nick in his arms. Carefully he put her on her feet, then climbed to his own. "Trickery doesn't count. I don't have time for a wife. I like what I do, and a wife would just get in the way." He was backing away as he talked. "I'm not good husband material, anyway. I—"

A little hand tugged on his pant leg. He stopped and looked down.

Nick stretched on tiptoe, holding the bouquet up to him with both hands. "Don't fordet oor fwowers," she said, beaming.

* * * * *

Dearest Friends,

My heart is singing the lyrics for "My Favorite Things." Christmas is by far my most favorite time of year. The hustle and bustle of shopping in stores filled with excitement and music. And the mail. How I love reading all those lovely Christmas cards. Christmas carols in church, and lighting the Advent wreath each night at dinner. The evergreen scent of a freshly cut Christmas tree never fails to stir my senses. I still have several homemade decorations carefully preserved from year to year. The cottonball snowmen Jenny made in Girl Scouts. The stamp-covered modified bleach bottle Ted crafted in Boy Scouts. Jody's preschool picture crocheted into a tree ornament. The treetop angel Dale constructed from a toilet paper roll in first grade. These are a few of my favorite things.

Something about Christmas frees the child within each one of us. I suspect that's what I love most. Like every family, ours has a number of traditions we celebrate from year to year. One of my favorites is gathering around the kitchen table so we can each sign the Christmas cards. There's generally popcorn and music and a lot of good-natured teasing.

As you might have already guessed, the Manning family is a great deal like my own. Many of you will remember Carrie, Jason Manning's stepdaughter, the fifteen-year-old who was instrumental in bringing her mother and Jason together. Carrie's all grown up now, and it only seemed fitting that she meet a romance-meddling teenager herself. I'm sure you'll enjoy the results.

My wish for you this Christmas is that you experience the love, joy and laughter of the season. Thank you for your continued loyal support of my books. Remember, Christmas is joy, laughter and memories. Be sure to plant a few of your own this year.

Debbie Macomber

SILVER BELLS
Debbie Macomber

Chapter One

"Dad, you don't understand."

"Mackenzie, enough."

Carrie Weston hurried through the lobby of her apartment complex. "Hold the elevator," she cried, making a dash for the open doors. Her arms were loaded with mail, groceries and decorations for her Christmas tree. It probably wasn't a good idea to rush, seeing that the two other occupants appeared to be at odds, but her arms ached and she didn't want to wait. Patience had always been one of her weaknesses, along with several other notable virtues.

The man kept the doors from closing. Carrie had noticed him earlier, and so had the other residents. There'd been plenty of speculation about the two latest additions to the apartment complex.

"Thanks," she said, sounding breathless and grateful all at once. Her eyes met those of the teenager. A girl, around thirteen, Carrie guessed. The two had moved into the complex a couple of weeks earlier, and from the scuttlebutt Carrie had heard from the other residents, they would be staying only until the construction on their new home was completed.

The elevator doors glided closed, with no particular hurry, but then those who lived in the brick three-story apartment building off Seattle's Queen Anne Hill weren't the type to rush. Carrie was the exception.

"What floor?" the man asked.

Carrie shifted the weight of her burden from one arm to the other. "Second. Thanks."

The thirty-something man offered her a benign smile as he pushed the appropriate button. He stared pointedly away from her and the teenager.

"I'm Mackenzie Lark," the girl said, smiling broadly. The surly tone was gone, Carrie noted. "This is my dad, Philip."

"I'm Carrie Weston." By balancing the groceries on one knee she was able to offer Mackenzie her hand. "Welcome."

Philip shook her hand next, his grip firm and solid, his clasp brief. He glared at his daughter as though to say this wasn't the time to be doing this.

"I've been wanting to meet you," Mackenzie continued, ignoring her father. "You look like the only normal person who lives in the entire building."

Carrie smiled despite her effort not to. "I take it you met Madam Fredrick."

"Is that a real crystal ball?"

"So she claims." Carrie remembered the first time Madam Fredrick stepped into the hallway, carting her crystal ball with her, predicting everything from the weather to a Nordstrom shoe sale. Carrie hadn't known what to think. She'd plastered herself against the wall and waited for Madam Fredrick to pass. The crystal ball hadn't unnerved her nearly as much as the large green emeralds glued above each eyebrow. She wore a modified caftan, with billowing yards of colorful material about her arms and hips, which hugged her legs from the knees on down. Her long, silver-white hair was arranged atop her head like a prom queen straight out of the sixties.

"She's really nice," Mackenzie remarked.

"Have you met Arnold yet?" Carrie asked. He was another of the more eccentric occupants of the apartment building, and one of her favorites.

"Is he the one with all the cats?"

"Arnold's the weight lifter."

"The one who used to work for the circus?"

Carrie nodded, and was about to say more when the elevator came to a bumpy halt and sighed loudly before the doors opened. "It was a pleasure to meet you both," she said on her way out the door.

"The same here," Philip grumbled, and although he glanced in her direction, Carrie had the impression that he wasn't really seeing her. She had the distinct notion that if she'd been standing there nude he wouldn't have noticed, or, for that matter, cared.

The doors started to shut when Mackenzie called, "Can I stop off and chat with you sometime?"

"Sure." The elevator closed, but not before Carrie heard the girl's father voice his disapproval. She didn't know if the two had continued on with their disagreement, or if this had to do with Mackenzie inviting herself over to visit.

Burdened with mail and groceries, Carrie experienced some difficulty unlocking and opening her apartment door without dropping everything. She slammed it closed with her foot and dumped the Christmas ornaments in the sofa's lap before hauling everything else into the compact kitchen.

"You'd been wanting to meet him," she said aloud, "now you have." She hated to admit it, but Philip Lark had been a major disappointment. He showed about as much interest in her as he would a loaf of bread in the bakery window. Well, what did she expect? That she anticipated anything was testament that she'd listened to Madam Fredrick one time too many. The older woman claimed to see Carrie's future and predicted that, before the end of the year, she'd meet the man of her dreams when he moved into this very apartment building. Yeah, right. She refused to put any credence into the prophecy. To do so would be ridiculous. Madam Fredrick was a sweet, old lady with a romantic heart.

Carrie reached for the mail, quickly scanned the envelopes, tossed the majority in the garbage and started to unpack her groceries when the doorbell chimed.

"Hello again," Mackenzie Lark said cheerfully when Carrie opened the door. The quickness of her return took Carrie by surprise.

"You said I could come see you," the teenager reminded her.

"Sure, come on in." Mackenzie walked into the apartment, glanced around admiringly and then collapsed onto the sofa.

"Are you still fighting with your dad?" Carrie asked. She'd had some real go-arounds with her mother before Charlotte had married Jason Manning ten years earlier. At the time, Carrie and her mother had been constantly at odds. Carrie knew that she was to blame, in part, but she was also aware that her mother had been lonely and unhappy. The two had grated against each other. Hindsight told her the root of their problem had been her parents' divorce. Carrie didn't remember a lot about her father—her parents had separated when she was four or five. For reasons that were never clear, Carrie blamed her mother. As she grew older, she came to resent that she didn't have a father. All this was buried deep in her subconscious, she realized now, years later, and reared its ugly head when she was thirteen or so.

"Dad doesn't understand." Mackenzie lowered her eyes; her mouth dropped.

"About what?" Carrie pried gently.

The girl stood and walked over to the kitchen and watched while Carrie put away groceries. She folded her arms atop the counter and then rested her chin there. "Everything. We can barely talk without fighting. It's tough being a teenager."

"You might find this difficult to believe, but it's just as difficult raising one," Carrie added.

Mackenzie's shoulders moved up and down with a deep sigh. "It didn't used to be this way with Dad and me. We were buds. It was hard when Mom left, but we got through it."

"So your parents are divorced?" She didn't mean to pry, but she was curious.

Mackenzie wrinkled her nose and nodded. "It was the pits when they split."

"It always is. My parents divorced when I was just a kid. I barely remember my dad."

"Did you see him very much afterward?"

Carrie shook her head. It had bothered her a great deal when she was younger, but she'd made her peace with it as an adult. It'd hurt to know that her father didn't want to be a part of her life, but that was his choice.

"I'm spending Christmas with my mom and her new husband." Carrie's eyes brightened. "I haven't seen her in almost a year. She's been busy," she offered as an excuse. "Mom works for one of the big banks in downtown Seattle and she's got this really important position and has to travel and it's hard for her to have me over. Dad's a systems analyst."

Carrie heard the pain in Mackenzie's voice. "You're fifteen?" she asked, deliberately adding a couple of years to her estimation, remembering how important it was to look older when one was that age.

Mackenzie's straightened, and looked self-important. "Thirteen, actually."

Carrie opened a bag of fat-free, cheese-flavored rice cakes and dumped the minishape round disks onto a plate. Mackenzie helped herself to one and Carrie did, as well. They sat across from each other on opposite sides of the kitchen counter.

"You know what I think?" Mackenzie said, her dark eyes brightening with intensity. "My dad needs a woman."

The rice cake stopped midway down Carrie's throat. "A woman?"

"Yeah, like a wife. All he does is work, work, work. It's like he can forget about my mother if he stays at the office long enough." She grabbed another rice cake. "Madam Fredrick said so, too."

"Madam Fredrick?"

"She looked into her crystal ball for me and said that she saw lots of changes in my future. I wasn't overly pleased. There've been too many changes lately with the move and all. I miss my friends and it's taking so much longer to build the new house than it was supposed to. Originally we were going to be in for Christmas, but now I wonder if it'll be ready before next Thanksgiving. Dad takes all the delays in his stride, but it bugs me. I'm the one who's attending a strange school and having to make new friends." Her chin returned to the countertop once again. "I want my life back."

"That's understandable."

Mackenzie seemed caught up in a fantasy world of her own for a moment. "You know, I think Madam Fredrick might have stumbled onto something here." Her voice elevated with enthusiasm.

"Stumbled onto something?" Carrie was beginning to think of herself as an echo. The teenager delivered one surprising statement after another.

"You know, about a relationship for my dad. I wonder how one goes about arranging that sort of thing?"

Carrie wasn't sure she understood. "How do you mean?"

"Finding a new wife for my dad."

"Mackenzie," Carrie said and laughed nervously. "A daughter can't arrange that sort of thing."

"Why not?" She seemed genuinely taken aback.

"Well, because marriage is serious business. It's love and commitment between two people. It's...it's..."

"The perfect solution," Mackenzie finished for her. "Dad and I have always liked the same things. We've always agreed on everything...well, until recently. I know what he likes better than he does himself. It makes perfect sense that I be the one to find him a wife."

"Mackenzie..."

"I know what you're thinking," she said, without a pause. "That my dad won't appreciate my efforts, and you're probably right. If I've learned anything from my father, it's the art of being subtle."

Carrie laughed. "I can't believe this," she whispered, and shook her head. This teenager was a reincarnation of herself eleven years earlier.

"What?" Mackenzie demanded, apparently offended.

"Take my advice and stay out of your father's love life."

"Love life?" she repeated. "That's a joke. He doesn't have one."

"He won't appreciate your help," Carrie warned.

"Of course he won't, but that's besides the point."

"Mackenzie, if you're not getting along with your father now, I hate to think of what would happen when he discovers what you're up to. My mother was furious with me when I offered Jason money to take her out and—"

"You were willing to pay someone to date your mother?"

Carrie didn't realize what she'd said until it was too late. "It was a long time ago," she said, hoping to leave it at that. She should have known better. Mackenzie's eyes brightened until they turned into huge spotlights as they zeroed in on her.

"You actually paid someone to date your mother?"

"Yes, but don't get any ideas. He refused." Already Carrie could see the wheels turning in the girl's head. "It was a bad idea, really bad, and like I said, my mother wasn't the least bit happy with me."

"Did she ever remarry?"

Carrie nodded.

"Anyone you knew?"

Again she nodded, unwilling to tell her it was the very man she'd tried to bribe into dating her mother.

Mackenzie's gaze cut into hers and Carrie looked away. "It was *him,* wasn't it?"

"Yes, but I didn't have anything to do with that."

Mackenzie's laugh was short and sarcastic. "I bet. You offered him money to date your mother; he refused, but dated her, anyway. That's great, just great. How long did it take before they were married?"

"Mackenzie, what happened with my mother and Jason is unique."

"How long?" she repeated, stubbornly pressing the question.

"A few months."

She smiled knowingly. "They're happy, aren't they." It was more a comment than a question.

Carrie nodded. She only hoped she would find a man who would make her as blissfully content as Jason Manning had made her mother. Despite ten years of marriage and two children, her mother and stepfather behaved like newlyweds. Carrie marveled at the strength of their love. It inspired her and in some ways had hampered her. She wanted that kind of relationship for herself and wasn't willing to settle for anything less. Her friends claimed she was too picky when it came to men, and she suspected they were right.

"My point exactly," the teenager declared triumphantly. "You knew your mom better than anyone. Who else was more qualified to find a husband for her? It's the same with me. I know my dad and he's in a rut. Something's got to be done, and Madam Fredrick hit the nail right on the head. He needs a love interest."

Carrie's smile was forced. "Madam Fredrick is one of my favorite people, but I think it's best to take what she says with a grain of salt."

"Well, a little salt enhances the flavor, right?" Mackenzie added. Excited now, she stood and started to pace. "What about you?" she asked all at once.

"Me?"

"Yeah, you. Would you be willing to date my dad?"

Chapter Two

"She's pretty, isn't she, Dad?"

Philip Lark glanced up. He sat at the kitchen table, filling out an expense report. His daughter sat across from him, smiling warmly. Something about the way her eyes focused on him told him she was up to something.

"Who?" he asked, wondering if he were being wise to inquire.

"Carrie Weston." At his blank look, she elaborated. "The woman we met in the elevator. We talked this afternoon." Mackenzie planted her chin in her hands and continued to look at him adoringly.

Philip's eyes reverted to the row of figures on the single sheet. His daughter waited patiently until he was finished. Patience wasn't a trait he was accustomed to seeing in Mackenzie. Generally she complained when he brought work home from the office, acting as though it were a personal affront. He cleared his mind, attempting to remember her question. Oh, yes, she wanted to know what he thought of Carrie Weston. For the life of him, he couldn't remember what the woman looked like. His impression of her remained fuzzy, but he hadn't found anything to object to.

"You like her, do you?" he asked instead, although he wasn't convinced pandering to Mackenzie's moods was a good thing. She'd been damn near impossible lately. Moody and unreasonable. Okay, okay, he realized the move had been hard on her; hell, it hadn't been all that easy on him, either. But it'd only be six to eight weeks. He'd assumed she was mature enough to handle the situation, but he was wrong.

Mackenzie's moods wasn't the only thing he'd miscalculated. Philip used to think they were close, but for the past several weeks she'd been a constant source of frustration.

Overnight his sane, sensible daughter had turned into Sarah Bernhardt, or more appropriately Sarah Heartburn! He swore she hadn't whined this much since she was three years old. Frankly, Philip didn't understand it. Even having her mother walk out on them hadn't caused this much drama.

"Carrie's great, really great."

Philip was pleased to have Mackenzie make new friends, although he would have been more pleased if it was someone closer to her own age. This move had been difficult on her, he realized, but the situation was only temporary. Gene Tarkington, a friend of his who owned this apartment building, had offered the furnished two-bedroom rental to him for as long as it'd take to complete the construction on his Lake Washington house. The apartment wasn't the Ritz, but then he hadn't been expecting any luxury digs. What he hadn't anticipated was the cavalcade of characters who populated the apartment complex. The woman with the crystal ball looked harmless enough. Even the muscle-clad sixty-year-old who walked around without a shirt, carrying hand weights, appeared innocuous. He wasn't as certain about some of the others, but then he didn't plan on sticking around long enough to form friendships with this group of oddballs.

"Dad," Mackenzie said wistfully, "have you ever thought of remarrying?"

"No," he answered emphatically, shocked by the question. He'd made one mistake, he wasn't willing to risk another. Laura and the twelve years he'd stuck it out had taught him everything he cared to know about that institution.

"You sound mad."

"I'm not," he commented, thrusting the expense report back inside his briefcase, "just determined."

"It's because of Mom, isn't it?"

Philip didn't know what had gotten into his daughter lately. "Why would I want to remarry?" he asked his own question, unwilling to be caught in a game of cat and mouse with Mackenzie.

"You might want a son someday."

"Why would I want a son when I have you?"

She grinned broadly, pleased with his response. "Madam Fredrick looked into her crystal ball and said she sees another woman in your life."

Philip laughed at the sheer ridiculousness of the idea. Remarry? Him? He'd rather dine on crushed glass. Wade through an alligator-infested swamp. Or, more appropriately, jump off the top of the Space Needle. No, he wasn't interested in remarrying. Not in this lifetime. Only recently he'd joked with Gene and said the next time he thought about marriage, he'd find an ugly woman he didn't like and buy her a house. He'd heard a comedian say that and felt an immediate kinship with the other man.

"Carrie's a lot like me."

So this was what the conversation was all about. Carrie and him. Well, he'd put an end to that right this moment. "Stop," he said, raising his palm outward. "I guess I'm a little slow on the uptake here, but the fog is beginning to clear. You're playing matchmaker with me and this—" being he couldn't recall a single thing about her, he couldn't think of a fitting adjective "—neighbor."

"Woman, Dad. Carrie's young, attractive, smart and funny."

"She is?" Funny he hadn't noticed that earlier.

"She's perfect for you."

"Who says?" The moment the words left his lips, Philip knew he'd made a mistake. He'd all but invited an argument.

Mackenzie's smile blossomed like a rose in the sun. "Madam Fredrick for one. Me for another. Just think about it, Dad. You're in the prime of your life and all you do is work. You should be enjoying the fruit of your labors."

"I'm building the house."

"Sure, to impress Mom, just so she'll know what a terrible mistake she made leaving you."

His daughter's words brought him up short. Philip sincerely hoped that wasn't true. He wanted a new home for plenty of reasons, none of which included his ex-wife. Or so he'd assumed.

"Why would your mother care about a home I'm building."

"Think about it, Dad."

"I am." He wasn't intentionally being obtuse.

She shot him a knowing look, one tempered with gentle understanding, which served to irritate him further. "Let's leave Laura out of this, all right?" His feelings for Mackenzie's mother were long dead. He'd tried to make the marriage work, God was his witness to that. Even when he discovered she was involved in an affair—the first time—he'd been willing to do whatever was necessary to get them back on track. With effort, it'd worked for a few years, but he'd been deluding himself because he'd so badly wanted the marriage to work.

The divorce had come long after there was any marriage left to save. He'd beat himself over the head emotionally for a long time before, and since. He had his daughter, and his dignity, and was grateful for both. The last thing he intended on doing at this point was risking that hard-won serenity.

"I want you to ask Carrie out for a date."

"What?" He couldn't believe the gall of his own flesh and blood. "Mackenzie, for the love of heaven, would you kindly stop. I'm not dating Carrie Westchester or anyone else."

"It's Carrie Weston."

"Her, either." He stalked into the kitchen and poured himself a cup of coffee. He took one sip, cringed at the bitter taste and dumped the rest in the sink.

"It's the least you could do..."

"Case closed! I don't want to hear another word about this, understand?" He must have added just enough authority to his voice for her to believe him because she didn't pursue the subject again. Frankly, Philip was grateful.

The next time he glanced at his daughter, he found her sitting in the middle of the living room, her arms folded around her as though she intended on squeezing the air from her own lungs. The sour look on her face was enough to curdle cream.

"Say, why don't we go out and buy a Christmas tree?" he suggested. Despite what Mackenzie might think, he didn't enjoy fighting with her.

With a look reserved for royalty, she turned to stare at him and consider his proposal. With what seemed to require an extraordinary amount of effort, she said, "No thanks."

"Fine, if that's the way you want to be."

"I thought you said a Christmas tree would be too much of a hassle this year?"

It would be, but he was willing to overlook that if it'd take his daughter's mind off this present topic of interest. "We could put up a small one." A compromise would go a long ways toward keeping the peace.

"She likes you, you know."

Philip didn't need to ask who she was talking about. He pressed his lips together to keep from saying something he'd later regret.

"She told me a story of what happened to her when she was about my age," Mackenzie continued, undaunted. "Her parents divorced when she was around five or so and her mother didn't date again or anything. She closed herself off from new relationships, just the way you're doing, and so Carrie felt she had to take matters into her own hands. Really, who could blame her, not me, that's for sure." She paused long enough to draw in a deep breath. "By the time Carrie was a teenager her mother had shriveled into this miserable, unhappy shrew." She stared pointedly at him before adding, "Sort of like what's happening to you."

"Come on now!"

"Like I said, Carrie felt she had to do something and so she offered to pay this guy to date her mother. Out of her own meager savings from baby-sitting jobs and walking a neighbor's dog. She took everything she'd managed to scrape together and selflessly paid this man. She told me she would have done anything to give her love-starved mother a second chance at happiness."

If he strained his ears, Philip could hear a violin playing softly in the background. "How noble of her."

"That's not the end of the story," Mackenzie informed him.

"You mean there's more?"

She ignored his sarcasm. "When her mother found out what she'd done, she was furious with Carrie."

"I can well imagine." Philip crossed his arms and leaned against the doorjamb. He glanced at his watch, indicating that there was only so much of this he was willing to listen to and he was already close to his limit.

"But she withstood her mother's outrage, withstood her tongue-lashing. Knowing she was right, Carrie gladly accepted the two-week restriction her mother placed on her."

The strains of the violin grew distinctly louder.

"Carrie didn't pick just any Tom, Dick or Harry to date her mother, though. She carefully, thoughtfully surveyed the eligible men around her and chose this really cool guy named James...or something like that. His name isn't really important—what is important is that Carrie knew her mother well enough to chose the perfect man for her. She chose the very best."

Now his daughter was beginning to sound like a Hallmark greeting card commercial. "This story does have a point, doesn't it?"

"Oh, yes." Her eyes gleamed with triumphant glee. "Not more than three months later, four at the most, Carrie's mother married Jason."

"I thought you said his name was James."

"His name doesn't matter. The point of the story is that he married her, and that they're both happy."

"That must have cost her a pretty penny, being that Carrie had already paid him everything she'd saved just for that first date."

"He married her for free."

"Oh, I see, she was on sale."

Mackenzie frowned at him. "You're not funny. Carrie told me that her mother's been happily married for going on eleven years now. Meeting Jason was the best thing that ever happened to her. Once a year, on the anniversary of that first date Carrie arranged, her mother sends her flowers out of gratitude that her daughter, the very one she'd restricted for two long weeks, had cared enough to search out the man of her dreams.''

The violin faded completely and was replaced with a full choral rendition of *God Bless America*. A lesser man would have taken pride in conducting the orchestra, but Philip managed to restrain himself. His daughter was Sarah Heartburn at her finest hour.

''Now,'' she said, and exhaled, ''will you ask Carrie out or not? She's perfect for you, Dad. I know what you like and what you don't and you're gonna like her. She's really nice and fun.''

''No.'' He yawned loudly, covering his mouth with his palm.

''I've never said anything, but I'd really love being a big sister, the way Carrie is to her two half brothers.''

''Thanks but no thanks.'' The kid was actually beginning to frighten him. Not only was she talking about dating a woman he'd briefly met, now she was talking about them having children together.

''Don't do it because I asked it of you. Do it for yourself. Do it before your heart turns into a hardened shell and you shrivel up into an old man.''

''Hey, hey, I'm not dead yet. I've got a good forty or fifty years left in me.''

''Maybe,'' Mackenzie challenged. With her nose leveled at the ceiling she exited the room with all the flair and drama of an actress walking offstage after the final curtain call.

Grinning to himself, Philip opened his briefcase. He removed a file, then hesitated and frowned. It was one thing to have his daughter carry on like a Shakespearean actress and another thing for an adult woman to be feeding her this bull. While he couldn't remember much about Ms. Carrie Weston, he did recall that she'd appeared plenty interested in him. Perhaps he'd best set the record straight with her. If she intended to use his daughter to get to him, then she was about to learn a thing or two.

Filled with purpose, he slammed his briefcase closed and headed toward the door.

"Where are you going?" Mackenzie asked.

"To talk to your friend," he snapped.

"You mean Carrie?" she asked excitedly. "You won't be sorry, Dad, I promise you. She's really nice and I know you'll like her. If you haven't decided where to take her to dinner, I'd suggest Henry's, Off Broadway. You took me there for my birthday, remember?"

Philip didn't think now was the time to inform his daughter that inviting Carrie to dinner wasn't exactly what he had in mind. He walked out the door and nearly collided with the old biddy with the crystal ball.

"Good evening, Mr. Lark," Madam Fredrick greeted with a knowing smile. She glanced at him and then the crystal ball and her smile grew wider.

"Keep that thing away from me," he told her, in clear terms. "I don't want you doing any of that hocus-pocus nonsense around my daughter. Understand?''

"As you wish," she said with great dignity, and moved past him. She proceeded like a queen before her subjects down the hallway. Philip glared at her and realized this was the very walk his daughter had used when she'd exited the room moments earlier. Exasperated, he sighed and headed for the stairs, taking them two at a time.

When he reached Carrie Weston's apartment, he was winded and short-tempered. She answered his knock almost immediately.

"Mr. Lark." Her eyes widened with the appropriate amount of surprise as though she'd spent the past five minutes standing in front of a mirror practicing. This woman had more tricks up her sleeve than Houdini.

"It seems you and I need to talk."

"Now?" she asked.

"Right now."

Chapter Three

Carrie Weston was lovely, Philip realized. For reasons he didn't want to analyze, he hadn't noticed how strikingly attractive she was earlier when they'd met in the elevator. Her eyes were clear blue, almost aquamarine. Intense. Her expression open and warm, expectant.

It took him an elongated moment to realize the reason he'd traipsed down to talk to her. Maybe, just maybe, what Mackenzie had been saying about him shriveling up contained a grain of truth. The thought sobered him.

"I need to talk to you about Mackenzie," he managed to stammer out.

"She's a delightful young lady. I hope I didn't keep her too long." Carrie's words were apologetic as she reached for her coat.

"It's about your discussion with her this afternoon."

"I'm sorry I can't chat just now. I feed Maria's cats for her on Wednesdays and I'm already late."

It could be a convenient excuse to escape him, but he was determined to see this through. "Do you mind if I tag along?"

She looked mildly surprised, but agreed. "Sure, if you want." She reached for a ten-pound bag of cat food. Ten pounds? Philip knew the older woman kept a ridiculous number of animals. Gene had complained to him more than once, but the retired schoolteacher had lived in the building for more than fifteen years and paid her rent on time. Gene tolerated her tendency to adopt cats, but he didn't like it.

"You might want to get your coat," she suggested as she locked up her apartment.

"My coat?" She seemed to imply that the old lady kept her apartment at subzero temperatures. "All right," he muttered.

She waited as he hurried up the flight of stairs, taking the steps two at a time. Mackenzie zoomed to her feet the instant he walked in the door. "What'd you say to her?" she demanded.

"Nothing yet." He yanked his coat off the hanger. "I'm helping her feed some cats."

The worry left his daughter's eyes. "Really? That's almost a date, don't you think?"

"Hell, no." He jerked his arms into the jacket sleeves.

"She asked me if I wanted to bake cookies with her and her two brothers on Saturday. I can, can't I?"

"We'll talk about that later." Already Carrie Weston was wheedling her way into his daughter's life. He didn't like it one damn bit.

Mackenzie didn't look overly pleased but agreed with a quick nod. The worried expression returned as he walked out the door.

Philip wasn't sure why he'd suggested he join her. It was important he clear the air, but it wasn't necessary to follow her around carting a bag of cat food to do so.

"Maria has a special love for cats," Carrie explained as they stepped into the elevator and rode to the ground floor. "I just don't think it's a good idea for her to be going out alone at night to feed the strays."

So that was what this was all about—feeding stray cats.

"Maria calls them her homeless babies."

Philip sure as hell hoped no one at the office heard about this. They stepped outside and cold air hit him like a slap across the face. His breath formed a small cloud of fog. "How often does she do this?" he asked, following Carrie down the well-lit street.

"Every day," she answered, and half a block later turned into an almost-dark alley. Carrie had claimed she didn't think it was safe for Maria to venture out alone at night. Philip wasn't convinced it was any less risky for her. He glanced about and saw nothing but a row of green Dumpsters.

They were halfway down the dimly lit alley when he heard the welcoming meow of a handful of cats. Carrie removed a cardboard container from a Dumpster and left a large portion of food there. The cats eagerly raced toward the feed. One tabby wove his way around her feet, his tail slithering about Carrie's slender calf. Squatting down, she ran her gloved hand down the back side of a large tomcat. "This is Brutus," she said, "Jim Dandy, Button Nose, Falcon and Queen Bee."

"You named them?"

"Not me, Maria. They're her friends. Most have been on their own so long that they're unable to adapt to any other way of life. Maria nursed Brutus back to health after he lost an eye in a fight. He was near dead when she found him. He let her treat him, but domesticated living wasn't for Brutus. Actually, I think he's the one that got Maria started on the care and feeding of the strays. I help out once a week. Arnold and a couple of the others do, too."

All this talk about cats was well and good, but Philip had other things on his mind. "As I explained earlier, I wanted to talk to you about Mackenzie."

"Sure." Carrie gave each of the cats a gentle touch, straightened and started out of the alley.

"She came back from her visit with you with some ridiculous idea about the two of us dating," Philip continued.

Carrie had the good grace to blush, he noted.

"I'm afraid I'm the one who put that idea in her head. Mr. Lark, I can't tell you how embarrassed I am over this. It all started with an innocent conversation about parents. My parents divorced, as well—"

"When you were four or five, as I recall," he said, filling in the details. He hated to admit it, but he enjoyed her uneasiness. Knowing Mackenzie, he was well aware of the finesse his daughter used to manipulate a conversation the way she wanted. Poor Carrie hadn't had a chance. "Mackenzie also said something about you paying a man to date your mother."

"Oh, dear." She briefly closed her eyes. "No wonder you wanted to talk to me." She glanced guiltily in his direction. "Jason was far too honorable a man to accept my offer."

"But he did as you asked."

"Not exactly... Listen, I do apologize. I'd best have another talk with Mackenzie. I'll do what I can to set the record straight. I was afraid she might do something like this. Actually, I should have realized her intent and warned you. But I didn't think she'd race upstairs and repeat every word of our conversation."

"My daughter has a mind of her own. She's taken quite a liking to you." For that, Philip was grateful. Mackenzie needed a positive female role model. Heaven knew her mother had taken little enough interest in her only child. Philip could do nothing to ease the pain of that. It hurt him to hear Mackenzie make excuses for Laura's disregard.

As they chatted, Carrie led the way into a vacant lot. He learned quite a bit about her in those few moments. She worked for Microsoft, the computer software conglomerate, had lots of family in the area and doted on her two half brothers.

The minute they stepped onto the lot, ten or so stray cats eased their way out of the shadows. It was clear they'd been waiting for Carrie. Talking softly, issuing reassurances and comfort, she distributed the food in a series of aluminum pie plates situated about the area.

"I saw a great deal of my teenage self in Mackenzie," she said when she rejoined him. She looked his way, but didn't hold his gaze long. "It wasn't just the fact my parents were divorced—broken homes were prevalent enough back then—but I'd been cheated out of more than the ideal family. In some ways I didn't have a mother, either.''

''Are you trying to say I'm not a good father?'' he asked tightly.

''No,'' she denied automatically. ''I think I'd better keep my mouth shut. I do apologize for what happened with Mackenzie. Rest assured, Mr. Lark, I have no intention of using your daughter to orchestrate a date with you.''

''Do you still want her over to bake cookies?'' he asked. He'd be in hot water with Mackenzie if she didn't.

''You don't mind if she comes?''

''Not if you and I are straight about where we stand with each other. I'm not interested in a relationship with you. It's nothing personal. You're young and attractive and will make some young man very happy one day—it just won't be me.''

''I wouldn't... You're not...'' She stopped abruptly and glared up at him. ''Rest assured, Mr. Lark, you have nothing to fear from me.''

''Good, as long as we understand each another.''

The gall of the man. Carrie removed her gloves and slapped her hands against her sides. She hung her coat in the closet and sat down, crossing her arms and her legs. She uncrossed both just as quickly, stood and started pacing. Remaining still was impossible.

Philip Lark actually believed she'd attempted to use his daughter to arrange a date with him. Talk about an egomaniac! This guy took the prize as the most conceited, egotistical, vain man she'd ever had the displeasure of meeting. She wouldn't date him now if he were the last man on the face of the earth.

The phone jingled just then and she glared at it accusingly, realized she was being ridiculous and reached for the receiver.

"Carrie?" Her whispered name came to her through the receiver.

It was her stepfather, Jason Manning. "Yes?" she answered in a barely audible voice. "Is there a reason we're whispering?"

"I don't want your mother to hear me."

"Oh?" Despite her agitation with Philip Lark she grinned.

"I ordered Charlotte a Christmas gift this afternoon," he boasted, sounding incredibly pleased with himself. From years past, Carrie knew buying Christmas gifts didn't come naturally to Jason. He'd been a confirmed bachelor until he'd met her mother, and buying gifts for a woman was foreign to him. The first Christmas after they were married he'd bought Charlotte a bowling ball, season tickets to the Seattle Seahawks and a vacuum cleaner. Since then, Carrie had helped steer him toward more personal items.

"You know how your mother likes to go to garage sales?"

"I'm not likely to forget." Jason had given her mother a lot of grief over her penchant to shop at yard sales. He liked to joke that Charlotte had found priceless pieces of Tupperware in her search for the treasure.

"Well, a friend of mine started a limousine service and I hired him to escort your mother on the Saturday of her choice. What do you think?" His voice rose several decibels in his excitement. "She'll love it, won't she?"

Carrie couldn't keep from smiling. "She'll have the time of her life."

"I thought so," he said proudly. "Jeff's giving me a twenty-percent discount, too."

"I think it's really sweet that you're taking Mom Christmas shopping in downtown Seattle."

"Yeah, well, that's the price a man pays to please his wife." He didn't sound very enthused.

"Doug and Dillon are coming to stay with me. We're baking cookies."

"I can't actually believe I'm voluntarily going Christmas shopping. There isn't another person in the world I let drag me into the city in the middle of the busiest shopping season of the year. Your mother's got to know I love her."

"She does know." Carrie had never doubted it, not from the first moment she'd seen her mother and Jason together. Rarely had any two people been more right for each other. In some ways it had hurt Carrie. From the day her mother had married Jason, Carrie had judged every man she dated against her stepdad. While Jason might not be the most romantic soul alive—she smiled every time she recalled the look on her mother's face when she unwrapped that bowling ball—he was a devoted husband and father.

Jason Manning loved and nurtured Carrie as if she'd been his own child. A teenager couldn't have asked for a better stepfather. After some of the horror stories she'd heard from other girls in her situation, she appreciated him all the more. It would take one hell of a man to fill his shoes.

The doorbell chimed.

"I'll let you go," Jason said. "Promise me you won't say anything to your mother."

"My lips are sealed." A limo to escort her to garage sales! She smiled when she thought about it. Carrie replaced the receiver and hurried across the living room to answer the door. Rarely had she spent a busier evening. She was hungry, disgruntled and in no mood for company.

"Hi," Mackenzie said, her eyes wide and eager. "So how'd it go with my dad?"

Carrie frowned.

"That bad, huh?" The teenager laughed lightly. "Don't worry, it'll get better once he gets used to the idea of dating again."

"Mackenzie, listen, you and I need to talk about this. Your father isn't pleased and frankly neither am—"

"Sorry, I can't chat now. Dad doesn't know I'm gone, but I had to talk to you before you lost heart. Don't be discouraged. All he needs is time." She beamed her a wide, ear-to-ear smile of encouragement. "This is going to be so great. Just wait until Jane hears about how I found my dad a wife. Jane's my best friend, or she used to be until we moved. I'll see you

Saturday." Having said that she promptly disappeared.

Carrie closed the door and shut her eyes, discouraged and depressed.

An abrupt knock sounded against the door.

"Now what?" she demanded, her patience shot.

Madam Fredrick smiled back at her. Arnold, with muscles bulging from his upper arms, stood with her. Both regarded her with open curiosity.

"Has she met him yet?" Arnold asked.

Madam Fredrick's face glowed that knowing look of hers. "You can answer that for yourself." She lifted her crystal ball and ran her hand over the smooth glass surface. "One look should tell you everything you need to know."

Chapter Four

A thin layer of flour dust covered the compact kitchen. Carrie fanned her hand in front of her face in an effort to clear the air. The scent of baking gingerbread men drifted though the apartment, smelling faintly of spices and fun.

Dillon stood on a chair, leaning over the electric mixer intently watching the blades stir the cookie dough. Doug was at the counter, his sleeves scooted up past his elbows, a rolling pin in his hand. Mackenzie scooped up the freshly baked cookies from the baking sheet and gently placed them on the wire rack to cool.

"Do you think anyone will taste the eggshell?" the teenager asked.

"The recipe said two eggs." Dillon's eyes gleamed defensively, "and Carrie said the whole egg. How was I suppose to know she didn't mean the shell?"

"You just should," his older brother informed him with more than a hint of righteousness. It went without saying that if he'd been the one adding the eggs the mistake wouldn't have been made.

"I already said we don't need to worry about it," Carrie inserted, hoping to smooth Dillon's dented ego. "A little extra protein never hurt anyone." She'd gotten the majority of the shell out and what had gotten crunched into the beaters had been pulverized to the point that it was no longer distinguishable.

Mackenzie expressively rolled her eyes, but it was clear she was enjoying herself. More and more the teenager reminded Carrie of herself eleven years earlier. Her neighbor had taken to Doug and Dillon immediately and they were equally enthralled with her. Within an hour the three were the best of friends.

"I want to decorate the cookies, too," Dillon cried, when he saw that Carrie had finished making the frosting.

"You can't lick the knife," his older brother remarked snidely, "not when we're giving the cookies to other people."

"There'll be plenty of frosting to go around for everyone."

"Who's going to taste the first gingerbread man?"

The three looked to one another. "Dillon should," Doug insisted.

"Okay," her youngest brother muttered bravely. "I don't mind. Besides, Carrie said no one would be able to taste the eggshell, anyway." He climbed down off the chair and reached for a cookie. "Maybe you should put a little frosting on it just in case," he said, looking to Carrie.

She slathered a thick layer across the top of the cookie and handed it back to him. Dillon closed his eyes and opened his mouth while the others waited in suspended animation for the outcome. One bite quickly became another.

"Maybe I should eat two just to be sure," the six-year-old suggested. "Just to be on the safe side."

Carrie winked and handed her youngest half brother a second cookie.

"I better try one myself," Doug said and grabbed one. He gobbled it down, head first, then smiled and nodded. "Not bad," he muttered, his mouth full of cookie.

"We're saving some for us, aren't we?" Dillon asked, reaching across the counter for the frosting knife.

"Of course, but I promised a plate to Arnold, Maria and Madam Fredrick."

"Can I frost now?" Dillon asked, and scooted the chair to the counter where Carrie stood.

"I want to decorate, too."

"Me, too," Mackenzie chimed in.

Two hours later, Carrie was exhausted. Doug and Dillon finished drying the last of the dishes and crashed in front of the television to watch their favorite video. Carrie sat on a bar stool, her energy gone, while Mackenzie finished adding tiny red cinnamon candy to the cookie faces.

"Dad's late," she said with a knowing sigh, "but then he's always longer than he says he's going to be. He has no life, you know." She glanced up from the task to be sure Carrie was paying attention.

"We agreed," Carrie reminded the girl, wagging her index finger.

"I remember." Hopelessness coated the teenager's voice. Carrie had insisted Mackenzie keep Philip Lark out of the conversation. It seemed like a drastic thing to do, but necessary, otherwise Mackenzie would use every opportunity to talk about her poor, lonely father, so desperate for companionship that he was literally shriveling up before her very eyes. Carrie could repeat the entire speech, verbatim.

It had taken the better part of two days to convince the teenager that Carrie wasn't romantically interested in Philip, no matter how perfectly matched they appeared to be in the girl's estimation.

Carrie suspected that Mackenzie was hearing much the same thing from her father. Philip wasn't thrilled with the idea of his daughter playing matchmaker any more than she was. In the three days since their first meeting the two had gone out of their way to avoid seeing or talking to each other. The last thing Mackenzie needed was evidence that her plan was working.

"It's a real shame," Mackenzie muttered, eyeing her carefully. "Madam Fredrick agrees with me and so do Arnold and Maria."

"Enough!" Carrie insisted, loud enough to draw the boys' attention away from the television screen.

When Mackenzie finished decorating the last of the cookies, Carrie set them on three large plastic plates, covered each with clear wrap and added a bright, frilly bow to the top.

"I want to deliver Arnold's," Doug insisted. The oldest of her half brothers had taken a liking to the former weight lifter. Arnold typified the stereotype to a T. From the top of his shiny bald head, handlebar mustache and bulging muscles, everything about him spelled out circus performer. His only consideration to modern times was colorful red spandex shorts, which he loved and wore over his blue tights. The first time Doug had met Arnold, he'd thought the older man was a bald Superman.

"Will Maria let me pet her cats?" Dillon wanted to know.

"I'm sure she will."

"I guess that leaves me with Madam Fredrick," Mackenzie said, not sounding the least bit disappointed. She cast her gaze toward the kitchen and Carrie understood that the girl was looking to make sure there were enough cookies left over to take home to her father. Carrie had already made up a small plate for the girl, and told her so.

"Thanks," Mackenzie said, her eyes glowing.

The three disappeared, eager to deliver their gifts, and Carrie collapsed on the sofa. She rested her head against the back cushion and closed her eyes, enjoying the peace and quiet. It didn't last long.

Doug barreled back into her apartment moments later, followed by Mackenzie. Dillon trailed behind.

"She's in here." Carrie heard her half brother explain before he entered her apartment. Philip walked in with him.

Carrie was immediately aware of how she must look. Flour had dusted more than the kitchen counters. She hadn't bothered with makeup that morning and dressed in her grungiest jeans. Rarely had she felt more self-conscious in front of a man. She was convinced she resembled an unflattering character out of a nursery rhyme. Probably *The Old Woman Who Lived in a Shoe*.

"Dad!" Mackenzie cried, delighted to see him.

Carrie stood and quickly removed the apron, certain the domestic look distracted from any air of sophistication she might possess. It might have been her imagination, but it seemed Philip's gaze zeroed in on her.

"I suppose I should have knocked," he said, and motioned to Dillon, "but your friend here insisted I come right in."

"Oh, sure, no problem." Each word seemed to stick to the roof of her mouth like paste. She clenched her hands together, remembering how uneasy her mother had been around Jason those first few times. Carrie had never understood that. Jason was the easiest person to talk to that she'd ever known.

Now she understood.

"Mackenzie behaved herself?" Once again the question was directed to Carrie.

"She was a big help," she assured him.

"Mom didn't call, did she?" Mackenzie advanced one step toward her father, her eyes wide and hopeful.

Philip shook his head, and Carrie watched as the weight of disappointment settled over the teenage girl. "She's real busy this time of year," Mackenzie explained to no one in particular. "I'm not surprised she didn't call, not with so much else on her mind... and everything."

Carrie resisted the urge to place her arm around the girl's shoulder.

"How about a movie?" Philip suggested abruptly. "I can't remember the last time we went together."

"Really?" Mackenzie's jerked her head up and her eyes brightened.

"Sure. Any one you want."

She mentioned the latest Walt Disney hit. "Can Doug and Dillon come, too?"

"Sure." Philip smiled affectionately at his daughter.

"And Carrie?"

"I . . . couldn't," she interjected before Philip could respond, saving him the embarrassment for them both.

"Why not?" Doug demanded. "You said yourself that we're all done with the cookies. A movie would be fun."

"You'd be welcome," Philip surprised her by adding. His gaze held hers and the offer appeared genuine. Apparently he felt that with three young chaperons there wouldn't be a problem.

"You're sure?"

"Of course, he's sure," Mackenzie insisted. "My father doesn't say things he doesn't mean, isn't that right, Dad?"

"Right." He sounded less sure this time, but his eyes were welcoming.

Carrie was half tempted to let him take the kids on his own, but changed her mind fast enough. Doug was right, getting out of the apartment would be fun, and a movie would be a great way to relax after the hectic activity of the morning.

The five of them together at the show would be innocent enough. In her naiveté she'd forgotten that it was taboo for kids past the age of ten to sit with their parents. The moment they entered the theater, the three kids promptly found seats several rows away from Philip and Carrie.

"But I thought we'd all want to sit together," Carrie said, loud enough for Doug and Dillon to hear. A small desperate ring echoed in her voice.

"That's for little kids," six-year-old Dillon turned around to inform her.

With the theater filling up so fast, soon the option of sitting together was taken away from them. Carrie settled uneasily in the padded seat next to Philip. Neither spoke. He didn't seem any more pleased at this turn of events than she did.

"Do you want some popcorn?" Philip offered, tilting the overflowing bucket in her direction.

"No thanks," she whispered, and glanced at her watch, wondering how much longer it'd be before the movie started. "I certainly hope you don't think I arranged this," she whispered out of the corner of her mouth.

"Arranged what?"

"The two of us sitting alone together." She'd hate to have him accuse her of anything underhanded, which, given his penchant for casting blame, he was likely to do. Not that she faulted him. She was the one who unwittingly put the matchmaking notion in Mackenzie's head. What a fool she'd been not to realize the impressionable teenager would pick up on the ploy she'd used against her own mother.

"Why would I blame you?" he asked, sounding exasperated with her for suggesting it.

His attitude rankled. "Might I remind you of our last conversation," she said stiffly. "You seemed to think there was some danger of me seducing you."

Philip laughed out loud and didn't have the good grace to look the least bit repentant. "It wasn't me I was worried about," he explained, "My fears revolved around Mackenzie making both our lives miserable. If I sounded rude earlier, I apologize, but I was protecting us both from the wiles of my headstrong daughter."

That wasn't the way Carrie remembered it.

"I'm not a man who'll let my daughter do my courting for me," he added, as though that explained everything. "Now relax and enjoy the movie." He tilted the popcorn her way once more and this time Carrie helped herself.

Philip grinned approvingly, and the theater lights dimmed as the curtain was drawn up for the show.

The movie was great. Carrie soon found herself completely immersed in the plot. Philip laughed in all the places she did and whatever tension existed between them melted with their shared enjoyment.

When the movie ended, Carrie was sorry that there wasn't more. While it was true that she enjoyed the story line, she also found pleasure sitting with Philip. She discovered that she liked him. She'd almost prefer to find something objectionable about him. A nervous habit, a personality trait she disliked, his attitude. Something. Anything that would help keep her mind off how attractive she found him.

He'd made it as plain as possible that he wasn't interested in a relationship with her. With anyone, if that was any comfort. It wasn't. She wanted him to be cold and standoffish, brisk and businesslike. The side of him she'd seen at the movie was laid-back and fun loving. She wasn't fooled. Philip hadn't developed a sudden desire to escort his daughter to the movies. He'd offered because he knew Mackenzie's disappointment over not hearing from her mother had been keen. He loved his daughter, and wanted to protect her from the hurts only a lackadaisical parent could inflict on an emotionally needy child.

"This was a nice thing you did," she said as they exited the theater. The youngsters raced on ahead of them toward the parking lot in front of the theater. "It helped take Mackenzie's mind off not hearing from her mother."

"I'm not so sure it was a good idea," he muttered, and dumped the empty cardboard popcorn container in the garbage can on their way out the door.

"Why not?"

He turned and stared at her for a long moment. "Because I find myself liking you."

Her reaction must have shone in her eyes because his own gaze narrowed fractionally. "You felt it, too, didn't you?" he quizzed.

She wanted to lie. If ever there was reason, it was now. "Yes," she whispered.

"I'm not right for you," he announced starkly.

"In other words, I'm wrong for you."

He didn't answer her for a long time. "I don't want to hurt you, Carrie."

"Don't worry," she answered brightly, "I won't let you."

Chapter Five

"What do you think?" Mackenzie proudly held up a lopsided snowflake with a thin thread dangling from the crochet hook. From the gleam in her eye one might think she'd created the *Mona Lisa* instead of a Christmas tree ornament. "Carrie's whole tree is decorated with snowflakes she crocheted," she added. "Her Grandma Manning taught her to crochet when she was about my age. It's a dying art, you know." She wound the thread around her index finger and awkwardly manipulated the hook, swashing her tongue from one side of her mouth to the other with the effort.

"It's lovely, sweetheart."

"Mom'll be pleased, won't she." Mackenzie turned the question into a statement, so certain was she of his response.

"She'll be thrilled." Philip's jaw tightened at the mention of Laura. His ex-wife had seen fit to contact Mackenzie and arrange a time for their daughter to spend time with her. Ever since she'd heard from her mother, Mackenzie had been walking five feet off the ground. Philip didn't know what he'd do if Laura didn't show. He wouldn't put it past her, but he prayed she wouldn't do anything so cruel.

"Carrie's been great," Mackenzie continued. "She taught me everything." She paused long enough to look up at him. "I like her so much, Dad."

The hint was there and it wasn't subtle. The problem was that Philip was discovering that his feelings for Carrie had aligned with those of his daughter. Although he avoided contact with Carrie, there was no escaping her. Mackenzie brought her name into every conversation, marching her virtues past him like a one-woman parade.

Carrie had become a real friend to Mackenzie. It used to be that his daughter moped about the apartment, complaining about missing her friends, badgering him about the move and generally making his life miserable. These days, if she wasn't with Carrie, she was helping Maria with her cats, having tea with Madam Fredrick—and having her leaves read—or lifting weights with Arnold.

"I'm going to miss the Christmas party," she stated matter-of-factly. "It's in the community room in the basement Christmas Eve." She glanced up to be certain he was listening. "Everyone in the building's invited. Carrie's going, so is Madam Fredrick and just everyone else. It's going to be a blast." Her shoulders moved up and down with heartfelt regret. "But being with Mom is more important than a silly ole party. She's really busy this time of year."

"I'm sure she is." Philip had forgotten about the Christmas party. He'd gotten the notice a day or so earlier, and would have tossed it if Mackenzie hadn't gone into ecstasy when she saw it. From her reaction one would think it was an invite to the Christmas ball to meet a bachelor Prince. As for him, he had better things to do than spend time with a group of friendly oddballs.

Philip reached for his car keys and his gym bag. "I'll only be gone an hour," he promised.

"It's okay. It'll take me that long to finish this." Her tongue worked as hard and fast as the crochet hook. "Oh, I almost forgot," she said, tossing everything aside and leaping out of the chair as if propelled forward by a buoyant spring. She raced into her bedroom and returned a moment later with a small white envelope. "It's for you," she said, watching him eagerly. "Open it now, okay?"

"Shouldn't I wait until Christmas?"

"No." She gestured for him to tear open the envelope.

Inside was a card in the shape of a silver bell, bright and cheerfully decorated.

"Go ahead and read it," she urged, and would have done so herself if he hadn't acted promptly. The card was an invitation to lunch at the deli on the corner. "I'm buying," she insisted, "to thank you for being a great dad. We've had our differences this year and I want you to know that no matter what I say I'll always love you."

"I don't always say what I mean, either," he murmured, touched by her words. "I'll be happy to pay for lunch."

"No way," she insisted. "I've saved my allowance and did a few odd jobs for Madam Fredrick and Arnold. I can afford it, as long as you don't order the most expensive thing on the menu.''

''I'll be sure and eat a big breakfast,'' he said, and kissed her on the cheek before he walked out the door. He pushed the button for the elevator and found himself grinning. He'd been doing a great deal more of that lately, he realized. In the beginning he thought moving into the apartment had been a mistake. No longer. The changes in Mackenzie since meeting Carrie had been dramatic.

The elevator arrived and he stepped inside, pushing the button for the lobby. It stopped on the next floor and Carrie entered, carting a laundry basket. She hesitated when she saw he was the only other occupant.

''I don't bite,'' he assured her.

''That's what they all say,'' she teased back. She reached across him and pushed the button for the basement, then stepped back. The doors closed with sluggish disregard for immediacy. It started to move, its descent slow and methodical, then it lurched sharply, dropping several feet.

Carrie gasped and staggered against the wall.

Philip was able to maintain his balance by bracing his shoulder against the side. The small compartment went dark.

''Philip?'' Carrie's soft voice inquired a moment later.

''I'm here.'' This was more than dark, it was pitch-black inside. Straining his eyes, he couldn't see a damned thing. ''It looks like there's been a power outage.''

"Oh, dear." Her voice sounded tiny and small.

"Are you afraid of the dark?"

"Of course not," she returned indignantly. "Well, maybe, just a little. Everyone is . . . I mean, it wouldn't be unusual under these circumstances to experience some anxiety."

"Of course," he agreed, and swallowed a smile.

"How long will it take for the power to come back on?"

"I don't know." Her guess was as good as his. "Give me your hand."

"Why?" She nearly bit his head off with the lone word.

"I thought it would comfort you."

"Oh. Here." If she offered it to him, he couldn't see it. He thrust his arm out and their fingers collided. She gripped hold of him like a lifeline tossed over the side of a cliff. Her fingers were cold as ice.

"Hey, there's nothing to be afraid of."

"I know that," she responded defensively.

He wasn't entirely sure who moved first, but before another moment passed he had his arm around her and held her protectively against his side. If the truth be known, he'd been thinking of little else but holding Carrie since the day they'd attended the movie. He hadn't allowed himself to dwell on the image, but it certainly felt right to have her this close. More right than it should.

Neither spoke. He wasn't sure why, then again he knew. For his own part, he didn't want reality interrupting his fantasy. Under the cover of the dark he was safe to lower his guard. Carrie, he suspected, didn't speak for fear she'd reveal how truly frightened she was. Philip already knew. He felt her tremble and welcomed the opportunity to bring her closer into his embrace.

"It won't be long."

"I'm sure you're right," she whispered back.

Without conscious thought, he wove his fingers into her hair. He loved the soft feel of it, the fresh, clean scent. He tried to concentrate on other matters and found his mind stubbornly clinging to the feel of the woman in his arms.

"Maybe we should talk," she suggested. "You know, to help pass the time."

"What do you want to talk about?" He could feel her breath against the side of his neck. Wistful and provocative. In that instant Philip knew he was going to kiss her. He was motivated by the equally strong emotions of need and curiosity. It had been a long time since he'd held a woman. For longer than he wanted to remember he'd kept any hint of desire tightly in check. He preferred living a life of celibacy rather than risk another failed marriage.

He would have ended it then and there if Carrie offered any resistance. She didn't. Her lips were moist and warm. Welcoming. He moaned softly and she did, too, slanting her head to one side.

"I thought you wanted to talk," she whispered.

"Later," he promised, and kissed her again, having trouble disguising his hunger. Sweet heaven, she tasted good, better than he dreamed, better than anyone he'd ever tasted.

At first their kisses were light, intriguing, seductive. This wouldn't be happening if they weren't trapped in a dark elevator, Philip assured himself. He felt he should explain that, but couldn't make himself stop kissing her long enough to form the words.

It wasn't supposed to be this damn good. He feared the taste and feel of her would soon become addictive. His head and his heart filled with the wonder and the surprise of it.

"Philip..."

He responded by brushing his moist lips against hers, gently rubbing back and forth, creating an exciting, tingling friction. His gut wrenched with the sheer awe of what they were doing. He coaxed her mouth open by stroking his tongue over hers. When her lips gently parted, he brazenly embedded it deeply, erotically, inside her mouth, swirling his tongue about on a journey of such intense desire that he heard himself moan. He wasn't the only one caught up in their love play. Carrie whimpered and squirmed in his arms.

She wrapped her arms around his neck, clinging tightly as if she needed to hold on. He eased her against the wall, kissing her ravenously. The strength of his erection throbbed against her thigh. She squirmed against him and he swallowed a thick groan. His hands moved to her hips, and he dragged the lower portion of her body intimately against the heat of his arousal. Cupping her buttocks, he lifted her slightly upward and ground the lower half of his body against her.

Before he could consider the wisdom of what he was doing, his hands roamed upward, under her sweater to capture her breasts, past the silky, smooth skin of her abdomen. Her breasts were full and lush. Her nipples instantly beaded under the soft manipulations of his fingertips. If he didn't touch and kiss them soon, he feared he'd go mad.

He was all thumbs in his rush to unfasten the back of her bra. It seemed to take an eternity to undo the small clasp. Her bounty spilled into his waiting palms and he rolled his head back at the sheer wonder of his discovery.

Philip was left to wonder what would have happened, how far their love play would have taken them, if the lights hadn't flickered just then.

They both froze as the electricity flashed on and off. It was as if they stood on a stage behind a curtain that was about to be raised before a full audience.

Carrie scrambled to right her clothes while Philip plastered himself against the wall, his hands flattened at his sides as he struggled to mentally deal with what they'd been doing. He wasn't a kid anymore, but he'd behaved like a hormonally love-starved seventeen-year-old.

For the first time since his divorce, Philip felt the walls he'd built around his heart start to crack. The barriers had been fortified by his bitterness, by resentment, mortared by his fears. This wasn't what he wanted. Following the divorce, he'd vowed not to get involved again. Carrie was young and sweet and deserved a man who came without emotional scars and a child in tow.

He was grateful that the electricity hadn't returned; he needed these few additional minutes to compose himself.

"Are you all right?" he asked, when he could speak without betraying all he felt.

"I'm fine." Her voice contradicted her words. She sounded anything but.

He thought to apologize, but he couldn't make himself say the words, fearing she'd guess the effect she'd had on him.

"You can't blame a guy for taking advantage of the dark, can you?" he asked, deliberately making light of the exchange. "I have to say you're one hot mama," he added, needing to demean their lovemaking before she made the mistake of placing any importance on the exchange.

The electricity returned at precisely that moment. He squinted against the flash of bright light. Carrie stood with her back braced against the wall opposite him, her fingers fanned out against the wood panel, her eyes wide and stricken. The laundry basket rested in the far corner where she'd dropped it.

"Is that all this was to you?" she asked in a hurt-filled whisper.

"Sure," he responded, and shrugged. "Is it supposed to mean anything more?"

Before she could answer, the elevator stopped at the lobby floor and the doors swished open. Philip was grateful for the chance to escape.

"Obviously not," she answered, but her eyes went blank as she stared past him.

He stepped out and waited as the doors closed, feeling both guilty and sad. He didn't mean to hurt Carrie. She was sweet and gentle and had touched Mackenzie's and his life with her generosity of spirit.

"Damn," he muttered, cursing himself for the fool he was.

"Go after her," the voice behind him advised.

Irritated, he turned to find Maria and Madam Fredrick standing behind him.

"She's a good woman," Maria said, holding a fat calico cat under her arm, gently stroking its fur. "You won't find another like her."

"You could do worse," Madam Fredrick added, then chuckled. "The fact is you already have."

"Would you two kindly stay out of my affairs."

Both women looked taken back by his gruff, cold response to their friendly advice.

"Well, I've never . . . !" the retired schoolteacher exclaimed righteously.

"Never mind, dearie. Some men need more help than we can give them." Madam Fredrick's words were pointed and sharp, hitting him square in the chest.

Disgusted with the two busybodies, and more so with himself, Philip hurried out of the apartment building determined that, from here on out, he was taking the stairs.

Chapter Six

"Did I ever tell you about Randolf?" Madam Fredrick asked wistfully as she poured Carrie a cup of tea. "We met when I was a girl. All right, I was twenty, but a naive twenty. I knew the moment our eyes met that I should fear for my virtue. I wanted him, but my girlish desires were no match for his suave maturity." She paused, her hand holding the top of the teapot in place, her eyes caught in the loving memory of forty years past. Laughing softly, she continued. "We were married within the week of meeting each other. We both knew we were meant to be together. It was useless to fight fate."

"He was your husband?"

"The man who stole my heart. We had thirty happy years together. We fought like cats and dogs and we loved. Dear God, how we loved. One look from that man could curl my toes. He could say to me with one sweeping glance what would take three hundred pages in a book."

Carrie added sugar to her tea and stirred. Her hand trembled slightly as her mind drifted back to the kisses she'd shared with Philip in the elevator. She'd taken the stairs ever since. She'd been kissed before, plenty of times, but it had never felt like it had with Philip. What unsettled her was how perfectly she understood what her neighbor was saying about Randolf.

"I never remarried after he died," Madam Fredrick mentioned as she slipped into the chair next to Carrie. "My heart wouldn't let me." She reached for the delicate teacup and raised it to her lips. "Not many women are as fortunate as I am to have found love at such a tender age."

Carrie sipped her tea and struggled to keep her mind focused on Madam Fredrick. Her thoughts remained tangled with the intense kisses she'd shared with Philip. She wanted to push the memories to the farthest reaches of her mind, but they refused to stay put. They continued to bob to the surface, like stubborn corks, reminding her of the blatant way in which she'd responded to his touch. It embarrassed her.

"I wanted to give you your Christmas present early," Madam Fredrick announced, and placed a small, wrapped gift in her lap.

"I have something for you, too, but I was going to wait until Christmas."

"I want you to open yours now."

The older woman watched eagerly as Carrie untied the gold ribbon and peeled away the paper. Inside the box was a small glass bowl with dried herbs and flowers. The scent reminded her of sage.

"It's a fertility potion," Madam Fredrick explained.

"Fertility!" Carrie nearly dropped the delicate bowl.

"Brew these leaves as you would tea, and—"

"Madam Fredrick, I have no intention of getting pregnant anytime soon."

The woman smiled and said nothing.

"I appreciate the gesture, really I do." She didn't want her friend to think she wasn't grateful, but she had no plans for having a child within the foreseeable future. "I'm sure at some point, a number of years down the road, I'll be brewing up this potion of yours." She took another drink of her tea and caught sight of the time. "Oh, dear," she said, rising quickly to her feet. "I'm supposed to be someplace else in five minutes." Mackenzie had generously offered to buy her lunch. Philip's daughter had crafted the invitation on a lovely card shaped like a silver bell.

"Thank you again, Madam Fredrick," she said, downing the last of the tea. She tucked the unwrapped Christmas gift inside her purse and reached for her coat.

"Come visit me again soon," Madam Fredrick insisted.

"I will," Carrie promised. She enjoyed her time with the older woman, although she generally didn't understand what determined the topic of conversation. Having her neighbor reminisce about her long-dead husband had seemed a bit odd, especially the comment about fearing for her virtue. It was almost as if Madam Fredrick knew what had transpired between her and Philip alone together in the darkened elevator. Her cheeks went red remembering the way she responded to him, how she'd allowed him to touch her breasts. There was no telling what might have happened had the lights not returned when they did.

Carrie hurried out of the apartment and down the windy street to the deli on the corner. It was a generous gesture on Mackenzie's part to ask her to lunch. It meant a great deal to the teenager, otherwise she wouldn't have gone to the trouble of printing up the invitation on a special card.

The deli was a beehive of activity. The food was excellent, and a neighborhood favorite. Inside she was greeted with a wide variety of mouth-watering smells. Patrons lined up against the glass counter that displayed a large assortment of sliced meats and tempting salads. The refrigerator case was decorated with a plastic swag of evergreen, dotted with tiny red berries.

"Over here." Carrie heard Mackenzie's shout and glanced across the room to find the teenager on her feet, waving her arm above her head. The kid was smart enough to claim a table, otherwise they might have ended up having to wait.

Carrie gestured back and wove her way between the tables and chairs to meet her special friend. Not until she reached the back half of the room did she realize that Mackenzie wasn't alone.

Philip sat with his daughter. His eyes revealed his surprise to find Carrie there, as well.

"Oh, good, I was afraid you were going to be late," Mackenzie said, and handed her a menu. "Tell me what you want and I'll get in line and order it."

Briefly Carrie toyed with the idea of canceling, but that would have disappointed Mackenzie and she didn't want to do that. Philip had apparently reached the same conclusion.

"Remember I'm on a limited budget," Mackenzie reminded them, speaking loudly to be heard over the hustle and bustle of the deli. "But you don't have to order peanut butter and jelly, either."

"I'll take a pastrami on whole wheat, hold the pickle, extra mustard."

Carrie set her menu aside. "Make that two."

"You like pastrami, too?" Mackenzie asked, making it sound incredible that two people actually found the same kind of meat to their liking.

"You'd better get in line," Philip advised his daughter.

"Okay, I'll be back before you know it." She smiled broadly before she left, expertly weaving her way across the room.

Carrie unwound the wool scarf from around her neck and removed her jacket. She could be adult about this. While it was true they hadn't expected to run into each other, it wasn't the end of the world.

While the noise about them was almost deafening, the silence between them was decidedly louder. When she couldn't stand it any longer, she said, "It's very sweet of Mackenzie to do this."

"Don't be fooled," he returned gruffly. "Mackenzie knew exactly what she was doing."

"And what was that?" Carrie hated to be defensive, but she didn't like his tone of voice, or his implication.

"She set this up so you and I'd be forced into spending time together."

He made it sound like a fate worse than high taxes. "Come on, Philip, I'm not a witch."

"As far as I'm concerned that's the problem."

His words lifted her spirits. She reached for a bread stick from the tall glass in the middle of the table and broke it in half. "Are you suggesting that I actually tempt you?" she asked, feeling downright chipper.

"Don't flatter yourself."

"I'm not." She knew a bluff when she heard one. "If anyone should be flattered it's you. First off I'm a good eight years younger than you, with endless possibilities when it comes to finding myself a man. Tell me what makes you think I'd be interested in an ill-tempered, unfriendly, nearing middle-aged frump?"

His eyes widened. "Ouch."

"Two can play that game, Philip."

"What game?"

"I almost believed you, you know. You were taking advantage of the dark? Really, Philip, you might have been a bit more original."

His eyes narrowed.

"But no one's that good an actor. You're attracted to me, but you're scared to let go of that tight rein with which you hold on to your emotions. I'm not sure what your hang-up is, but my guess is that it probably has something to do with the divorce. So be it. If you're content to spend the rest of your days alone, far be it for me to stop you." She took a bite of the bread stick, chomping down hard.

Mackenzie had their order. She carried the tray high above her head as she expertly manipulated herself through the crowd. Her eyes were bright with excitement and joy when she rejoined them.

She lifted a thick ceramic plate and handed it to Carrie. "Pastrami on whole wheat, no pickle and extra mustard."

"Perfect," Carrie said, taking the thick white plate from her. She was grateful Mackenzie had returned when she did, unsure if she could continue the bluff much longer. As it was, Philip didn't have an opportunity to challenge her statement, which was exactly the way she wanted it.

Mackenzie distributed the rest of the sandwiches, set the tray aside and flopped down in the seat between Carrie and Philip. "Don't you just love the holidays?" she asked, before biting into her sandwich.

Philip's gaze locked with Carrie's. "Sure do," he said, and Carrie noted that he was gritting his teeth.

From the way Philip tore into the sandwich, one would think he hadn't eaten in a week. It was as though they were involved in a contest to see which could finish first.

Philip won. The minute he swallowed the last bite, he stood, thanked his daughter and excused himself.

"He's going back to work," Mackenzie explained sadly as she watched her father leave. "He's always going back to the office."

"Inviting us both to lunch was a thoughtful thing to do," Carrie said, "but your father seems to think that you asked us to suit your own purposes."

Mackenzie lowered her gaze. "All right, I did, but is that such a bad thing? I like you better than anyone. It's clear that my dad's never going to get married again without my help. My parents have been divorced two years now and he's never even gone out on a real date."

"Mackenzie, your father needs time."

"Time? He's had more than enough already. He can't continue to go through life with his head buried twenty feet below the surface of life. It's like he's put everything on hold while he tries to forget what my mother did. I want him to marry you."

"Oh, Mackenzie." Carrie exhaled sharply. While she didn't want to disappoint the teenager, she couldn't allow the girl to continue to believe dealing with human emotions was this simple. "I can't marry your father because you want me to."

"Don't you like him?"

This was far more difficult than she thought it would be. "Yes, I do, very much, but there's so much more to committing to marriage than me liking your father."

"But he cares about you. I know he does, only he's afraid to let it show."

Carrie had already guessed as much herself, but it could be that she wanted to believe it so badly that she'd made it so in her mind.

"My mom is really pretty," Mackenzie said, and she lowered her gaze to her hands, which clenched a paper napkin. "I think she might have been disappointed that I looked more like my dad's side of the family than hers. She's never said anything, but I had the feeling she would have stayed married to my dad if I'd been prettier."

"I'm sure that isn't true." Carrie's heart ached at the pain she heard in the girl's voice. "I used to feel those kinds of things, too. My dad never wanted anything to do with me. He never wrote or sent me a birthday gift or remembered me at Christmas and I was convinced it was something I must have done."

Mackenzie raised her gaze until it was level with Carrie's. Her eyes were round and sympathetic. "But you were just a little kid when your parents divorced."

"It didn't matter. I felt that somehow I was the one to blame. It didn't have anything to do with me. I realize that now. Your parents didn't divorce because you took after your father's side of the family. Your parents' problems had nothing to do with you."

Mackenzie didn't say anything for a long moment. "This is why I want you to marry my dad. You say all the things that make me feel better. In the past couple of weeks you've been more of a mother to me than my real mother ever was."

Carrie reached out and squeezed Mackenzie's hand.

"I didn't say anything last week, but did you know that was the first time I've ever baked homemade cookies? Dad helped me bake a cake once, but that came in a box."

From the inept way Mackenzie had completed the tasks given her, Carrie had suspected as much.

"I like the way we can sit down and talk. You seem to understand everything that's in my heart," Mackenzie murmured. "I'm probably the only girl in my school who knows how to crochet, although all I can do is those snowflakes. You taught me that, too. The house is going to be finished soon, and Dad and I are going to move away. I'm afraid that if you don't marry my dad, I'll never see you again. Won't you please, please marry my dad?"

"Oh, sweetheart," Carrie whispered, and wrapped her arm around the girl's neck. She leaned forward and braced her forehead against the top of Mackenzie's head. "It isn't as simple as that. Couldn't I just be your friend?"

Mackenzie sniffled and nodded. "Will you come visit me when we move?"

"You bet."

"What about what Madam Fredrick says?" the girl asked.

Carrie groaned inwardly. "Madam Fredrick means well, and she's a dear, dear person, but I'm going to tell you something that I want to be a secret between you and me."

"Okay." Mackenzie stared at her intently.

"Madam Fredrick can't really see anything in that crystal ball of hers."

"But—"

"I know. She says what she thinks, and in doing so puts the idea in other people's minds and lets the suggestion take root there. If her predictions come true, it's because the people have steered the course of their lives in the direction she pointed."

"But she seems so sure of things."

"Her confidence is all part of the act."

"In other words," Mackenzie said after a thought-ful moment, "I shouldn't believe anything she tells me."

Chapter Seven

If Carrie hadn't seen it with her own eyes, a dozen times or more, she wouldn't have believed any two boys could be more like their father. Doug and Dillon sat on the sofa next to their father, watching the Seahawks football game. Three pairs of feet, each clothed in white socks, were braced against the coffee table, crossed at the ankles. Jason had the remote control resting at his side, a bowl of popcorn in his lap. Each one of his sons held a smaller bowl. So intent were they on the hotly contested play-off game that they barely gave Carrie more than a hurried nod of acknowledgment.

The sight of Jason with his sons never ceased to amaze Carrie. The boys were all Manning, too. Smaller versions of their father in both looks and temperament.

Carrie found her mother in the kitchen, whipping up a batch of fudge for the Manning family get-together. "Carrie, this is a pleasant surprise." Charlotte's face relaxed into a smile when she saw her daughter.

"I came for some motherly advice," Carrie admitted, seeing no need to traipse around the point of her impromptu visit. She'd left Mackenzie less than an hour before and hadn't been able to stop thinking about their conversation, or about Philip's reaction to her being there. He hadn't been able to escape fast enough.

"Sure. What's up?" Charlotte continued to stir the boiling liquid into the chocolate chips. The effort produced a sheen of perspiration on her forehead.

Carrie scooted the padded stool to the countertop where her mother worked. "I'm afraid I'm falling in love."

"Afraid?"

"Yes." She'd purposely chosen that word. That was exactly the way she felt about it.

"This wouldn't happen to have anything to do with your friend Mackenzie, would it?"

Carrie nodded, surprised her mother even knew about the thirteen-year-old girl. But then the boys must have said something. "Do you remember how it was when you first started dating Jason?" she asked.

Her mother paused and a hint of a smile bounced against the edges of her mouth. "I'm not likely to forget. I wasn't sure I wanted anything to do with the man, while you invented excuses to throw us together."

"You weren't interested in him at first, right?"

Charlotte chuckled softly. "That's putting it mildly, but gradually his gentle patience won me over."

Carrie realized there was a great deal more that her mother wasn't telling her. She'd long suspected that her mother and Jason's courtship had been anything but smooth.

Charlotte resumed stirring, her smile growing a tad wider. "As I said earlier his patience won me over. His patience and his drop-dead kisses," she amended. "If ever a man has a talent for kissing, it's your stepfather." She grinned shyly and looked away.

"Philip shares the same gift," Carrie whispered, feeling a bit shy about sharing this aspect of their relationship with her mother.

Charlotte didn't say anything for a long moment, as if digesting this latest bit of information. "I take it you've been seeing a good deal of Mackenzie's father."

"Not as much as I'd like," she admitted. "He's been divorced for two years and according to Mackenzie he hasn't gone out on a single date." Her guess was that well-meaning friends had tried to set him up. His own daughter had made the effort, too. With Carrie.

"So he comes with a suitcase load of emotional trauma. Has he ever talked about what happened in his marriage?"

"No." Carrie hated to admit how little time they'd actually spent together. Feeding Maria's homeless cats was as close as they'd come to an actual date. She wasn't sure how to measure the time in the elevator. Although she'd managed to make him think his callous attitude afterward hadn't fooled her, in truth she didn't know what his reaction had been.

"You're afraid he's coming to mean more to you than is sensible, after so short an acquaintance."

"Exactly. But, Mom, he's almost constantly on my mind. I go to bed at night, close my eyes and he's there.

I get up in the morning and take the bus into the office and all I can think about is him.''

"He's attracted to you?''

"I think so ... I don't know anymore, but my guess is that he is, but he's fighting it. He doesn't want to care for me. If anything he'd rather I lived on another planet than share the same building with him. We both work hard at avoiding each other—we probably wouldn't see each other at all if it wasn't for Mackenzie. The girl's made it her mission in life to make sure we don't escape each other.''

Charlotte dumped the warm fudge into a buttered cookie sheet. "This is beginning to sound familiar.''

"In what way?''

Charlotte giggled. "Oh, Carrie, how soon you forget. It was you who pushed, pulled and shoved me into a relationship with Jason. It would have been horrible if he was a different kind of man. As it was, he was patient and nonthreatening. Like Philip, I came into the relationship with enough emotional trauma to fill a matched set of luggage. He was exactly the kind of man I needed. You've always been a sensitive, intuitive child. Out of all the men you might have picked for me, you chose the one man who possessed the gentle patience I needed most.'' She reached over and cupped the side of Carrie's face. Her eyes grew warm and tender. "In my heart of hearts I'm confident you've done the same thing for yourself. Philip needs you just as much as I needed Jason. Be patient with him, Carrie. Your heart is bound to take a few jabs before this is finished, be prepared for that, but don't be afraid to love him because it's your love that he needs most. Mackenzie, too. I promise you, your patience will be worth the wait."

How wise her mother was, Carrie realized as she left the family home. How wise and wonderful. Not for the first time, Carrie was grateful for a mother she could talk to, a mother she could confide in, a mother who didn't judge, but listened and advised.

"What are you doing here?" Gene Tarkington asked, stepping into Philip's office. He leaned against the doorjamb, striking a relaxed pose. The entire floor was empty. Row upon row of desks stretched across the carpeted floor outside his office.

"I thought I'd come in and run through these figures one last time," Philip murmured, staring into the computer screen. Although he considered Gene one of his best friends, he'd rather be alone just then.

"Hey, buddy, it's almost Christmas. Haven't you got anything better to do than stop by the office?"

"What about you?" Philip challenged. He wasn't the only workaholic in this company.

"I stopped by for some papers and saw the light on in your office. I thought you were having lunch with Mackenzie this afternoon. A little father-daughter tête-à-tête. That kid's a real sweetheart, you know?"

"We had our lunch," Philip muttered, "but I wasn't the only one Mackenzie saw fit to invite."

"You mean to say she brought along that neighbor friend of yours. The woman who works for Microsoft."

"That's the one." Philip frowned anew, remembering how upset he'd been when he realized what Mackenzie had done. From the way she'd acted, he should have guessed she'd try something like this. What distressed him even more was the glad way his heart had responded when Carrie walked in the deli.

He didn't want to feel these things for her. It'd taken effort to steel himself against those very emotions. He'd been burned once, badly enough to know better than to play with fire. Carrie Weston wasn't an innocent book of matches, either. Every time he was with her he felt as if he was standing too close to a bonfire.

"Mackenzie's got a level head on her. What have you got against this neighbor woman? She's not ugly, is she?"

"No." He recalled what a shock it was when he realized exactly how lovely Carrie was.

"If you want my opinion, I'd say count your blessings. Generally the friends I have involved in the dating scene would welcome a woman their daughters know and like. Remember what happened to Cal. His daughter and second wife hate each other. Any time they're out together, Cal has to keep the two from physically coming to blows."

"I'm not Cal."

"It seems to me that if your daughter's that keen on this neighbor lady, then you should take the time to find out what she likes about her so much. I'm no expert when it comes to matters of the heart...."

"My thoughts exactly," Philip said pointedly. He'd come to the office to escape Carrie, not to have her name tossed in his face from someone he considered a good friend. "I appreciate what you're trying to do."

Gene rubbed the side of his face and chuckled. "I doubt that. But I hate to see you wasting time in this office when Christmas is only a few days away. If you want to hide there are better places to do so than here."

Although Gene's tone was friendly enough, the words tightened Philip's jaw. He bit down hard on his back molars to keep from saying something he might regret later. It was all he could do to keep from blaming his friend for his troubles. Gene was the one who owned the apartment complex, and it was because of him that Philip and Mackenzie were living there.

"Well, I've got to get back to the car. Marilyn's waiting. You know how it is this last weekend before Christmas. The malls are a madhouse and naturally my wife thinks this is the perfect time to finish up the last-minute shopping. She wouldn't dream of going alone. I told her there'd better be a Husband of the Year Award in this for me somewhere," he said, and chuckled. "But she promised me another kind of reward, one she knows I won't refuse." From the contented, anticipatory look on his friend's face one would think Gene was headed for the final game of the World Series and not a shopping mall.

"I'll see you later," Philip said.

"Later," Gene returned. "Just promise me you won't be here long."

"I won't."

Gene left and the vacant room had never seemed emptier. The walls echoed with loneliness, a constant reminder that Philip was by himself. His friend was right; it was almost Christmas and here he was at the office hiding. That was what he had been doing for a very long time. While Gene was out fighting the Christmas crowds with his wife, Philip had dug himself a grave and conveniently climbed inside whenever life threatened to offer him something he couldn't handle. Even a gift.

In so many words that was what Gene had told him Carrie was. A woman Mackenzie not only liked, but championed. Many a man would advise him to count his blessings. Instead of thanking his daughter for lunch, he'd chastised her for using the time as an opportunity to shove Carrie under his nose.

Carrie.

Every time he mentally said her name a chill raced through his blood. Correction, his blood didn't go cold, it heated up. He barely knew the woman, but then his daughter had spent a copious amount of time with their neighbor. A twenty-four-year-old was more of a mother to her than her own had ever been.

Philip rolled his chair away from his desk, stood and walked over to the large picture window. The view of downtown Seattle and Puget Sound was spectacular from his twentieth-story viewpoint. Breathtaking. The waterfront, the ferry dock, Pike Place Market, all alive with activity. Philip couldn't count the number of times he'd stood exactly where he was and looked out and saw nothing, felt nothing.

He returned to his desk and turned off his computer, feeling more confused now than when he'd arrived. It was a sad day when he was reduced to the level of accepting his thirteen-year-old daughter's advice, but in this case, Mackenzie was right. She'd told him to get a life. Instead, Philip had dug himself deeper into his rut, fearing that any life there was to be gotten would include making peace with the past and moving forward. It wasn't that the past held any particular allure. He'd married too young, unwisely. That didn't mean he would repeat the same mistake, although that was what he'd feared for a good long while.

Locking up, Philip headed back toward the apartment building. He parked in the garage across the street and was walking toward the entrance when he saw Carrie. There was a natural buoyancy to her step, a joy that radiated from inside her. He sometimes wondered what it was she had to be so happy about. That no longer concerned him, because he wanted whatever it was she had and so willingly shared.

"Carrie." Unsure what he'd say when he caught up with her, Philip charged across the street.

Carrie paused midway up the steps outside the building and turned around. Some of the happiness drained from her eyes when she saw it was him. She waited until he'd reached her before she spoke. "I want you to know I had no idea Mackenzie had invited us both to lunch."

"I know that," he said, regretting his angry mood earlier.

"You do?"

Every time he saw her it was a shock to realize how beautiful she was. Her intense blue eyes cut straight through him. "I was wondering...I know it's the last minute and you've probably got other plans, but..." He paused, realizing he was making a mess of this. "Would you go Christmas shopping with me?" He feared if he invited her to dinner or a movie she'd turn him down flat and he wouldn't blame her. "For Mackenzie," he added for incentive. "I haven't got her much and I could do with a few suggestions."

His invitation had apparently taken her by surprise because she opened and closed her mouth a number of times before asking, "When?"

"Is now convenient?" he asked hopefully. He was as crazy as his friend Gene to even consider going shopping at this time of the year.

"Now," she repeated, then smiled, that soft, gentle smile of hers that caused his heart to quiver. "Okay."

Okay. It was crazy how one small word could produce such undiluted exhilaration. If this were a play, he'd break into a song about now, Philip realized. His heart felt like singing.

She walked down the three or four steps to join him on the sidewalk. That little bounce of hers was back. The bounce that said she was glad to be alive and glad to be with him.

He was the one who should be grateful, Philip decided. He tucked her arm in the crook of his elbow and led her back to the parking garage.

Life was good. It had been a very long time since he'd believed that, but he did now.

Chapter Eight

Hours earlier, Carrie had been telling her mother that she barely knew Philip Lark and now she doubted that there were many men she knew better. They sat in an Italian restaurant, their feet crowded with Christmas packages, and talked until there wasn't anything more to say. Their dinner dishes had long since been removed and Philip poured the last bit of red wine into her goblet.

The room gently swayed from side to side, but her light-headedness wasn't due to the Pinot noir. Philip was the reason. He'd told her things she felt would take months if not years for him to reveal. He spoke hesitantly of his marriage, and his career as a systems analyst. She listened, a lump in her throat, as he heaped the blame for the failure of his marriage upon his own shoulders. She marveled that he allowed none of his own disappointment to bleed through.

"You're friends with Laura?" she asked at one point.

"Yes. Beyond anything else, she's Mackenzie's mother. I made more than one mistake in this marriage, but my daughter wasn't one of them. I'll always be grateful to my ex-wife for Mackenzie."

Tears formed in the corners of Carrie's eyes at the sincerity with which he spoke. How easy it would be for him to blame his ex-wife for their problems. Carrie was sympathetic to his side, and knew from the things that Mackenzie had told her that her mother wasn't exactly June Cleaver. Carrie suspected that Laura hadn't been much of a wife, either.

"What are you doing tomorrow?" Philip asked unexpectedly.

"Sunday," Carrie responded, thinking aloud. She pressed her elbows against the white linen tablecloth as she mentally sorted through her social calendar. "The Mannings are getting together. Mom and I married into this large, wonderful family. Jason has four other brothers and sisters. There are so many grandchildren these days it's difficult to keep track of who belongs to whom. Why don't you and Mackenzie come along and meet everyone?" Carrie couldn't believe she'd carelessly tossed out the invitation. While she wanted him to attend the outing, there was sure to be speculation if he did.

"You're sure?"

"Positive...just... Never mind," she said, stopping herself in the nick of time. Her gaze held his. "It would mean a great deal to me if you would."

"Then we'll come." He reached for her hand and squeezed her fingers.

Philip had given up the effort of remembering everyone's names. After cataloging the first ten or so relatives Carrie had introduced him to, the others became lost in the maze of personality types.

Mackenzie had disappeared almost the minute they arrived. Doug and Dillon had greeted him cheerfully and then quickly vanished with his daughter. Holding a cup of eggnog, Philip found himself a quiet corner and made himself comfortable. He was lucky to find a place to sit.

From his vantage point, he watched Carrie interact with her family. His eyes followed her as she expertly wove her way across the room, ostensibly to find her mother so she could introduce her parents to Philip. He found it difficult to take his eyes off Carrie. Her face was flushed with happiness, her eyes bright with excitement. She'd married into this family, but it was clear they thought of her as one of their own.

"Do you mind if I join you?" a woman unexpectedly approached him and asked.

"Please do." He stood to offer her his seat.

"No, no. Sit down, please. I can only stay a moment. You must be Philip."

"Yes." The dark-haired beauty had to be Carrie's mother. "You're Charlotte Manning?"

"How perceptive of you. Yes." She held out her hand, which he shook.

"Philip Lark."

"I assumed you must be."

Now that he had her full attention, it was a wonder he hadn't recognized the resemblance sooner. Charlotte and Carrie shared the same intense blue eyes, and a gentleness of spirit that was unmistakable.

They spoke for a few moments, of little, unimportant matters. Although Philip had the impression he was being checked out, he also had the feeling that he'd passed muster. He liked Charlotte, which was understandable since he definitely liked Carrie.

"So this is Carrie's young man." Charlotte's husband, Jason Manning, joined his wife and slipped his arm around her waist. "Welcome. Where's Carrie? I take it she's left you to fend on your own?"

"From what I understand, she went in search of you two."

The three spoke a number of minutes before Jason glanced over his shoulder and called, "Paul, come and meet Carrie's beau."

Soon a group had gathered around Philip, more faces than he ever hoped to remember. He stood and shook hands with Carrie's two uncles. Once again he felt their scrutiny.

Soon a loud, "Ho, ho, ho," could be heard in the background. Jason's father had donned a Santa suit and paraded into the room, a bag of goodies swung over his shoulder. The children let out a cry of glee and raced toward Santa.

Philip was grateful to have everyone's attention focused elsewhere. He sat back down in the large overstuffed chair and relaxed, grateful not to be the center of attention. Soon Carrie was close. She sat on the padded arm and cast him an apologetic look.

"Sorry, I got sidetracked."

"So I saw." He patted her hand. "I met your stepfather and two uncles."

"Aren't they great?" Her eyes gleamed with pride.

"I need a degree in computer science to keep track of who's married to whom."

"Don't worry, it'll come in time. Be grateful not everyone's here."

"You mean there's more?"

Carrie grinned, and nodded. "Taylor and Christy live in Montana. Between them they have six children now."

"My goodness." Adding ten more names to his repertoire would have overwhelmed him even more than he was already. "Mackenzie certainly seems to fit right in."

"Doug and Dillon think she's the best thing since cookie-dough ice cream. Knowing her gives them the edge over their cousins."

While the youngsters gathered around their grandfather, dressed in an ill-fitting red suit, Mackenzie made her way toward them. Philip understood. At thirteen she was too old to mingle with the kids who believed in Santa Claus, and too young not to be caught up in the excitement. Furthermore, Santa wouldn't have a gift for her.

"Are you having fun?" Philip whispered when she sat down on the padded chair arm, across from Carrie.

"This is so great," she whispered. "I didn't know families could get this big. Everyone is friendly and nice."

Santa dug deep into his bag and produced a package. He read the tag and called out the name. Doug leapt to his feet and raced forward as if he had only a limited amount of time to collect his prize.

Santa reached inside his bag a second time and removed another gift. "What's this?" he asked, lowering his glasses to the far reaches of his nose in order to read the tag. "This gift is for someone named Mackenzie Lark? I do hope Mrs. Claus didn't mix up the gifts with those of another family."

"Mackenzie's here," Dillon shouted. He stood and pointed toward Philip and Carrie.

"Me?" Mackenzie slid off the chair arm and planted her hand across her chest. "There's a gift in there for me?"

"If your name's Mackenzie, then I'd say this present is meant for you."

His daughter didn't need a second invitation. She hurried toward Santa as eager as Doug had been moments earlier.

Philip's gaze sought out Carrie's. "I'm sure my mother's responsible for this," she told him.

"We talked briefly," he told her.

Carrie's gaze widened. "What did she have to say?"

"Nothing much, it was your stepfather who put the fear of God in me."

"Jason? Oh, dear. Listen, whatever he said disregard. He means well and I love him to death, but half the time his head's in some sports cloud and he doesn't know what he's saying."

Philip loved it. He didn't know when he'd seen Carrie more unnerved. Even when they'd been trapped in the elevator without electricity she'd displayed more composure then this.

"Carrie, good grief, what did you think he said?"

She clamped her mouth closed. "I—I'm not entirely sure, but it would be just like him to suggest you take the plunge and marry me."

"Oh, that, well..."

"Are you telling me he actually..."

Philip had to work to keep from laughing out loud. "He didn't, don't worry about it."

Mackenzie traipsed forward to claim her gift and walked back, holding the package in both hands.

"You can open it," Carrie assure her.

"Now?" His daughter didn't need a second invitation. She tore into the wrapping as though waiting a second longer was sheer torment. Inside was a vanity mirror with a brush and comb set. "It's perfect," she whispered, crushing the brush and comb against her bosom. "I've always wanted one of these. It's so...so feminine."

"How'd your family know?" Philip asked. He'd never have thought to buy something like this for his daughter.

"I have one," Carrie whispered out of the side of her mouth. "She's sat down with it a number of times."

"Oh." More and more he felt inadequate when it came to understanding his daughter. She was in that awkward stage when it was difficult to know exactly where her interests lay. Half the time she talked about wanting a horse someday, and the other half she inquired about ballet lessons. Philip didn't think she knew herself any longer. Half tomboy, half woman. Mackenzie was trapped somewhere in between, traveling uneasily from one desire to the next. It wasn't just wanting a horse and ballet lessons that confused him, either. One minute she'd be her jovial self and the next be in tears over something he considered trivial. He wished Laura had taken more of an interest in the girl. Often he felt completely inadequate in dealing with Mackenzie's frequent mood swings.

Philip didn't know about anyone else, but he was happy when the party let up for the evening. He thanked the elder Mannings for having him and Mackenzie.

"You're welcome anytime," Elizabeth Manning said, clasping his hand between both of her own. On what seemed an impulsive gesture, she leaned forward and kissed his cheek. "You'd be a welcome addition to our family," she whispered in his ear. "Just promise me one thing?"

"What's that?" he asked.

"I want a nice, big wedding," she said, this time loud enough for half the room to hear.

Philip heard a murmur of approval behind him. "Ah..."

"Thanks again, Grandma," Carrie said, saving him from having to come up with an appropriate response.

Carrie hugged the elderly couple and led the way outside. Jason, Charlotte, Doug and Dillon followed them to the driveway for a second go-around of farewells and hugs. This had to be one of the most outwardly affectionate families Philip had ever known, but it didn't bother him. These were good people, hardworking and family oriented. He hadn't seen himself in that light, although it was what he'd always wanted. Laura hadn't been raised that way, and frankly neither had he.

They sang Christmas carols on the drive home. Carrie's sweet voice blended smoothly with that of his daughter's. His own was a bit gruff from disuse and slightly off-key, but no one seemed to mind, least of all Mackenzie, whose happiness spilled over like so much fizz in a pop bottle. He parked in the garage and they walked across the street to the apartment building.

"I had a wonderful time," his daughter told Carrie, and hugged her close as they waited for the elevator.

"I did, too."

"I'm so pleased your family get-together was tonight instead of tomorrow. I'll be with my mother, you know."

"I do," Carrie said. "You'll miss the party here, but I'll be sure and tell you all about it."

"Do you think Madam Fredrick will made a prediction for me, even if I'm not there?"

"I'm sure she will," Carrie answered.

"She'll have to make one for me, as well," Philip added.

"You aren't coming?" This news appeared to catch Carrie by surprise. She'd mentioned the Christmas party earlier and he'd managed to avoid answering her one way or another.

"No," he said, pushing the button to close the elevator door.

"But I thought, I hoped . . ." Her disappointment was evident.

Philip didn't want to say anything negative, but as far as he was concerned the majority of those who lived in the apartment complex were a group of friendly, harmless eccentrics. He didn't have anything against them, but he didn't want to socialize with them, either.

"Talk him into it," Mackenzie advised when the elevator stopped on Carrie's floor.

He wished now he hadn't said anything. "Would you like a cup of coffee?" Carrie asked.

What he wanted was time alone with Carrie.

"Sure he does," Mackenzie answered for him, and shoved him out of the elevator. The doors closed before he could respond.

"I guess I do," he answered, chuckling.

Carrie's eyes shyly met his. "I was hoping you would."

She unlocked the door and stepped inside, but he stopped her before she turned on the light switch. With his hand at her shoulder, he guided her into his arms. "I've been waiting all night for this," he whispered, and in an exercise of anticipation claimed her lips.

He meant it to be a soft, gentle kiss. One that would tell her that he'd enjoyed her company, enjoyed their evening together. But the minute his mouth settled over hers he experienced a barrage of desire so strong that it was all he could do to keep it in check. No woman had ever affected him like this. He wove his fingers into her hair and tilted her head to one side in order to deepen the kisses.

She groaned softly, then again, it could well be the sound of his own pleasure that rang in his ears. He thrust his tongue forward, breaching the gap between her lips, swirling it around. His knees jerked at her immediate, welcoming response. This woman could make him weak in areas he'd always considered himself strong.

"Why won't you come to the party tomorrow night?" she asked between hot, breathless kisses.

The party was the last thing on Philip's mind. He led her through the darkened living room, sat down in the chair and brought her into his lap. "Let's talk about that later, all right?" He didn't give her time to respond, but directed her lips back to his for a series of slow, drugged kisses.

"Why later?" She nibbled the side of his neck, sending delicious shivers scooting down his back.

"I'm not sure I like Madam Fredrick."

She laughed softly, and he felt her breath against his sensitized skin. "She's completely harmless."

"So they say." He placed his hands on either side of her head and brought her lips down to meet his. The kiss was long and deep, leaving him breathless when they'd finished. "The people in this apartment are a bunch of oddballs. Half of them are candidates for the loony bin," he said.

Carrie stiffened in his arms. "You're talking about my friends."

"No offense meant," he said. Surely she recognized the truth when she heard it.

Carrie squirmed out of his lap and stood in front of him. "I live in this apartment complex. Is that the way you think about me?"

"No. If it means so much to you, I'll attend this silly party."

"No thanks," she returned stiffly. "I wouldn't want you to do me any favors."

From her tone of voice, Philip realized that he'd managed to offend her. That was the last thing he wanted. It had taken the conversation with Gene to realize that he'd been building a barricade against her when she was a blessing in his life. A gift.

"Carrie, I'm sorry. I spoke out of turn."

"Is that what you really think, Philip?" she asked, her voice small and uncertain.

He didn't respond right away, afraid anything more he said would only dig him in deeper.

"That's answer enough. I'm tired...I'd like it if you left now."

"Carrie, for the love of heaven, be reasonable."

She walked over to the door and opened it, sending a shaft of cruel light directly across his face. Philip squinted and did as she asked. "We'll talk about his later, all right?"

"Sure," she returned in a soft, sarcastic murmur.

Rather than wait for the elevator, Philip took the stairs to his apartment a floor above Carrie's. He'd talk to Mackenzie, get her advice on how to handle this situation. His daughter was sure to know what he should say. He never thought he'd be reduced to seeking advice for the lovelorn from his own teenage daughter.

The apartment was silent and dark when he entered. He switched on the light and walked down the hall to Mackenzie's bedroom. Her bed was slightly mussed as if she'd sat on it.

"Mackenzie," he called.

No response.

He checked the other rooms of the house, and found a note from her on the kitchen table.

Dad,

Mom left a message on the answering machine. She said she wouldn't be coming for me, after all, and that I couldn't spend the holidays with her. I guess I should have known she'd be too busy for me. She has time for everything else but me. I need some time alone to think.

Mackenzie

Chapter Nine

Carrie wasn't certain what had distressed her so much about Philip's comment about Madam Fredrick and the others. While it was true they were her friends, she couldn't deny they all *were* a bit on the weird side. But they were also affectionate, warmhearted people and it hurt to have Philip dismiss them with such carelessness. She was still sorting through her feelings when the doorbell chimed. Whoever it was seemed impatient because it chimed again almost immediately afterward in short, restless bursts.

"Just a moment," she called out.

To her surprise it was Philip. "Have you seen Mackenzie?" he demanded, without exchanging greetings.

"Not since we returned from the party."

He forcefully exhaled and rubbed his hand along the back of his neck. "Her mother left a message for her on the answering machine. She won't be coming for Mackenzie the way she'd planned," he explained.

Carrie noted a muscle along the side of his jaw jerked with the effort it took to control his anger.

"She was looking forward to spending time with Laura," he continued. "It was all Mackenzie could talk about."

Carrie knew. She'd spent a good deal of time with the teenager, going over her hairstyle and wardrobe for the impending visit. It had been important to Mackenzie that everything be perfect for her mother. She'd wanted to impress Laura with how grown-up she was, how stylish and hip. She wanted to make herself as attractive as possible, Carrie realized, hoping her mother would notice and approve.

"Mackenzie left a note that said she needed time alone." He checked his watch, something Carrie knew he'd probably done every five minutes since discovering the note. "That was an hour ago. Where the hell would she go?"

"I don't know," Carrie whispered. Her heart clenched with the hurt the teenager must be suffering. These few days scheduled with Laura had meant the world to the girl. Mackenzie had talked of little else for days on end.

"I thought she'd come to you." He rubbed a hand over his eyes. "Now I don't know where to look. Think, Carrie, think."

"She probably doesn't want to be around people just yet," she murmured, doing her best to clear her head of worry and fear in order to be of help.

Philip nodded. "Do you think she went for a walk? Alone in the dark?" He cringed as he said the words.

"I'll look with you."

His eyes told her he was grateful. Carrie reached for her jacket and purse, and they both rushed out of the building.

Soon after she'd graduated from high school, when Carrie was a young eighteen, she'd decided to seek out her father. It had been a mistake. He seemed to think she wanted something from him, and in retrospect, she realized she had. She wanted him to love her, wanted him to tell her how proud he was of the woman she'd become. It had taken her the better part of a year to realize Tom Weston was incapable of giving her anything. Even his approval.

In the five years she'd known Jason Manning, he'd been more of a father to her then her biological one would ever know how to be. She hadn't had any contact with her biological father since. It had hurt to realize that the man responsible for her birth wanted nothing more to do with her, but after several months she accepted his decision. If anything, she was grateful for his honesty, as hurtful as it'd been at the time.

Not really knowing where they were going, they walked crisply from one spot to another, trying to make intelligent guesses on where Mackenzie might choose to escape. Their fears mounted, but Carrie noticed how they struggled to hide them from each other. Instead, they offered one another flat reassurances neither believed.

"I hate to think of her out in the cold, alone and hurting," Philip murmured, his hands buried in his coat pockets against the cold.

"Me, too." The cold air stung her cheeks.

"I could hate Laura for doing this to her," Philip said defiantly, "but I refuse to waste the energy. She can treat me any way she damn well pleases, but not Mackenzie.''

Carrie knew it would do no good to remind him that he had no control over his ex-wife. Laura would behave as she pleased when it came to her relationship with their daughter.

''Perhaps I should have said something to Mackenzie,'' Philip said, ''warned her not to count on anything her mother says. I didn't because, well, because I didn't want Mackenzie to think I'd purposely do or say anything to influence the way she thinks about her mother.''

''I find that both admirable and wise.''

''I don't feel either just now.'' Anger and frustration coated his words.

''Mackenzie's smart enough to figure out what her mother's really like on her own. She won't need you or me to tell her,'' Carrie assured him.

His gaze locked with hers. ''I hope you're right.''

They searched everywhere they could think to look, to no avail. By the time they returned to the apartment building it was almost midnight. The building was dark and silent, arming their fears even more.

''You don't think she'd do anything stupid, do you?'' a worried Philip asked. ''Like run away and find her mother on her own?''

''I don't know.''

When they stepped into the lobby, Carrie noticed that the door leading to the basement was open. As she stepped closer, she could hear voices below.

''Let's check it out,'' Philip suggested.

Carrie followed him down the stairs. As they descended, the sound of voices became more distinct. She recognized Madam Fredrick, chatting away with Arnold. Carrie guessed that they were putting the finishing touches on the decorations for the Christmas party, which was to take place the following night.

They found Mackenzie busy pinning streamers of bright red and green papier-mâché in the center of the room, and fanning them out to the far reaches of the ceiling. The teenager didn't so much as blink when she noticed Carrie and Philip.

"Oh, hi, Dad. Hi, Carrie," she said, and leapt down from her chair.

"Just where have you been, young lady?" Philip demanded gruffly.

Carrie placed her hand on his arm, silently pleading with him to display less anger and more compassion. She felt some of the tension leave his muscles and knew it took a great deal not to cross the room and fiercely hug the teenager.

"Sorry, Dad. I forgot to tell you where I was."

"Carrie and I've been looking for you for a good hour."

"Sorry," Mackenzie returned contritely.

"Are you all right?" Carrie asked. "I mean, with not being able to spend the holidays with your mother?"

Mackenzie hesitated and her lower lip trembled slightly. "I'm disappointed, but then as Madam Fredrick said, 'Time wounds all heels.'" She laughed and wiped her forearm under her nose. "Mom's got to make her own decisions about what role I'll play in her life. All I can do is give her the freedom to choose. I've got my dad and my friends.'' Her gaze fell about the room, pausing on each person.

Arnold was there in his spandex shorts and bulging muscles. Madam Fredrick with her crystal ball and her age-old wisdom, and Maria with her tenderhearted care for cats. And her, Carrie realized. She was there, too.

Mackenzie wrapped her arms around her father's waist and hid her face in his chest for a couple of moments. ''I'll be here for the party,'' she said, making an effort, it seemed, to look at the bright side of things. ''You don't have to come, Dad. I understand.''

''I want to come,'' he said, his gaze reaching out to Carrie. He held his hand out to her and their fingers locked together. ''It takes moments like these for a man to recognize how fortunate he is to be blessed with such good friends.''

To her surprise, Mackenzie chuckled and glanced over her shoulder at Madam Fredrick.

''What did I tell you?'' the older woman said, smiling broadly. ''The crystal ball sees all.''

''It didn't do me a damn bit of good when it came to deciding which mutual fund to invest in,'' Arnold snootily reminded her. ''And it didn't help me pick the winning lottery numbers, either. You can take that crystal ball of yours and store it in a pile of cow manure for all I care.''

''I told you it wouldn't help you for personal gain,'' Madam Fredrick returned with more than a hint of defensiveness.

"What good is that silly thing if it doesn't make your friends rich?"

"It serves its purpose," Philip surprised everyone by responding. He wrapped his arm around his daughter's shoulders. "I'd say we've had enough excitement for one night, wouldn't you?"

Mackenzie nodded. "'Night, everyone."

"Good night," Arnold called.

"Don't let the bed bugs bite," Madam Fredrick advised.

"Good night, little one. You stop by and visit me sometime, you hear?" Maria called.

"I will," Mackenzie promised.

Carrie left with Philip and Mackenzie. "I'm baking cookies for the party in the morning," she said, when the elevator reached her floor.

"Do you need any help?" Mackenzie offered eagerly. "You won't have to worry about any eggshell getting in the dough this time."

"I'd love it if you stopped by."

Content that all was well, Carrie entered her apartment and undressed for bed. She slipped the nightgown over her head when the phone rang. It was Philip.

"I know I was with you less than ten minutes ago, but I wanted to thank you."

"For what? I didn't do anything." She'd shared his helplessness in searching for Mackenzie, his frustration and anger.

"You helped me find my daughter, in more ways than one."

"I wish I could take credit for that, but I can't. Your love for her paved the way."

"I was wrong about your friends."

She grinned, wondering how long it would take him to admit as much.

"They're as wonderful as you. Not spending time with her mother was a big blow to Mackenzie. She was devastated to have Laura put her off once again. I don't know what Madam Fredrick said, but apparently it was exactly what Mackenzie needed to hear. Exactly what I needed too."

"You're a fast learner."

Philip's amusement echoed over the telephone line. "Don't kid yourself. I was with the slow reading group in first grade. I'm not exactly a speed demon when it comes to relationships, either. My marriage is a prime example."

"You'll come to the Christmas party?" she quizzed.

"With bells on." He hesitated, then chuckled. "The thing is, I'll probably fit right in."

Epilogue

Six months later

"This is probably the most exciting day of my life!" Mackenzie declared, waltzing around the small dressing room in her full-length pink chiffon dress. A wreath of spring flowers adorned her head, a silk ribbon streamer falling down the middle of her back. "You're actually going to be my stepmother just the way Madam Fredrick said you would."

"It's a wonderfully exciting day for me, as well." Carrie planted her hands against her stomach to calm her jittery nerves. The church was full of family and friends, waiting for her to make her appearance. Jason, dressed in a tuxedo, would soon escort her down the aisle.

"Dad was so cute this morning," Mackenzie said, laughing softly. "I thought he was going to throw up his breakfast. He's so much in love he can hardly eat."

Carrie closed her eyes in an effort to compose her own set of nerves. She hadn't so much as attempted breakfast, and applauded Philip the effort. As for being in love, she was crazy about him and Mackenzie.

This day was a dream come true, worthy of the finest fairy tale. Prince Charming and his Lady Fair.

"Gene and his wife are here and lots of people from the office," Mackenzie said, after checking out the inside of the church. "I didn't know that many people knew my dad." Gracefully she waltzed her way around Carrie once again, in a wide circle. "You're going to be the most beautiful bride there ever was. That was what Dad said, and he's right."

"Thank you, sweetheart."

"I think it's extra special that you're letting me be in the wedding party. Not everyone would do that. My first wedding," she said, and her eyes held a dreamy, faraway look.

"You're a good friend, Mackenzie."

"You probably wouldn't be marrying my dad if it wasn't for me," Mackenzie reminded her. "But then Madam Fredrick was the one who gave me the idea first so I guess I should give her the credit."

"Remember what I told you about Madam Fredrick and her crystal ball."

"I remember, it's just that this seems mighty convenient. It really does seem that you and Dad are perfect for each other. Madam Fredrick couldn't have known that."

"I'm pleased *you* think so."

"If I were to handpick someone to be my mother, I'd choose you." Her eyes grew dark and serious. "The best part is you're perfect for my dad. He needs you almost as much as I do. You're perfect for me, too. I'd rather spend time with you than anyone, with the exception of Les Williams.'' Her shoulders moved up and down with an expressive sigh. ''But then Les doesn't know I'm alive.''

''Don't be so sure of that.''

''Are you two ready?'' Jason called from outside the small dressing room.

Carrie drew in a deep breath. ''As ready as I'll ever be.''

Mackenzie handed her the floral bouquet and Carrie squared her shoulders and opened the door. Jason was working the black tie at his throat back and forth in an effort to loosen it. He stopped mid-action and his jaw sagged.

''You're . . . you're lovely,'' he whispered.

''Don't act so surprised,'' Carrie teased.

''You look so much like your mother on our wedding day, it's hard to believe. I can't get over it . . .''

Mackenzie beamed her a smile and hurried to join Carrie's friends for the procession down the aisle.

''Be happy, little one,'' Jason advised, his voice suspiciously low. He tucked her hand in the crook of his arm.

When Carrie glanced his way, she noticed a sheen of tears in his eyes.

''In some ways you'll always be my daughter,'' he murmured, fidgeting with his tie once more. ''I couldn't be more proud of you than I am right this moment. You've done your mother and me proud.''

''Thanks, Dad,'' she whispered tightly.

They stood at the back of the church and waited for their cue, which came when the organ burst into music. Carrie took a tentative step forward. Toward Philip. Toward love. Toward their life together.

* * * * *

A WILD WEST CHRISTMAS

Linda Turner

Dear Reader,

Christmas has always been sort of wild in my family. There are always a lot of secrets, hectic shopping, then wrapping presents till midnight or later on Christmas Eve. Of course, sometimes waiting so late to wrap the presents can backfire. One year, when I was about five or six, my mother was so tired when she finally finished that she forgot to put the presents from Santa out before she went to bed. When my brother and sister and I woke up the next morning—before dawn, I might add—we were shocked to discover that Santa had passed us by. My mother, always fast on her feet, suggested that we go with my father to the convenience store for milk and cookies for Santa while we were waiting for him to get there. We were just kids and never thought to point out that all the stores were closed. I can still remember driving up and down San Antonio streets with my father, looking for a store that was open and watching the dark sky for Santa! Lord, how he and my mother must have laughed about that afterwards. When he finally took us home, Santa had come, of course, and my mother had helped him put our presents under the tree. We were so disappointed we'd missed him!

And that's what Christmas is to me—laughter, magic and surprises. I hope your holidays are full of things that memories are made of and filled with love. Merry Christmas!

Linda Turner

Prologue

Ten Years Ago

It was the hottest part of the day, when the shadows were short and there wasn't so much as a whisper of a breeze to stir the dust off Priscilla Rawlings's boots. When she'd first come to the Double R to spend the summer with her cousins at their ranch, she was sure she'd never be able to survive the hot New Mexican sun that baked the earth until it was granite-hard and bleached the very color from the sky. It hadn't, however, taken her long to appreciate the heat . . . and the men who worked out in it day after day.

But it was one man in particular who made her smile. One man in particular who stole her breath and weakened her knees. Wyatt. Wyatt Chandler. Five years her senior, he, too, was a cousin to the Rawlings—but on their mother's side, which made him no relation to her—and was, like her, spending the summer at the Double R. She'd taken one look at him and fallen like a ton of bricks.

He hadn't wanted anything to do with her, of course. Not at first, anyway. She was only seventeen and off-limits to a man who had his future all mapped out for him. He'd graduated from college in May and would head for L.A. at the end of August and a job he already had lined up with one of the largest architectural firms in California. He'd taken one look at her and labeled her a little girl looking for someone to sharpen her flirting skills on. He'd sworn to her face that it wasn't going to be him. He'd called her "baby" and "jailbait" and everything else he could think of to discourage her, but all the while his eyes had held a hunger that had called to her like something on the wind. In the end, he hadn't been able to resist her anymore than she had him.

What had followed was, without a doubt, the most wonderful summer of her life. Under the very noses of their watchful—and very protective—cousins, they'd laughed and played and fallen in love without anyone being the wiser. But nothing lasted forever, and their time together was almost over. August was only two weeks away and soon Wyatt would be leaving for L.A. and his future.

And she meant to go with him.

The decision had come to her while she was swimming at the creek with her cousin Kat an hour ago, and suddenly nothing had been as important as finding Wyatt and telling him. She'd left a stunned Kat at the creek and rushed back to the house, taking time only to change before searching the ranch for him. In her haste, she'd overlooked one of their favorite meeting places—the barn—until Alice, the family housekeeper, had told her he was waiting for her there with an old college friend who had dropped in unexpectedly while she was at the creek.

Hesitating at the shadowy entrance to the barn, she knew she probably shouldn't intrude. Whoever his friend was, he obviously had something important to say to him or he wouldn't have driven halfway across the country to see him. She could wait until tonight to speak with Wyatt, she decided reluctantly. She'd just step inside, meet the man, and make arrangements to talk to Wyatt later.

A smile of welcome already stretching across her face, Priscilla stepped into the darkened interior of the barn and waited for her eyes to adjust to the change in light. Blinking, she caught sight of Wyatt standing by the horse stalls and started forward, but she'd only taken three steps when she stopped short, shock strangling the gasp that rose in her throat. A woman, she thought dully. Wyatt's visitor wasn't a man as she'd so foolishly assumed, but a long-legged blonde in a short skirt and a halter top. And they weren't talking... they were kissing.

Chapter One

"Well, I did it," Priscilla said grimly as soon as her cousin answered the phone. "I broke things off with Tom this afternoon."

"Oh, no," Kat gasped. "Not on Thanksgiving Day, Cilla!"

"I know—my timing stinks. But he insisted on going over the wedding music, and something in me just snapped."

"How did he react? Was he devastated?"

"Furious is more like it," she retorted dryly. "He fired me...after he told me that his mother warned him months ago that I would leave him high and dry at the altar. That old lady never did like me."

Kat chuckled. "And now you've gone and proved her right. Talk about having a happy Thanksgiving. You just made hers."

As miserable as she felt, Cilla had to laugh. "I've finally done something she approves of." Her smile fading, she said quietly into the phone, "Tom's a good man. I hated hurting him, but I know this was the right decision. He has all the qualities I thought I wanted in the man I married, but something was always missing between us. I'm fond of him, but that's not enough."

"Of course it's not!" her cousin replied with satisfying indignation. "Hold out for the fireworks. I did, and it was worth the wait. So what are you going to do now?"

With a will of their own, Cilla's eyes drifted to the princess-style wedding dress hanging on the door to her bedroom. God, how had she ever gotten herself into this mess? "Take back an unused wedding dress, then see about getting another job, I guess. Though God knows where I'm going to find one this time of year. Most places don't hire until after the holidays."

"Speaking of the holidays, what are you doing about them? Are you going to go home or what?"

"And listen to Mom go on about what a mistake I'm making in letting a dependable man like Tom go? I don't think so."

"Then why don't you come to the ranch and stay for awhile? Don't wait for Christmas—come now. You said yourself no one hires in December, so there's no reason for you to stay in Denver. You can stay at the main house and go riding whenever you like and just veg out. And no one will even mention Tom's name— I swear it."

Cilla hesitated, tempted. She hadn't been back to the Double R for an extended stay since she was a teenager, but she could still remember the sound of the wind in the grass and the peace of the wide open spaces that stretched in all directions for as far as the eye could see. Right now that sounded like heaven, but it was the holidays and she didn't want to ruin it for anyone.

"Oh, I don't know, Kat. I'd be lousy company—"

"Then we'll cheer you up. It's settled, Cilla. You're coming within the week. I'll call Gable and Josey and let the rest of the gang know. Okay?"

What could she say? Kat could be as stubborn as a rock when the mood struck her, and when she spoke in that don't-mess-with-me tone, she wouldn't take no for an answer. "Okay," she laughed. "I'll see you soon."

At the ranch headquarters, Gable picked up the phone on the second ring and grinned at the sound of his cousin's voice. "Hey, man, what's going on? How was your turkey day?"

"Let me give you a hint," Wyatt said. "Does 'the holiday from hell' tell you anything?"

"Uh-oh." Gable chuckled. "Sounds like you've got a problem. What's her name?"

"Eleanor." He fairly spit the name out in distaste. "And it's not what you think."

"Yeah, yeah, that's what all you diehard bachelors say."

"No, I mean it. She's not a girlfriend. Hell, I don't even really know her. She saw me at a building site in Beverly Hills and decided I was just the man she'd been looking for all her life."

"So what's wrong with that? Maybe it was love at first sight."

Wyatt snorted. "Make that *Fatal Attraction* at first sight. I tell you, Gable, she's a nut case. And a spoiled brat whose daddy has more money than God. I took one look at her and knew she was trouble, but when I tried to be nice and explain that I wasn't interested in a relationship right now, she got nasty. She had her daddy make some calls and almost got me fired from a government project.''

"Are you kidding me? Dammit, Wyatt, she sounds dangerous. Have you talked to the police?''

"Yeah, for all the good it did me—they didn't do jack squat. Her old man's best buddies with the police commissioner. Now she's started showing up wherever I go. If I stay home, she calls day and night to make sure I haven't got another woman with me. I've already had the number changed twice, and she's found out what it was both times. She's driving me crazy.''

"You need to get out of Dodge, man. I mean it. I know you're tied up with work—''

"Actually, I'm finishing up a project by the middle of the week and don't have another one starting till after New Year's, and it's in Oakland. How would you feel about having a visitor for a month or so? I know it's a lot to ask—''

"Stuff it, Chandler," Gable growled. "You're family, remember? Stay as long as you like. We've got plenty of room.''

"Thanks, man. I owe you. I'll see you in a couple of days.''

Her mother hadn't exactly been thrilled with her decision not to spend Christmas with her, but as Cilla drove through the simple, unadorned gates of the Double R late Wednesday afternoon, she felt as if a huge weight had been lifted from her shoulders. The ranch had always been a refuge for her, a place to go to get away from the world, and that was something she really needed right now. Here, there would be no pressure to make a decision about what she was going to do with the rest of her life, no questions about what went wrong in a relationship that had seemed so right for her. She could, for a while at least, take this time for herself and forget a wedding that was never going to be.

As she left the highway behind and drove deeper into the ranch, civilization was left far behind. There were only miles and miles of grass-covered grazing land and the shadowy, rocky ridge of mountains that marked the western boundary of the ranch. Rolling her window down so she could hear the whisper of the cold wind across the open plain, Cilla smiled for what felt like the first time in days. She felt like she was coming home.

Then the huge Victorian house that had been the ranch headquarters for more than a century came into view, the lighted windows a welcoming beacon in the gathering twilight, and suddenly she couldn't get there fast enough. Pressing down on the accelerator, she raced toward it, dragging a rooster tail of dust behind her.

There was a sports car parked in the circular drive in front of the house, the kind that cost the earth and ate up the road with intimidating ease, but Cilla hardly had time to lift a brow at the sight of it before a very pregnant Kat and the rest of her cousins were pouring out of the house to greet her, all talking at once.

"Cilla! You look wonderful!"

"How was the drive? We heard it was sleeting up north. D'you have any problems?"

"You must be tired. What time did you leave this morning?"

They were all there, Gable and his wife, Josey, Cooper and Susannah, Flynn and Tate, and Kat's husband Luke. And the children, of course. There seemed to be more every time she came, and for the first few moments, it was a madhouse as everyone hugged her, then passed her onto the next Rawlings. Then Alice, hovering around them all like a mother hen, waved them toward the porch as she tossed out orders like a drill sergeant. "Don't keep the poor girl outside in the cold. Can't you see she's freezing to death? And Kat, you need to put your feet up—you haven't rested today like you're supposed to. Gable, get Cilla's suitcases. Cooper, help her with that bag of presents. Land sakes, it looks like she's been to the North Pole."

Laughing, Cilla hugged the housekeeper affectionately. "Alice, you never change. Arc you going to make me a Mexican chocolate cake while I'm here?"

"It's already on the kitchen table," she admitted with a grin. "And let me tell you, you're lucky it's still in one piece. These cousins of yours would have already had it half-eaten if I hadn't take the broom to a few of them."

"We were only trying to do you a favor," Flynn told Alice innocently as they all started up the porch steps. "We just wanted to test it to make sure it was done before you served it to company."

"Yeah," Cooper added. "We know how you pride yourself on your baking. We didn't want you to be embarrassed."

When the older woman only snorted at that, they all laughed and swept Cilla along with them to the front door. Kat, however, wasn't laughing when she pulled Cilla to the side just before she could step inside. "Cilla, there's something you should know—"

Surprised by the worried glint in her cousin's blue eyes, Cilla frowned. "What is it? The baby? Is there a problem? Alice said something about you resting—"

"No, no, I'm fine," she said, distracted. "I should have called you back after I found out you both called the same night, but I thought it might be better if I stayed out of it. Now I'm not so sure, and it's too late—"

"Too late?" she repeated with a confused laugh. "Too late for what? Kat, you're rambling. Just spit it out—"

But Kat didn't have to. An abrupt, apprehensive silence from the rest of the group caught Cilla's attention, and she looked up...only to stop dead in her tracks at the sight of the man standing just inside the front door in the entrance hall.

Wyatt.

The smile that curled her mouth froze, then vanished completely. No! she cried silently. It had been ten years since she'd seen him last, ten years since he'd broken her heart. Determined not to lay eyes on him ever again, she'd timed her visits to the ranch when she knew he wouldn't be there. But she hadn't even thought to ask this time because the last she'd heard, he was tied up with some big government project in L.A. What was he doing here?

She wanted to turn and run. Now! But she'd be damned if she'd give Wyatt Chandler the satisfaction of seeing her run for cover like a scared rabbit. With her heart thumping crazily in her breast, she stood her ground and lifted her chin, reminding herself that he no longer had the power to hurt her. But it didn't feel that way when her gaze met his.

He'd changed. She'd have given anything not to have noticed or cared, but much to her dismay, her eyes were already searching his face, noting the differences between the man she'd loved and the one who stood before her. There was no boyishness to his lean, angular face now, no softness in the sharp green eyes that boldly met hers. His wavy black hair was still as dark as midnight, but the sun had carved lines at the corners of his eyes and weathered his skin. He'd matured, filled out, hardened.

And he was still the best-looking thing she'd ever seen in cowboy boots and jeans.

The thought hit her like a stray bullet in the dark, catching her off guard. Horrified, she stiffened, but it was too late. He'd always been able to read her like a book and that, apparently, hadn't changed. His green eyes suddenly glinting with amusement, he grinned at her. "Well, if it isn't Prissy all grown up," he drawled. "Long time no see, cousin."

They weren't cousins and he knew it, but like a trout rising to a fly, she took the bait so beautifully, he almost laughed aloud. "The name is Cilla, *cousin,*" she snapped, glaring at him. "And just for the record, absence doesn't make the heart grow fonder. What are you doing here?"

"The same as you," he chuckled. "Spending Christmas here."

"What? You can't be!"

He laughed, not the least offended by her outburst. "'Fraid so. Knocked me for a loop when I heard you were coming, too. Did you bring me a present?"

Not amused, she gave him a withering look. "What do you think?"

What he thought was that she still hated his guts, and he couldn't say he blamed her. He hadn't forgotten what had happened between them that summer ten years ago, any more than she had. She had been just a kid, barely old enough to drive, and still finding herself. He shouldn't have given her a second look, but she was cute and so outrageous, he hadn't been able to resist her. He'd told himself he wouldn't lose his head or do something stupid—just flirt with her and kiss her a couple of times. But one taste and she'd gone straight to his head. The next thing he knew, he was making love to her. When he finally came back to his senses, she was looking up at him with wedding bells in her eyes. It had scared the hell out of him.

Looking back now, he readily admitted that he'd handled the situation badly. But he hadn't been much more than a kid himself and he'd panicked when she started talking happily-ever-after, and all he could see was her father coming after him with a shotgun. So he'd done the only thing he could to convince her they weren't made for each other. He'd called a friend from college and arranged for Cilla to find the two of them in a hot clinch.

He wasn't proud of what he'd done, but his back had been against the wall. And even though she'd never believe it now, he'd done it for her own good. She'd gone home that very day and had managed to avoid him ever since. Until today.

Shaking his head over the quirks of fate, he couldn't help wondering if it had all been for nothing. Here they both were, back at the ranch and snipping at each other like two kids again. Only this time she wasn't seventeen.

And that could be a problem, he thought with a frown as the others quickly stepped in then to fill the awkward silence. All these years, whenever her memory had slipped up on him unaware, he'd pictured her frozen in time with freckles dusting her cheeks, her long, auburn hair caught up in a ponytail, cutoffs hugging her slim hips and a faded T-shirt molding her slight breasts. But that girl was long gone and in her place was a Priscilla Rawlings he could have passed on the street and not known.

Sophisticated. Over the course of the last ten years, he'd never once pictured her as sophisticated, but the woman who stepped around him like he was a bug to be avoided had somehow acquired polish and grace. Where was the little hoyden he remembered so fondly? The wild Indian who used to ride hell-bent for leather across the ranch, her laughter trailing behind her in her dust? There was no sign of her in this Cilla, who was a city girl through and through. Dressed in black wool slacks and a sapphire-blue angora sweater, with her hair cascading to her shoulders in soft curls that glinted with fire, she was a stranger.

Dear God, when had she become so beautiful? And why hadn't anyone told him? The family had kept him apprised of every boyfriend she'd had since her senior year in high school, dammit, but no one had thought to tell him that she could stop traffic with a smile. If he'd known, he could have least prepared himself for the sight of her, he told himself, then snorted at his own wishful thinking. Yeah, right. Who was he trying to kid? With her oval face, high cheekbones and flawless skin, not to mention a mouth that looked more kissable than ever, the lady was drop-dead gorgeous. And nothing anyone could have said could have prepared him for that. Somehow, over the course of the next month, he was going to have to deal with that. He had a sinking feeling it wasn't going to be easy.

Her stomach knotted with nerves, Cilla escaped upstairs to her room to unpack and tried to convince herself she could do this. Just because she was staying in the same house with the man didn't mean she had to be anything more than polite to him. After all, it wasn't as if they'd even see each other that much. Wyatt had never been the type to hang around the house in the past, and the ranch was a big place. If she was lucky, she wouldn't have to deal with him except at mealtimes, and then the others would be around.

"All you have to do is smile and make small talk so the rest of the family won't be uncomfortable," she told her reflected image in the mirror as she put the last of her things away and checked her appearance. "It'll be a piece of cake."

It sounded easy enough, but the second she stepped out into the hall, the door to the guest room directly across from hers opened and she once again found herself face-to-face with Wyatt. For a second, he looked as surprised as she felt, then that slow, maddening grin of his propped up one corner of his mouth. "We've got to stop meeting like this, sweetheart," he taunted softly. "The cousins will start to talk."

Heat blooming in her cheeks, Cilla just barely resisted the urge to hit him. "I agree," she retorted. "So why don't you do us both a favor and go back to where you came from?"

"Why should I do that?" he chuckled. "I was here first."

"Dammit, Wyatt, this isn't a game! I'm serious. You're not any happier to see me than I am you. If you were a gentleman, you'd leave."

For all of two seconds, he actually considered her suggestion. She was right—neither of them was thrilled to see the other and that would make for an awkward holiday for the rest of the family. But his gut knotted just at the thought of going back to L.A. right now. He could handle Cilla and her hostility. Eleanor and her insane fanaticism was something else entirely. If he never saw the woman again, it would be too soon.

"Sorry, darlin'," he drawled, "but you should know better than most that I'm no gentleman. But you don't have to stay just because I am. I'm sure the family would understand if you decided the house wasn't big enough for the two of us. You could always go to your mother's in Florida."

"And let everyone think you scared me off?" she snapped, arching a delicate brow at him. "Not on your life, Wyatt Chandler. If you can suffer my company, I can stomach yours."

Satisfied, he only grinned. "Have it your way, honey. Whatever makes you happy."

She gave him a withering look, not the least impressed. "Please...spare me. If you really wanted to make me happy, you'd do the decent thing and at least go stay with Flynn or Cooper for awhile."

"Why? So you won't have to worry about running into me every time you turn around? What's the matter?" he teased. "Afraid you'll fall for me again?"

"Fat chance," she retorted with a laugh, truly amused. "I'm over you, cowboy. So if you're sticking around in hopes of rekindling an old flame, you're wasting your time. It ain't going to happen."

Chapter Two

When the entire Rawlings clan got together for a meal, they had to put two tables together and use every chair in the house. Even then, they sat shoulder to shoulder, crowded in like a herd of calves at a feeding trough. You could hardly move without bumping the person next to you, and at times, the different conversations going on around the combined tables were so loud that you couldn't hear yourself think. Cilla loved it.

The family hadn't been nearly as large when she was a teenager. No one had been married then and there'd just been Gable, Cooper, Flynn and Kat. And Alice, of course, who had fussed over them like a mother hen and helped Gable keep them all in line and the family together after their parents died. To Cilla, who had never had any brothers or sisters of her own, every visit with her Rawlings cousins had seemed like something out of "The Brady Bunch." And meal times had been the best of all. The Double R had always been known for its hospitality, so there'd always been a place at the table for anyone who cared to drop by. The more the merrier.

Glancing around at the laughing faces of her cousins, Cilla was glad to see that that hadn't changed.

There were seven children now—good Lord, when had that happened?—who ranged in age from Flynn and Tate's sixteen year old Haily all the way down to Cooper and Susannah's Holly, who would be two on Christmas Eve. As close as brothers and sister, they were a lively group and kept everyone laughing with their antics. Especially Holly. An unabashed flirt, she grinned across the table at Wyatt and giggled as he rolled his eyes at her playfully.

Watching him under lowered lashes, Cilla couldn't help but notice he was still a flirt, still a ladies' man, and it didn't matter if the lady was two or eighty—he could still charm the pants off her. All of their cousins were happily married and settled in life, but Wyatt showed little interest in marriage or having a family. Oh, he was great with the kids, just like a favorite uncle. But when the holidays were over, he'd go back to L.A. and a life that didn't require commitment or responsibility.

And that irritated her no end. He was still footloose and fancy-free, and she was, she told herself, lucky she'd gotten over him long ago.

Seated at the far end of the table from him, she tried to ignore him but Holly and the other kids' laughter made that impossible. Fighting the urge to smile, she watched him blow the toddler a kiss, and just that quickly, his eyes were on *her*. Her heart skipped a beat, then thundered frantically in her ears. Damn him, she fumed, glaring at him. How did he do this to her? She'd deliberately taken a seat as far away from his as possible, but his wicked, dancing, *knowing* eyes pinned her in her chair and just reached out and physically stroked her, stealing her breath.

So you're over me, are you? he seemed to taunt silently. *Well, we'll just see about that.*

He was staring and he didn't care who noticed. She wanted to kill him.

Seated across from her, Kat gently tapped her tea glass with her fork. "Hey, everybody, I need the floor for a second," she said over the low roar of the different conversations making their way around the table. "I have an announcement to make."

"Oh, God, here it comes," Flynn groaned teasingly. "She's come up with another name for the baby. What is it this time, brat? Michelangelo Valentine or Abraham Lincoln Valentine? They've both got a ring to them."

"Cute, Flynn. Real cute," she retorted, grinning as the others laughed. "Actually, I was thinking about Michelangelo *and* Lincoln. That sounds better than Fred and Barney, don't you think?"

Puzzled, he frowned. "You're going to give the kid two names?"

Her eyes twinkling, she reached for her husband, Lucas, who sat next to her, and smiled as his strong fingers closed around hers. "No, we're going to give the *kids* names of their own."

For a moment, there was nothing but stunned silence. Then her words really registered, and in the next instant pandemonium broke out as all the adults seemed to surge to their feet at once.

"Twins?" Cilla whispered, thrilled. "You're having twins?"

Tate and Josey, the two doctors in the family, immediately started throwing questions at her. "Are you okay? Are you still seeing Thompson in Silver City? What does he say about you working with those longhorns of yours?"

"Should you even be working?" Gable asked, frowning. "Josey spent the last four months in bed before the boys were born. Are you sure you're following the doctor's orders?"

"Yes, for once in my life I'm following orders," Kat laughed as she was swept from her brothers to her sisters-in-law to her cousins for a round of hugs and kisses. "Lucas is making sure of it. And yes, I'm seeing Thompson, and no, I'm not working anymore, not since last week. Give me a chance to catch my breath and I'll tell you everything."

Wyatt, the last to congratulate Lucas and hug his cousin, drew back suddenly to grin down at her. "You're going to make a hell of a mother, brat. But two? Lord, if they're anything like you, they're going to lead you a ragged chase. Think you're going to be able to keep up with them?"

Her blue eyes twinkling, she only grinned. "What do you think?"

Alice, beaming like a proud grandmother, swept in then with champagne and the cake she'd been guarding all afternoon. Just that easily, dinner became a party, and long after the cake and the champagne were history, they sat around the table talking and laughing and discussing everything from the most outlandish names everyone could think of to where the new babies would go to college when the time came.

"College is the least of our worries," Kat laughed. "Right now, I'm just worried about where we're going to put them if we get a mixed set instead of two of a kind. The cabin's only got one spare room."

"Well, that's easily solved," Wyatt said. "I'll draw you up some plans while I'm here, if you like."

"But you're on vacation. We couldn't let you do that."

"I don't know why not if I want to do it," he said reasonably. "Consider it my present to the new arrivals."

Kat hesitated, looking to Lucas for help, who said dryly, "That's a pretty expensive present, Wyatt. Most people give a stuffed teddy bear. You sure you want to do this?"

"I wouldn't have offered if I wasn't sure. Anyway, I can't sit around here all month and just twiddle my thumbs. I'll go nuts."

Lucas glanced back at Kat, a silent message passing between them before he finally shrugged and grinned. "Well, if you're sure you want to do it, I guess we'd be crazy to turn you down. Thanks, Wyatt. We appreciate it."

"Things are pretty slow around here right now," Gable said thoughtfully. "If we all pitched in, we could have that room up and finished in no time once the plans are drawn up."

That started a discussion on who could do what and when they could start and soon Wyatt was drawing a sketch of the cabin on his paper napkin while Kat described her dream nursery. Watching them from the far end of the table, Cilla found herself staring at what could have been. *She* could have been the one who was pregnant and it could have been a nursery for his own child that Wyatt was designing.

Not in a million years, Cilla Rawlings, a voice growled in her ear. *Don't even think it.*

But it was too late. Old dreams and forbidden needs flashed in front of her eyes, teasing her, taunting her with yearnings that she had locked away in a secret part of her heart eons ago. A baby. Wyatt's baby. At seventeen, she'd imagined and fantasized and dreamed of the day in the far distant future when she would hold a tiny infant in her arms, an infant that would have a fascinating combination of her and Wyatt's features, a precious baby that would be the embodiment of their love for each other. But that dream had shriveled up and died—she'd thought forever—when she found him in the arms of another woman.

God, what was she doing?

Pale, suddenly in desperate need of some time to herself, she pushed her chair back and immediately drew the attention of every adult at the table. Including Wyatt's. Avoiding his sharp gaze, she pushed to her feet with a smile that wasn't quite as easy as she would have liked. "Sorry to be a killjoy, but I'm really bushed, guys. It's been a long day, and if I don't go to bed, I'm going to crash right here."

"You do look a little pale," Josey said with a frown. "Are you feeling all right?"

"The flu's been going around," Tate added, studying her in concern. "Josey and I have been tripping over patients all week. Have you had any kind of a fever?"

"No, Dr. Tate. I'm fine. Really," she insisted with a smile as she rose to her feet. "It's nothing that a little sleep won't fix. I started at five this morning and I finally ran out of gas. So don't break up the party on my account. I'll see you all in the morning."

Promising to catch up on all the family gossip in the days and weeks to come, she hurried upstairs to her room, sure she would be out like a light the second her head hit the pillow. But long after she'd showered and crawled into bed in her favorite flannel gown, her thoughts were still jumping around like popcorn in a hot skillet.

Downstairs, she heard the sleepy good-night calls of the children and their parents as Flynn and Cooper and their families left for their own nearby homes, which were also part of the Double R. Kat and Lucas followed soon after that, and then the house started to quiet down as Josey and Gable got their own brood ready for bed. One by one, Cilla heard them all come upstairs, the whisper of their feet on the hall runner, the quiet thump of doors shutting up and down the hall. Finally there was nothing but the silence of the night, and still she lay flat on her back and stared up at the ceiling, sleep a thousand miles away.

Across the hall, she caught the muted sounds of Wyatt getting ready for bed—the running of the water in the bathroom, the sound of boots dropping, first one, then the other, to the floor—and suddenly she'd had enough. She couldn't do it. She couldn't lie there and listen to those intimate sounds without imagining him undressing, stretching out on the bed with a tired sigh, thumping his pillow into a comfortable shape... not without dreaming about him and that was something she hadn't done in years. She didn't intend to start now.

Her heart thumping crazily in her breast, she bolted up and reached for her robe. Seconds later, she carefully eased open her bedroom door and cautiously peered out into the hall. There was a night-light on at the top of the stairs, providing the only illumination. As quiet as a mouse, she hurried downstairs in her bare feet to the den and switched on the TV. She needed a movie, something old and draggy and preferably in black and white that would bore her to death inside of five minutes. Maybe then she'd be able to go to sleep.

But what she got was *It's a Wonderful Life*. And it was just starting.

She groaned. Of all the miserable, rotten luck. It was her favorite holiday movie, the only one she made a point to watch religiously at least once every year. Frowning at the stark black-and-white images of Jimmy Stewart and Donna Reed, she reminded herself that she needed to get some serious sleep if she was going to hold her own with Wyatt tomorrow. But she was a real sucker when it came to the holidays and traditions. And *It's a Wonderful Life* was definitely a tradition. Unable to resist, she sank down onto the couch, her chenille robe flaring out around her, and tucked her bare feet up under her folded legs. Clutching one of the throw pillows to her breast, she hugged it to her, her eyes glued to the screen.

That was the way Wyatt found her twenty minutes later.

On his way to the kitchen for another piece of Alice's Mexican chocolate cake, he heard the muted sounds of the TV coming from the den and stepped into the doorway to see who was still up. At the sight of Cilla huddled on the couch with tears streaming down her cheeks, a slow, crooked smile tugged at the corners of his mouth. She always had been a pushover for a sappy movie.

He should have left her alone. She was enjoying the movie and her tears and wouldn't appreciate his showing up in the middle of either. But he wasn't going to go away; he couldn't. Not when there were tears sliding down her cheeks and they were the only two people awake in the house. Alice's chocolate cake forgotten, he walked silently into the den and dropped down onto the couch beside her. Without a word, he reached into his pocket, pulled out a handkerchief, and held it out to her.

Startled, she stared at the folded cotton handkerchief as if it was a snake that was going to strike any second. "Go ahead, take it," he said, laughing softly as he reached for her hand and closed her fingers around the cloth. "It's not going to bite you."

She took it . . . warily. "What are you doing down here? I thought you'd gone to bed."

His smile flashed in the darkness, wicked and teasing. "I was just about to ask you the same thing. What's the matter? Can't sleep for dreaming of me?"

"Fat chance, Chandler," she snorted. "I know this may come as something of a shock to you, but my every thought doesn't begin and end with you."

Grinning, he pressed a hand to his heart like a man who had just taken a mortal blow. "No kidding? And here I had the distinct impression that just being around me made you nervous. Guess I was wrong."

"You're darn right you were wrong," she retorted. "I couldn't care less what you do. Now, if you'll excuse me, I'm going up to bed."

"Oh, no, you don't. The movie's not over yet." His eyes dancing, he settled his arm about her shoulders and leaned back, all his attention innocently focused on the movie.

Cilla wasn't fooled for a second. Wyatt Chandler didn't have an innocent bone in his body. And the day he actually wanted to watch a sentimental movie like *It's a Wonderful Life* was the day he'd been out in the sun too long.

But God, his arm felt wonderful around her! It had been so long. She'd thought she'd forgotten what it felt like to be held by him, to lean against him and draw his scent in with every breath and know that nothing in the world could hurt her when he was this close.

Except him.

And it took nothing more than the throb of a hurt that even now, ten years later, hadn't quite healed to make her reach hurriedly for the arm around her shoulders and shrug out of it. "You haven't changed, Wyatt Chandler. You'll use any line, any situation, to get a woman in your arms. Let go! I'm going to bed."

He made no move to stop her, but his taunt followed her across the den. "Go ahead. Cut and run like a scared little girl. And here I thought you were all grown up."

Later, she told herself she should have ignored him and gone on upstairs. At the very least, she should have held on to her temper and given herself time to think before she answered him. But his needling words struck a nerve, and before she had time to ask herself why she cared what he thought, she was whirling and bearing down on him with fire in her eyes.

"Don't pull that garbage on me, Chandler. I know what you're doing and it's not going to work. I *am* all grown up, and in case you haven't noticed, I'm not running scared from you or anyone else. I'm tired. T-i-r-e-d. Got it?"

Not the least impressed, he only grinned up at her crookedly as he sprawled against the couch with his arms spread wide against the back. "A likely story," he drawled. "You've been avoiding me ever since you got here. Admit it, cousin, you've still got a thing for me—"

"A thing for you! God, I don't know why I even bother to try to hold a rational conversation with you. You always were the most insufferable, conceited—"

"And it's got you all shook up," he finished, chuckling, as insults fell from her tongue. "Why else would you be spitting at me like a scalded cat? You're scared."

She gave him a scornful look that would have felled a lesser man. He didn't even blink. Annoyed, frustrated, she wanted to shake him until his teeth rattled ... and, just once, shake up that irritatingly smug self-confidence of his. Glaring at him, she said, "I couldn't care less what you do or where you go and I can prove it."

His mouth twitching, he arched a dark brow at her. "Oh, really? And how do you plan to do that?"

"Like this," she retorted, and sank down beside him on the couch. A heartbeat later, she grabbed him by the ears and kissed him.

Chapter Three

Somewhere in the back of her head, she told herself she could do this. She could lay a kiss on him that would curl his hair and leave him panting, then walk away without a second glance. After all, it was no more than he deserved. He might think he was God's gift to women, but not where she was concerned. By the time she got through with him, he wouldn't know what hit him. And she wouldn't feel a thing.

At least, that was the way it should have happened. But nothing, she discovered too late, was that easy with Wyatt. The second her mouth settled on his, she felt things she hadn't allowed herself to even think about for a very long time. Things like need, the kind that came from her very soul. And a hunger that was immediate and fierce, as familiar as the sound of his name on her tongue. Stunned, she should have pulled back right then and there, but she couldn't think, couldn't move, couldn't tear herself away from the wonder that was and always had been Wyatt. His arms came around her, snatching her close, wrapping around her like he'd never let her go, and between one heartbeat and the next, she felt like she'd come home. Finally.

Dizzy, her heart doing somersaults in her breast, she swallowed a whimper as the truth slipped into her heart like a switchblade between the ribs. *This* was what had been missing in her relationship with Tom. This instant heat, this fire in the belly that threatened to burn you from the inside out, this passion that swept over you like a crashing breaker and dragged you down into full blown raging desire before you even thought to note the danger. A passion that she'd never come close to finding with Tom, not even when she'd thought she loved him with all her heart.

She'd known something was missing, something that she'd been yearning for, searching for, something she'd never felt for any man...except Wyatt. Something that, in spite of everything, was still there and stronger than ever.

Have you lost your mind, Cilla Rawlings? a caustic voice demanded in her head. *This isn't Prince Charming you've got in a lip-lock, you know. He's the worst kind of rat, and he'll break your heart again if you give him a chance. Last time you were a kid—you didn't know what you were doing. But you're not seventeen anymore. What's your excuse this time?*

The painful words forced their way through the cloud of need that shrouded her brain, tugging at her until they got her attention and brought her up short. Horrified, she stiffened. Dear God, what was she doing? She was supposed to be teaching the man a lesson, not melting in his arms and kissing him like there was no tomorrow!

She jerked back abruptly, her breathing ragged and the thunder of her heartbeat loud in her ears. She'd eat dirt before she'd let him see what he could do to her with just a kiss. Calling on all her self-control, she looked him right in the eye and gave him a cool smile that was guaranteed to set his teeth on edge. If her blood was still hot, her pulse racing, no one but she knew that. "Not bad, Chandler. Your technique's improved with age."

His eyes narrowed slightly, but he only grinned. "So has yours. But if that little demonstration was supposed to show me how indifferent you are, I think I missed the point. Maybe we should try it again."

"Oh, no you don't!" Her laugh shakier than she would have liked, she quickly shied out of reach. "Nice try, but if you think I'm going to stand here and trade kisses with you, all those years of working in the sun must have fried your brain. I'm not interested."

"Oh, really? That's not what your body was telling me just a few seconds ago."

"Oh, I didn't say I didn't enjoy it," she said with an airiness that was nothing but pure bravado. "I enjoy hot fudge sundaes, too, but that doesn't mean I want a steady diet of them. Some things just aren't good for me, and you're one of them. So you see," she continued with an easy smile, "I'm over you, cousin. Totally and completely. I can enjoy the company—and occasional kiss—of a man who's not good for me, but I no longer fall head over heels like a teenager with a bad case of hero worship. So you don't have to worry about me making a fool of myself over you again. It's not going to happen."

Watching him closely, she saw his usually laughing eyes darken with irritation and grinned cheekily. "Now that we've got that cleared up, I think I'll go to bed. It's been a long day. 'Night, Wyatt. See you in the morning.''

Turning on her heel, she walked away from him with unhurried grace. She could feel his eyes drilling into her back, but he didn't move, didn't say a word, for which she was profoundly grateful. Because if he'd just have called her name, he could have tempted her to change her mind. But he didn't, and she didn't spare him a glance. She didn't dare.

With the sound of her footsteps loud in the quiet of the night, it seemed to take her forever to cross the length of the den. Then she finally reached the door and quietly stepped into the hall. It wasn't until she was around the corner that she realized how shaky her knees were. Alone, out of his sight, she ran for the stairs and the privacy of her room.

Long after she disappeared from view, Wyatt stared after her like a man who had just been flattened by a stampeding herd of longhorns that had come out of nowhere. For the life of him, he couldn't say what the hell had just happened. One second he was teasing her, lighting that fire in her eyes that always delighted him, and the next, she was kissing him with a determination that set every nerve ending he had humming.

He should have pushed her away. If nothing else, he damn sure shouldn't have kissed her back. She was trouble—she always had been. The second he realized they'd both been invited to the ranch, he should have gotten the hell out of there. But by then, she'd been walking through the front door with that glint in her eye that warned him not to come anywhere near her, and something deep inside him had balked at the idea of conveniently disappearing just so *she* could be more comfortable. He had just as much right as she did to be there.

Damn his stubborn pride, he thought irritably. If he hadn't stayed, he would have put her out of his head the minute he drove away, but there was no way in hell that was going to happen now. Not after that kiss.

She'd just caught him by surprise, he tried to tell himself. That was the only explanation for his response. After all, he wasn't a monk. When a beautiful woman laid one on him, he was damn well going to enjoy it.

As far as excuses went, it sounded good. But his common sense wasn't buying it. It wasn't just any beautiful woman he'd kissed. It was Cilla. And there was enough electricity in that kiss to light up the whole West Coast.

Over her? he thought grimly. Like hell!

Damn! Now what was he going to do? She wasn't the only one who'd thought the past was dead and buried. Oh, he'd never really forgotten her—even at seventeen, Cilla hadn't been the type of woman a man walked away from unscathed. She'd stuck like a burr to his memory, pricking his consciousness at the most inopportune times and refusing to let any other woman push her from his head.

But it'd been ten years, dammit! And you couldn't look back. Time had a tendency to blur the memories, to enhance them, to make them better than they were. A long-ago summer was always longer, hotter, the music better, the romance sweeter than anything in the here and now. Which was ridiculous, he tried to tell himself, because it couldn't have been that good. Nothing ever was.

So where did he go from here? Regardless of the need that was still churning in his gut from that damn kiss, he wasn't looking for a relationship with Cilla or anyone else. It wasn't that he didn't ever plan to settle down—he did when the right woman came along, but so far, he'd run into nothing but one roadblock after another. If they weren't too young—as Cilla had been when they'd first met—they were too old or too afraid of getting hurt or too career-minded.

And then there was the problem he'd left behind in California. Eleanor. Just thinking about her made his gut clench. He'd searched his memory a dozen times, trying to pinpoint some innocent word, some unsuspecting action, that had led her to believe not only that he was available, but that he was interested in her. But there was nothing, not even a smile. He didn't deny that he had a reputation for flirting, but he didn't encourage anyone that he wasn't first attracted to. And Eleanor had left him stone-cold. There'd been something about her that he hadn't liked from the second his eyes had met hers, and he'd been as curt as he could without being rude. She hadn't taken the hint. If anything, she'd somehow seen his coolness as a challenge and had given him misery ever since.

Compared to Eleanor, Cilla didn't come close to being a problem. She wasn't, thankfully, jailbait anymore. She'd grown up, filled out, and learned to control that impulsive streak that had once nearly gotten them both into serious trouble. And she despised him—he'd made sure of it by setting up that kiss with Sharon all those years ago. The sparks might still sizzle between them, but he'd destroyed her youthful illusions and flung her love back in her face, and no woman forgot or forgave that. And that just might be both their salvations.

Still, when he locked up and went upstairs, he couldn't stop his gaze from drifting to Cilla's closed door. All too easily, he could picture her getting ready for bed, slowly stripping out of her sweater and slacks, revealing inch by inch that beautiful body that had only gotten better with the passage of time. Was she still shy about that mole on her hip? And still so sensitive—

Suddenly realizing where his thoughts had wandered, he swore under his breath and wondered whose brainy idea it had been to put them at this end of the hall together. It wasn't as if these were the only two available rooms. The house was as big as a small hotel. They could have easily been given rooms at opposite ends of the house. So why hadn't they?

If he were a suspicious man, he'd swear someone was playing matchmaker, but that was downright ridiculous. The entire family knew that Cilla couldn't stand the sight of him—she'd been avoiding him for years, for God's sake! She'd even, according to Gable, planned her visits to the ranch at times she knew he wasn't going to be there. No one in their right mind could possibly think there was anything between them but hostility.

Unless they'd happened to witness the kiss they'd just shared downstairs. Whatever he'd felt for the lady at that moment, it hadn't been hostility. Swearing, he turned away from her room and went into his own, determined to put Cilla and that damn kiss out of his head.

The lady, however, didn't make it easy for him. He'd barely drifted off to sleep when she wandered into his dreams as if she owned them, teasing and touching and kissing him until he was hot and hard and reaching for her, only to come up with nothing but sheet. He'd dreamed of her before, of course, but that was in the past, and the Cilla who had tormented him then was little more than a girl who was just discovering her powers as a woman. She'd tied him in knots with her innocent seduction, and he hadn't resisted her as he should have, but in the end, he'd found a way to walk away from her because it was for her own good. This Cilla was something else entirely. Older, wiser, more sure of herself, she was a grown woman who knew exactly what she wanted and how to get it. And that was what made him more than a little bit nervous. How was a man supposed to handle a woman like that without getting burned?

Disturbed by the thought, he rolled over on his stomach and punched his pillow into a more comfortable shape, determined to put the lady out of his head once and for all and get some sleep. They were going to spend the next month together under the watchful eye of the family, and he had no intention of dreaming of her or any other woman every night. He had better things to do with his time...like come up with the plans for the addition to Kat and Lucas's cabin.

Over the course of the next six hours, he designed additions to half a dozen cabins and even came up with plans for an office complex in L.A. But it didn't help. Nothing did. Every time he drifted into sleep, Cilla was there, waiting for him with a smile that was as distracting as hell. He woke reaching for her, cursing her, cursing himself. If she'd really been there beside him in bed, he didn't know if he would have kissed her or shook her until her teeth rattled. He just knew that in all the years since that long-ago summer, he'd never once met a woman who could fascinate and irritate him at one and the same time the way Cilla could.

Giving up all pretense of trying to sleep, he was up before dawn and standing under the shower by the time the first rooster crowed. The hot water didn't do a thing for his dull head, though, so as soon as he was shaved and dressed, he headed downstairs to the kitchen. Coffee. He needed lots of coffee.

The house was quiet as a tomb—with the slower pace of winter, it would be another hour before the rest of the family started to stir—but he was no stranger around his cousins' kitchen. For as long as he could remember, Alice had insisted that everyone help get the meal on the table and clean up afterward, and he hadn't been spared that chore when he was a kid just because he was visiting. Retrieving the ground coffee from the pantry, he put on a pot and sat down at the old oak kitchen table to wait for it to brew.

Thirty minutes later, he was on his second cup and enjoying the sight of the first streaks of morning sunlight creeping over the ranch when Gable appeared in the doorway wearing nothing but his jeans and a frown. "I thought I smelled coffee," he said in a voice gravelly with sleep. "What are you doing up so early, man? You're on vacation!"

"Someone forgot to tell my brain," he said, sipping at his steaming cup. "Sorry I woke you."

"Hey, don't worry about it. I needed to get up, anyway. Josey's got the early shift at the clinic this morning, and she needs a ride. Her water pump went out yesterday, and I've got to run into town to get her another one. Any more of that coffee?"

"A whole pot," Wyatt said with a grin. "I figured it would take that much to jump-start my motor this morning. Help yourself. I hope you like it strong."

Strong didn't even begin to describe the brew Gable poured into the mug he'd grabbed from the cabinet. Black as tar, it could have, in a pinch, served as battery acid. Filling his mug to the rim, Gable took a cautious sip and sighed in satisfaction, a slow grin stretching across his rugged face as the potent liquid hit his stomach. "This stuff damn near ought to be outlawed," he growled. "Where'd you learn to make coffee like this?"

"Visit any construction site anywhere in the world, and this is pretty much what you're going to get,"

Wyatt replied, his green eyes glinting with amusement. "I've been told it puts hair on your chest."

"Then remind me not to let Josey have any," he chuckled as he settled into the chair across the table from him and took another cautious sip. "Damn, that's good. So tell me," he said casually, studying him with eyes that missed little, "what kept you awake last night? Cilla or the woman in California?"

Caught in the act of swallowing, Wyatt choked. "Cilla? What's she got to do with anything?"

"I don't know," his cousin replied. "You tell me. It's been—what? Ten years since you've seen each other? And you didn't exactly part on the best of terms. I guess it was no surprise that she wasn't thrilled to see you."

"That's putting it mildly," Wyatt snorted. "If looks could kill, I'd have dropped dead on the spot."

"Probably," Gable agreed, grinning. "But she's sure grown into a fine-looking woman, hasn't she? She was engaged, you know."

Wyatt took the news like a man who had just been shot. Stunned, he blurted out, "Engaged! To who? When? How come I wasn't told about this?"

"I guess because no one thought you'd be interested one way or the other. After all, it's not as if you two have kept up with each other over the years. Anyway, nothing came of it. She broke things off last week."

"Why?"

Gable shrugged. "I don't know. I guess she decided she didn't love him. She told Kat all about it, how the guy was her boss and fired her when she gave him his ring back. That's why she's here. She's trying to decide where to go from here. I think she's sort of had it with Denver."

Still reeling from the news that she'd actually been on the verge of getting married, Wyatt hardly heard him. All these years, he'd known she wasn't standing still in time. She'd gone on with her life just as he had. He'd pictured her growing up, graduating from high school and college, getting a job, a place of her own, even a boyfriend or two. But he'd never pictured her loving another man. And he found, to his disgust, that he didn't like the images that sprang to mind. He didn't like them at all.

"Have you got a problem with her being engaged?"

Lost in his thoughts, it was a minute before Gable's words even registered. When they did, he retorted sharply, "Why the hell would I care if she was engaged or not engaged? She's nothing to me."

"Good, I'm glad to hear it," Gable said easily. "I wouldn't want to see her get hurt again. Or you. So your problem must be the woman in California. Right? I know if I had someone like that showing up every time I turned around, I wouldn't be able to sleep nights, either."

It was a logical conclusion, but still Wyatt hesitated, considering. In the end, however, there was nothing left to consider, not if he was going to get any sleep at all the next month. "Right," he said, taking another bracing swig of coffee. What else could he say?

Chapter Four

"Daddy, can we get the Christmas tree today? Ple-e-a-ase? You said we'd do it this weekend."

"I want to drive. Can I drive the wagon, Daddy? Brian got to do it last year."

"Did not! Mandy did. She always gets to do things like that cause she's the oldest."

Gable, grinning at his kids as they argued good-naturedly about who did what and when, lifted an inquiring brow at Josey, who was seated across the breakfast table from him. "Well, Mom, what'da you say? It's your day off. Do you want to spend it getting the tree and putting it up or did you have something else planned?"

Her dark green eyes twinkling, Josey pretended to consider. "Well, I was going to go through everybody's sock drawers today and sort them out—"

"Aw, Mom, you can do that any time!" Joey grumbled.

"And Cilla and Wyatt really want to go with us to get a tree," Mandy pointed out. "They've been here nearly a week already and haven't got to do anything fun."

In the middle of spreading jam on one of Alice's homemade biscuits, Cilla glanced up in surprise. "Oh, but I have,'' she told the eight-year-old. ''I've slept late every morning and visited your mom and Tate at the clinic, and caught up on all the gossip with Kat. Tomorrow, I'm having dinner with Cooper and Susannah, and later this week, I'm going shopping with your mom. I'm having a great time.'' And in the process, she'd successfully stayed out of Wyatt's way. Life couldn't be better.

''Yeah, she's hardly been here at all,'' Wyatt said dryly, the glint in his eyes warning her he knew exactly what she'd been doing. ''And neither have I. I've been working on the plans for the addition to Kat's cabin and ordering all the supplies, but that doesn't mean I haven't been having a good time. And we don't need to be entertained, anyway. We're family.''

''Does that mean you don't want to go with us to get the tree?'' Brian asked, hurt.

''Oh, no!''

''Hey, sport, you know better than that. I love picking out Christmas trees.''

Cilla almost choked on her coffee at that one—the Wyatt she'd known in the past had been cynical and mocking about anything that had to do with tradition and sentiment and holidays—but before she could remind him of that, Gable was rising to his feet with a grin. ''Well, then, it looks like we're all taking a trip to the canyon to get a tree. Who's going to help me hitch up the wagon?''

''I will!''

''Me first!''

''I'm the oldest!''

Grabbing their father's hands, the kids were off like a shot, laughing and shouting in excitement as they dragged him off to the barn while Josey yelled after them not to forget their coats. His green eyes twinkling, Wyatt glanced down the table at Cilla and arched a brow at her. "Does this mean we're going to have the pleasure of your company today, Prissy?"

The nickname was old and hated and no one knew that better than him. Put on the spot, Cilla gritted her teeth and gave him a smile that should have lowered his body temperature ten degrees. She was trapped, and if she hadn't known better, she would have sworn he'd somehow finagled the whole thing. "It looks that way, Earp," she said sweetly, returning tit for tat when it came to hated nicknames. "We can sing Christmas carols and everything. It'll be fun, don't you think?"

"Oh, yeah," he drawled, his grin broadening. "I intend to make sure of it."

Cilla didn't like the sound of that—or the wicked mischief dancing in his eyes—but what could he possibly do in front of Gable and Josey and the kids? Oh, he would tease her, but she could handle that. It was the touching—and the kissing, God help her—that stole her breath and turned her into putty in his hands. She didn't, however, intend to be an easy mark. She'd just keep her distance and everything would go fine. And it wasn't as if she'd have to spend the entire day with him. How long could it take to pick out a tree?

It was a cold morning, but clear, with a playful wind that grabbed at hats and hair and chilled any exposed skin. Thankful that she'd brought her mittens and stocking cap, Cilla started to pull them on as she stepped outside with Josey a few minutes later, only to stumble to a halt as her gaze fell on the old wagon pulled up before the front steps. She'd assumed that the wagon Gable had gone with the kids to hitch up was some kind of modern ranch trailer that was pulled behind the family Jeep to carry the Christmas tree back to the house. But the wagon parked in the drive was definitely the old-fashioned wooden kind, complete with a pile of hay in the back and a team of horses hitched to the front. Gable was already lifting the kids up to the long bench seat they would share with him so they could take turns driving, while Wyatt stood by the open tailgate to lift her and Josey up into the back.

"It's a great day for a hayride," he said with a grin. "Of course, I wouldn't complain if it was night and we had a full moon, but that's a different kind of hayride. Up you go, Josey." With no effort at all, he helped her up, then turned to Cilla. "Ready?"

Cilla took one look at his roguish grin and knew she should run, not walk, for safety. He was up to something, and if she got into that wagonload of hay with him, she was just asking for trouble. But the whole family was waiting on her, and she couldn't back out now without a darn good excuse, which she didn't have.

Her pulse pounding, she forced a smile and held out a hand, expecting him to steady her as she stepped up into the wagon. But instead of taking her hand, he grabbed her around the waist and swung her up into the hay before she could do anything but gasp and latch on to his arms.

"Dammit, Wyatt, stop that!" she hissed in a low voice that didn't carry to the others.

"What?" he asked innocently, releasing her. Holding his hands away from her, he looked pointedly at where her fingers still curled into his arms. "You're the one holding on to me, sweetheart."

Heat stinging her cheeks, she snatched her hands back and glared at him, but he only laughed and vaulted up into the wagon beside her. Cilla wanted to hit him, but she had no intention of touching him again. Edging away from him, she moved to the opposite side of the wagon and sat cross-legged in the hay.

"Everybody in?" Gable called over his shoulder.

"Yeah," Wyatt said. "Let's get this baby in gear."

"All right!" the kids yelled.

Laughing, Gable clicked his tongue, gave the reins a light flip and set the wagon in motion. Wyatt, to the delight of the children, pretended to lose his balance, stumbled, then toppled over into the hay...and landed face-first in the hay mere inches from Cilla's hip.

Cilla's heart jumped into her throat, then seemed to lodge there permanently when his hand brushed against her jean-covered thigh as he moved to push himself up out of the hay. Swallowing a gasp, she tried to tell herself that it was just an accident. But then he looked up at her and winked.

If he hadn't looked so funny, she might have given him a disapproving frown and pushed his hand off her knee, where it had casually slipped. But his hair was a mess, with hay poking out of it in every direction, and he scratched at his chest like a monkey to make the kids laugh. Before she knew how it happened, Cilla found herself laughing. Damn the man, what was she going to do with him?

"Hey, how about some Christmas carols?" Josey suggested. The boys broke into "Jingle Bells," and soon the whole family was singing...everybody but Cilla. Settling next to her, his own deep baritone carrying easily over the children's sweet tones, Wyatt waited for her to join in. When she didn't, he leaned over to whisper in her ear, "You got a frog in your throat or what? You're not singing."

At the first touch of his warm breath against her ear and neck, Cilla shivered. Lord, why hadn't she moved once he sat next to her? Hugging herself, she whispered back, "Believe me, it's better that way. My singing has been known to make grown men cry."

He chuckled, his green eyes crinkling attractively with amusement. "Can't carry a tune in a bucket, huh?"

"Make it a wheelbarrow and you're closer to the mark," she retorted as his nearness seeped through her like a tropical breeze, heating her blood all the way to her toes and back. Fighting the sudden unexpected urge to melt against him, she tore her gaze from his and held herself stiffly erect, but it took more than that to discourage the infuriating man. He didn't touch her, but he didn't have to. Aware of every breath he drew, she could feel the touch of his eyes on her, stroking her.

"And here I thought you had the voice of an angel to go along with that face of yours," he murmured teasingly. "You've grown into a beautiful woman, Cilla Rawlings."

She gave him a withering look and prayed he couldn't hear the pounding of her heart. "I don't know what you think you're doing, *cousin*, but it's not going to work," she said in a voice that was pitched too low to carry to the others. "Go find yourself someone else to sweet talk."

His dimples flashed, drawing her gaze to his mouth. "Now why would I do that when you're right here and so easy to tease? Do you know you're blushing?"

"I am not!"

"You are, too. Right here."

He reached out and traced a finger over the curve of her cheek, instantly intensifying the heat that stung her cheeks. Instinctively, Cilla grabbed at his hand, and the second she touched him, his smile faded. Something flared in his eyes, something that made her throat go dry and heartbeat quicken. "Don't—"

A sharp wind suddenly swirled around the wagon as they entered the rocky canyon that formed the western boundary of the ranch, tugging at hats and scarves and hay and abruptly dragging them both back to their surroundings. Gable's and Wyatt's cowboy hats went sailing through the air into the trees that crowded the canyon, Cilla's and Josey's hair flew into their eyes, and the kids laughed as the loose hay flew up around their heads.

"I guess this is where we'll get the tree," Gable laughed as he reined in the horses and set the wagon's hand brake. "Remember, everybody, this year we're getting a tree that fits in the house. Okay? No giants!"

"Ah, Dad, that's no fun!"

"You always say that."

"And we always get one we have to practically cut in half to get in the living room," Josey said, grinning. "Face it, honey, you're as bad as the kids when it comes to getting a big tree."

Laughing, he didn't deny it. "Guilty as charged."

"You've got to have one big enough to put all the presents under," Wyatt pointed out with a broad grin. "Come on, kids. Let's see what we can find."

They didn't need a second urging. Yelling excitedly, the kids tumbled over the side and took off into the trees with Wyatt right behind them. Watching them, Gable shook his head. "I'd better go with them. I've got a feeling Wyatt's going to be as bad as they are."

"He's changed, you know," Josey confided as Gable, too, was swallowed up by the thick patch of juniper that covered the entrance to the canyon. "I can't believe how much."

Cilla lifted a brow. "Gable?"

"No, silly. Wyatt. Don't tell me you haven't noticed."

What Cilla had noticed was that he was just as much of a flirt as he had always been. He had hurt her in the past and he would do so again if she made the mistake of trusting him. But that wasn't something she could obviously tell Josey. "No, I guess I haven't," she admitted cautiously. "But then again, I haven't seen much of him. He's been pretty busy coming up with the plans for Kat's cabin, and I've been on the move visiting with everyone."

"That's what I mean," Josey explained. "I wasn't surprised that he offered to design a room for Kat and Lucas, but I don't think anyone expected him to spend so much time on the plans. He's really given it a lot of thought and come up with a wonderful design for the babies. And he's been here a week and hasn't been to the Crossroads once. The last time that happened during one of his visits, he was sick with a stomach virus the entire time he was here."

"Yeah, but that was when everyone was footloose and fancy-free," Cilla pointed out. "Flynn even had his own stool at the bar, didn't he? Things are different now that everyone's married. Maybe he doesn't want to go by himself."

"And maybe he's growing tired of the bars and single scene and thinking about settling down. He's in his thirties now. He wouldn't be the first man his age who decided bachelorhood wasn't what it was cracked up to be."

It sounded good, but so did winning the lottery. The chances of either were slim to none. "Maybe," she said with a shrug. But she didn't think so.

The new, improved version of Wyatt Chandler might have fooled Josey, but Cilla knew better. The man she'd fallen in love with at seventeen hadn't cared about holidays or family traditions or anything remotely connected with sentiment. She was the sap for those types of things, and he'd always kidded her about being a Pollyanna in search of a white picket fence and the man and babies that went with it. If he appeared to have had a change of heart, it was only to get past her defenses. A skunk didn't change its stripes.

"Hey, this is it! I found it, everybody! Come look!"

Joey's triumphant shout brought them all running. Arriving on the scene two steps behind Josey, Cilla couldn't help but grin at the sight of Gable standing with his arms around his two sons and his daughter as the four of them turned expectantly to Josey. "Please, Mom," they all begged. "Ple-e-a-ase?"

"C'mon, Mom," Wyatt joined in teasingly. "It's not that big. Only twenty feet or so."

Cilla followed his gaze to the tree and almost choked on a laugh. Twenty feet wasn't much of an exaggeration. The thing wouldn't fit in the barn, let alone the house. "Uh, yeah, Mom," she chuckled, turning to Josey in anticipation. "It's not that big. All we have to do is trim it up a little."

"Trim?" Josey snorted. "You trim your toenails. We'll have to take the chain saw to that thing just to tie it to the back of the wagon. Are you guys sure this is what you want?"

As bad as the kids, Gable nodded and spoke for the group. "C'mon, honey. We can put every decoration we've got on this sucker. Whatdaya say?"

"What I say is Alice is going to kill us, but what the heck," she laughed. "I don't imagine she'll be too surprised."

"All right!"

"Quick, Wyatt, get the chain saw before she changes her mind!"

"Does this mean Santa's going to bring us more presents because we've got a bigger tree to put them under?"

Mandy, in the process of hustling her little brothers out of the way, looked down at Joey and grinned. "Only if you're a big sister, which you're not."

"Mom!"

The adults laughed and assured the boys that nobody knew for sure what Santa was going to bring, and then the chain saw was started, drowning out the kids' moans. Cilla and Josey circled the tree, pointing out spots that needed to be trimmed and shaped while Gable applied the saw where they directed. Minutes later, the huge juniper crashed to the ground like a freshly shaved but drunken cowboy.

"Now comes the hard part," Josey said once Gable hit the kill switch on the saw. "Getting it on the wagon. It's going to take up most of the back. Where are we all going to sit?"

"You can have our seat, Mom," the boys said quickly. "We want to walk."

"Me, too," Mandy chimed in. "It's not that far back to the house."

That left the front seat of the wagon for the adults, but there was no way it could hold all four of them. Voicing the thought, Gable's eyes began to dance. "We'll just have to double up. Josey can sit on my lap—"

"And Cilla can sit on mine," Wyatt finished for him, grinning like a cat with the canary feathers still sticking out of his mouth.

"Oh, no you don't," Cilla snapped, her brown eyes flashing. "I'll walk, thank you very much. Like the kids said, it's not very far."

Amused, he arched a brow at her. "What's the matter, Prissy? Scared?"

"Of you?" she tossed back. "Fat chance."

"Then there's no problem, is there? You can ride with the rest of us."

Too late, Cilla realized she'd walked right into a trap. And before she could find a way out, Gable and Wyatt were lifting the tree into the back of the wagon and tying it down. Minutes later, Gable was back in the driver's seat with Josey perched on his knee, and a grinning Wyatt, seated next to him, was leaning down to offer her a hand up.

Standing on the ground and staring up at him, her gaze caught on his mischievous grin, Cilla fought the need to step up into the wagon and into his arms. He was the only man who had ever been able to push her buttons and make her want him at one and the same time, and she'd missed him in her life. She hadn't realized how much until just now.

Staggered by the thought, she stared blindly at his broad, strong hand, her heart jumping crazily in her breast. How could he still have the power to do this to her? she wondered in confusion. She'd thought she was over him, through with him. Why, then, did just the thought of placing her hand in his and sitting on his lap make her go weak at the knees?

She should run, get out of here, and not stop until half the country was between them. It was the only way she knew for sure to protect her heart from him. But she was a woman now, not a seventeen-year-old child who wore her heart on her sleeve, and she didn't run from her emotions anymore. She stayed and faced them head-on, then put them behind her where they couldn't hurt her. And that, she promised herself, was what she was going to do with Wyatt.

Her chin lifting to a determined angle, she placed her hand in Wyatt's and had the satisfaction of seeing surprise flicker in his eyes. A slow smile curled the corners of her mouth. So he'd expected her to chicken out, had he? Maybe it was time she showed him that the Cilla Rawlings who had followed him around like a puppy during that long-lost summer could now hold her own with him or any other man. He wanted to flirt—she'd be more than happy to oblige him.

"Are you sure you want to do this?" she asked with a grin as he tugged her up in front of him and she settled gingerly on his knee. "People will talk."

"What people? There's nobody around but Gable and Josey and the kids."

Her lips twitching, Josey said solemnly, "And we won't say a word. Will we, honey?"

"Sure we will," he retorted teasingly. "As soon as we get back, I'm going to call Sydney and have the story put on the front page of the *Gazette*. By this time tomorrow, the whole county will know there's another hot romance brewing out at the Double R.''

His eyes only inches from Cilla's, Wyatt flashed his dimples at her. ''Is that what we've got going here, cousin? Another hot romance?''

She wanted to flat out deny it, but her heart was knocking so loudly against her ribs as he settled her more comfortably against him that she couldn't quite manage the lie. Instead, she leaned back as if she didn't have a care in the world and laughed with an ease that cost her more than he could possibly know. ''In your dreams, Chandler. In your dreams.''

Chapter Five

How she rode all the way back to the house without going quietly out of her mind, Cilla never knew. All her senses were on red alert and throbbing with awareness. And it was all Wyatt's fault. His arms and scent surrounded her, and every time the wagon hit a rut in the rough track, she was thrown back against the hard wall of his chest. She laughed along with the others, but inside, her heart was flip-flopping like a salmon at low tide.

This close, she could feel the power in him, the strength that left her breathless. He laughed at something Gable said, and she could almost trace the sound as it rippled through him like a summer wind through the desert grasses. It was unnerving, exhilarating. Her mouth suddenly dry, she couldn't stop herself from closing her eyes and savoring the feeling.

"She's gone off into the ozone again. Look—she's nodding off." Snapping his fingers in front of her face, Wyatt grinned. "Earth to Prissy. You with us, sweetheart? What planet are you on?"

Cilla blinked and came back to earth to find herself nose to nose with him. And from the glint in his eyes, she had a horrible feeling he knew exactly what she'd been doing. Mortified, she felt hot color surge into her cheeks and snapped, "Don't call me that!"

"What?" he quipped. "Prissy or sweetheart?"

"Both!"

"Don't tease her, Wyatt," Josey scolded, her lips twitching. "You know she hates to be called Prissy."

"That's why he does it," Cilla retorted, glaring at him. "Small minds are easily amused."

Unrepentant, his eyes laughed into hers. "Are you calling me a pea-brain?"

Despite her best efforts, Cilla felt her own lips twitch. "If the shoe fits . . ."

"Now, children, don't fight," Gable said with a chuckle. "Santa won't bring you any presents if you're bad."

His arms tightening playfully around Cilla, Wyatt drawled suggestively, "Then I guess I'll have to be very, very good. What do you say, sweetheart? Do you think I can be good?"

Unbidden, images of a long ago loving flashed before her eyes, taunting her. Good? she thought wildly. That didn't begin to describe what he could be when he set his mind to it. But she had no intention of telling him that. Looking down her nose at him, she drawled, "Not in a million years, Chandler."

The rest of the ride home passed in a blur for Cilla. Sitting stiff and straight on Wyatt's lap, she stared straight ahead, tension crawling through her like a troop of ants. Then the house came into view, and she felt they couldn't reach it fast enough. She needed some time to herself. Now! The second Gable brought the horses to a stop at the porch steps, she jumped up from Wyatt's lap.

"Cilla, wait—"

He reached to help her, but she was too quick for him. Scrambling over the side, she ignored his muttered curse and turned to Josey as she joined her on the porch. "Why don't I get the decorations out while the guys are getting the tree?"

Her eyes knowing, Josey nodded. "They're in the attic, but you won't be able to carry them all down by yourself—there are enough boxes of lights alone to fill a small truck. Let me supervise getting this monster onto its stand and into the house, and then I'll be up to help you."

The minute she stepped into the attic, Cilla saw it had changed little over the last ten years. Tucked up under the eaves and isolated from the rest of the house, it was filled with shadows and old furniture and musty smells of the past. It was here, as children, that she and Kat had spent hours playing dress-up in the vintage clothes they'd pulled from the dusty trunks that had belonged to long-forgotten Rawlingses. Then later, when they'd outgrown such childish games, the two of them had claimed the attic as their own special hideout from the boys. Here, they'd talked about school and boys and dances and first loves. They'd confided secret crushes to each other and dreams of the future and fantasized about the men they would marry.

Until that last summer Cilla had spent at the ranch. Then she'd never once mentioned Wyatt to her cousin or anyone else.

Stepping into the thick shadows that rose to the rafters, Cilla stared blindly at the cardboard boxes and discarded antiques and saw instead the past and a perfect summer—up until the end—stolen out of time. Long hot days. Secret kisses. Touches that nobody saw.

She'd been so young, so naive, so much in love that she'd thought no one else but Wyatt had suspected a thing. But looking back on it now, she knew she and Wyatt had been anything but discreet, and even the lowest ranch hand must have known what was going on. Now that horrified her. Then, she'd wanted him so badly that she wouldn't have batted an eye if the whole world had known.

Regrets and a sweet melancholy for what might have been stirred in her. Stepping over to an ornate dresser that had belonged to some nameless Rawlings woman near the turn of the century, she drew a heart in the thick coating of dust on the top with her index finger, then added C + W in the middle. A children's rhyme about a boy and girl sitting in a tree played softly in her head, bringing the sting of foolish tears to her eyes.

The sound of footsteps on the stairs behind her cut through her musings, jerking her roughly back to the present. Hastily swiping at her cheeks, she dragged up a shaky smile as she turned to face Josey. "I'd forgotten how much junk there was up here—"

But it wasn't Josey standing on the threshold watching her every move—it was Wyatt. And his sharp eyes had already picked up the tracks of her tears in the poor light. "Josey said you could use some help. What's wrong?"

"Nothing."

"Then why are you crying?"

"I'm not," she lied, turning away. "I just..." Frantically searching for an excuse, she froze as her gaze dropped to the dresser top where she'd traced their initials in the dust.

C + W

Lord, what was she going to do now? If he saw that childish message, he'd never let her live it down. She had to do something...erase it. But even as she glanced around for a rag to wipe it away, a voice in her head mocked, *You came up here for Christmas decorations, not to clean house. He'll think you've lost your mind.*

"You just what?" he prodded, stepping up behind her.

Panicking, she snatched an old straw hat from its hook on the wall. "I was just looking at all this old stuff and dust must have gotten in my eye," she said with a shrug. Pretending to examine the hat, she tossed it casually over the dust tracings on the dresser. "I guess Alice hasn't cleaned up here in awhile."

It was a logical explanation, but something about it didn't quite ring true. Frowning, Wyatt reached up to brush at the cobwebs that had caught in her hair. "You go downstairs looking like that, and everyone's going to be wondering what we've been doing up here."

It was a mistake, of course, touching her and thinking about what they could do together in the intimate, shadowy confines of the attic—he knew it the second his fingers brushed her forehead and the words left his mouth. He felt her stiffen, saw her eyes widen slightly, and should have let her go immediately. But suddenly images from the past—*need*—was there between them, as strong as the pull of the moon on the tides, and he could no more walk away from her than he could cut off his own arm.

His hand moved from the wisp of her bangs to the back of her neck. "Oh, God, Cilla, I've got to do this."

He didn't know if he was apologizing or warning her, he just knew that he had to kiss her. Now. Lowering his head, he swooped down and covered her mouth with his.

Like a chocoholic in desperate need of a fix, he promised himself that all it would take to satisfy him was one simple kiss. Nothing more. After all, the family was waiting downstairs—there wasn't time for anything else. If they didn't get down there soon with the decorations, someone would come looking for them. And while he didn't care who caught him kissing Cilla, he had a feeling Cilla wouldn't be too thrilled with the idea.

But the minute his lips touched hers, every logical thought he had slipped right out of his head. It seemed he'd been waiting days to hold her again, taste her again, lose himself in the heat and scent of her. Growling low in his throat, he gathered her close and nearly lost it right there and then. God, she felt good against him. So damn good. She fit in his arms as if she was made for him, the crush of her full breasts against his chest burning him from the inside out, her slender hips enticingly flush with his, trapping his arousal between them.

And then there was her mouth. No woman with such a seductive mouth had a right to be walking around free. He nipped at her full, sexy lower lip and something in her seemed to shatter. His name a hoarse, lost cry on her tongue, she kissed him back like a woman who had been alone too long, lonely too long. With heart and soul and all the scorching heat she had in her, she clung to him as if she would never let him go.

His arms tightened around her, madness pulling at him. He could have her . . . here, now, as he'd dreamed of having her ever since that first day when she'd stepped up on the porch and just the sight of her had nearly knocked him out of his shoes. She was as hot, as eager, as hungry as he was. And they were finally alone. All he had to do was sink down to the floor with her and give into—

"Hey, Wyatt! Cilla!" Gable suddenly called up the stairs teasingly. "What are you guys doing up there? Making the decorations from scratch?"

Lost to everything but the ache of desire that she had been denying for days, Cilla heard nothing but the rush of her blood in her ears. This was what her body had cried out for in the dark of the night for too long. Aching, yearning, she crowded closer, then Gable's words abruptly penetrated the sensuous fog that enveloped her brain and she thought she heard footsteps on the stairs. Jerking back with a gasp, she stared up at Wyatt in horror.

Quickly calling out to Gable that they'd be right down, he murmured, "Now don't get all bent out of shape on me, sweetheart. Gable doesn't suspect a thing. And it was just a kiss—"

"Just a kiss!" she squeaked, hurt squeezing her heart. God, if that wasn't just like him. He'd always dismissed what they'd shared as just a kiss, just a summer romance, just a fling. It—*she*—had never meant anything to him and never would. How many times did he have to hurt her before she got the message?

Angry tears stinging her eyes, she glared at him accusingly. "You haven't changed at all. Oh, you may have fooled the rest of the family, but I know better."

"Then you know more than I do. What the hell are you talking about?"

If she hadn't known him so well, she might have been fooled by his very real-looking confusion. But she knew better. "This perfect-family-man act of yours," she snapped in growing frustration. "Designing a room for Kat's babies, offering to help build it, getting the Christmas tree when you know you don't care two cents about the holidays—none of it fits. Josey thinks you've mellowed, that you might be ready to settle down—"

"But you don't think so," he said in a gravelly voice, his narrowed eyes locked with hers. "Do you?"

"No." She couldn't, because if she did, she'd lose her heart to him all over again, and that was a chance she couldn't take. Not again. "I've got to get out of here!" Turning her back on him, she looked distractedly around. "The decorations...God, I forgot all about them."

"They're over in the corner. Dammit, Cilla, if you'll just wait, I'll help you!"

But she had no intention of letting him get close enough to help. Hurrying over to the corner and the pile of boxes labeled Christmas Decorations, she snatched up as many as she could carry, then stepped around Wyatt as if he were a snake that could reach out and bite her any second. Uncaring that she was practically running from him, she hurried down the stairs.

His blood still hot, Wyatt stared after her and wondered what the hell had just happened. Except for earlier in the wagon, he had, much to his satisfaction, been careful to keep his distance all week. He hadn't touched her, flirted with her, or even made eye contact with her. He'd been damn proud of himself, and as the week had passed, he'd convinced himself that whatever feelings the lady still stirred in him, he could handle them with one hand tied behind his back. So sure of himself was he that when he'd come upstairs to help her, he'd have sworn kissing her was the last thing on his mind.

Dammit, he didn't even remember reaching for her!

Feeling like a man who had just fallen down a flight of stairs, he tried to tell himself that it was just chemistry. She'd grown into a beautiful woman, and his body had responded to her just as it would to any other gorgeous female. It was nothing personal.

Yeah, right. That's why you can't close your eyes at night without dreaming about the lady. Face it, man. You're lying through your teeth. All this time you thought you'd gone on with your life, you were really marking time, just waiting for the chance to see her again. You never got over her and you know it.

The truth hit him right between the eyes, stunning him. No, dammit! he thought, scowling. That was bull. He'd gone on with his life and left whatever he'd once felt for her far behind. But even as he tried to deny it, he couldn't forget the feel of her in his arms. She'd felt right, in a way no other woman ever had.

The sound of footsteps on the stairs intruded on his thoughts and he looked up to see Gable standing in the doorway, a puzzled look on his rugged face. "I thought you were getting the rest of the decorations. You need some help?"

"Yeah," he muttered grimly. "What I need is my head examined, but I don't think you can do much about that. You want to carry the little boxes or the big one?"

Blinking at the swift change of subject, Gable raised a brow in amusement. "The big one. Why do I feel as if I missed something here?"

"Because you did," Wyatt retorted, passing the largest of the boxes to him. "And that's all I'm going to say on the matter." Scooping up the last of the decorations, he headed for the stairs, only to give his cousin a fierce glare when he grinned knowingly at him. "What the devil are you grinning at?"

"Oh, nothing." Gable laughed, not the least offended. "You just look like you're coming down with something, and it hasn't been that long since I suffered the same symptoms. All I can tell you is that it's not nearly as fatal as it seems right now.''

"What the hell is that supposed to mean?''

Gable chuckled again, enjoying himself. "You'll figure it out soon enough. C'mon. We've got a tree to decorate.''

Wyatt followed him downstairs, half tempted to find some excuse to go off somewhere by himself rather than inflict his foul mood on the rest of the family. But the second he reached the living room, the kids surrounded him, chattering like magpies as they tore the boxes open and showed him their favorite ornaments.

"Look, Wyatt,'' Mandy said eagerly. "Uncle Cooper gave me this for my first Christmas. I've had it for years and years and years. Isn't it pretty?''

"It's just an old pony,'' one of the boys said dismissingly, crowding her out of the way. "My dinosaur is a lot better. Look, Wyatt. It's a T-rex. Isn't it great?''

Unable to spoil their fun, he grinned and ruffled the five-year-old's hair. "Yeah, great. I don't think I've ever seen something that fierce on a Christmas tree before, though. This is gonna be some tree.''

"You ain't seen nothing yet,'' Josey replied, chuckling. "Their uncles have this competition between them to see who can buy them the most outrageous ornament. So far, the T-rex seems to be the winner.''

"Are you guys going to stand there talking all day?'' Gable drawled from across the room. "Cilla and I could use some help with these lights. It looks like whoever put them up last year just threw them in the box for a rat to nest in.''

At his pointed look, a slow smile spread across Josey's face. "You took the tree down last year, honey," she reminded him gently. "Remember?"

Nonplussed, he just looked at her, then had the grace to laugh. "Like I said, someone just threw them in the box and I don't want to hear another word about it."

"Are you kidding?" Wyatt retorted teasingly as he and Josey both moved to help. "What else have you been blaming Josey for? Or don't you remember?"

Josey was quick to name a few things, and that started them all laughing as they untangled the lights and began the daunting job of decorating the huge tree. With the kids helping and everyone talking, no one but Wyatt seemed to notice that Cilla not only didn't once speak to him, but also managed not to get anywhere near him the entire time they were decorating the tree. Her conversation was directed to Gable or Josey, her laughter to the children. And when they were hanging bulbs and she looked up to find herself on the same side of the tree, she shied away from him and gave the ornament she held to one of the kids to hang. Seconds later, she disappeared to the other side of the tree.

Unable to take his eyes off her, Wyatt knew he couldn't put it off any longer. He had to give serious thought to what he was going to do about her. She thought he was the same man who had betrayed her ten years ago and she wasn't prepared to believe that he was anything but what she'd thought he was back then—an unprincipled bastard. She wanted to believe she hated his guts, but that hadn't stopped her from responding to him. He could, he knew, talk her into an affair, but that wasn't what he wanted, dammit! He wanted ... hell, he didn't know what he wanted!

Disgusted with himself, blaming Cilla for the sudden restlessness that was like an itch under his skin, he had withdrawn to the far side of the room to scowl at her when Flynn and Tate arrived. Tate immediately laughed over the size of the tree and waded through the boxes to help while Flynn, claiming he was going to supervise, joined Wyatt on the couch.

Taking one look at his cousin's set face, Flynn raised his eyebrows, his sapphire eyes dancing. "Something's got your tail in a snit. You want to talk about it?"

"No."

His answer was curt and tight and had Back Off written all over it. Not the least discouraged, Flynn followed Wyatt's gaze to Cilla and back again, the laughter in his eyes spreading to a broad grin. "Cilla's getting to you again, isn't she?"

"The hell she is!"

Stretching his legs out, Flynn nodded as if he hadn't spoken. "Yep, that's what it is. And it's damned uncomfortable, isn't it? Believe me, I know. When I found myself falling for Tate, it really shook me up. But nobody falls harder than a flirt, and now I wonder why I even tried to fight what was so right."

His jaw set in granite, Wyatt said through his teeth, "I never said I was falling for anyone."

"You didn't have to—it's written all over you." Flynn laughed. "And it couldn't happen to a more deserving guy. Come on, cousin, jump right in. Trust me. The water's fine."

Chapter Six

Half-expecting Wyatt to ambush her again the first chance he got, Cilla spent the next week looking over her shoulder. But he spent most of each day at Kat's with the rest of the men, working on the room addition, and she didn't know if she was relieved or disappointed. When they did chance to run into each other, he was always the one to end the conversation as soon as possible. And in his eyes was a wariness that hadn't been there before. A wariness that cut her to the bone.

Hurt, she tried to convince herself it was for the best. But still, she found herself looking for him, waiting for him, dreaming of him . . . and longing for the teasing banter they had once shared. It was gone, however, apparently forever, and Christmas was quickly approaching. She didn't see any way it was going to be a festive one.

If the family didn't notice that they were hardly speaking, they had good reason. For the second time in a week, Gable announced over supper, "Someone decorated another cactus."

That got everyone's attention. Over the course of the last seven days, someone had been decorating cactuses around the ranch with garlands and paper decorations. Flynn had discovered the first one near the ranch entrance the day after the Christmas tree was put up and everyone on the ranch had been questioned about it. No one had claimed responsibility, however, and since then, three more cactuses, including the latest, had been decked out for the holidays. The whole ranch was abuzz with the mystery.

"Where?" Mandy asked excitedly, her mouth full of Alice's chicken enchiladas.

"Just south of the clinic," her father said. "Wyatt and I saw it when we went over to Flynn's this afternoon."

"Is it like the last one?"

"Can we go see it after supper?"

"Were there any tracks?" Josey asked over the excited questions of the kids. "Whoever's doing this is bound to leave some kind of clue to his identity eventually."

"You'd think so," Wyatt agreed. "But we scouted the whole area and didn't find so much as a footprint. Whoever's doing this is darn clever."

"Maybe Santa sent one of his elves," Brian said hopefully, his supper forgotten at the thought.

Joey, wide-eyed as only a five-year-old can be, nodded. "Elves don't leave footprints, you know. They can come and go and no one ever sees them."

Cilla, struggling to hold back a smile along with the rest of the adults, nodded solemnly. "I've heard that, too, sweetie. You just may be right. Those elves can be pretty sneaky."

The children were more than willing to accept that explanation, but when small presents were left for all the kids on the front porch the following morning, the grown-ups started looking at each other with suspicious grins. Cilla knew she was innocent, though she wished she'd thought of the idea. Secrets were part of the fun of the holidays, and someone was making sure that this was a Christmas the Rawlings kids would never forget. The question was . . . who?

"Don't look at me," Josey said when Cilla confronted her as the two of them cleared the table after supper. "With the flu that's been going around and the clinic packed to the rafters from dawn until after dark, I haven't had time to turn around, let alone decorate cactuses or shop for extra presents. I thought you were doing it. Or Wyatt."

"Wyatt?" Cilla echoed, surprised. "I don't think so. Not that he hasn't been great with the kids and shown them a lot of attention, but frankly, I just can't see him playing one of Santa's helpers in the middle of the night. Flynn, maybe, but not Wyatt."

Josey shrugged. "You could be right about that. Flynn's just like one of the kids when it comes to surprises. When I see Tate at the clinic tomorrow, I'll ask her if he's been slipping out in the middle of the night." Cocking her head, she listened to the thunder of little feet running down the upstairs hall. "Speaking of kids, it sounds like mine are playing football in the hall again with their daddy instead of taking their baths. I'd better get up there. Save the dishes and I'll do them after I get the tribe in bed."

Cilla nodded, but she had no intention of acting like a pampered guest while everyone else worked. Alice had taken some food to a friend who was down with the flu and would be gone the rest of the evening, and Josey had had a long hard day at the clinic. The least she could do to help her, Cilla thought, was the dishes. So as soon as she was out of sight, she started loading the dishwasher.

With the water running and the clatter of dishes drowning out most of the sounds from the rest of the house, she never heard Wyatt step into the kitchen doorway from the dining room. Her attention focused on what she was doing, she rinsed out the pan that the enchiladas had been cooked in, then turned to load it in the dishwasher, only to jerk to a stop at the sight of Wyatt leaning against the doorjamb silently watching her every move.

Her heart stumbled to an abrupt stop in her chest, then jumped into an uneven rhythm that suddenly made breathing difficult. Dragging her attention back to the task at hand, she quickly placed the pan in the bottom rack, then turned off the water. In the sudden silence, the only sound was that of the kids upstairs calling to Gable for a bedtime story.

When she glanced back to the doorway, he was still there, his gaze steady and unblinking. He stared at her as if he was seeing her for the first time in years, and something about his very stillness caused her throat to tighten in apprehension. "What?" she demanded with a quizzical smile as she glanced down at herself, then back up again. "What is it? Do I have on two left shoes or what? Why are you looking at me that way?"

He straightened but never moved away from the doorway. "I've been thinking about the other day in the attic."

Caught off guard, she frowned. "We've already discussed this, Wyatt. There's nothing left to say."

She started to turn back to the dishes, but he stopped her without even touching her. "You think so? Then try this on for size. I've been giving it a lot of thought, and I realize that I never really got over you."

Wide-eyed, Cilla stared at him as if he'd lost his mind. "This is a joke, isn't it? You're just pushing my buttons again, the way you always do."

He should have laughed, or at the very least, gotten that wicked glint in his eyes that always made her want to smile. But he merely looked at her, his expression dead serious. "Do I look like I'm joking?"

No, God help her, he didn't. Her heart pounding out a frenzied jungle beat in her breast, she paled. "Then I'd say you've got a problem," she retorted. "Because you may think you never got over me, but I *know* I got over you. So this conversation is pointless."

For the first time, the glimmer of a smile flirted with the corners of his mouth. "Somehow I had a feeling you'd say that. But in case you've forgotten, there's the matter of a couple of kisses—"

"I haven't forgotten anything!" she retorted. "Not a single moment of that day when I walked in the barn and found you with another woman. So don't talk to me about a couple of kisses. I lost my head—that's all. It won't happen again."

Undaunted by her sudden fury, he said, "For someone who claims to hate my guts, you've got an awful lot of passion in you, sweetheart. And I can think of only one reason for that—you feel the same way about me that I feel about you—"

"No!"

"Yes," he insisted. "I thought I'd gone on with my life and forgotten all about you, but the minute I saw you again, I knew I'd just been killing time for the last ten years, waiting until our paths crossed again. And I'm willing to bet you've been doing the same thing. Face it, honey. We were made for each other, like it or not."

Caught in the trap of his steady gaze, she wanted to laugh, to scoff at the very idea that she could still be carrying a torch for him after all these years. But somewhere deep inside her, his words struck a nerve, scaring her to death. Suddenly terribly afraid he might be right, she lifted her chin. "The only thing I'm facing right now is these dishes." Turning her back on him, she deliberately reached for another pot.

She appeared totally focused on the task at hand, but all her senses were tuned to where Wyatt stood frowning in the doorway silently watching her. She didn't need to look over her shoulder to know that he was still there—she could feel his eyes on her, touching her, watching her, studying her. Then, in a voice as rough as the gravel road that led from the highway to the main house, he growled, "Fine, if that's the way you want it. But I'm giving you fair warning, Cilla. I'm not giving up on you. One way or the other, I'm going to win you back."

Cilla didn't hear him walk out, but she knew the second he was gone. Suddenly the kitchen was empty and quiet, and she was alone, just as she had been for the last ten years. The pride that had refused to let her tremble before him vanished. Shaking, she dropped the pot she'd been holding and hugged herself.

She didn't care what he said, he wasn't serious, she told herself fiercely. At least not about pursuing what they had once had. A rattler didn't change its spots and he'd proven a long time ago that he was nothing but a snake in the grass. He talked about winning her back, but all he really wanted was her back in his bed. That's all he'd ever wanted from her, and once she'd given him her heart and soul, the thrill had gone out of the chase and he'd turned to someone else. History was not going to repeat itself, she vowed grimly. A man who had done that to a woman once would do it again, and there was no way on earth she was going to let herself fall for him a second time. She didn't care how desperately he made her want him.

Her spine stiff with resolve, she heard Gable and Josey coming down the stairs and quickly finished the dishes, then joined them in the family room, where they usually relaxed over cups of hot chocolate after the kids were in bed. Wyatt was already there and looked up the minute she entered. Her eyes locked with his, the thumping of her heart loud in his ears. She was half-afraid he would say something about their conversation in the kitchen, but he only asked Gable about a renegade bull that kept making a break for it every chance he got. From there, the conversation shifted to the newest pepper hybrid the family planned to plant in the spring to speculation on when and where the mysterious cactus decorator would strike again.

Not once over the course of the next few hours did Wyatt say or do anything that could be considered the least bit flirtatious. He rarely even looked at her. Still, Cilla was a nervous wreck. Seated as far from him as possible, her heart tripping over itself every time he opened his mouth, she kept waiting for something that never happened. By the time ten o'clock rolled around, she was exhausted.

"I hate to break up the party, guys, but I've got to call it a night," she said the second there was a lull in the conversation. "I'm bushed."

"Ah, c'mon," Josey protested. "It's early yet."

Uncomfortably aware of Wyatt's eyes following her every move, she set her barely touched hot chocolate on the serving tray Josey had carried from the kitchen earlier and rose to her feet. "Blame it on the hot chocolate," she said, forcing a smile. "I can hardly keep my eyes open."

"Party pooper," Gable teased. "Admit it, it was the shoptalk about the peppers that did it, wasn't it? You're not sleepy. You're just bored out of your mind."

"If I was bored, I would have been snoring by now," she retorted, grinning. "'Night, guys. See you in the morning."

She turned, only to have her gaze clash with Wyatt's. Her smile faltered, but Josey was already rising to her feet and talking about going up, too, and nobody else saw. Feeling as if she'd just escaped a close brush with something she didn't even want to put a name to, she hurried up the stairs.

Midnight had come and gone when Wyatt soundlessly opened Cilla's bedroom door and slipped inside. Silence engulfed him, thick and warm and hushed, making the drumming of his heart loud in his ears. Giving his eyes a few seconds to adjust to the change in light, he leaned back against the closed door and waited until the shadows that filled the room sharpened into recognizable shapes. With the glow of a full moon streaming through the open curtains at the wide windows that took up half of the far wall, it didn't take long.

The room, he saw in a single, all-encompassing glance, was pretty much the same as his. Large and airy, with nine-foot ceilings and old cedar-plank flooring, it was furnished with a massive, intricately carved antique walnut bedroom set that would have overpowered a room in a more modern house but hardly made a dent here. The bed was tall, with posters, and at least two feet off the floor. And lying in the middle of the huge mattress, covered by a patchwork quilt that was at least a hundred years old, was Cilla.

With her face half-buried in the pillow she clutched to her breast, and her hair a tangle of dark curls around her head, she looked like a little girl who had simply run out of gas at the end of the day. Soft and vulnerable, her lips parted softly in sleep, she was dead to the world.

Transfixed, Wyatt couldn't drag his eyes away from her. He'd never seen her like this. All those years ago, when they hadn't been able to keep their hands off each other, they'd snatched every stolen moment they could together, but they'd never actually slept together. Not once. And he hadn't noticed the loss until now.

Unable to resist her, he pushed away from the door and quietly moved to the side of the bed. Itching to touch her, to crawl under the covers with her and slowly bring her to wakefulness, he clenched his hands into fists and had to be content with stroking her with his eyes instead. Because if he made the mistake of giving in to the need to touch her, he'd never be able to stop with just that.

God, she was beautiful! Now that he was closer, he could see the flush of sleep that stained her cheeks, the way her lashes lay like sooty smudges against her skin. She murmured something, then sighed and drifted deeper, and never had a clue that he was there. Was it him she dreamed of? he wondered, then had to grin. Fat chance. If she did, she'd probably cast him as the main monster in a nightmare.

But his time was coming, he promised himself confidently. She could ignore him, run from him, look him right in the eye and lie through her teeth about her feelings for him, but they both knew that what they'd once felt for each other was as strong as ever. And it was only a matter of time before he made her admit it. Where they went from there, God only knew.

For now, though, he had another problem. He had to find a way to wake her without giving in to the yearning that burned low in his gut.

"Cilla?"

His voice sounded loud in the darkness in spite of the fact that he kept it pitched deliberately low so that he wouldn't scare her. But she didn't move by so much as a flicker of an eyelash. Frowning, he stepped closer to the bed, stopping a good two feet away. "Priscilla? Wake up. Do you hear me? I need to talk to you."

His only answer was a soft snore.

He was, he promised himself, going to kill her. But first he had to wake her up. His jaw clenched on an oath, and he eliminated the distance between the bed and himself with a single step and reached for her. "Dammit, Prissy, why didn't anybody tell me you were such a deadhead? What do I have to do to wake you up? Throw a glass of water in your face?"

From the dark depths of sleep, Cilla thought she heard Wyatt call to her from a long way off. Stirring slightly, she turned her face more fully into her pillow, a frown skimming across her brow. He'd followed her into her dreams, she told herself groggily. Again. And this time she didn't have the strength to wake up and make him leave her alone. Later, she promised herself. When she wasn't so tired.

"Dammit, woman, don't make me crawl into bed with you. Wake up!"

What did he mean...*crawl into bed with her?* He was a dream, so he was already in bed with her, she thought drowsily. Then he touched her, his hand settling at her shoulder to give her a quick shake, and a frown furrowed her brow. He felt so real! But that was impossible, she silently argued as she swam up from the depths of sleep. He might dare just about anything, but not even Wyatt would sneak into her room in the middle of the night when Gable and Josey and the kids were sleeping just down the hall.

"I can't believe this," he muttered. "The one time I'm trying to do the right thing—"

She felt the bed dip, his breath against her face, and suddenly she was wide awake. Her eyes flew open and she looked up to see Wyatt bending over her in the dark, his jaw set with determination. Startled, she gasped. "What do you think you're doing?"

"Now, don't get all bent out of shape," he began quickly. "I can explain—"

"Explain?" she echoed in growing outrage as she scrambled to sit up and jerk the covers up to her chin. "What's there to explain? I caught you red-handed, crawling into my bed!"

His mouth twitched at that. "Believe me, sweetheart, if I really was crawling into your bed, I wouldn't have to sneak around to do it—you'd invite me in. And you wouldn't be complaining about it, either—I'd make sure of it. I was trying to wake you up, dammit!"

"Sure you were. Tell me another one, Chandler. I didn't just fall off the hay wagon yesterday, you know. I know what you're up to."

"You don't know squat, sweetheart. The only reason I'm in here is to tell you Kat's gone into labor."

"What? Don't be ridiculous. The babies aren't due for another couple of months."

"You can tell them that when they get here later in the morning," he tossed back, grinning. "In the meantime, Cooper and Flynn are bringing their tribes over here so the two of us can baby-sit while everyone else goes to the hospital. So get your pretty little butt out of that bed, honey. We've got work to do."

Chapter Seven

It was three o'clock in the morning and the family room at the back of the house was wall-to-wall kids in their pajamas. Gable's three should have been asleep in their beds, but somehow they'd instinctively known the second their cousins arrived, and within minutes, they were downstairs and ready to play. Cilla had tried to talk them all into going back to bed, but her pleas had fallen on deaf ears. The boys had dragged out their toy trucks, Mandy and Haily had pulled out building blocks for the toddlers, and before Cilla quite knew how it happened, they had a day care up and running in the middle of the night.

"C'mon, guys, I know you're not used to being up at this time of the night. Why don't you put up the toys and go on up to bed? It's way past your bedtime."

She might as well have been talking to herself. The only one who paid the slightest bit of attention to her was sixteen-year-old Haily, who was building a castle for the younger kids. "It's okay, Cilla. Mandy and I are the only ones who have to go to school tomorrow, and it's our last day before Christmas vacation starts. No one will care if we're a little sleepy. We're not going to do anything, anyway."

"But—"

"You're wasting your time, sweetheart," Wyatt drawled in her ear as he came up behind her from the kitchen with a bowlful of popcorn. "You don't try to reason with rug rats—you bribe 'em." The smell of the popcorn preceding him into the family room, he walked over to the couch and immediately had everyone's attention.

"Popcorn! All right! Can we have some?"

They rushed him like a bunch of young puppies that had just spotted dinner, all of them chattering at once. Laughing, he held the huge bowl of popcorn out of reach. "Hold it! Nothing's free in this world, you greedy little beggars. We're going to make a deal first. You get popcorn and a story and then everyone goes to bed. Okay? And that means no arguments. Got it?"

Six heads nodded solemnly. Holly, Cooper and Susannah's toddler who would be two on Christmas Eve, couldn't have cared less about making a deal. Climbing up on Wyatt like he was some type of jungle gym, she scrambled up his chest and balanced herself by grabbing his hair. "Gimme," she said with a big baby grin. "Now."

Laughing, he dropped two pieces into her free hand, then arched a brow at the others. "Well? What's it gonna be?"

"Aw, Wyatt, do we have to?"

"We get two new cousins tonight. Can't we at least wait up to see if they're going to be boys or girls or one of each?"

"Nope," he said emphatically. "Popcorn, a story, then bed. Take it or leave it."

Grumbling, they gave in, but only after Mandy warned with a cheeky grin, "We're talking about a really cool story, right? Not Goldilocks or something silly like that?"

His lips twitched, but he held back the smile that threatened and nodded. "No Goldilocks. Scout's honor." Scooping Holly down into his lap, he plopped the bowl of popcorn down in front of her so the rest of the kids could reach it. "Okay, who wants to hear about the night Santa forgot his glasses and got lost when he was delivering presents?"

"I do! I do! Where did he get lost?"

"Right here in New Mexico," he said promptly. "Just down the road, in fact. It was a cold and rainy night...."

Silently slipping into a chair across the room, Cilla watched the children's rapt faces as they quickly settled in a circle around Wyatt, spellbound as he began a story about the year Santa ended up just miles from the Double R because he didn't have his glasses and couldn't read his map. According to him, it was Cooper, Flynn and Gable who found him, acted as his navigators, and helped him deliver presents all over the world.

He was doing this for her benefit, Cilla desperately tried to tell herself. This was just another trick to make her think he was no longer the irresponsible flirt who flitted from one girl to the next without a thought to the one he left behind. If she was gullible enough to fall for it, he would be all over her like candy on a candied apple the first chance he got. Then when Christmas was over and they both went home to their own lives, she would once again be the one with the broken heart because he would walk away without a backward glance. All this talk about having changed was just that...talk. And talk was cheap.

But even as she tried to convince herself that she couldn't trust him as far as she could throw him, her eyes kept drifting to the children's faces. As he got to the part about their parents helping Santa when they were kids, the popcorn was forgotten. They stared up at him in hushed silence, hardly daring to breathe and chance missing a word, totally captivated. Cilla wanted to believe that it was just the part about Santa and their parents that fascinated the kids, but her conscience balked at that. Kids were pretty smart and it wasn't easy to fool them. They could see through a phony in the blink of an eye. If they thought Wyatt was stringing them along, they wouldn't just sit there and let him weave a spell around them. They trusted him and were just as charmed by him as they were by the story.

If this was the type of father he would make, his kids would adore him.

The thought slipped past her guard as silently as Santa slipped from one house to the other every Christmas Eve, catching her unaware, intriguing her before she could dismiss such a foolish notion. Too late, she found herself looking at him with different eyes, and it was all too easy to imagine that at least some of the kids surrounding him were his own. And hers.

Alarm bells went off in her head so loudly she was sure he must have been able to hear them from where he sat. But when he glanced up at her, he only grinned and winked, then went back to the story without ever noticing that she was staring at him like a woman who had just been run over by a Mack truck. No! she cried silently. Dear God, what was she doing? She didn't want to think about him that way. She didn't want to imagine what their children would look like or see his face and hers in the features of babies that didn't even exist. It was too painful, too intriguing, too late.

Caught up in her imaginings, she never noticed that the story had ended or that most of the younger children had quietly fallen asleep. Then he looked over at Cilla and grinned, his green eyes sparkling with satisfaction. "Looks like it worked," he said softly. "Think we should leave them down here or carry them up to bed?"

Cilla blinked at the sight of Holly and Christopher, Flynn's three-year-old, asleep in his lap. Lainey and Gable's boys were yawning and fighting a losing battle to keep their eyes open, and Mandy and Haily weren't far behind. Warmed by the glint in his eyes, she flushed and quickly bolted to her feet. "They're probably going to be here for the rest of the night, so we might as well take them up. They'll sleep better. Haily, sweetie, can you help us get everybody upstairs?"

A sixteen-year-old version of her mother, Tate, Haily nodded sleepily and reached for Christopher. "Sure. Gosh, it's really late, isn't it? You think Aunt Kat's had the babies yet?"

"Probably not," Wyatt said as he struggled to his feet with a limp Holly in his arms. "We would have heard something, and babies like to take their own good time getting here, especially when there's two of them."

Putting an arm around Mandy's shoulders when she stared blankly at the stairs as if she had never seen them before, Cilla chuckled and said, "Come on, Mandy, girl. Up to bed, sweetheart, before you fall on your face."

"I'm okay. Really."

The eight-year-old was weaving on her feet and would never be able to navigate the stairs alone, but Cilla only fought back a grin and suggested, "Then maybe you could help me up. It's been a long night and I'm bushed."

"Oh...sure," she said, shuffling in the general direction of the stairs. "I'm kinda tired, too."

With Haily's help, they finally got everyone into bed and tucked in, all without a single word of protest out of anyone. The upstairs was hushed and dark, with only a small table lamp left on in the hall in case anyone woke up and was scared. Hesitating at the top of the stairs after Wyatt had gone back downstairs and Haily had quietly wished her a good-night and gone off to her own bed, Cilla knew she should do the same. But she was wide awake, and something in her rebelled at the thought of scurrying off to her room just because she didn't want to go downstairs and be alone with Wyatt. After all, Kat was her cousin, too. If she wanted to stay up and wait for word from the hospital, she could.

Defiantly, she went down to the family room, only to find it empty. Surprised, she went looking for Wyatt and found him pouring himself a cup of coffee in the kitchen. At her entrance, he arched a brow. "I thought you went to bed."

"I wouldn't be able to sleep, worrying about Kat," she said simply. "I was hoping we would have heard something by now."

"We would have if something was wrong," he assured her. Pouring her a cup, he pushed it across the breakfast bar. "Here. Have some coffee."

She hesitated. She really didn't want any caffeine this late at night, but she couldn't just stand there and stare at him. Moving to the breakfast bar, she took a seat, then spent the next thirty seconds stirring creamer into her coffee. When she looked up, Wyatt was openly staring at her and making no apologies for it.

Her heart suddenly skipping a beat, she frowned at him. "What are you doing?"

He grinned. "Looking at you. You know, Prissy, you grew up into a darn good-looking woman. Any of the men in your life take the time to tell you that?"

"If they did, it's none of your business," she retorted, fighting the smile he pulled from her so easily. "Dammit, Wyatt, stop that! I know what you're doing and it's not going to work."

"Oh, I don't know about that," he drawled, his dancing eyes crinkling with amusement at her over the rim of his coffee cup as he took a sip. "Looks like it's working to me. You wear a blush better than any woman I know."

"And you know a lot, don't you?" she replied sweetly.

If she'd hoped to put him in his place, she might as well have saved herself the trouble. Not the least offended, he only grinned in pleased delight. "Jealousy rears its ugly head. And here I thought you didn't care."

That struck too close to the bone. Irritated with herself for letting him get to her, she set her coffee cup down with a snap. "I think I'll play some cards to pass the time. Solitaire," she said pointedly.

Not giving him time to comment, she strode out of the kitchen into the den and found a pack of cards in the built-in cabinet by the fireplace. She heard Wyatt moving around in the kitchen, but she studiously ignored him and sat down on the floor at the coffee table to shuffle the cards.

Her concentration was shot, but she laid the cards out and frowned down at them as if her only care in the world was matching a red queen to a black king. She never looked up, but all her senses were attuned to Wyatt as he followed her into the den and laid a couple more logs on the fire. Seconds later, a light on the far side of the room was switched off, then another one by the TV. Just that easily, the atmosphere was warm and intimate.

But it wasn't until he sat down on the couch, though, his feet just inches behind where she sat on the carpeted floor, that her nerve endings vibrated in warning. He was close. Too close. She only had to lean back mere inches to find herself resting intimately against his knee and thigh. Her hands suddenly trembling, she turned up a card and automatically moved it to an open spot without sparing it a glance.

"You can't put that there. A red seven has to go on a black eight."

Startled by his soft, husky growl, she jumped. "What?"

"The red seven," he repeated patiently. "You laid it on a red eight. You can't do that. It has to be a black one."

Lost, hardly hearing him for the thumping of her heart in her breast, Cilla frowned down at the cards spread out before her. "What red seven?"

"This one." Leaning over, he reached around her, his arm brushing hers and nearly circling her shoulders as he pointed out her mistake. "See?"

Her mouth dry, Cilla couldn't have answered if her life had depended on it. Unable to drag her eyes from the strong masculine hand that hovered mere inches from hers, she nodded dazedly. When had he moved so close? He wasn't touching her, not really, yet she would have sworn she could feel his hard chest against her shoulders and the heat of him seeping into her, warming her, melting her bones.

And his scent...God, it was just as she remembered it. Clean and spicy and all man. She'd tried her best to forget him over the years, but nothing had driven the scent of him from her head. She'd lost track of the number of times over the years when she'd stepped into a crowded elevator or restaurant and found her senses assaulted by a whiff of a cologne that was all too familiar. And every time, her heart took off at a gallop and her eyes looked for him before she could stop herself.

There'd been so many things about him that she'd missed, and she hadn't even realized it until now. The size and strength and sheer magnetism of him, not to mention what it felt like to have him hold her. How could she have forgotten? Other men had held her, but no one had ever made her feel the way he did when he put his arms around her. Safe and treasured. Needed. If she leaned back a few centimeters, she could feel that way again....

Don't you dare, Cilla Rawlings! a voice snapped in her ear. *You let that man touch you now, and you're a goner for sure. Wake up and smell the coffee, for God's sake. He's already warned you he wants to take up where you left off. That means* bed, *Cilla.* B-e-d. *A roll in the sack, nothing more. Is that what you want?*

She never remembered moving, but suddenly she was across the room and switching on the TV. She wanted noise, and lots of it. Enough to drown out the frantic cadence of her heart and her jumbled thoughts. "I was never very good at card games anyway," she said in a shaky voice she hardly recognized as her own. "I'd rather watch an old movie on TV."

Not bothering to hide a grin, Wyatt gathered up the cards and propped his feet on the coffee table. His arms stretched out on either side of him along the back of the couch, he drawled, "Oh, good. Why don't you turn the rest of the lights out and we'll neck."

Damn him, he would not make her laugh! Struggling to keep her expression impassive, she said, "I'd rather kiss a randy goat."

"B-a-a-a-a."

"Dammit, Wyatt—"

Grinning, he clicked his tongue at her. "No cussing, sweetheart. The children are just upstairs."

She laughed. She couldn't help it. What was she supposed to do with such an impossible man? "Then don't push your luck, Chandler. And don't call me sweetheart." Choosing a seat at the far end of the couch, she stared pointedly at the television and silently promised herself she wasn't going to say another word to him. Then the opening credits for *White Christmas* rolled onto the screen.

Stifling a groan, Cilla couldn't believe her miserable luck. First *It's a Wonderful Life* the night she arrived, now this. Why did they have to show all the sentimental movies at Christmas, for heaven's sake? Didn't they know that some people just couldn't take it? She knew the whole movie by heart and could quote the dialogue word for word, but she still got misty-eyed at the end. And it wasn't a movie she watched with a man. Especially one like Wyatt. He would make fun of the singing and the hokiness of the story and all the parts she loved, then tease her about crying over a movie that wasn't even a tearjerker.

She couldn't take it, she decided. Not tonight, when they were alone together and the house was dark and quiet and she only had to reach out to touch him. She was too vulnerable, too aware of him, too emotional. Leaning forward, she reached for the remote control on the coffee table.

"Hey, what are you doing that for? I thought you liked that movie!"

"I do, but I've seen it a zillion times. There's bound to be something else on."

"But you love all that syrupy holiday stuff. Turn it back on."

"I'd rather watch a spaghetti western," she retorted, deliberately switching channels and scanning the airwaves. "There's bound to be one on somewhere. There always is this time of night."

"But I want to watch Bing!"

"You do not. You just want to make fun—hey, give that back!"

He snatched the remote out of her hand before she could do anything but gasp, switched the channel back to *White Christmas,* then shoved the remote into the back pocket of his jeans. His grin wicked, he taunted softly, "You want it? Go for it, sweetheart. I dare you."

He didn't think she would—she could see the cockiness in his eyes, but it was the middle of the night and she was too tired to think clearly. Impulsively rising to the bait, she threw herself across his lap and reached around behind him for the remote.

Like a well-oiled trap that was sprung by a whisper of movement, his arms instantly closed around her.

Grinning down into her startled eyes, he growled, "Gotcha."

Her heart stopped in mid-beat, then stumbled into a frenzied flutter as he tangled his hand in her hair and slowly started to lower his mouth to hers. Stiffening, she wedged a hand against his chest and glared at him. "Is this the latest Chandler technique? You have to trick a woman in order to kiss her?"

"Only you, sweet pea," he admitted with a chuckle. "And I wouldn't have to do that if you gave me any other choice. Every time I think I've got you to myself, you take off running the other way. Kiss me, honey. You wouldn't believe how long I've been starving for another taste of you."

"No—"

His mouth smothered hers, cutting off her protests, scrambling her brain. Every time he held her, kissed her, it was like the first time. She didn't understand it, couldn't explain it. She just knew she couldn't resist the need he stirred in her so effortlessly. With a murmur that could have been his name, she wrapped her arms around him, hugging him as if she would never let him go. But still, she wasn't close enough. Shifting restlessly, she kissed him back hungrily, wanting, needing, more.

Wyatt groaned low in his throat as she moved against him, the feel of her breasts against his chest setting him afire. God, she was sweet. And so hot she made him ache. She could have made him beg if she'd only known it, and that was something he could say about no other woman.

And he had to have her. Now! Muttering a curse, need clawing at him, he pulled her completely across his lap and rolled with her on the overstuffed couch. A split second later, he had her right where he wanted her...under him.

Chapter Eight

The sudden ringing of the phone was like the scream of a fire alarm in the heated silence. His hand already sliding under the hem of Cilla's T-shirt, Wyatt froze, the string of rough, muttered curses that fell from his tongue turning the air blue. "I don't believe this! Ignore it, dammit!"

But even as he said it, he knew they couldn't. At this hour of the night, it couldn't be anyone but one of the cousins at the hospital with Kat. "Forget I said that," he said through his teeth as he rolled off her and pushed to his feet. "It's probably Gable."

Stepping into the kitchen, he jerked up the receiver of the wall phone and growled, "Yeah?"

For a moment, there was nothing but silence, then Gable said wryly, "I'm not going to ask if I interrupted anything—obviously, I did."

"Stuff it, Rawlings," Wyatt grumbled, reluctant amusement easing the tight set of his jaw. "How's Kat?"

"Beaming like a proud mama. She came through it like a champ, but she's a whipped puppy. We're going to get out of here in a couple of seconds and let her get some sleep."

"And the babies? Everything okay there?"

"Yeah, thank God. She had two boys—Nathan and Alex—and they barely topped out at four pounds apiece. Right now their names are bigger than they are, but the doctors say they're healthy. They won't be able to go home for a couple of weeks, but that seems to be par for the course with preemies."

"Good. Tell her congratulations for Cilla and me. Lucas holding up okay?"

Gable laughed softly. "I don't think he's going to want to repeat the experience anytime soon, but right now, he's ten feet off the ground. Did the kids give you two any trouble?"

"Not after they got popcorn and a story," he said with a chuckle. "Everybody crashed after that, and we haven't heard a peep out of any of them in the last hour."

"Good. Since it's so late, we thought we'd all just stay in town for the rest of the night—if that's all right with you and Cilla," he quickly added. "It's already going on four and even if we left right now, we wouldn't get in till close to dawn."

"Don't sweat it," Wyatt assured him. "There's no need for you to rush back when everybody's asleep. We'll just go on to bed and see you in the morning."

"Good idea," Gable agreed. "If you need to get in touch with us, we'll be at the Town and Country Motor Lodge. The number's in the book."

Standing in the kitchen doorway listening to Wyatt's side of the conversation, Cilla watched him hang up the phone and assured herself that he couldn't have possibly just told Gable that they were going to bed together. He still had her on her heels from that kiss, that was all. She'd just misunderstood. Frowning, she said carefully, "Kat had the babies? Are they okay? What did you mean we'd see Gable in the morning? Is there a problem? Is that why no one's coming home tonight?"

"Yes, Kat had two little boys, and no, there's not a problem." Giving her a quick rundown of the situation, he added, "I didn't think you'd mind if I told them to go ahead and stay in town for the rest of the night. The kids are out for the count. Considering how late they went to bed, they probably won't start straggling downstairs in the morning until at least ten, and by then, their parents will be back."

Mind? she almost echoed shakily. Of course she minded! But not because she didn't want to baby-sit. Things had already nearly gotten out of hand and that was when they both knew that Gable and the others could have returned at any moment. Now they were going to be alone for the rest of the night, and the only chaperons were seven sleeping kids upstairs. God, what was she going to do?

Nothing, she decided, squaring her shoulders. If she showed the least nervousness, he would tease her unmercifully and take the first opportunity to get her back in his arms. And if he touched her again tonight, she didn't think she'd be able to summon up the strength to push him away. Not when she still ached for him deep inside.

"Of course I don't mind," she lied easily. "I would have suggested the same thing if I'd talked to Gable.

Everyone's had a long night and there's no use anyone getting on the highway at this time of night unless it's an emergency, which it isn't. Why don't you lock up down here and get the lights while I check on the kids?''

"No problem," he said just as easily. "I'll be up in a few seconds."

Cilla planned to be safely in her own room by then, but she didn't tell him that. Quickly hurrying up the stairs, she started at the first room on the left, where the lights of Flynn and Tate's eyes—Haily and Christopher—were sleeping. Checking on them should have been as simple as opening the door and taking a quick peak inside, but Christopher was out from under the covers and already curled up like a puppy. By morning, he'd be chilled. Rushing over to him, she pulled the quilt up, waited a second to make sure she hadn't disturbed him, then stepped back out into the hall.

The whole procedure took all of twenty seconds and shouldn't have slowed her down. But at every other room she came to, there was something that wasn't quite right that drew her inside. Holly, who still slept with a pacifier, had lost it in the dark and was whimpering in her sleep as she searched for it. And then there was Joey, who had a reputation for being a restless sleeper. He'd kicked all the covers off his bed and hung half off the mattress himself. One wrong move and he'd go tumbling to the floor and no doubt wake the whole house with his howls.

"What are you doing?"

In the process of trying to lift the five-year-old back onto the bed without waking him, she didn't hear Wyatt soundlessly step into the room. Startled, she gasped and nearly dropped Joey, who was rock-solid and limp as a dishrag. "I was afraid he was going to roll off the bed," she gasped in a hushed whisper.

"Here, let me help you."

Lightning quick, he was at her side and taking most of the boy's weight as they lifted him back onto his pillow. Sighing in contentment, he snuggled down, hunched his little bottom in the air, then didn't move so much as an eyelash again.

Cilla couldn't help but grin at him, but when she quietly stepped out into the hallway with Wyatt right on her heels, her heart was thundering with expectations she didn't dare analyze too closely. "Well, that seems to have been the last of them," she said with a cheerfulness that sounded more than a little forced. "Guess we might as well turn in."

"Good idea," Wyatt agreed. Grinning broadly, he reached for her. "Now, where were we?"

She moved, but not quickly enough. Scowling at him, she tried not to laugh. "*We* weren't anywhere."

"Oh, yes we were. If I remember correctly, we were right here." Pulling her into his arms, he smiled down into her eyes. "Now all we have to do is get horizontal."

When he looked at her like that, it was all she could do not to go boneless in his arms. Feeling herself weakening, she warned, "I'm not going to bed with you just because we've got the place to ourselves except for the kids.''

''Of course you're not,'' he said promptly, lowering his head to nip playfully at her ear. ''You're going to bed with me because it's what we both want.''

''No!''

''Yes,'' he murmured against her neck. ''Admit it, honey. You know it's true. We've both been waiting for this moment ever since you got here.''

She wanted to deny it. She would, in fact, have given anything to tell him that the only thing she'd been waiting for was for him to realize that whatever feelings she'd once felt for him had long since been left behind with ankle socks and her high-school pompoms. But the words just wouldn't come. Because, God help her, he was right. There'd always been a sense of inevitability about her relationship with him. From the first moment she'd met him all those years ago, she'd known he was the only man for her. And nothing had changed. She wanted him, heart and soul. In spite of the past. In spite of the fact that he didn't seem to be interested in anything but a steamy holiday affair. He would hurt her again; she knew that as well as she knew just where to touch him to make him groan. But when he held her and kissed her like there was no tomorrow, none of that seemed to matter.

''I used to wait up for Santa on Christmas Eve, too,'' she told him huskily, holding him off even as she fought the need to melt against him, ''but I always woke up disappointed in the morning.''

He laughed softly, the sound a moist, erotic caress against her throat. "I can't promise that you'll see Santa, but I'm not bragging when I guarantee that you won't wake up disappointed. Where are you going?"

"To my room." Slipping out of his arms before he could stop her, she almost made it. But two steps from her door, he quickly sidestepped around her and she plowed right into his chest. Chuckling, he gathered her close. "Sweetheart, you don't have to throw yourself at me. I'm not going anywhere without you."

"Dammit, Wyatt, I am *not* going to bed with you!"

Even to her own ears, the protest sounded pitifully weak, but instead of pressing her, he said simply, "Fine. Then how about a kiss? C'mon, Cilla, honey, what's one little kiss between old lovers?"

"More than you're going to get," she tossed back, struggling to hold back a smile. "Let me go."

"In a minute," he promised.

"Wyatt!"

"Hear me out first. All I'm asking is one kiss. You set the rules."

That got her attention. Studying him speculatively, she said, "Let me get this straight. You get one kiss, and I start it and end it whenever I want? With no argument from you?"

He nodded. "You got it. Take your best shot, honey. I'm ready when you are."

She could see by the glint in his eye that he expected her to make it short and sweet, but she had no intention of doing any such thing. He would only protest that it wasn't a real kiss and expect another. No, she was going to kiss him, all right, and knock his socks off in the process. To do that, she was going to have to put more than a little effort into it.

Blatant seduction was what she was going for, and for a while there, she almost pulled it off. Linking her arms around his neck, she pulled his mouth down to hers and kissed him with a wantonness she hadn't known she was capable of. Focusing all her attention on his reaction, she nibbled and nipped and took his mouth with a pent-up hunger that came from the very depths of her being. And he loved it. His arms snapped around her, crushing her close, his heart pounded out a frantic rhythm against hers, and with nothing more than the teasing trail of her tongue along his bottom lip, his breathing grew short and ragged. Muttering a curse, he backed her up against her bedroom door and kissed her back with a wildness that delighted her.

Somewhere in the back of her brain, the thought registered that she should end this madness now—while she still could. But it was already too late. Instead of running, she was rubbing up against him with a daring that would shock her in the light of day. And then there was this crazy need to kiss him...everywhere. With a will of its own, her mouth wandered to his ear, his brow, the V-neck of his T-shirt, the hard line of his jaw and the sandpaper roughness caused by a night's growth of beard. She loved the feel of him against her, his hardness against her softness, the sinewy strength of him, the arousal he made no attempt to hide. Desperate for another taste of him, she went up on her toes and fitted her mouth hungrily to his.

With that single kiss, she told him things that nearly brought him to his knees. Like how she had forgotten that she intended to stop with just one kiss, that *he* was the reason that she'd forgotten, that the need that had once burned so hot between them was nothing compared to the inferno they lit in each other's blood now.

God, he wanted her. Every time he held her like this, it was harder to let her go. And while she may have forgotten that she'd only bargained for one kiss, he hadn't. Before they went any further, she had to know what she was getting into. They weren't kids anymore who got caught up in the heat of passion and could claim later that they didn't know what they were doing. If they made love now, it would be a joint decision or nothing.

Tearing his mouth from hers, he held her tight and buried his face in the dark cloud of her hair, his breathing loud and ragged in the quiet stillness of the night. "You're not making this easy for me, sweetheart," he said thickly. "I thought you just wanted one kiss."

Blindly nuzzling against him, she tightened her arms around his waist. "So did I," she murmured. "I don't know what happened."

She sounded so bewildered, he almost smiled. He knew exactly how she felt. Just when he thought he could control his response to her, she turned around and did something that cut him off at the knees.

Drawing back slightly, he captured her face in his hands and stared down at her, his thumb lightly rubbing her bottom lip in a caress he could have no more denied himself that he could have stopped the beating of his heart. "This is your call, honey. You know I want you. There's not a night that goes by that I don't dream about making love to you. But you've got to want it, too—here, tonight, right now—or we're not going any further until you're ready."

Caught in the heat of his tender gaze, she couldn't believe what she was hearing. The brash, young Wyatt she'd known in the past had been just as caught up in the uncontrollable passion that had sparked between them as she had. Even if he'd thought to make such a suggestion, he would have never been able to carry it off. But the Wyatt who held her before him was a man, not a twenty-two-year-old kid. And he meant what he said. One word from her, and he'd leave her to her lonely bed.

But she couldn't say it. She might regret it in the morning, but she couldn't send him away and deny what they both wanted so badly. "I do want it," she said huskily. "I want *you*. Please . . . don't go."

She didn't have to say it twice. He swept her off her feet and up into his arms before she could do anything but gasp. "God, sweetheart, you don't know how glad I am you said that," he groaned, kissing her fiercely. "If you'd really wanted me to leave you alone, I would have, but don't ask me how. Open the door, honey. I've got my hands full and it's going to be a long time before I'm ready to let you go."

With his words alone, he warmed her inside and out. Touched, unable to stop smiling, she kissed him softly while she reached behind her for the door handle. A split second later they were in her room with the door closed, shutting out the world, and there was nothing but the two of them and the dark.

She expected him to set her on her feet then, but he carried her to the bed and laid her on it, his mouth smothering hers as he followed her down. Feeling like a kid again, urgency firing her blood, she reached for the hem of his T-shirt. But his hands were there before hers, closing around her fingers to draw them up and press them into the mattress by her shoulders. "No," he murmured, giving her a slow, languid kiss that liquified her bones. "I've dreamed of taking this slow and easy and driving you right out of your mind, sweet girl. Let me."

She stared up at him in the darkness and felt her heart turn over in her chest at the sight of the need glinting in his eyes. Emotion, sweet and hot, clogged her throat, making it impossible for her to tell him that that was what she'd dreamed of, too, for longer than she could remember—Wyatt in her bed and loving her the whole night through. Her hands still trapped in his, she squeezed his fingers and gave him the only answer she could manage.

She thought she knew what to expect . . . of herself and him. It had been ten years, but there were some things a woman didn't forget. Like every touch, every kiss, every heated moment of the times they'd been together over the course of that long-ago, magical summer. Since then, she'd cursed him and tried to hate him for clinging to her memory so vividly, but she hadn't been able to push a single second from her mind. But the loving they shared now was like nothing out of the past.

He loved her as if she was the most precious thing in the world to him, a treasure that had been lost and was now found, a piece of his heart that he'd carelessly misplaced and never intended to let get away from him now that he'd finally found her again. Without saying a word, he told her with long, heated kisses how much he'd missed her, how much he needed her, how impossibly lonely the nights had been without her. Then he showed her.

She never knew when her clothes or his melted away or when he moved them both under the covers. She couldn't think, couldn't feel anything but his hard body against hers, his hands and mouth moving over her, seducing her, loving her, enchanting her. He touched her and she shuddered, then kissed her and she moaned. He'd released her hands, but she couldn't have said when. Dazed, mindless, every nerve ending in her body tight with need, she reached for him with a hoarse cry, lost to everything but the fire he'd slowly built in her blood.

"Easy, sweetheart," he growled against her breast, curling his tongue around a sensitive nipple. "I'm right here."

But his lady was no longer satisfied with slow and easy. She surged toward him, her mouth hot and eager, nipping at him, her hands demanding as they swept over him, seeking, searching, rubbing, determined to crack the iron control he'd imposed on himself. He could have told her all it took was one touch from her, but she didn't give him the chance. With a push of her hand, she sent him rolling over onto his back, and then she was covering him like a dream, delighting him, dropping kisses wherever she could reach, straddling him and loving him with a fierce sweetness that burned hotter than a forest fire. Control, what little he had left, was lost in the flames.

Seizing her hips, he brought her down to him and took her like a man possessed. He should have been gentler, he should have at least tried to slow the pace, but she was as caught up in the madness as he was and would have none of it. Her wet, hot heat surrounding him, she caught his rhythm and urged him on, riding him, racing with him in the dark to a destination that was theirs and theirs alone. And when they reached the edge and plunged headlong into ecstasy, it was his name she called in the night, his arms she trusted to catch her as the mindless pleasure took them both, his heart she claimed as her own.

Chapter Nine

Bright winter sunlight was streaming through the bedroom window when Cilla opened her eyes hours later. Lying on her stomach on the side of the bed nearest the window, she didn't have to check the mattress next to her to know that she was alone. Sometime near dawn, she had a vague, shadowed memory of Wyatt easing away from her and stopping to kiss her softly on the cheek before silently making his way back to his own room. If she hadn't been so tired, she would have reached for him and pulled him back to her, but now she was glad that she hadn't. He knew her too well. One look at her face and he would know that she'd done the one thing she'd sworn she'd never do again. She'd fallen in love with him for the second time in a lifetime.

Denial rose up in her like a tidal wave, threatening to choke her. No! She had to be mistaken. No one had ever hurt her like he had; there was no way she'd be stupid enough to let him do it again. She was just being fanciful because of the holidays. That had to be it. She always got sappy at this time of the year, this year especially with the unexpectedly early arrival of Kat's babies. No wonder she couldn't think straight—her emotions were up and down the scale.

Nice try, Cilla, a voice drawled sarcastically in her head. *But it's not going to wash. You love him. You always have. Deal with it.*

Panic seized her, urging her to run. To pack her bags and get the heck out of there. Now, while she still could. But where would she go? Back to Denver? To a job she no longer had? To a life that no longer seemed hers? Her whole world was in an upheaval; she didn't even know where she belonged anymore.

Trembling, she hugged herself and readily admitted she was scared. What she'd felt for Wyatt at seventeen was nothing compared to what she felt now. And he wasn't the marrying kind. Dear God, what was she going to do?

Staring with unfocused eyes out the bedroom window, she toyed with the idea of going back to bed and just pulling the covers over her head for the rest of the day. But that would only bring Josey and Tate running with their medical bags to see what was wrong. And there were two new babies to meet and love and fuss over. Only a self-centered, whiney baby would hide in her room like a spoiled brat while the whole family celebrated. Reluctantly pushing back the covers, she reached for her clothes.

"Well, looky here," Flynn greeted her with a wicked grin as she stepped into the dining room thirty minutes later and found everyone but the new parents gathered there. "Sleeping Beauty arises. And I just bet Cooper we wouldn't see hide nor hair of you until at least noon. I'm out ten bucks, cousin."

Every eye turned her way, but it was Wyatt's narrowed gaze that she was achingly aware of. Cursing the sting of a blush that rose to her cheeks, she avoided looking directly at the entire end of the table where he sat and turned thankfully to Flynn with an impudent flash of her dimples. "That's what you get for betting against your favorite cousin."

"You tell him, Cilla," Tate laughed. "I told him he was throwing his money away, but he wouldn't listen. You ready for breakfast or you want to wait awhile? Alice saved you some biscuits and gravy. They're warming on the stove."

Cilla's stomach curdled at the mere thought of food. "No, thanks. I just need a shot of coffee to get my motor running this morning."

"Don't you mean this afternoon?" Cooper teased.

"Don't you start, too, string bean," she tossed back, using the nickname she'd tacked on him as a kid. "Not until I get some caffeine in my bloodstream." Grabbing a cup from the sideboard, she filled it to the rim, then turned back to the table and took the seat that was farthest from Wyatt. Her smile as bright and phony as a ten-dollar Rolex, she said, "Okay, who's going to tell me about the new babies? Are they as gorgeous as the rest of the Rawlings men?"

That, thankfully, started everyone talking at once, and no one noticed that she said very little after that and Wyatt said nothing at all. The conversation naturally revolved around the new additions to the family and the type of mother Kat would be, which everyone agreed would be wild and wonderful. There was a lot of laughter and reminiscing, then the discussion turned to the work that had to be done to the new room addition before the babies came home. By the time breakfast broke up, the fact that Cilla had overslept had long since been forgotten.

By everyone, that is, except Wyatt.

She only glanced at him in passing, but she could feel his eyes on her, dark and brooding, surreptitiously watching her every move. He didn't do anything to draw her attention to himself—he didn't even force her to speak to him, which he very well could have done just by asking her a question. But Cilla wasn't fooled. He was biding his time, waiting for the chance to get her alone, which was the last thing she wanted.

So as soon as breakfast started to break up, she was on her feet. She intended to follow Josey into the kitchen and ask her what Kat needed for the babies, but before she could take a step away from the table, Wyatt was right behind her. "We need to talk," he growled in a low voice that didn't carry to anyone's ears but her own.

Startled, she glanced over his shoulder and found him just inches behind her. Her heart thumping crazily, she quickly turned away. "I can't," she said stiffly. "Not now. I'm going shopping in Tucson."

"I didn't mean now—I've got an errand to run anyway. Later—"

"I'm going to be busy most of the day."

"Dammit, Cilla—"

Ignoring his muttered curse, she hurried to catch up with Josey in the kitchen. "Josey? Have you got any idea what Kat needs for the babies? I wanted to buy them something special, but I don't know what Kat's already got.''

In the process of returning a jar of Alice's home-made jelly to the refrigerator, Josey frowned. ''I think she still needs a stroller, but she and Lucas may have already bought one....''

Wyatt didn't follow them into the kitchen, but Cilla could feel him scowling daggers at her from the hall. He was more than a little miffed at her, but he didn't force the issue. For what seemed like an eternity, he just stood there, waiting. Then, without a word, he turned and stormed off.

Releasing the breath she hadn't even realized she was holding, Cilla almost wilted in relief. She'd wasn't foolish enough to think she'd put him off indefinitely, but she'd bought herself some time...at least for now. With luck, by the time she did have to face him one-on-one, she'd be more in control of her emotions.

When she walked into Kat's hospital room six hours later, she was pushing a twin stroller that was loaded down with flowers and presents. Kat, in the process of giving one of the babies a bottle, laughed in delight. ''A stroller! How did you know we needed one?''

''Josey suggested it.'' Grinning, Cilla hugged her, making sure not to squash the baby. ''Congratulations, Mama! Who do we have here?''

Fairly beaming with pride, Kat eased back the re-ceiving blanket from the infant's face and head and said, ''This is your new cousin Nathan. Nathan, open your eyes, sweetheart, and meet Cilla. She's brought you and your brother some presents."

"And you," Cilla added. "Since you weren't planning on this little one and his twin showing up so early, I figured you weren't quite prepared to spend a night or two in the hospital, so I bought you a gown and robe." Dropping her gaze to the baby, she felt her heart melt. "Oh, Kat, he's beautiful! Look at that hair! Where's Alex?"

"In the nursery. They're both on oxygen except when I'm feeding them. It's just a precautionary measure since they decided to check in so early."

"Are they identical?"

"Carbon copies," her cousin confirmed with a rueful grin. "God knows how we're going to tell them apart. Lucas is terrified we'll get them mixed up and warp them for life."

"No, you'll do fine," Cilla laughed. "If worse comes to worst, you can always do like Gable and Josey did with the boys and leave their hospital bracelets on them until they outgrow them. If you can't tell them apart by then, you never will." Looking her cousin over, she shook her head. "I don't know how you can look so rested when you just spent most of the night in hard labor. When are they letting you out of here?"

"Tomorrow morning, but I really won't be going anywhere. Tate wants the babies to stay another week or so, just to make sure their lungs are developed properly, so I'll be here most of the time." Shifting the baby to her shoulder so she could burp him, she sent Cilla a teasing look. "Enough about me. I want to hear all about you and Wyatt alone at the ranch last night with the kids. How'd you manage it without killing each other?''

Cilla knew she should have come back with a teasing retort and found a way to change the subject, but her cheeks were already hot. Turning away to wander aimlessly around the small private room, she said, "The kids kept us busy for awhile. Wyatt finally bribed them into going back to bed with popcorn and a story."

At her stiff tone, the teasing smile faded from Kat's face. "Cilla? Why do I feel like I just put my foot in my mouth? Are you okay? What happened last night?"

"Nothing," she said quickly, but the lie stuck in her throat, and before she could stop herself, the truth—or at least all she was willing to talk about—came spilling out. "No, that's not true. Wyatt wants to pick up where we left off, and he's not going to take no for an answer. I don't even know if I want him to. I don't know what I want. I just know I can't go through losing him again. It hurt too much the first time."

Leaning back against her raised pillow, Kat let out her breath in a huff. "Well! This is certainly a surprise. I thought you were over him a long time ago."

"So did I," Cilla replied, her shaky laugh holding little humor. "Surprise, surprise. The joke's on me. All he had to do was kiss me again and I knew why I couldn't marry Tom."

"You still love him."

It was a statement, not a question, one that Cilla couldn't deny. Hugging herself, she nodded miserably. "Yeah. I guess I'm just a glutton for punishment."

"Not necessarily. If you love him and he loves you—"

"But he doesn't. At least he never mentioned the *L* word. To be perfectly honest, I don't think it's even in his vocabulary. He *wants* me," she said flatly. "He wants to pick up where we left off. I don't know about you, but that doesn't sound like a declaration of undying love to me, not when all we had before was a hot summer romance."

She thought she had her emotions firmly in check, but suddenly tears were welling in her eyes and spilling over her lashes. Giving Kat a watery smile, she felt her heart squeeze at the sight of her and the baby. "I want what you have, Kat. You and Cooper and Flynn and Gable. I want the ring and the babies and going to sleep and waking up with the same man every day for the next fifty years. But I don't think that's ever going to happen—not with Wyatt. He likes his freedom and other women too much."

"But just because he hasn't mentioned anything permanent doesn't mean he's going to let you just walk away after Christmas," Kat pointed out quietly. "He's changed, Cilla. Haven't you noticed? He's not the same man he was ten years ago. He's more settled, more...I don't know—family oriented, I guess."

"That's what Josey said," Cilla replied. "Personally, I haven't seen it. He's just as much a flirt as he always was."

"With *you,* silly. But not with anyone else, at least not that I've noticed. Has he been going out? Hanging out at the Crossroads looking for babes?"

"No, but—"

"No, but nothing. That doesn't sound like a man who's on the prowl. Face it, cuz. The guy's nuts about you—everybody but the two of you seem to know it. He can't take his eyes off you whenever you're in the same room together."

Cilla wanted desperately to believe her, but she'd learned the hard way that she couldn't put much stock in what she *thought* Wyatt's feelings for her were. Ten years ago, she would have sworn on all that was holy that he loved her with all his heart. Then she'd found him with another woman. "I don't know. God knows I want to believe it, but right now I'm so confused, I can't be sure of anything."

"Then ask him what his intentions are," Kat said bluntly. "It's the 1990s, not the Gay Nineties. You've got a right to know if he's planning just a roll in the hay or a walk down the aisle. Of course, he may not know yet himself, but you've got a right to know that, too. Then you can make up your mind about what you want to do about it."

It was good advice, and long after she'd left Kat and the babies at the hospital and headed back to the Double R, Cilla chewed over the idea, liking it more and more the closer she got the ranch. Why shouldn't she ask him his intentions? She wasn't some Victorian maiden who had to sit around twisting her hands waiting for a man to take the initiative that would affect the rest of her life. She'd find him, demand some answers . . . and pray they were the right ones.

Her chin set at a determined angle, the light of battle in her eyes, she pulled up in front of the house and marched inside, all set for a confrontation. But there wasn't a soul in sight and the place was as quiet as a tomb. Surprised—with three kids in the house, the only time you ran into silence was in the middle of the night—she yelled, "Hey, anybody home?"

"In here," Alice called in a muffled voice from the nether regions at the back of the house. "I'm in the pantry."

Following her voice into the kitchen, she found the housekeeper up to her ears in jars of homemade canned goods that she was transferring from the large walk-in pantry to the kitchen table. Eyeing her flushed face in amusement, Cilla hurried forward to help her with the armload of pint jars she was struggling not to drop. "Lord, Alice, what are you doing?"

"Getting out all my Christmas presents for the neighbors," she huffed as she set the last of the lot on the table. "I usually make homemade jam for everybody, but this year I tried making my own picante sauce." Behind the lenses of her bifocals, her faded eyes twinkled. "It'll strip the hair right off a man's tongue."

"Alice, I've never seen hair on a man's tongue and hope I never do," Cilla said with a laugh.

"You won't if you feed him my picante sauce," she retorted, grinning. Suddenly realizing that Cilla was home long before she expected her, she said, "What are you doing back so early, anyway? I figured you and

Kat would talk the afternoon away about those new babies.''

"I didn't want to tire her out," she explained. "And I need to talk to Wyatt. Have you seen him? Where is everybody?"

"God only knows. They've all been going every which way since breakfast, with everybody keeping secrets—you know how it is at Christmas. And then the phone's been ringing off the wall with everyone calling about Kat's babies, and sales people, and someone doing a survey, and everything in between—"

Wound up, she would have gone on, but Cilla stopped her with a gentle reminder. "What about Wyatt? Did he say where he's going? His truck's not out front."

"Last I saw him, he was headed for Kat's. That was over two hours ago, though. He could have gone anywhere since then. That's what I told that—hey, where're you going?"

"To see if he's still there," she called over her shoulder as she hurried out the door. "I need to talk to him. See you later."

She was gone before Alice could stop her, before she could finish what she'd started to say—that she'd told the unknown woman who had shown up on the doorstep looking for him the same thing only moments before. Worried, she started after her. Maybe she could catch her before she pulled out of the driveway. But then the phone rang—again!—and the opportunity was lost.

* * *

Kicking up a cloud of dirt, Cilla raced toward the rocky canyon where Kat's cabin was, unable to hold back the smile that kept insisting on tugging at the corners of her mouth. Right or wrong, she was taking the bull by the horns and she felt good about it. Kat was right. She loved Wyatt—why shouldn't she tell him so, and ask him if he felt the same way?

He did, she told herself. He had to. Anything else was unacceptable. Her hands unconsciously tightening on the steering wheel, she pressed down on the accelerator and fairly flew across the desert, the inexplicable need to hurry pushing her on.

She would have sworn nothing on earth could have made her check her speed until she reached him, but at the rocky entrance to the canyon, she slammed on her breaks, unable to believe her eyes. The trees and the cactuses lining the road all the way to Kat and Lucas's cabin were decorated with ribbons and bows and garlands.

Stunned, her smile broadening into a grin, Cilla could do nothing but stare. Wyatt had done this. And the other cactuses near the house. It had to be him. He'd said this morning that he had an errand to run, and Alice had seen him heading this way. And he had no other reason to come to the canyon by himself since Kat was still in the hospital at Silver City and when Lucas wasn't with her, he was catching up on his sleep at a nearby hotel.

Foolish tears stinging her eyes, Cilla laughed shakily and blinked them away. Kat and Josey were right—

he *had* changed. Afraid he'd break her heart again, she hadn't wanted to see it, but suddenly all the pieces fell into place. The evenings with the family, the play time with the kids, the total lack of interest in carousing with the ranch hands the way he usually did—he hadn't hung around the house all those nights just to make an impression on her. He really had changed.

Suddenly anxious to see him, to tell him how she felt and to feel his arms around her, she hit the gas, her heart knocking crazily as she imagined his reaction to her announcement that she still loved him, had always loved him. God, the time they had wasted! Just thinking about it made her want to cry, but they'd both needed to grow up and mature and find each other again. Now that they had, they had nothing but clear sailing in front of them.

Driving as fast as she dared through the brightly decorated trees, she burst into the clearing where Kat's cabin sat, her face lighting up like a star on top of one of the Christmas trees when she spied Wyatt's sports car parked at the side of the house. Only when she braked to a stop behind his Corvette, though, did she see the dusty red Mercedes with California plates parked next to it.

Surprised, she looked around and started to call out for him when she suddenly spied him in the trees at the edge of the clearing. And he wasn't alone. There was a tall blonde with him, and he was kissing her for all he was worth.

Chapter Ten

Feeling that she'd just been swept back into a nightmare from the past, Cilla stood as if turned to stone while a scream of pain and outrage echoed in her head. *No!* This couldn't be happening! Not again. She couldn't have fallen in love with the same man twice in a lifetime only to have him betray her twice in that same lifetime. How could she have been such a fool? Like a naive schoolgirl caught up in the thrill and rush of first love, she'd wanted to believe so badly that he'd changed that she'd let her guard down and convinced herself he loved her. God, what a crock! Wyatt Chandler didn't love anyone but himself. How many times did he have to stab her in the back before she realized that?

No more, she thought, swallowing the hot tears that threatened to choke her. This was it, the last time he hurt her, the last time she let him hurt her. Some things just weren't meant to be, and she and Wyatt were evidently one of them. Trying to force the issue wasn't doing anything but torturing her and she couldn't take it anymore.

Fury hit her then, hot and quick and cleansing. How dare he do this to her! It was just last night that they…that the two of them… Shying away from that thought and the heated images it dragged up, she seriously considered storming over there, jerking him away from the hussy who was plastered all over him, and tell him exactly what she thought of him. It was the least he deserved, the rat! But she didn't even want to look at him, let alone tell him off. Whirling, she headed for her car.

Glaring, nose-to-nose, at the woman who had snuck up on him while he was decorating the last cedar and laid a kiss on him before he even knew she was on the property, Wyatt stood unmoved, unresponsive and revolted, his lips as cold as a dead fish and his arms at his side. He could have pushed her from him, but the lady had more moves than an octopus and he'd have had to hurt her to do it. As much as she infuriated him, he had to draw the line at that. So he waited her out, not giving her the least encouragement. He didn't know how the hell she had found him, but she'd made a wasted trip. And he was going to tell her that just as soon as she finished making a fool of herself.

But the lady was nothing if not persistent. His patience growing thin, he was on the verge of telling her to give it up when he suddenly heard the sound of tires spinning in the drive and kicking up gravel. Jerking his head back, he looked up just in time to see Cilla's Honda racing wildly down the road that led back to the main ranch house.

"Ah, hell!" Curses rolling off his tongue, he pushed Eleanor to arm's length, furiously untangling himself from her. "Damn you, woman, *let go!*"

Undaunted, Eleanor only smiled and tried to rewind her arms around his neck. "You know you don't mean that, Wyatt, honey. C'mon, give me a kiss. You know you're dying to."

What he was dying to do was go after Cilla—God, he had to explain!—but first he had to deal with this little witch once and for all. A muscle jumping along his rock hard jaw, he laid his hands on her shoulders and looked her dead in the eye. "Listen to me, Eleanor, because I'm only going to say this once. You're an attractive woman. I'm sure there're a lot of men out there who would like to get to know you better if you'd give them the chance, but I'm not one of them. I'm never going to be one of them."

"Don't say that, sweetie. If you'd just—"

"I'm in love with someone else," he said with brutal honesty.

"Don't be ridiculous!" She laughed, the sound more than a little desperate. "You love me."

"No, I don't. I never loved you. I never even gave you any encouragement. Not once. Hell, I even left the damn state so you would finally realize that I wasn't interested, but you found a way to track me down—"

"I hired a private investigator," she said simply. "I thought you were playing some kind of a game."

"I don't play games. Not those kind, anyway." Unwrapping her arms from around his neck, he stepped back and this time she let him go. "I don't want to hurt you," he said quietly, "but the truth is that you don't love me. No, you don't," he said quickly when she opened her mouth to protest. "You love the thrill of the chase. The hunt. So find yourself somebody else to chase, because I'm out of the race. I love somebody else and I plan to spend the next fifty or sixty years proving it to her. So if you'll excuse me, I've got to go. I've got a lot of explaining to do. Just go back the way you came and you won't have any trouble finding your way back home.''

Stepping around her, he strode quickly toward his Corvette, his thoughts already jumping ahead to Cilla. Of all the rotten, miserable luck! Dammit, how could he have let this happen? He knew how resourceful Eleanor was. She left no stone unturned when she wanted something and for some crazy reason that only she could understand, she thought she wanted him. God, what must Cilla be thinking? He'd never thought to tell her about Eleanor because she never had been and never would be a part of his life, but there was no way he was going to be able to convince Cilla of that now. Not after she'd witnessed that one-sided kiss. She'd think that he'd invited the woman here on purpose, that history was once again repeating itself, when nothing could have been further from the truth. He had to find her, had to make her understand!

But when he raced back to the house, there was no sign of Cilla's Honda. Swearing, he braked to a screeching stop in the front drive and just sat there with the motor running, trying to figure out where the hell she could have gone. She wouldn't have left without her things, and she hadn't had time to pack. Dammit, where was she?

But even as he hit the steering wheel in frustration, he knew. Praying he was right, he wheeled around and headed back to the canyon.

The line cabin was located miles from Kat's place, at the opposite end of the canyon. A simple structure that consisted of four bare walls and a roof, its weathered logs had never seen a coat of paint, and electricity was just a dream. The only running water was the nearby creek, which ran the entire length of the canyon, the only furniture a roughly built bunk and a crude table and chairs. It hadn't been designed for comfort but as a refuge for cowboys who had wandered too far from the ranch headquarters and suddenly found themselves caught up in a storm.

Braking to a stop in front of it, Cilla cut the engine and just sat there for a long time, staring at the rough-hewn cedar walls with eyes that were stark with despair. She shouldn't have come here. Not now. She was too hurt, too vulnerable. And there were too many memories here. Memories of her and Wyatt, here, together, swimming in the creek, exploring the canyon, teasing and playing and falling in love.

Well, at least one of them had fallen in love... then and now, she thought bitterly. God, she had to get out of here! But instead of starting the motor and heading back to the house, she reached for the door handle and stepped out of the car.

The wind that always swirled through the canyon immediately grabbed at her hair, blowing it into her face with a playfulness she would have normally laughed at. But not today. Then she heard the creek. As the clear, cold water tumbled over the rocks that lined the creek, it murmured and bubbled and whispered secrets to the wind.

Stopping in her tracks, Cilla cocked her head to listen, her lips twitching into the barest semblance of a smile, and suddenly she knew why she'd come here. The water. How could she have forgotten it? She's always loved the sound of it, the soothing murmur that never stopped. It called to her soul, seeped into her bones, calmed her as nothing else could.

That long-ago summer, she'd spent more hours here than she could remember. Most of the time, she'd been with Wyatt, but she'd also come here by herself, drawn to the peace of the place, the privacy, the solitude. Here, she'd fantasized and dreamed and built castles in the sky. And when all that had come tumbling down around her ears, it was here she'd come to cry her eyes out.

Nothing, it seemed, had changed.

Emptiness spread through her like a cold, creeping fog, chilling her to the bone. Shivering, she hugged herself, but it didn't help. She'd never felt so alone in her life. She wanted to believe that she'd get over this, but if this time with Wyatt had proven anything, it was that she was and always would be a one-man woman. And an idiot. How many times did she have to catch him with other women before she got the message that he didn't have a faithful bone in his body?

Anger, sharp and biting, coiled in her gut. The man was a skunk, lower than dirt, she decided as she wandered through the trees to the creek. He'd used up all his chances and hurt her for the last time. Reaching down for a small rock, she tossed it into the water and watched it sink to the bottom. She didn't pretend that she didn't still love him—evidently that was to be her lot in life, like it or not—but she wasn't a masochist. She could love him and not let him be a part of her life. After all, wasn't that what she'd been doing for the last ten years?

Lost in her misery, trying to figure out what she was going to do with the rest of her life, she didn't hear the sports car that quietly rumbled into the canyon and drew up next to her Honda. But then the sound of a vehicle door being slammed carried easily to her over the gurgle of the creek, and she whirled to see Wyatt striding toward her, the angles of his lean face set in somber lines.

Her heart kicked into gear at the sight of him, irritating her no end. Lifting her chin, she glared at him from twenty feet away. "I don't know why you followed me, but I came here to be alone. So go back to your hot-to-trot little blonde from California. We've got nothing to say to each other."

"The hell we don't," he growled, stalking toward her. "She's not my hot-to-trot little anything!"

"Oh, really?" she taunted, standing her ground. "That's not the way it looked to me. She was plastered all over you like a heat rash—"

"You're damn right," he agreed. "*She* was plastered all over me. And *she* was kissing me, not the other way around."

She laughed at that, but there wasn't a trace of humor in the painful sound. "And you were fighting her off with a stick, right? Tell me another one, Wyatt."

"Dammit, Cilla, if you'll just let me explain! That wasn't what you thought it was—"

"Oh, yes it was," she retorted. "So save the fairy tale for someone who's interested. I'm not." Presenting him her back, she headed for the cabin.

The tears she was so sure she wasn't going to shed thankfully held off as she stepped inside and slammed the door behind her. But once the silence closed around her, once she was well and truly alone, her eyes burned and suddenly she was shuddering with sobs she couldn't control. With a muffled cry, she threw herself onto the bunk that was built against one wall and cried her eyes out.

When Wyatt soundlessly opened the cabin door, his heart twisted in his chest at the sight of her misery. In two strides, he reached the bunk and went down on one knee beside Cilla. "Ah, honey, don't do this to yourself," he said thickly. "You're crying over nothing."

"G-go away," she choked, burying her face in the bare mattress. "J-just g-go a-waaay."

"Not on your life," he growled. "I'm not going anywhere until we get this straightened out."

He didn't give her a chance to argue, but simply scooped her up and settled her in his lap as he sank down onto the bunk with his back against the wall. She cursed him and tried to wiggle free, but he was ready for her. Wrapping his arms around her, he crushed her against his chest and just held her. "I'm not letting you go, honey. Not now. Not ever. So you might as well get used to it.''

She stiffened, her slender body as rigid as a broom handle in his arms, and for a second, he thought she was going to haul off and belt him one—she was that upset. He couldn't have said he'd have blamed her, not after she'd found him with another woman just hours after they'd made love. As far as she knew, he was guilty as sin and deserved anything she could dish out. But instead of letting him have it with both barrels, all the fight just seemed to go out of her. A sob caught in her throat, and suddenly she pressed her face against his throat and cried as if she was never going to stop.

His arms tight around her, Wyatt just held her, emotion clogging his throat. He couldn't lose her, not again. He loved her too much even to consider the possibility. The words rose to his tongue, the need to tell her almost more than he could bear, but first he had to explain about Eleanor and make her understand that the woman had never been anything to him but an aggravating problem that he'd tried his damndest to avoid.

''I wasn't lying to you, honey,'' he said gruffly as her sobs gradually quieted and she lay spent against him. ''I never gave Eleanor the time of day, but somehow she got it in her head that she was in love with me.'' He told her everything then, how Eleanor showed up uninvited at work, how she followed him whenever he went out, even when it was just with friends, the telephone calls in the middle of the night to make sure he wasn't with someone. ''I'm telling you, she's nuts.

Certifiable. She stalked me everywhere I went and even announced our engagement in the paper. And I don't even really know her! That's why I came here for Christmas. I thought if I got out of California for awhile and didn't tell anybody where I was going, she would become fixated on somebody else and leave me alone. I should have known better. The lady is nothing if not stubborn.''

At his bitter tone, Cilla pushed back just far enough so that she could see his face. "Are you serious?"

"Do I look like I'm kidding?"

No, she had to admit he didn't. She'd never seen him more somber. "How did she find you?"

"Apparently she hired a private investigator. I never thought she'd go that far, which shows how stupid I am. The lady's rolling in it and used to getting anything and everything she wants. When I first told her I wasn't interested, I guess she saw me as a challenge.''

Even to his own ears, it sounded like a half-baked story that was an insult to any woman's intelligence, and Cilla was no exception. He saw the doubt in her eyes and it hurt, dammit! He was telling the truth and somehow he had to make her believe him. "If I was going to lie, I'd come up with a hell of a more believable story than this," he said flatly. "I know it sounds farfetched, but if you don't believe me, ask Gable. When we talked at Thanksgiving, I told him all about Eleanor and how she was driving me crazy. He was the one who suggested I get out of L.A. for awhile and come here for the holidays.''

Her eyes searching his, Cilla wanted desperately to believe him, but she was afraid to take the chance and let him shatter her heart again. "Why would she think she's in love with you if you didn't encourage her? Did you ever go out with her?"

"Not once. I swear it!"

"Oh, come on, Wyatt," she scoffed. "I know what a flirt you are. The family's been keeping me apprised of the women in your life for years. You had to have done something to make this woman think you were interested in her."

Grinning at the sudden temper that flashed in her eyes, he caught her hands and held them firmly against his chest. "So you've been keeping tabs on me, have you? I'm glad to hear it. Yeah, there were women, but not that many and I wasn't serious about any of them. As for Eleanor, all she ever got from me was a smile, and I've been regretting even that ever since. That's the truth. I can't prove it—you'll just have to take it on faith."

She could have told him that was a lot to ask of her, considering the number of times she'd found him with another woman, but when she stared into his eyes, she couldn't doubt the sincerity she saw in his steady gaze when he spoke about Eleanor. If he was lying, he was much better at it now than he had been in the past when he couldn't fib and look her in the eye at the same time. As for his heartthrobs over the years since she'd last seen him, that was another matter.

"You don't have to prove it," she said quietly. "I believe you... at least about Eleanor. But you're really pushing it if you expect me to believe you've been a monk all these years. I know better."

His smile faded. "I meant for you to. A man's got his pride, you know. I exaggerated things because I knew the news would get back to you through the family, and I didn't want you to think that I missed you or anything. But I did. I just didn't realize how much until I saw you again."

His words echoed her own feelings so exactly that she felt as if he'd reached out and squeezed her heart. All the lonely years rose up in her throat, thick and hot, threatening to choke her. "Don't."

"Don't what?" Frowning at the tears that once again sparkled in her eyes, he released one of her hands to cup her cheek in his palm. "Sweetheart, what is it? What did I say? Please don't cry again. I love you, dammit! You've got to believe me!"

God, how long had she waited to hear those words? It seemed like a lifetime. Hope lightening her heart, she could only stare at him. "You love me?"

"Well, of course I do! I've only fallen in love twice in this lifetime and both times were with you."

"But—"

"I know what you're thinking. If I loved you, how could I have fooled around on you ten years ago? I didn't. That was all a setup, honey, staged for your benefit."

"A setup? What are you talking about? Are you saying you weren't involved with that girl I caught you kissing?"

"She was my roommate's girlfriend. I had to do something, Cilla. You were only seventeen, for God's sake! You were already planning a wedding and picking out china, and I knew you wouldn't believe me if I just told you I didn't love you. So I talked to Kurt and Sharon and we came up with this plan." His eyes dark with entreaty, he said gruffly, "I had to let you go so you could grow up, sweetheart. If you want to hate me for it now, I can't stop you. But it was just as hard on me as it was on you. All these years, I thought I'd lost you for good."

Shaken, Cilla couldn't believe what she was hearing. All this time, she'd thought she knew him, the type of man he was, what being loved by him meant. But she hadn't had a clue. He'd nearly sacrificed them for what was best for her, and she didn't know many men who would have done that. She wanted to rail at him for putting them both through such pain, but she knew he was right about one thing. At seventeen, she never would have believed he simply didn't love her, not without the "proof" that Sharon provided.

Cocking her head at him, she smiled. "You decorated the cactuses for the family, did you? Don't try to deny it. I'd already figured it out when I saw Eleanor giving you a tonsillectomy."

The abrupt change of subject caught him off guard, but only for a second. Shrugging, he grinned. "Maybe I did, and maybe I didn't. Why?"

"Because I've got a feeling the man I love did," she said simply. "I didn't know it before, but I think that's just the type of thing he'd do."

Tightening his arms around her, he lifted a teasing brow at her, his green eyes alight with love. "The man you love, huh? You sure about that?"

"Surer than I've ever been about anything in my life," she replied confidently, and kissed him.

It was a kiss of promise, of renewal, of a love that had withstood the test of time and was better for it. Without saying a word, forgiveness was given, the past forgotten, trust shared. And when they both came up for air, there was nothing but the future in front of them.

"I was going to wait until Christmas Eve to propose, but I can't wait," he said thickly. "I love you more than you'll ever know, Cilla Rawlings. Will you marry me?"

All her dreams coming true, she laughed with joy. "Well, it's about time! I thought you'd never ask!"

"Can I take that as a yes?"

"You'd better," she retorted, hugging him fiercely. "You're mine, cousin. Now that I've found you again, I'm not ever letting you go."

"Good. Because I'm not going anywhere." His grin broadening, he shifted on the bunk and drew her down beside him. "Now, what was that you were saying about the man you love?"

* * * * *

THESE THREE BESTSELLING AUTHORS

LINDA HOWARD
DEBBIE MACOMBER
LINDA TURNER

bring you *more* great romance!

This holiday season,
Linda Varner brings three very special couples

HOME
FOR THE HOLIDAYS

where they discover the joy of love and family—
and the wonder of wedded bliss.

❄✳❄✳❄✳❄✳❄✳❄✳❄✳❄✳❄✳❄✳❄✳❄

WON'T YOU BE MY HUSBAND?—Lauren West and
Nick Gatewood never expected their family and friends to get
word of their temporary engagement and nonintended nuptials. Or
to find themselves falling in love with each other. Is that a *real*
wedding they're planning over Thanksgiving dinner?
(SR#1188, 11/96)

MISTLETOE BRIDE—There was plenty of room at Dani Sellica's
Colorado ranch for stranded holiday guests Ryan Given and his
young son. Until the mistletoe incident! Christmas morning brought
presents from ol' Saint Nick...but would it also bring wedding bells?
(SR#1193, 12/96)

NEW YEAR'S WIFE—Eight years after Tyler Jordan and
Julie McCrae shared a passionate kiss at the stroke of midnight,
Tyler is back and Julie is certain he doesn't fit into her plans for
wedded bliss. But does his plan to prove her wrong include a lifetime
of New Year's kisses? (SR#1200, 1/97)

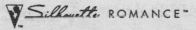

Silhouette ROMANCE™

The collection of the year!
NEW YORK TIMES BESTSELLING AUTHORS

Linda Lael Miller
Wild About Harry

Janet Dailey
Sweet Promise

Elizabeth Lowell
Reckless Love

Penny Jordan
Love's Choices

and featuring
Nora Roberts
The Calhoun Women

This special trade-size edition features four of the wildly popular titles in the Calhoun miniseries together in one volume—a true collector's item!

Pick up these great authors and a chance to win a weekend for two in New York City at the Marriott Marquis Hotel on Broadway! We'll pay for your flight, your hotel—even a Broadway show!

Available in December at your favorite retail outlet.

NEW YORK
Marriott®
MARQUIS

HARLEQUIN® *Silhouette*®

NYT1296-R

For the Janos siblings

Three Weddings and a Gift

leads to a lot of loving!
Join award-winning author

Cathie Linz

as she shows how an *unusual* inheritance leads to
love at first sight—and beyond!—in

MICHAEL'S BABY #1023
September 1996

SEDUCING HUNTER #1029
October 1996

and

ABBIE AND THE COWBOY #1036
November 1996

Only from

SILHOUETTE® Desire®

'Tis the season for holiday weddings!

This December, celebrate the holidays
with two sparkling new love stories—
only from

V SILHOUETTE YOURS TRULY™

 ### A Nice Girl Like You
by Alexandra Sellers

Sara Diamond may be a nice girl, but that doesn't mean
she wants to be Ben Harris's ideal bride. But she might
just be able to play Ms. Wrong long enough to help this
confirmed bachelor find his true wife! That is, if she
doesn't fall in love first....

A Marry-Me Christmas
by Jo Ann Algermissen

All Catherine Jordan wanted for Christmas was some
time away from the hustle and bustle. Now she was
sharing a wilderness cabin with her infuriating opposite,
Stone Scofield! But once she stood under the mistletoe
with Stone, she was hoping for a whole lot more
this holiday....

 Don't miss these exciting new books,
our gift to you this holiday season!

The Calhoun Saga continues...

in November
New York Times bestselling author

NORA ROBERTS

takes us back to the Towers and introduces us to
the newest addition to the Calhoun household,
sister-in-law Megan O'Riley in

MEGAN'S MATE
(Intimate Moments #745)

And in December
look in retail stores for the special collectors'
trade-size edition of

THE
Calhoun
Women

containing all four fabulous Calhoun series books:
COURTING CATHERINE,
A MAN FOR AMANDA, FOR THE LOVE OF LILAH
and *SUZANNA'S SURRENDER.*
Available wherever books are sold.

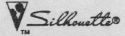

Silhouette®
TM
Look us up on-line at: http://www.romance.net   CALHOUN

This December keep your eyes open for

Royal Weddings

Marriages fit for a king or a queen—three
complete novels by three of your favorite authors,
all in one special collection!

Diana Palmer
Kathleen Korbel
Marion Smith Collins

Available wherever
Harlequin and Silhouette books are sold.

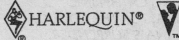